to LOVE *a*
TEXAS RANGER

LINDA
BRODAY

sourcebooks
casablanca

Published by Sourcebooks Casablanca, an imprint of Sourcebooks,
Inc.
P.O. Box 4410, Naperville, Illinois 60567-4410
(630) 961-3900
Fax: (630) 961-2168
www.sourcebooks.com

Printed and bound in Canada.
MBP 10 9 8 7 6 5 4 3 2 1

To my editor, Mary Altman. Thank you for your faith in me. It brings great joy to work with you. You see my vision with each story and help me attain it as no one else has ever done. And you don't scratch your head in confusion at my Texas slang.

One

Central Texas
Early Spring 1877

DEEP IN THE TEXAS HILL COUNTRY, WIND SIGHING through the draw whispered against his face, sharpening his senses to a fine edge. A warning skittered along his spine before it settled in his chest.

Texas Ranger Sam Legend had learned to listen to his gut. Right now it said the suffocating sense of danger that crowded him had killing in mind. He brought the spyglass up to his eye and focused on the rustlers below. All fifteen had covered their faces, leaving only their eyes showing.

Every crisp sound swept up the steep incline where he crouched in a stand of cedar to the right of an old gnarled oak. He'd hidden his horse a short distance away and prayed the animal stayed put.

"Hurry up with those beeves! We've gotta get the hell out of here. Rangers are so close I can smell 'em!" a rustler yelled.

Where were the other rangers? They hadn't been separated long and should've caught up by now.

Letting the outlaws escape took everything he had. But there were too many for one man, and this bunch was far more ruthless than most.

He peered closer as they tried to drive the bawling cattle up the draw. But the ornery bovines seemed to be smarter. They broke away from the group, scattering this way and that. Sam allowed a grin. These rustlers were definitely no cattlemen.

A lawman learned to adjust quickly. His mind whirled as he searched for some kind of plan. One shot fired in the air would alert the other rangers to his position if they were near. But would they arrive before the outlaws got to him?

Or…no one would fault Sam for sitting quietly until the lawless group cleared out.

Except Sam. A Legend never ran from a fight. It wasn't in his blood. He would ride straight through hell and come out the other side whenever a situation warranted. As a Texas Ranger, he'd made that ride many times over.

From his hiding place, he could start picking off the rustlers. With luck, Sam might get a handful before they surrounded him. Still, a few beat none. Maybe the rest would bolt. Slowly, he drew his Colt and prepared for the fight.

Though winter had just given way to spring, the hot sun bore down. Sweat trickled into his eyes, making them sting. He wiped away the sweat with an impatient hand.

"Make this count," he whispered. He had only one chance. It was all or nothing.

The first shot ripped into a man's shoulder. As the outlaw screamed, Sam quickly swung to the next target and caught the rider's thigh. A third shot grazed another's head.

Damn! The next man leaned from the saddle just as he'd squeezed the trigger.

Before he could discharge again, cold steel jabbed into his back, and a hand reached for his rifle and Colt. "Turn around real slow, mister."

The order grated along Sam's nerve endings and settled in his clenched stomach. He listened for any sounds to indicate his fellow rangers were nearby. If not, he was dead. He heard nothing except bawling steers and men yelling.

Sam slowly turned his head. Cold, dead eyes glared over the top of the rustler's bandana.

"Well, whaddya know. Got me a bona-fide ranger."

Though Sam couldn't see the outlaw's mouth, the words told him he wore a smile. "I'm not here alone. You won't get away with this."

"I call your bluff. No one's firing at us but you." The gun barrel poked harder into Sam's back. "Down the hill."

Sam could've managed without the shove. The soles of his worn boots provided no traction. Slipping and sliding down the steep embankment, he glanced for anything to suggest help had arrived, but saw nothing.

At the bottom, riders on horseback immediately surrounded him.

"Good job, Smith." The outlaw pushing to the front had to be the ringleader. He was dressed all in black, from his hat to his boots. "Let's teach this Texas

Ranger not to mess with us. I've got a special treat in mind. One of you, find his horse and get me a rope. Smith, march him back up the hill. The rest of you drive those damn cattle to the makeshift corral."

The spit dried in Sam's mouth as the man holding him bound his hands and pushed him up the steep incline, back toward the gnarled oak high on the ridge.

Any minute, the rangers would swoop in. Just a matter of time. Sam refused to believe that his life was going to end this way. Somehow, he had to stall until help arrived.

"Smith, do you know the punishment for killing a lawman?" Sam asked.

"Stop talkin' and get movin'."

"Are you willing to throw your life away for a man who doesn't give two cents about you?"

"You don't know nothin' about nothin', so shut up. One more word, an' I'll shoot you in the damn knee and drag you the rest of the way."

Sam lapsed into silence. He could see Smith had closed his mind against anything he said. If he ran, he'd be lucky to make two strides before hot lead slammed into him. Even if he made it to the cover of a cedar, what then? He had no gun. No horse.

His best chance was to spin around and take Smith's weapon.

But just as he started to make a move, the ringleader rode up beside on his horse and shouted, "Hurry up. Don't have all day."

Sharp disappointment flared, trapping Sam's breath in his chest. His fate lay at the mercy of these outlaws.

They grew closer and closer to the twisted, bent

oak branches that resembled witch's fingers. Those limbs would reach for a man's soul and snatch it at the moment of death.

Thick bitter gall climbed into his throat, choking him. The devil would soon find Sam had lost his soul a long time ago.

The steep angle of the hill made his breathing harsh. The climb hurt as much as his looming fate. He'd always thought a bullet would get him one day, but to die swinging from a tree had never crossed his mind.

As they reached the top, an outlaw appeared with Sam's horse. The buckskin nickered softly, nuzzling Sam as though offering sympathy or maybe a last good-bye. He stroked the face of his faithful friend, murmuring a few quiet words of comfort. He'd raised Trooper from a foal and turned him into a lawman's mount. Would it be too much to pray these rustlers treated Trooper well? The horse deserved kindness.

"Enough," rasped the ringleader with an impatient motion of his .45. "Put him on the horse."

Sam noticed a crude drawing between the man's thumb and wrist—a black widow spider. Not that he could do anything with the information where he was going.

One last time, he scanned the landscape anxiously, hoping to glimpse riders, but saw only the branches of cedar, oak, and cottonwood trees swaying gently in the breeze. He strained against the ropes binding him, but they wouldn't budge.

Panic so thick he could taste it lodged in his throat as they jerked him into the saddle. His heart pounded against his ribs. He sat straight and tall, not allowing so much as an eye twitch. These outlaws who thrived on violence would never earn the right to see the turmoil and fear twisting behind his stone face.

Advice his father had once given him sounded in his ears: *When trouble comes, stand proud. You are a Legend. Inside you beats the heart of a survivor.*

Sam Legend stared into the distance, a muscle working in his jaw.

The ringleader threw the rope up and over one of the gnarled branches.

Bitter regret rose. Sam had never told his father he loved him. The times they'd butted heads seemed trivial now. So did the fights with big brother Houston over things that didn't make a hill of beans.

Yes, he was going to die with a heart full of regret, broken dreams, and empty promises.

The rope scratched, digging into his tender flesh as the outlaw settled the noose around Sam's neck.

"You better find a hole and climb into it, mister," Sam said. "Every ranger and lawman in the state of Texas will be after you."

A chuckle filled the air. "They won't find us."

"That wager's going to cost you." Sam steeled himself, wondering how long it took a man to die this way. He prayed it would be quick. He wondered if his mother would be waiting in heaven to soothe the pain.

"Say hello to the devil, Ranger."

With those words, he slapped the horse's flank. Trooper bolted, leaving Sam dangling in the air. The rope violently yanked his neck back and to the side as his body jerked.

Choking and fighting to breathe, Sam Legend

counted his heartbeats until blackness claimed him. As he whirled away into nothingness, only one thing filled his mind—the vivid tattoo of a black widow spider on his killer's hand.

Two

A MONTH AFTER TEXAS RANGER SAM LEGEND ALMOST died, an ear-splitting crash of thunder rattled the windows and each unpainted board of the J. R. Simmons Mercantile. The ominous skies burst open, and rain pelted the ground in great sheets. A handful of people scattered like buckshot along the Waco boardwalk in an effort to escape the thorough drenching of a spring gully washer.

Sam paid the rain no mind. The storm barely registered—few things did, these days. The feeling of the rope around his neck was still overpowering. He reached to see if it was there, thankful not to find it.

The nightmare had him in its grip, refusing to let go. More dead than alive, he moved toward his destination. When he reached the alley separating the two sections of boardwalk, he collided with a woman covered in a hooded cloak.

"Apologies, ma'am." He glanced down by rote, then blinked. All at once, the world and its color came rushing back as Sam stared into blue eyes so vivid they stole his breath.

A pocket of fog drifted between them. Was she just a dream? He could barely see her.

She nodded and gave him a smile for only a brief second. He reached out to touch her, to see if she was real, but only cold damp air met his fingertips.

The man beside her took her arm and jerked her into the alleyway.

"Hey there!" Sam called, startled. He'd been so focused on those blue eyes he hadn't realized anyone else was there. "Ma'am, do you need help?"

He received no answer. Through the dense fog, he watched her companion force her toward a horse at the other end of the alley where a group of mounted riders waited. The hair on the back of his neck rose.

Intent on stopping whatever was happening, Sam lengthened his strides. Before he could reach them, the man threw her onto a horse, then swung up behind her. Within seconds, they disappeared, ghostly riders in the mist.

Sam stood in the driving rain, staring at the empty alley. It had all happened so fast he could hardly believe it.

Hell, maybe he'd imagined the whole thing. Maybe she'd never existed. Maybe the heavy downpour and gray gloom had messed with his mind…again. Ever since the hanging, he'd been seeing things that weren't there. Twice now he'd yanked men around and grabbed for their hands, thinking he saw a black widow spider between their thumbs and forefingers. The last time almost got Sam shot. Folks claimed he was missing the top rung of his ladder and now, his captain was sending him home to find it.

Crippled. The word clanked around in his head, refusing to settle. But even though he had full use of his legs, that's what he was at present. The cold fear washing over him had nothing to do with the air temperature or rain. What if he never recovered? Some never did.

His hand clenched. He'd fight like hell to be the whole man he once was. He had things to do—an outlaw to hunt down, a wrong to right—a promise to keep.

Sam squared his jaw and drew his coat tight against the wet chill, forcing himself to move on down the street toward the face-to-face with Captain O'Reilly. Again. It stuck in his craw that they thought him too crazed to do his job. The captain thought him a liability, a danger to the other rangers. Wanted him to take a break.

His heart couldn't hurt any worse than if someone had stomped on it with a pair of hobnail boots. Maybe the captain was right. If he'd imagined that woman just now—and he really couldn't be certain he hadn't—then maybe he *needed* the break. Sam Legend, who had brought in notorious killers, bank robbers, prison escapees, and the like, had become a liability.

But one thing he knew he hadn't imagined, and that was the blurred figure of Luke Weston standing over him when he'd regained consciousness that fateful day. There had been no mistaking those pale green eyes above the mask. They belonged to the outlaw he'd chased for over a year—he'd have staked his life on it.

When his fellow rangers had ridden up, Weston

disappeared into the brush, leaving Sam with questions. Had Weston cut him down from the tree? Was he with the rustlers? And why had the outlaws left Trooper behind? Awful considerate of them.

So what the hell had happened, dammit?

Rangers who'd ridden up told Sam they'd seen no one. He'd lain on the ground with the rope loosened around his neck, drifting in and out of consciousness.

Those questions and others haunted him, and he wouldn't rest until he got answers. Somehow he knew Weston was the key.

At ranger headquarters, he took a deep breath before opening the door. He pushed a mite too hard, banging the knob against the wall. Captain O'Reilly jerked up from his desk. "What the hell, Legend? Trying to wake the dead?"

"Sorry, Cap'n. It got away from me." It seemed a good many things had, recently.

The tall, slender captain waved him to a chair. "I haven't heard this much racket since the shoot-out inside that silo with the Arnie brothers down in Sweetwater."

Sam removed his drenched hat, lowered into the chair, and stretched his long legs out in front of him. "I hope I can talk you out of your decision."

O'Reilly sauntered to the potbellied stove in the corner and lifted the coffeepot. "What's it been? A month?"

"An eternity," Sam said quietly.

"Want a snort of coffee? Might improve your outlook."

"I'll take you up on your offer but doubt it'll improve anything. I need this job, sir. I need to work."

Revenge burned hot. He'd not rest until he found the men who'd try to hang him, and when he did, they'd pay with their blood.

"What you *need* is some time off to get your head on straight. I can't have you seeing things that aren't there." O'Reilly sighed. "You're gonna get yourself or someone else killed. I'm ordering you to go home. Rest up, then come back ready to catch outlaws."

"Finding the rustlers and catching Luke Weston is my first priority."

"That wily outlaw has been taunting you for the last year." O'Reilly's eyes hardened as he handed Sam a tin cup. "It seems personal."

"Hell yeah, it's personal!"

Weston had been there. That much he knew for damn certain. The outlaw could have strung him up himself. Why else would Sam remember those green eyes, so pale they appeared silver?

In addition to that, and though it sounded rather trivial when compared to a hanging, Weston had taken Sam's pocket watch during a stagecoach holdup a year ago. Sam tried to protect a payroll shipment, but Weston did the oddest thing. The outlaw took exactly fifty dollars, a paltry sum compared to what remained in the strongbox, and left the passengers' belongings untouched. He did, however, seem to take particular delight in pocketing Sam's prized timepiece. The way the wily outlaw singled Sam out was downright eerie. Weston knew exactly where to find the treasured keepsake. No rifling his pockets. No fumbling. No uncertainty. Memories of how Weston had flipped it open and stared intently at the inscription for almost a full minute before tucking it away drifted through Sam's mind.

"Makes me mad enough to chew nails." The thought filled Sam's head with so many cuss words he feared it would burst open.

The captain leaned back in his chair and propped his boots on the scarred desk that Noah must've brought over on the ark. To make up for a missing leg, someone had cut a crutch and stuck it under there. "Sometimes we all get cases that sink their teeth into us and won't let go."

"I just about had him the last time." And now the captain was forcing him to take time off. Sam would lose every bit of ground he'd gained.

Luke Weston had led him on a chase this past year from one end of Texas to the other. To this day, other than a vague outline of his figure, Sam had yet to glimpse anything solid except a pair of cold, pale green eyes glaring over the top of a bandana. Eyes that only held contempt and anger. Except for this last time, when they'd seemed to hold concern. But maybe he'd imagined that.

Damn! He really didn't know what was real and what wasn't anymore.

Maybe the captain was right.

Reaching for a poster that lay atop a pile on his desk, Captain O'Reilly passed it to Sam. "Got this yesterday." Bold lettering at the top of the page screamed: *WANTED! $1,000 reward for capture and conviction of notorious outlaw Luke Weston. Sought for robbery and murder. Armed and considered extremely dangerous.*

The murder charge was new since the last poster

Sam had seen. The reward had been only two hundred dollars then. He stared at the thick paper and narrowed his eyes, wondering whose fate had intersected with Luke Weston's.

"Who did he kill?"

O'Reilly's face darkened. "Federal judge. Edgar Percival."

"Stands to reason Weston would turn to outright murder eventually. Seems every month he's involved in a gunfight with someone, though folks say they were all men who needed killing."

And yet the new charge did shock Sam. He'd come to know Weston pretty well. A period of four months separated each of the outlaw's robberies, with only fifty dollars taken each time. And in every single instance, Weston had never shot anyone. Maybe he robbed out of boredom…or to taunt Sam.

"A bad seed." The ranger captain's chair squeaked when he leaned forward. "Some men are born killers."

This poster, as with all the others, didn't bear a likeness, not even a crude drawing. There were no physical features to go on. Frustration boiled. The lawman in him itched to be out there tracking Weston. The need to bring him to justice rose so strong that it choked Sam. Weston was *his* outlaw to catch, and instead, he'd been ordered home.

Hell! Spending one week on the huge Lone Star Ranch was barely tolerable. A month would either kill him, or he'd kill big brother Houston. The thought had no more than formed before guilt pricked his conscience. In the final moments before the outlaw had hit his horse and left Sam dangling by his neck, regrets had filled his thoughts. He'd begged God for a second chance so he could make things right.

Now, it looked like he'd get it. He'd make the time count. He'd mend bridges with his father, the tough Stoker Legend.

Family was there in good times and bad.

Despite his better qualities, Stoker had caused problems for him. Sam had driven himself to work harder, be quicker and tougher, to prove to everyone his father hadn't bought his job. Overcoming the big ranch, the money, and the power the Legend name evoked had been a continuing struggle.

Captain O'Reilly opened his desk drawer, uncorked a bottle of whiskey, and gave his coffee a generous dousing. "Want to doctor your coffee, Sam?"

"Don't think it'll help," he replied with a tight smile.

"Suit yourself." The hardened ranger put the bottle away. The white scar on his cheek had never faded, left from a skirmish with the Comanche.

Sam studied that scar, thinking. Although Sam had intended to keep quiet about the woman he may or may not have bumped into on the way over, out of fear of being labeled a lunatic for sure, he felt a duty to say something. He wouldn't voice doubts that he'd imagined it. "Cap'n, I saw something that keeps nagging at me. I collided with a young woman a few minutes ago. All I said was sorry, but a man grabbed her arm and shoved her into the alley between the mercantile and telegraph office. I saw fear in her eyes. When I followed, they got on a waiting horse and rode off. Can you send someone to check it out?"

Sam winced at how quickly doubts filled O'Reilly's eyes. The captain was wondering if this was one more example of Sam breaking with reality. Hell! If he'd conjured this up, he'd commit himself into one of those places where they locked up crazy people.

O'Reilly twirled his empty cup. "After the bank robbery a few weeks ago, we don't need more trouble. I'll look into it."

"Thanks. I hope it was nothing, but you never know." Relieved, Sam took a sip of coffee, wishing it would warm the cold deep in his bones.

"When's the train due to arrive, Legend?"

"Within the hour." Sam would obey his orders, but the second his forced sabbatical was over, he'd hit the ground running. He'd dog Luke Weston's trail until there wasn't a safe place in all of Texas to even get a slug of whiskey. He'd heard the gunslinging outlaw spent time down around Galveston and San Antone. That, Sam reckoned, would be a good starting point.

O'Reilly removed his boots from the desk and sat up. "I seem to recall your family ranch being north-west of here on the Red River."

"That's right."

"Ever hear of Lost Point?"

Sam nodded. "The town is west of us. Pretty law-less place, by all accounts."

"It's become a no-man's-land. Outlaws moved in, lock, stock, and barrel. Nothing north of it but Indian Territory. Jonathan Doan is requesting a ranger to the area. Seems he's struggling to get a trading post going on the Red River just west of Lost Point, and outlaws are threatening."

"I'll take a ride over there while I'm home. Weston would fit right in."

"No hurry. Give yourself time to relax. Go fishing. Reacquaint yourself with the family, for God's sake. They haven't seen you in a coon's age."

"Sure thing, Cap'n." The clock on the town square chimed the half hour, reminding him he'd best get moving. Relieved that O'Reilly had softened and allowed him to still work a little, Sam set down his cup. "Appears I've got a train to catch."

O'Reilly shook his hand. "Get well, Sam. You're a good lawman. Come back stronger than ever."

"I will, sir."

At the livery, Sam hired a boy to fetch his bags from the hotel and take them to the station. After settling with the owner and collecting his buckskin gelding, Sam rode to meet the train. He shivered in the cold, steady downpour. The gloomy day reflected his mood as he moved toward an uncertain future. He was on his way home.

To bind up his wounds. To heal. To become the ranger he needed to be.

And he would—come hell or high water, mad as a March hare or not.

Right on time, amid plumes of hissing white steam, the Houston and Texas Central Railway train pulled up next to the loading platform.

Sam quickly loaded Trooper into the livestock car and paid the boy for bringing his bags. After making sure the kerchief around his neck hid his scar, he swung aboard. He had his pick of seats since the passengers had just started to file on. He chose one two strides from the door.

Shrugging from his coat, he sat down and got comfortable.

A movement across the narrow aisle a few minutes later drew his attention, as a tall passenger wearing a low-slung gun belt slid into the seat. Sam studied the black leather vest and frock coat. Gunslinger, bounty hunter, or maybe a gambler? Bounty hunter seemed far-fetched—he'd never seen one dressed in anything as fine. Such men wasted no time with fancy clothing. A gunslinger, then. Few others tied their holster down to their leg. No one else required speed when drawing. Likely a gambler too. Usually the two went hand in hand.

His coloring spoke of Mexican descent. Lines around the traveler's mouth and a gray hair or two in his dark hair put him somewhere around the near side of thirty. Though he wore his black Stetson low on his forehead, he tugged it even lower as he settled back against the cushion.

The fine hairs on Sam's arm twitched. He knew this man. But from where? For the life of him, he couldn't recall. He leaned over. "Pardon me, but have we met?"

Without meeting Sam's gaze, the man allowed a tight smile. "Nope."

Darn the hat that bathed his eyes in dusky shadows. "I'm Sam Legend. Name's not familiar?"

"Nope."

He'd been so certain the man looked familiar. "Guess I made a mistake." Maybe his madness had taken over again. Odd that the man hadn't introduced himself, though.

"Appears so, Ranger."

How did he know Sam was a ranger? He wore no badge. "My apologies," Sam mumbled.

The train engineer blew the whistle and the mighty iron wheels began to slowly turn.

Sam swung his attention back to the gunslinger. A few more words, and he'd be able to place him, surely. "Would you have the time, Mr....?" Sam asked.

"Andrew. Andrew Evan." The man flipped open his timepiece. "It's ten forty-five."

"Obliged." Finally, a name. Not that it proved helpful. Sam was sure he'd left his real one at the Texas border, as men with something to hide tended to do. By working extra hard trying to make himself invisible, Evan had as much as declared that he had things to conceal.

Worse, the longer Sam sat near Andrew, the stronger the feeling of familiarity grew. And that was something Sam's brain had not conjured up. He glanced out the window at the passing scenery, trying to make sense of the thoughts clunking around in his head. When he next looked over at Andrew Evan, Sam wasn't surprised to find the slouching gunslinger's head against the seat with his hat tilted over his eyes.

The hair on his neck rose. Sam felt Andrew's eyes watching from beneath the brim of the Stetson. Then he saw a muscle twitch in Andrew's jaw and watched his Adam's apple slide slowly up and down.

Tension electrified the air.

As Sam stared at Evan's hands, searching for the tattoo, a woman rushed down the aisle. She came even with them just as the train took a curve and tumbled headlong into his lap. He found himself holding soft, warm curves encased in dark wool.

Stark fear darkened the blue eyes staring up at him, and her bottom lip quivered.

A jolt went through him. Lucinda? But no—it couldn't be her. Yet this girl had Lucinda Howard's black hair and blue eyes framed by thick sooty lashes.

His body responded against his will as he struggled with the memory. Hell! At last, he realized this girl was not the faithless lover he'd once known.

But she *was* the woman he'd collided with on his way to Ranger headquarters.

"Are you all right, miss?"

"I–I'm so sorry," she murmured.

He felt her icy hand splayed against his chest through the fabric of his shirt, where it had landed when she tried to break her fall.

"Are you in trouble? I can help."

"They're—I've got to—" The mystery woman pushed away, extricating herself from his lap. With a strangled sob, she ran toward the door leading into the next car.

Sam looked down. Prickles rose on the back of his neck.

A bloody handprint stained his shirt.

Three

HE KNEW FOR DAMN SURE HE HADN'T MADE HER UP this time. Sam grabbed his coat and hurried after the woman. If she was injured, she'd possibly need the coat. A muscle worked in his jaw. He'd make any man rue the day he tried to harm a woman.

Not seeing her among the group in the next coach, he hurried through. Maybe she was out on the small platform separating them from the baggage car.

A pair of fearful blue eyes framed by thick dark lashes swam in his mind, along with the faint fragrance of wild honeysuckle. He had to find her. He had a feeling her life depended on it. But she wasn't on the platform either. That left one option. She could only be hiding with the mailbags and luggage, and sooner or later, whoever was after her would figure that out too.

And when they did, they'd find themselves staring at his Colt.

Sam put on his coat to free his hands. Sliding his weapon from the holster, he opened the door. Swollen by the rain, the wood scraped loudly against the floor. He flinched. So much for trying to keep quiet.

Shadows greeted him and it took a moment for his eyes to adjust to the dim light.

"Don't be afraid, ma'am. I'm Texas Ranger Sam Legend." Movement behind a stack of luggage drew his attention. "I'm here to protect you. Are you injured?"

Please let her answer and quiet the doubts in my head that she is real.

She stood. Even from his position in the doorway, her fear rolled over him, engulfing Sam like thick fog.

"You can trust me." He shut the door and moved slowly toward her. "Are you hurt?"

"Not badly. A cut on my hand—my throat." She moved out of her hiding place. "They'll do worse if they find me."

"Who?"

"Isaac Ford and his gang," she whispered.

Sam's mouth tightened in anger. He might've known. Ford had a reputation for terrorizing folks, women in particular. Sam had dealt with the man over the years and even put him away for a time. Trouble was, Ford never stayed behind bars long.

"I won't let him get you." As Sam's thoughts flew to finding a plan, the train began to slow. "I'm going to get you off this train when we stop at the water station just ahead. What is your name?"

"Sierra Hunt. Thank you, Ranger." She rested a trembling hand on his arm. "They mean to kill me."

Though cold, her touch warmed something deep inside Sam. Sierra Hunt settled his mind and grounded him in a way nothing else had before or since the hanging.

"Ain't gonna happen if I have anything to say about

it, Miss Sierra. You're shivering." He removed his coat and draped it around her shoulders. Where was the cloak he'd seen her in earlier? She'd need something on her head when they went out into the storm.

Sam directed her to a seat on a large trunk. "I'm guessing you lost your cloak."

"Forgot it when I saw my opportunity and ran."

He spied an empty mailbag hanging on a nail. Grabbing it, he took the knife from his boot and sliced the thick burlap up the side. "That's a pretty name you've got. Don't think I've ever heard it before on a woman. Only know Sierra from the large mountain range."

"That's where my parents got it from."

Sam noticed the smile that trembled on her lips. But then, Ford could frighten anyone half to death. "Here's what's going to happen. When we come to a complete stop, we're heading to the livestock car for horses. Then we're leaving Ford and the train behind. It's still storming out, so put this burlap on your head. Maybe it'll help."

Sierra took the bag and started to remove the coat.

"No, keep it. You need it worse. Why is Ford after you?"

"I don't know. Last evening, just after dark, he burst into my brother's office and took me. I tried to escape, but Ford caught me and forced me onto a horse. I spent the cold night in a cave with him and the other six gang members. They…" She put a trembling hand to her mouth. "We rode back to town this morning, and that's when I ran into you."

"And you have no idea why he wants you?"

"He held a gun to my head and kept yelling something about giving him a map. Crazy talk about treasure. I've never seen a map. My brother only runs a modest newspaper. I don't know anything."

No telling with Ford. Maybe he had a rung or two missing from his ladder, too. But the way she lowered her eyes and the little hitch in her breath said she knew more than she was saying. He considered pushing for the truth, then decided to let it be. No use trying to get more out of her just now.

Sam sat down beside her. "It doesn't take much for outlaws to get something in their heads, and when they do, there's no getting it out."

The faint scent of honeysuckle circled him. He wished he could put his arm around her shoulders, but seeing as how they'd just met, it seemed wrong. She'd probably box his ears. Suddenly, his mouth quirked at the corners. Maybe that would fix his fool head.

"I feel safe here with you, Ranger."

"Sam. Call me Sam."

They sat in companionable silence, listening to the rain pounding on the metal roof. She'd talked of feeling safe. He didn't know many people who made him feel that way. His father, his brothers—the men of Legend.

Stoker Legend had been one of the first settlers to North Texas and took up arms in the war for independence. He'd fought Comanches, braved fires, floods, and outlaws to plunk down roots so deep nothing short of a twenty-mule team and thirty pounds of dynamite could yank them out. No stronger, tougher, more fearsome man walked the earth than Stoker Legend. He'd carved his name on Texas land with his blood.

That name would survive long after they were dead.

Although ranching had never appealed to Sam, pride filled him each time he rode beneath the huge crossbar with the words *Lone Star Ranch* emblazoned on it. Sam still called it home whenever he got tired of chasing outlaws and needed to rest...or when he was stove up in the head. Yeah, his father made him feel safe.

If only the man would bend a little and see that Sam was no longer a kid. That would go a long way in ending their head butting. Sometimes he wanted to walk away and never return. But then in times like now, he needed his father, and no one else would do.

Screeching wheels protesting, the train jerked to a stop at the desolate water tank in the middle of nowhere.

"Time to go." Sam went to open the door and jumped down into the pounding rain. Reaching up, he placed his hands around her waist and swung her to the muddy ground. The thick muck immediately buried her high-top boots.

The struggle to free herself would waste precious time. He scooped her up and carried her to the livestock car. She waited in the rain with the mailbag over her head while he lowered the ramp and went to get the horses. With the mounts still saddled, he only had to untie their reins. In no time, he led out every animal in there. Although conscious of possibly facing a trial for horse stealing, Sam wasn't about to leave the outlaws any way of following. He'd report the horses taken and make sure their owners received compensation.

Without asking questions, Sierra pulled herself into the saddle of a mare. Handing her the reins of the other horses, he lifted the ramp back into place.

Sudden gunfire burst through the curtain of rain before Sam had finished. He jerked around and saw Andrew Evan standing on the five-foot-wide platform at the end of the passenger car, plastered to the side of the door, trying to dodge bullets from inside. Ear-splitting screams of women and children rose above the sound of the storm.

Thankfully, Sierra made herself small against the mare's neck. Sam admired her quick thinking. Water poured from the brim of his hat as he wasted no time mounting Trooper and relieving Sierra of the extra sets of reins.

"We have to help him," she yelled above the noise.

He glanced at Andrew, then back at her. He knew he should leave the gunslinger to battle Ford by himself. There was no time—not if he wanted to get Sierra to safety. But then, seven against one wasn't very good odds, even for a man with lightning-fast reflexes. Sam couldn't leave him.

A string of cusswords colored the soggy air. Sam ground out, "The damned fool is trying to save us."

At the last minute, he dug his heels into Trooper's side and swung around. Just as two of the Ford gang burst through the passenger door of the train car, Sam spurred the horse. He rode hard toward Andrew Evan and pulled him onto the back of his horse.

Bullets flew around them as the shaggy-haired outlaw,

Isaac Ford, stood with his legs braced apart, guns blazing, looking for all the world like the devil he was.

Sam prayed Sierra had some skill at riding a horse and that she could keep up, at least until they got out of range.

But even if not, he'd make sure she and Andrew were safe. Another fight, another tough spot to escape, another outlaw to test Sam Legend's mettle.

Calm washed over him. He'd do whatever he must.

❧

Rain stung Sierra's face, soaking her through and through except for where the coat protected. Her teeth chattered, though she didn't cry out from the cold. It was no use. The men were just as miserable, and Sam didn't have anything to shield him, not even a collar to turn up around his neck. So she rode in silence, thankful to be alive.

Once out of Ford's range, Sam stopped to let off the man he'd saved. Selecting a black gelding from the horses, the man mounted up and, with the skies opening up with a pounding fury, they set off again. Sierra held tight to her reins. She'd lost the makeshift head covering somewhere in the mad dash, and the rain stung her face, blinding her. She followed the dim shapes for what seemed like miles until they slowed again.

"We can't keep going," Sam shouted over crashing thunder. Lightning flashed around them, showing his grim features. "Too dangerous for the horses."

"I agree," his partner answered. "There's a place a little farther. Ford and his gang are afoot, and they'll have to stop too, so we should be safe."

Whatever it was would be better than this. Sierra couldn't control her shivers, couldn't feel the reins in her frozen hands. She closed her eyes, picturing a warm fire.

They took off at a trot through the downpour. She fought to stay in the saddle. After crossing one hill and rounding a bend, she could make out a structure through the fog. Thankfulness rushed over her when they stopped at last in front of what appeared to be an abandoned shack. The stranger was right—it offered little in the way of comfort, but she welcomed whatever it could provide. After tying the horses in a thick grove of cedar and oak where the overlapping branches offered respite from the weather, they took shelter in the dark, ramshackle dwelling. Sam held the door for Sierra and she rushed inside. While water steadily dripped from the ends of her limp hair and streamed off the men's hats, she struggled to focus.

Her heart sank. From what she could tell, it was little better than outside.

Water poured through the roof of the shack on one side, splattering the plank floor and creating mud in the thick layer of dirt. Barely able to see in the heavy gloom, she stumbled over a broken chair. Sam's quick reflexes saved her from a fall. After making sure she was steady, he and the gunslinger struck matches, and she got her first real glimpse of the moldy, decaying room. Other than the broken chair, a barrel, a small bench, and a mound in the corner under a piece of canvas completed her inventory. They were dismal surroundings, to say the least.

"What was that fool stunt back there, Evan?" Sam shot angrily.

"You're welcome." The gunslinger stood with his hands tense at his sides. "I bought you a little more time. Thought you could use it."

"No one asked you to. You could've gotten us all killed."

"Yeah, but I didn't. You stole my damn horse, Ranger."

Though Sam had pushed back his hat, Evan still wore his so low it hid his eyes. Uneasiness crawled up her spine. She needed to see men's eyes, to see what they held. Danger oozed from Evan, from the way he walked and talked and how his hands fell at his sides within easy reach of the gun.

Sam replied hotly, "I made sure Ford had no way of coming after us."

"Well, it's a good thing for you I didn't keep my seat in that passenger car. That black gelding is mine, and any man wants to take him will answer to me."

Her breath stuck in her chest. She stared at Evan's low-slung holster and the deadly gun hanging at his side, fearing he'd draw and send a bullet into Sam. Freezing in her wet clothes, Sierra desperately tried to defuse the situation. "Gentlemen, would either of you have another match so we can get warm?" Theirs were nearly burned down now.

With a silent nod, Sam knelt in front of a fireplace made of river rocks to start a fire. "Sierra Hunt, meet Andrew Evan."

"Pleasure to meet you, ma'am." Andrew Evan shook her hand.

The two men were as opposite as night from day. She'd seen Evan's type before, and usually steered clear of such men. Most women would think him handsome, with his dark features, high cheekbones, and a day's growth on his jaw. His long, slender fingers drew her attention as he easily broke the rickety chair apart for kindling and handed the pieces to Sam. Those fingers, his elegant hands—they probably had as much power to end a life as to shuffle cards.

On the other hand, a Texas Ranger made his living riding into danger and saving people like her. True, he was familiar with his weapon also, but didn't wear his gun belt low around his hips, relaying a deadly message.

A tiny smile curved her lips. The dark-haired, gray-eyed ranger cast a tall shadow. She'd read a dozen or more articles about Sam Legend. Her brother had written about his exploits, and some of those stories she'd helped him publish in the paper. From those thrilling accounts, she'd come to know a little about Sam. He was all business and duty and sacrifice, proving it each time he rode out.

She'd asked Rocky once if he'd interviewed Sam. Her brother had said he'd tried several times, but the ranger had turned him down. Sam had insisted he was no hero.

She admired a man who sidestepped attention. The world was full of those who sought to be noticed. Maybe one day, after this was over, he might favor her with his story.

But first, she had to stay alive. Stay alive and find her brother. Everything else could wait.

Thoughts of Isaac Ford and his gang flooded back, bringing uncontrollable trembles. Staying alive would take some doing, because they were out to kill her over a map she didn't have. Something told her she probably hadn't seen the last of the gang.

They were still out there somewhere.

Sierra anxiously watched Sam still laying the fire. "I owe you both for risking your lives on my account. Isaac Ford meant to kill me."

Though Sam kept working, he nodded. "I wouldn't be much of a man if I hadn't. I'm happy to help."

"All the same, I owe you." She moved to the overturned barrel and sat down.

Evan turned. "No thanks needed, pretty lady. We'll have you warm in a minute. I'll see if I can find some dry firewood, Legend. Or do I need to ask your permission first?"

"Of all the... I'm sure it won't make any difference how I answer. You'll do what you want anyway. Your kind always does." With a scowl, Sam swung back to his task. Tension coiled between them, reminding Sierra of a deadly rattlesnake. She tried to keep her teeth from chattering as she studied the two, waiting for the strike. The hostility reminded her of everything she'd left behind in the mountains.

Everything that had sent her running for Texas.

And she was still running. When would it stop?

Four

HEAVY SILENCE SATURATED EVERY INCH, EVERY DUST particle of the small dwelling. Only the crackle of the fire and the spatter of water from the leaky ceiling provided relief as the two men faced each other.

Sam's face hardened as he stood. "Whatever you're trying to prove is out of line, Evan. Miss Sierra doesn't need this. After I get her to safety, you and me will settle up."

Though color crept up the gunslinger's neck, he refrained from a reply. He swung to her. "My apologies, Miss Sierra. I've truly seen the error of my ways." He stalked to the canvas-covered bulk in the corner and revealed a stack of old firewood. "Appears I don't need to go out after all, Legend. Or do I need your permission to use it?"

"Please, I don't want to cause trouble between you." She hated discord, always had. From experience she knew anger made men say foolish things, which led to violent acts. But why were these two men at odds?

"You're not," Sam said firmly, building the fire

up with the newly discovered wood. "Just a slight disagreement. Come and get warm." He pulled the bench over for her.

Shivering, Sierra went to share the fire with him. He seemed far safer than Evan, with his taunting anger and face half wreathed in shadow. She turned to Sam, a question on her tongue. She was a practical woman and needed to get a clear picture. "Now what?" she asked quietly. "Where are you taking me?"

"I haven't thought beyond getting you safe." Sam's gray eyes met hers in the firelight. "Is there anywhere I can take you? Any secure place?"

"No." Sierra shivered as fear washed over her anew. "I won't be safe anywhere as long as Ford runs free," she whispered.

His glance steadied her. "You're safe with me. That's a promise." Sam swung to Andrew Evan. "If anything happens to me, you take her to the safety of the Lone Star. It's—"

"I know the place."

"Then you won't have a problem," Sam snapped.

"Except for one. I'm parting company here."

Sam's eyes turned as icy as a winter's day. "Might be an excellent idea. Why you didn't stay on the train, I'll never know."

The dangerous undercurrent rippling between the two men filled Sierra with renewed unease. As one who kept secrets, she recognized all the signs of others who did, and the gunslinger had a fat, juicy one.

"I had no intentions of getting off until I saw you with the horses." The edge in Evan's voice sliced the air. "You seemed to have everything under control."

"And yet, here you are," Sam pointed out.

"Isaac Ford stomped into the passenger car with blood in his eye, saying he'd kill anyone helping the girl. Then he saw me and started shooting. Returning fire would've put a lot of people in harm's way, so I ran to the exit."

"What does Ford have against you? Did you meddle in his business too? You seem to make a habit of that."

"What's stuck in your craw, Legend?" Evan spewed. "Spit it out."

Her breath caught as Sam scowled at the gunslinger. "Not in front of a lady," he said quietly.

"Please, this hasn't been easy for either of you and I'm to blame." Sierra leaned closer to the fire to dry her hair. Funny, the power that small word held. *Blame.* Though her father hadn't exactly said it in so many words, she'd seen blame in his eyes day after day until finally he'd put her on the stage in Billings. Something else had filled his eyes before he coldly turned his back...disgust, loathing. Then he'd climbed on his horse.

"Can't you just trust each other? For me? Please?" she cried.

Sam scrubbed his face and turned, softening his voice. "You're not to blame for anything. You're a refreshing breath of air, and I didn't realize how much I needed that until today. Meeting you reminded me of what I've lost of myself. I truly owe you a debt of thanks. And yes, Evan and I will learn to trust each other. For you."

The fire knocked off a layer of chill in the cabin, and Sierra removed Sam's coat. She handed it back to him. "Thank you—for trying to get along and the loan of this. Although the wool is damp, it's better than nothing."

He nodded his appreciation, sliding his arms into the sleeves. "Anything will help when I check the horses."

Andrew stood. "I'll go take a look around outside if it's all right with the lawman. See if we have any visitors. Would you like anything, *amiga*?"

"*Amiga*"? What did that mean? His voice had softened when he'd addressed her, so she gathered it must be some kind of endearment. Her cheeks grew hot. Confused, she offered a smile and kept working on drying her hair. "Thank you, but I'm fine."

Relief swept through Sierra when the door closed behind him. She reached to move the bench a little closer to the fire, only to catch her palm on the rough wood. Stinging pain raced through her. The cut Isaac Ford had made reopened.

Sam noticed the blood and gently lifted her hand. His eyes hardened as he examined the jagged cut. "You didn't say how Ford did this."

"He sliced my palm with a knife," she whispered.

Sam touched the wound on her throat above her collar. "This as well?"

The steely grit of his tone might've frightened her if not for the concern in his gray eyes. She nodded.

"I'll make him and his men pay for what they did."

The bold statement took her aback. "I only want to distance myself from them, nothing more."

"That's not the way the Texas Rangers do things." He removed a bandana from around his neck. "Best clean your cuts before they get infected."

She reached for the bandana, but her attention swept to an angry red scar around the base of his throat.

A forgotten memory hurled her back to Montana. She'd been twelve years old when she stumbled across a shepherd dangling from the gnarly branch of a white-bark pine. Chills had wracked her body. She'd never forgotten the terror on his bloated face, in his bulging eyes that stared unseeing into the beyond.

Sam Legend had faced that darkness.

The hair on her arms rose with the knowledge. Memories circled in her head: how she'd run to get her father, cutting down the poor shepherd, burying him under that same tree.

On unsteady legs, she stumbled to the steady stream of water pouring from the buckling ceiling. Wetting the cloth, she washed the blood from her hands, then her throat. She couldn't shake that horrible image. Sam dangling by the neck, choking, facing the end. Her body trembled. She wondered if, at least in part, it would be similar to drowning. Nothing could be more agonizing than fighting to live in the face of death.

The despair that came in the end of knowing it wasn't to be.

Sierra didn't realize she stood rooted in place until a loud popping made her jump.

Sam met her worried gaze. "It's okay. You're safe." He paused. "But maybe you don't feel safe anymore, the way me and Evan… I apologize for our bickering. This weather seems to have put us both in a foul mood."

"You don't owe me an explanation."

"You should knock our fool heads together." Sam

rubbed his knee as though the joint ached. "What was the name of your newspaper?"

"My brother, Rocky, named it *The Waco Explorer Inquisitor*."

Surprise—and maybe admiration—filled his gaze. "I've heard of it. You give an honest accounting of the facts, no matter how it rankles some. I have to say you hide your ink stains well."

Sierra felt heat rush to her cheeks. "I try."

"Then I should take you back to him. I'm sure he's worried, wondering what's happened to you."

She shook her head, struggling to stay calm and matter-of-fact. "He's disappeared. My brother has made enemies."

"Are you speaking of Ford?"

"Among others. But yes, him for sure. I think he or some of his associates may have kidnapped Rocky." Was he alive? Or dead? Though a sob tried to rise, she raised her chin, determined to meet whatever came head-on.

"When did your brother go missing?"

Memories swept her back to the chaotic scene in the newspaper office and the little room above it with Rocky's bed not slept in. "Two days ago."

"Did you report it?"

She nodded, holding her hands to the fire that didn't seem to warm her. "First thing. I can't say for sure Ford bears the blame, because I didn't see him take my brother, but it seems logical."

Sam crossed his arms. "Yep. He probably thought Rocky had that treasure map, and when he didn't find it, Ford took you, hoping to make you talk. Or Ford could have planned on using you as leverage against Rocky. I wouldn't put anything past that outlaw."

A lump blocked Sierra's throat. "Look, Ranger, I can't ask you to solve this."

"You're not asking—I'm volunteering. While Ford had you, did you see Rocky?" The firelight brought out Sam's strong profile that seemed to have been chiseled from a piece of granite.

How long it had been since she'd had someone to talk to who would listen? Even Rocky had shut her out with his distractions. She'd been alone for so long. Confiding in Sam and releasing some of her troubles felt nice.

"No. He wasn't in the cave where the outlaws took me. But I overheard Ford mention Rocky's name when talking to one of his men."

"What do you think? Could your brother, or someone else in your family, be involved in anything illegal?"

"No, absolutely not. Our father is an explorer. He and my mother traveled the far reaches of the American West, cataloguing what they found."

"And Rocky?"

Sierra gave her head an emphatic shake. "My brother is many things, but a lawbreaker is not one of them."

"Don't worry. I'll help you find him. We'll get to the bottom of this. But how did Ford come in contact with you and your brother?"

A shiver passed through her even though she stood in front of the warm blaze. "It all began last week. You might as well know our sordid secret. Rocky is…" She paused for a second, wishing Sam didn't have to know how far her family had sunk. "He's a bit of a drinker. He frequents the saloons…looking for worthy news, he says, though I know better.

"He stumbled across some details that bore proof of Ford's crimes and, while quite inebriated, foolishly published them." She dragged the overturned barrel closer and sat down again. "Ford was enraged. He and his men busted into the office, beat Rocky, and threatened to kill us both."

Sheer terror flooded her mind. She took several deep breaths, fighting tremors, remembering the feel of that gun pressed to her head. "I got loose and ran out screaming for help. They escaped out the back way."

"I'm sure you were terrified. So they came at you twice." Sam's quiet reflection banished some of the chill. "When did you last see Rocky?"

"Two nights after that incident. We closed the shop, and he walked me to my room at the boarding-house. He told me good night, and that's the last time I saw him. When I went to open the next morning, his bed hadn't been slept in. I didn't notice anything missing. I haven't seen him since." Now it was too late. Everything was too late. That foolish, foolish article had put them in untold danger. *Oh, Rocky, what have you done?*

Fear knotted her stomach. She'd spoken with the sheriff, but his interest had waned once he'd learned of Rocky Hunt's restless feet. When she found her brother, would he be alive? Or dead?

Rocky shared her father's obsessive nature, except that her brother's passions were drinking and the newspaper.

Was it possible he'd ridden out following a story and gotten waylaid? Or had he simply forgotten the way back? Forgotten about her?

He'd been overjoyed to see her when she arrived a few weeks ago. She'd settled into a nearby board-inghouse and immersed herself in her work, feeling as though she'd truly left her past behind. Or had she? Maybe a person never outran their mistakes. Maybe problems simply followed behind on an invisible leash.

At any rate, now Rocky was gone, and she was running for her life.

The door banged open, and Andrew Evan tried to maneuver inside with another load of wood. Sierra hurried to help.

Water gushed from his hat when he dropped the wet logs. "No sign of letting up. Found a woodpile out back, just like I thought there would be. Maybe this will have time to dry some before we use up the other."

"With luck it will." Sierra grabbed for a piece that tumbled from the top.

"*Gracias, amiga.*" Evan took it from her. "For your smile, I would walk barefoot across hot desert sand."

Sierra blushed.

"The lady doesn't want to listen to a bunch of foolish drivel," Sam growled. She could tell that Sam itched to say more. Judging by his black glower, eating the unsaid words appeared to leave a bad taste on his tongue. She appreciated the effort.

That tension was back, stretching Sierra's nerves. She looked at him out of the corner of her eyes and spotted the rope mark about his throat. She yearned to offer sympathy but didn't know how. Maybe it was best to pretend she hadn't seen it. She returned Sam's bandana and thanked him instead.

With a grin, Evan reached into his coat pocket and pulled out six apples. "Found an apple tree within spitting distance of the shack. Lots of fruit on the ground." He handed her one. "A special one for you, *amiga*."

Sierra gave him a bright smile. "This is wonderful. I haven't eaten since yesterday."

"Seems you've saved our bellies, along with our lives," Sam drawled, catching an apple Andrew pitched. "Miss Sierra, earlier you asked where I was taking you. Where do you want to go? Name it, and I'll make it happen."

Evan lowered to the floor in front of the fire and stretched out his long legs. "Have a husband waiting?"

"No."

"Parents?" Evan pressed.

The old panic climbed up her spine. Why wouldn't they change the subject?

Thoughts of her father flashed through her head. Avoiding the ranger's questioning stare, she polished her apple on her wet skirt. "Like I said, I have no one, no place." No life.

"Then I'll take you to my family's ranch, the Lone Star, until I find your brother. You'll be safe there."

His gaze steadied her. "Again, I'm not sure such a place exists, but thank you."

"Just makes sense." Sam leaned forward and rested his arms on his knees.

Could he also save her from other perils? She wanted

to ask if they'd have to cross any rivers to get to the ranch, only the words were stuck in her throat.

With this heavy rain, creeks and rivers would be swollen.

Dangerous.

Deadly.

A cold shiver ran up Sierra's back.

Evan swung his attention to Sierra. "I'd like to hear about your life."

Sierra frowned, wishing they wouldn't ask. "I don't like to talk about it, but I can see you're not going to let it go. From my earliest memory, my parents dragged us from pillar to post. William and Daisy Hunt saw no need to let a bunch of small kids tie them down as they traveled the American West. I quickly found unpacking to be a useless endeavor."

She focused on the thick layer of dirt on the floor, remembering how she used to beg to have a normal home, permanence…friends…a suitor. "The longest we ever stayed in one spot was high in the Sierra Nevada. We wintered there only because we got snowed in and couldn't leave." Four lovely months spent in that one place had sparked a fierce dream that refused to die. She knew she couldn't live as a wanderer.

Sam leaned toward the fire, warming his hands. "How do you like Texas?"

Sierra lifted her gaze and fell headlong into his stare. "It's beautiful. Nowhere is the sky this big and the sunsets as vivid. The wide-open spaces enchant me. Although I've seen amazing things others can't begin to dream about, I've had more than enough. From now

on, I'll settle for nothing less than permanence and putting down deep roots."

And a chance for her dream to become a reality. A
chance to forget and learn how to live with the pain
of her choices.

"Roots are good." Sam tossed his apple core into
the fire. "Let me see your hand. I want to check the
bleeding." He spoke as he examined the cut, holding
her hand in his. "Your experiences prepared you for
everything life will throw your way. I admire you,
Sierra. You showed real gumption today."

"You give me far too much credit." She studied the
hand that held hers. He wouldn't think her worthy of
admiration if he learned what she'd done.

She was a coward and despised herself for it.

A coward didn't deserve to be safe and warm with
shiny apples to eat.

Five

SIERRA GLANCED AT HER FINGERS CURLING INSIDE SAM'S large palm. Hands told so much about a woman. Or man. Sam's had thick calluses, telling of a good portion of life spent outdoors. Whereas Andrew Evan's had seemed smooth and more suited to saloons, gambling dens, and the ability to quickly draw a pistol.

Two men. Total opposites.

She drew a shaky breath, noticing that even her fingers showed her cowardice. They hid, cowering inside the warm pocket he'd created. She swallowed the choking lump in her throat.

Andrew opened the door and stood looking at the raging storm. Every few minutes, lightning slashed across the sky and thunder rattled every board of the cabin.

Sierra leaned closer to Sam so Andrew wouldn't hear. "What does 'amiga' mean, and why does he call me that?"

"It's nothing. Want me to tell him to stop?"

She shook her head. "No."

"If you change your mind, let me know. I'll be happy to set him straight."

No doubt. But she didn't want trouble. Changing the subject seemed best. She prayed it erased his stormy expression and that piercing gray stare that saw too much. "What time do you suppose it is?"

The ranger released her hand. "I figure early afternoon."

"It's so gloomy in here with only the fireplace. And the heavy clouds outside block any light that might drift through the chinks in the walls."

Where would she...*they* sleep? She felt Sam's gaze follow her as she poked around the ramshackle one-room dwelling that had probably once served as someone's homestead. Thick spiderwebs hung from the corners like gray ghosts, watching her. A shiver raced along her spine. She knew how it was to have eyes following her every move.

"You're worried about your brother," Sam said.

Was Rocky out in this rain, cold and hungry? Her chin quivered. She desperately needed to know he was safe. "No matter the cost, I'll do anything to save him," she whispered.

Like an old letter that was read and reread, she'd been over everything until it wore thin. If she had a map, she'd gladly turn it over to Ford and his gang. In saving Rocky, maybe she could find some sort of redemption. But if he died, her father would be right.

"I've been mulling this over, and something doesn't fit. If they have Rocky, why did they kidnap you?" Sam's stare made her fidget.

"I can't say. Look, I can't ask..." Fear spread through her. Sierra swallowed the last of the sentence as her throat closed around the words.

Sam rose. Slipping his arms around her, he pulled her against him. Unable to resist, she leaned her head on his chest, if only for a moment. "It's all right," he murmured, smoothing her hair. "I'm not going to let Ford near you. I'll keep you safe while we figure things out." His voice had a hard edge as he added, "But there *will* be a reckoning for Ford in the end."

It had been so long since anyone had held her or spoken comforting words. Still, she couldn't let him get too close, or he would see all the pain. Men like him tried to fix things and right wrongs. Nothing could fix this. With an upward glance, she attempted a smile that wavered and died before it formed. "You're a good man, Ranger."

A sudden grin deepened the crow's-feet at the corners of his eyes, softening his features. "I'll bet you tell every banged-up lawman that."

Sensing Andrew watching, she pushed away.

Sam buttoned his coat. "I'll go check on the horses. This storm is probably making them nervous."

"I'll go with you," Andrew said.

The fire crackled and popped, breaking the silence in the wake of their departure.

Sierra sat beside the fire. With her hair now dry, she tried to braid it, but it had become a tangled mess. The task was hopeless without a comb, and she gave up. She faced an uncomfortable night ahead. Her wet clothes made her cold and miserable; rain had drenched the many layers and would take a long while to dry on her.

She glanced at the thick layer of dirt on the floor.

Well, she supposed she'd slept on worse. A blast of thunder made her jump. Where were the men? She wished they'd hurry back.

After what seemed like an hour, the door swung open, and Sam strode in with rain running off his coat and hat onto the floor. Bedrolls and saddlebags loaded him and Andrew down.

Sierra went to help. "Where did you get all this stuff?"

"The horses," Sam said. "We unsaddled the mounts and removed the gear. The overlapping branches of the trees kept most of it pretty dry."

"All for you, *amiga*." Andrew gave her a grin, pulling out a shiny ribbon.

"That's wonderful! You're amazing, Andrew Evan."

"Yeah, downright amazin', all right," Sam said dryly.

Sierra pulled back her hair and secured it with the ribbon. The strip of satin helped immensely, even though tangles still made her hair nigh unmanageable. "How long have you known each other?" The ranger and the gunfighter mixed like oil and water.

Sam snorted. "Not until today on the train. Although I believe I know him from somewhere."

"Nope," Evan murmured. He'd squatted down and was rummaging through one of the saddlebags he'd brought in. Bedrolls, nine in all, lay on the floor. That would help pass the night in comfort. Sam sat down and reached for one.

Sierra didn't know what to believe. Utter strangers didn't get their backs up at each other for no reason, but plainly they weren't going to discuss it.

Several times over the last two hours, she'd caught

Andrew staring at Sam with an odd look on his face. And why did he wear his hat all the time, even in the dim room lit only by the fire? Her certainty that he was hiding something became stronger with each passing moment.

Releasing an exasperated sigh, she turned to the bounty Andrew had brought in. They didn't hold secrets.

The saddlebags from the Ford gang yielded the most: jerky, a beat-up coffeepot with the makings for more, extra ammunition, and two bottles of whiskey. Some of which would come in handy.

Out of one saddlebag, Sam lifted an oilskin-wrapped piece of frayed burlap. Removing the layers, he brought a big stack of currency into the light.

"How much do you think is there?" Sierra asked quietly.

"Got to be at least five hundred dollars, maybe more."

Andrew gave it a glance. "Outlaw loot."

A piece of paper fluttered to the floor. Sierra picked it up. "Looks like a telegraph." She opened it and read aloud:

BRING THE PACKAGE TO ME IN TEN DAYS STOP
FIND THE MAP STOP YOU KNOW WHAT HAPPENS
IF YOU DON'T STOP FB

The threat tightened her already fragile nerves. That blasted map! It came up every way she turned. Her life and that of her brother's hinged on that one mysterious item.

"Sounds like the Ford gang answers to a boss." Sam turned to Sierra. "You don't have to speculate any longer on why they took you and Rocky."

"I wish I knew what the sketch looked like or where it is. I'd give it to them in a heartbeat."

Evan leaned forward. "What map are you talking about?"

"One Ford thinks I have and will do anything to get." Sierra stared into the flames, wondering if Rocky had one and didn't tell her. It would hold true to form.

"How come the person who sent this telegram thinks you have it?" Sam asked.

Sierra met his gaze. "I wish I knew."

The scowl on Evan's face shot fear through her as he passed a hand across his eyes. "The gang will come after this money. And you, *amiga*."

"Without a doubt," Sam agreed.

Chills raced along Sierra's spine. Her hand flew to her throat, where she felt the rapid thud of her heartbeat. The time she'd spent as their captive flooded back. The hardness of their eyes. The thin blade against her throat. The cold steel of the gun pressed to her head.

If they got her again, they'd kill her.

In an effort to take her mind from the looming threat, she opened two more saddlebags and found clothes. With a little squeal, she stood, holding a pair of pants against herself. They looked to fit her petite frame. They must belong to a very slight man. There were other trousers also. A pair of longer ones appeared close to Sam's six-foot-plus size.

"We can get out of our wet things," she said, grinning.

The tall Texas Ranger smiled back. "I'll go for that."

While she hugged the treasure to her, Andrew pulled a fancy set—black trousers that had silver conchas up the sides and a black shirt—from his own saddlebag. Then, without a word, he gathered one of the bedrolls and got to his feet. Striding to a corner, he draped the fabric on nails sticking from the wood to create a tiny dressing area.

"Your privacy awaits, *dulce*." Evan stepped back, bowing from the waist with a flourish.

There was another strange word. A look at Sam's glower told her to let it pass.

"Thank you, Andrew. You're a perfect gentleman." Maybe she'd been too quick to mistrust him, secrets or no. She quickly grabbed the pants and one of the smaller shirts from the pile and disappeared behind the hanging bedroll. She peeled off the wet wool of her dress and chemise. Thank goodness she had never worn one of those corsets she'd seen on other women. Living in the mountains and not seeing anyone for months at a time, she'd had little need of such. It didn't take long to slip into the dry clothes. Warmth spread throughout her limbs.

She shyly stepped out, clutching the extra material around her waist. With the pants hugging her curves, she felt exposed but free at the same time. "I need a piece of rope."

"Coming up." Sam laid down the stack of money he'd finished counting, took out his knife, and picked up a coiled lariat.

Minutes later, she rewarded Sam with a smile as he cinched her waist. She loved the feel of his hands brushing against her and hummed as she retrieved her wet clothes.

Moments later, with the clothes in front of the fire, she caught Sam's stare.

"You have the smile of an angel," he murmured, then flushed with embarrassment. The soft words he evidently hadn't meant to say brought heat to her cheeks.

An angel? Lord knew she was far, far from that.

"Thank you, Ranger." Maybe not using his name would remind him not to get too familiar. Still, her heartbeat had picked up speed.

Andrew pitched Sam one of the whiskey bottles. "This'll warm us up."

The ranger made a one-handed catch. Sierra watched him stare at the bottle a long moment as though pondering something. He finally opened it and took a long swallow. Andrew uncorked the other and took a drink.

A little while later, all three sat in dry clothes, watching the coffee boil. The aroma of the hot brew wound through Sierra, bringing the first optimism she'd known in days. Maybe more than she had a right to, given their situation.

"Coffee's almost ready. A few more minutes." Using Sam's wet shirt to protect her hand, she removed the pot from the embers so the grounds would settle.

"I'm all for that. It'll taste mighty good," Sam said.

The gray-eyed lawman drew her admiration. From beneath her lashes, she took in his hair, a shade that reminded her of rich coffee beans. The firelight played on the dark strands, bringing out a luster. She suspected he was unaccustomed to the length brushing his shoulders. Strands kept falling into his face, and each time, he impatiently shoved them back. She relished the ruggedness it added, though he certainly didn't need anything extra to set her heart racing.

Andrew was handsome, with hair the color of midnight. But the dark stubble on his jaw whispered danger. He didn't make excited quivers run through her body with a look.

Sam had quiet confidence and a strength that made her feel safe and protected. She knew he'd put his life on the line for her with no questions asked. After all, he already had. And something told her it would take more than a bullet to stop him. He was the kind who kept on coming, despite the odds, bad weather, and any physical challenges. When a brave man took a stand, it stiffened the spines of others. That described the Sam Legend she'd read so much about. She felt braver simply being next to him.

"I don't know how I can ever repay you," she said. "Just last night, I froze in a cave, fearing for my life. Now, I'm warm and dry and safe."

"You don't owe me anything, and we aren't home yet," he answered.

A change rippled in his gray eyes at the word *home*. They'd held a flash of fire when he and Andrew had words, and she'd seen them take on the coldness of a wintry day when he spoke of Isaac Ford. Sam Legend was a man with hard edges, yet he'd shown great gentleness when he held her and stroked her hair. He made her feel safe from every threat, even the ones she'd locked away in a far corner of her heart.

And the way he said *home* made her long for one of her own.

Part of her wished…

But he'd never want a woman like her, someone too opinionated by half. And short. She was short. A woman with long legs and an elegant frame would suit his height better. A woman like everything she'd never be—tall and cultured and pretty. Those women would always have male attention.

Her chin quivered. All she needed was one chance, one person to say *You matter to me. I'll stand beside you to the end of time. Your happiness is the most important thing.* No one had ever said that in twenty years, and she was far too old now. Her time had passed.

Since she was a little girl, she'd dreamed of owning a small house with a white picket fence around it. She had pictured rows of pretty flowers across the front and a garden in the back where she could grow things. A place of her own where she'd never have to pull up stakes. Strong roots called to her like a robin to his mate, rich soil that could feed her starving soul as well as her stomach.

Except Isaac Ford stood between her and that dream. And it may never be hers to claim.

Six

SAM SPENT A SLEEPLESS NIGHT IN THE DRAFTY SHACK WITH Sierra and Andrew lying beside him on their bedrolls.

Once he'd dozed off, only to jerk awake, gasping for air. He'd sat up, drenched with sweat. When would it end? Over and over he relived the moment when he knew he was going to die. The feel of the rope tightening around his neck, the second his feet dangled helplessly in the air was embedded in his memory. He recalled everything about that day—the color of the cloudless sky, the temperature of the air... and the taste of fear that sat on his tongue like a rotted piece of meat.

Eventually, his heartbeat slowed, and the sweat dried.

With a troubled sigh, Sam turned his thoughts to Sierra Hunt and his limited options. They could ride back to the watering station and wait for a train to Fort Worth, but Ford likely stood between them and the tracks.

Maybe angling north, intersecting the tracks farther up and catching a train there?

Damn his aching head that clouded his judgment!

Tired of his muddled thoughts, he glanced at his nearest sleeping companion. In the firelight, Sierra's cloud of dark hair billowed out around her head like the wings of a delicate bird. He'd loved when she'd removed the ribbon before bed and let the strands flow down her back.

He doubted she even knew how beautiful she was. But it was more than outward appearance. Beauty also shone from the inside and her kind heart.

Though the liberties Andrew Evan had taken with her made him mad enough to cuss, it was no wonder the man called her *amiga* and *dulce*. She *was* a friend—and a very sweet one.

Sam was still amazed at the effect she had on him. Almost from the moment they'd met, he became more settled, surer of himself, more confident in his abilities. She grounded him in reality, and the doubts that plagued him before had begun to fade.

She lay so near, tempting, pulling him toward her. Unable to resist, he lightly touched the back of her hand, resting only inches away on the bedroll. The woman had been through sheer hell, but her enormous will to survive had given her the strength and courage to escape Isaac Ford.

A lesser woman would've folded.

His eyes swept to the cuts Ford had made on her palm and throat, which were barely visible in the dim light, and his resolve hardened. There *would* be a reckoning, even if he had to track Ford and his gang to the ends of the earth. He'd make them pay.

An ache in his gut formed as he focused on Sierra's soft, perfectly shaped lips. A sudden hunger to kiss her consumed him. He couldn't help but imagine what it would be like. She was kind and sweet like honey, but with wild passion burning in her eyes.

Sierra Hunt would definitely taste like wild honey.

The thought teased the edges of his mind. When she'd come out wearing those figure-hugging trousers, he'd had to force himself to keep breathing. From that moment until the time they'd crawled into the bedrolls, he'd made a damn fool of himself because he couldn't take his eyes off her curves.

Then every time she'd bent over, oh Lord! His heart hammered so hard he felt sure it would jump out of his chest.

It was more than that, though. She was genuine with a heart that beat true. She also would see Evan's pretty words for what they were—an attempt to turn her head.

Anyone could see through that.

Sierra's fresh scent swirled around him, making him think of things better left alone. Rubbing his eyes, he forced his thoughts away from temptation.

A safer subject was how to get her to the Lone Star. Instead of the train, maybe he should put her on a stagecoach somewhere? If he did, one thing for sure, he wasn't going to let her go alone. He'd stable Trooper until he could get back for him. Only one problem—how far would he have to go to find a stagecoach? The one-horse towns between them and the ranch probably wouldn't be on a route.

Finally he settled on a plan of action. He'd try the train first. If that failed, they had horseback as a last resort.

But with or without Andrew Evan remained to be seen. The man had vowed to go his separate way—but would he? Whoever or whatever the mysterious gunslinger really was, Sam didn't trust him. And damned if he knew why. He was still sure he knew him. Positive.

The lawman in him prayed he found the answer before it was too late.

After they'd changed into dry clothes last evening, he'd again felt that familiar thing pass between them. The feeling burrowed deep into his mind like some kind of rat, gnawing at the elusive memory niggling in his brain. Those dark trousers with the silver conchas up the side that Evan pulled from his saddlebag seemed familiar. But admittedly, they seemed to be the fashion among males of Mexican descent, which Evan clearly was.

Slender fingers of light squeezed through some of the chinks in the wall. Daylight must be near. With the water no longer streaming from the ceiling, he knew the rain had stopped. At least that was welcome news. He closed his eyes, hoping to catch a few more winks. If he got up now, he'd wake the others, and Sierra needed her rest for the grueling day ahead.

The fire popped as the soaked wood he'd thrown on in the wee hours finally dried enough to catch.

The creaking floor seemed to send a warning that the ramshackle abode was about ready to fall in.

Sam rolled over and focused on his breathing, reaching for calm, trying to quiet the whispers in his head.

The door eased open. He jerked to attention and reached for his Colt. As he made it to his feet, he caught sight of Andrew Evan disappearing outside with his bedroll under one arm and saddlebags thrown over his shoulder. The gunslinger was up to something!

But what? Evan had threatened to part ways here. Maybe he was getting an early start.

Sam hurried toward the largest chink in the wall to peer out. Evan stood, looking toward the horses as though contemplating taking one or all. He removed his black hat and rubbed his eyes before swiveling to face the eastern horizon.

Familiar pale green eyes—ones that had stared at Sam more than once over the top of a bandana rocked him backward.

Luke Weston!

Fury crawled up the back of his neck. He should have pressed the issue and forced the man to remove that damn hat hours ago. He'd put Sierra's fate into the hands of a wanted man, an outlaw. A murderer no less.

One who had a thousand-dollar bounty on his head.

Sierra had asked him to trust Evan, and now look what it got him. The outlaw had been right under his nose the whole time. Laughing about it. All the strange statements, the sly grins, the flashes of anger, the familiar fancy trousers suddenly made sense.

Hell! The string of silent cusswords left a blue streak across his mind.

The arrogance of the cocky outlaw. The joke would be on him. Sam intended to slam his butt behind bars so fast his head would swim. One thought bothered him, though. Could Luke be in cahoots with Ford? Had he been luring them into a trap all along?

Sam scrambled toward his gun belt lying next to his

bedroll and slung it around his waist. Weston hadn't seen him. He was sure of that. That gave Sam the advantage. But he needed to pretend ignorance a bit longer or he'd spook Weston. This was his best chance to date of finally catching him. His heart raced.

Sierra rose up from her bedroll and smiled. "Good morning."

"I didn't mean to wake you."

"It's time to get moving. Besides, my bones are tired of lying here. I heard you cry out in your sleep. Are you all right?" She threw aside the extra bedroll she'd used for a blanket and stood.

"I'm fine," he murmured quietly.

Keeping Sierra in the cabin was crucial. But how to do that? She'd have to go out to take care of personal needs. Sam had seen more than one instance where the criminal grabbed the person nearest to use as a shield, sometimes ending with the hostage's death.

"Where's Evan?" she asked.

Getting ready to run? Getting ready to meet up with the Ford gang? Or getting set to shoot when they walked out the door? Weston had already added murder to his list of crimes. They could hang him only once.

"Went out," Sam said. Simple and plain.

"I'll fetch water." She moved toward the pot. "I can't wait to feel the sun on my face."

He froze. He couldn't let her face any danger.

"No. I'll go. It's muddy and you'll ruin your shoes. Stay in here, pretty lady, where it's warm and dry." Sam took the pot, leaving before she could object, praying she wouldn't follow.

Outside, his jumpy nerves settled into a familiar calm. He slid his Colt from the holster, scanning the area. But his quarry had already disappeared. Sam dropped the coffeepot and raced toward the horses, wondering if Weston had seen him through the chink in the wall after all.

Or was it his damn bad luck at work again? Hell!

With his heart pounding, he didn't slow until he reached the cool shadows of the trees.

Would the horses be there?

If Weston *had* ridden off, he wouldn't hesitate one second in taking them all, leaving him and Sierra afoot.

Gripping his Colt, Sam crept closer.

The sound of cushioned hoofbeats reached his ears a second before a black gelding galloped past a hundred yards away.

"Stop, Weston! Stop, damn you!" Sam raised his gun and fired. A large tree trunk shielded the outlaw as he rode by, the bullet splitting the bark. Weston never looked back.

Only one thing remained—to see if the outlaw had left them a horse, or untied and run them all off.

The overlapping branches had kept back much of the deluge. Though water dripped from the leaves, the ground was firmer here. He moved forward, afraid to hope. It wasn't for him but for Sierra. She wouldn't last long afoot.

He finally glimpsed movement through the leafy forest and made out the shapes of horses.

Sam gave a sigh of relief. At least they had a way to travel.

That Weston had again shown a smattering of

compassion came as a shock. He'd done wrong but had turned around and tempered it with good. Just like the time he'd shot Sam in the leg then sent help.

Damn, if he could only figure the outlaw out!

A sound from behind alerted him. Luke doubling back and sneaking up behind him? He whirled, his finger tightening on the trigger, and shoved his Colt into the person's face.

A jolt raced through him as he stared at Sierra.

She gasped, her eyes wide in fear.

"Thought I told you to stay in the shack." He hated the angry words, but he reeled from the shock of how close he'd come to ending her life.

His jagged nerves had trouble settling for several beats of his heart. He could still feel his finger pulling back on the trigger that would've sent a bullet into her. Sam's hand shook as he returned the Colt to his holster.

"I couldn't wait. Something's going on. What's wrong, Sam?" A quiver in the words spoke of Sierra's fear. "Where's Andrew?"

"Andrew Evan is the outlaw Luke Weston, and I've been chasing him nigh onto a year." At her soft cry, he put his arm around her and held her next to him. "I recognized him this morning when I finally saw him without his hat. Those eyes are burned into my memory."

"I liked him. He seemed real nice. You suspected, didn't you? That was the reason for the tension I kept feeling."

"I knew he was familiar, but it's been hard trusting my instincts lately." He smoothed back her tendrils of dark hair. "Forgive me? I almost shot you. Lady, you scared me out of ten lives."

"Of course. I should've done as you told me, only I heard shots. It's my fault."

Sam tried to drag his stare from her tousled hair and soft curves that the trousers did little to hide. She was a sight for sure. He swallowed hard, trying not to think about running his hands over her satiny skin and kissing her until neither had an ounce of breath left.

He felt more like his old self, and he realized it was because of her. She'd fixed him by pushing back the darkness and allowing light into his life. By giving him something—someone—to be a hero for. A swell of deep gratitude rose as he struggled to contain his emotions.

"No, no. I beg to differ, pretty lady. I see no fault at all with you." He looked deep into her blue eyes that saw only goodness. "Since you're here, can you help me bring the mounts to the shack?" Somehow, someway, he'd return the horses that didn't belong to the Ford gang to their rightful owners.

"Sure, Sam." Pride, and maybe a little sadness too, rippled in her pretty eyes. They reminded him of a pale blue sky. In fact, he wasn't sure if they were blue or gray. Maybe a combination of both. Whichever, he loved looking at them.

Her softly parted lips beckoned like a light that guided sailors on a dark, storm-tossed sea.

Kissing her was the only thing on his mind. Not Luke Weston. Not the trials they faced ahead. Not the time he'd have to spend twiddling his thumbs on the Lone Star Ranch. He knew he had to taste her mouth or die wanting.

Placing his large hands below her jawline, Sam lowered his head and gently pressed his lips to hers. Heat pooled low in his gut as he tasted the tangy sweetness that *did* faintly resemble wild honey. Just as he'd imagined.

He tried to hold back, to make the kiss light and meaningless, but his need for her made it impossible. In seconds, the gentle kiss turned urgent, demanding a response.

And Sierra did answer his invitation. With a smothered cry, she leaned into him, clutching a handful of his shirt, holding him to her. The passion and desire that filled Sam seemed to have swept her along.

That she didn't pull away sent joy through him.

A low moan rumbled in his throat as he slid his hand into her dark hair. The satiny strands wrapped around his fingers, tethering her to him. Closing his eyes, he savored the feel of her soft curves molding against the hard planes of his body.

In that second he knew heaven wasn't only golden streets and angels playing harps.

Heaven was Sierra Hunt in his arms.

Seven

OVERWHELMING HUNGER FOR SIERRA SHOOK SAM ALL the way to his toes. The need to scoop her up and never let go spread through him.

That hunger charred the deadness inside him and turned it to ash. As his arms tightened around her, he felt each time her heart beat, each tiny quiver of her body, and each flutter of her pulse that sent blood rushing through her veins. He could almost hear the whooshing sound. It was as if he could see inside her, past the skin and muscle, and had become a part of her.

The kiss aroused burning desire, creating a fire inside like he'd never felt. He'd never been touched, never been kissed by a woman without first paying for the privilege in some form or another—money, favors, or gifts.

Sierra asked for nothing. Not one cent, one pretty bauble, more deeply or one request to do something for her other than protect and keep her safe. Not that she'd asked then. He'd volunteered.

Though he'd yearned for this ever since she fell

into his lap on that train, it was unplanned, and maybe the freedom of it intensified the excitement racing through him.

Or maybe nearly dying had made him feel things more deeply. All he knew was that an unexpected bond had formed between him and this woman.

He slid his hand down her back to her waist, just below the black curtain of her hair. A little moan slipped from her mouth and mingled with his breath. The tips of those silky strands brushed his knuckles.

Sam's senses reeled in the whir of the emotion rushing through him. She smelled of fresh rain and dew-laden honeysuckle. With a growing need to breathe, he ended the kiss. She sighed and rested her head on his chest. His ragged breath ruffled her hair, and surprise that she stayed locked in his embrace wound through him.

He rested his chin on top of her dark head and wrapped his arms tight around her. Sierra was different from any woman he'd ever met. He'd seen the horror in her eyes yesterday when she'd noticed his scar, yet hadn't drawn back in alarm as others had done.

The bandana he always wore hid the ugliness from the world. Concern for her cuts had made him forget the scar for the first time in a long while.

She made him forget a good many things.

"What do we do now?" Sierra whispered.

"About the kiss? Or about Luke?" His question came out bruised. He hoped he wouldn't have to apologize, because her tenderness meant more than she'd ever know.

The shake of her head set her long black hair rippling like a dark waterfall. "I don't regret the kiss."

Good. He allowed a quick grin before he turned serious. "Luke Weston can crawl through a briar patch for all I care. But when I get you to safety, I'm going after him."

Once and for all, Sam would put the man where he belonged—either in jail or a grave. Didn't much matter which.

She moved out of his arms, and a sense of sudden loss enveloped him. Noticing her shiver, Sam removed his coat, draping it around her. "Right now, you're cold and we're going to have coffee. You can change back into your own clothes. Then we'll cut a trail to the Lone Star."

It took real effort to suggest she shed the trousers that clung to her curves, but he knew it would be far safer.

For both of them.

A bright smile made her blue eyes sparkle like stars. "I knew you'd have a plan, but I really was talking about the kiss."

He didn't even want to allow himself to think of what could come after. The touch of his lips on hers had seared itself into his brain.

"Oh," he said, feeling like a jackass. "As for what we do now—I'd like to kiss you again sometime. If you're willing." He sighed. "You made me feel better than I have in a very long time."

"It was special for me too," she whispered. "No one has ever kissed me before."

Shock probably showed on his face. It was hard to fathom. Suitors should've been swarming a pretty woman like her like bees to honey. "No one?"

"You're the first."

Sam grinned and put an arm around her waist. The privilege of offering Sierra her first kiss was all his. But a quiet part of him whispered a prayer that he be the *last*. "Let's gather these horses and get some coffee."

With her lending assistance, he had the horses saddled and ready to ride in no time. A comfortable silence enveloped them as he led the animals to the shack. While she got back into her dress and petticoats, Sam took the horses to the creek and let them drink.

The sudden memory of Luke going out the door with saddlebags over his shoulder flashed across his mind.

The outlaw loot!

Leaving the horses, he raced inside to the pile of leather Sierra had neatly stacked. Finding his saddlebag, he emptied the contents and froze.

The frayed burlap bundle of money he'd stuck inside was gone.

Hell and be damned!

Another thought followed. Could Weston be the F. B. in the telegraph they'd found tucked in with the money?

The wanted man went by a slew of names, and that fact did nothing to reassure Sam. Clearly F. B. was the brains of the Ford gang, the one they answered to. Luke had smarts—that much he knew.

In the past, Sam had only known Luke to be a loner…with the possible exception of the rustlers who'd tried to hang him. But, to be fair, his involvement with them wasn't a proven fact. Not yet, though he meant to ask first chance he got. The outlaw would definitely be a leader if he were in a gang. Maybe the loner part was just the impression the outlaw *wanted* people to believe.

Sam's temples throbbed. "Just wait until I get my hands on you."

A second later, Sierra strode from the private area Weston had made. "Were you saying something?"

He turned and was struck anew by her beautiful features and the simple wool dress that couldn't hide the flare of her hips.

It took several moments to unglue his tongue from the roof of his mouth. Finally he managed, "Talking to myself."

"What's wrong?"

"The outlaw loot—it's gone. Weston took it."

"No, I refuse to believe that of him. I think I saw it when I returned the contents to the saddlebags earlier."

"I know I put the bundle into mine last night," Sam insisted.

Sierra knelt and began going through them again. "Two of these look alike. In the dim light, maybe you got them mixed up."

It *was* possible, he supposed. Yet, after she'd searched them all, she failed to find the missing money.

"Could you have been mistaken and stuck it inside your boot, thinking it would be safer?"

Willing to try anything, he pulled off his boots and dumped them upside down.

Nothing except his knife fell out.

They were wasting time. He could sort it all out later. Weston had the money. Besides, they had to get moving down the trail. Sam had to get her to safety. Even though Ford had no horse, he'd be coming soon.

A fellow ranger had once told Sam that Isaac Ford scaled a steep cliff four hundred feet straight up just to get to him. The outlaw had climbed all through the night, slowly inching rock by rock. His hands were a bloody mess, but he'd made it and took the ranger by surprise.

Nope, Ford wouldn't stop until he got Sierra and that loot.

And Weston might come back.

Sierra stood. Giving a cry, she reached into the shadows next to the overturned barrel and lifted something. "Here it is," she said, handing it to him. "I just knew Andrew…Luke didn't take it. He had kind eyes."

The odd statement brought a wry smile. Sam had known many an outlaw whose kind eyes had hidden a killer's black heart, including Weston's.

Wondering how the bills had gotten next to the barrel, he counted them. Though he expected the tally to be short, the entire six hundred and fifty dollars was there. They must've fallen out of the saddlebag when they moved them to spread the bedrolls last night.

Seems he'd been wrong about Weston. At least this time. Not about anything else concerning the outlaw, though. A mistake three years ago that had cost a fellow ranger his life had turned Sam hard and bitter. The sudden memory rose up—holding Pete Walker in his arms, listening to the gurgle, wiping the trickle of blood oozing from his mouth.

Pete's last words echoed in his head. *Promise you'll take care of Amy. And promise you'll always try to see the good in people. Some aren't bad. You have a good heart, Sam. Use it.*

Look for the good in men? Not anymore. His jaw clenched. He'd messed up then, and now he'd let Weston outsmart him. Sam poured Sierra some coffee. "Drink up. We have a long way to go before night."

❧

Sierra hurriedly ate a bit of jerky and an apple. Downing the last of her coffee, she helped Sam take out the saddlebags and finished tying bedrolls onto the horses.

He seemed lost in thought.

The man who'd kissed her so deeply a little while ago was gone, and she didn't know the one who'd taken his place. He was a stranger who had no tenderness inside.

After helping her onto the little mare she'd ridden yesterday, he stuck his foot in the stirrup and threw his leg over his buckskin's broad back. "Ready?"

Before she could answer, a horse and rider galloped into view from around the grove of trees.

Her breath stilled when she recognized the horseman.

Sam pulled his Colt, leveling it at the rider. "You're a dead man, Weston."

A chill swept up Sierra's spine. His hard, brittle words hung in the crisp morning air.

Yet the crazy man kept coming as though Sam had invited him to tea.

"Should've kept riding," Sam barked.

A yard away, Luke reined up and squinted. "Thought about it." Though he tried to sound relaxed, Sierra noticed the tense set of Luke's shoulders.

"Couldn't do it. You need me," Luke went on. "The

only way you're going to keep Miss Sierra safe is if I help you."

"Here I thought I was the crazy one. You've lost your mind to think I'd need your kind of help." The horse shuffled its feet, tossing his head. Sam spoke low, and the animal calmed.

"Fair enough, but two is always better odds than one."

When Sierra thought the tension couldn't get any thicker, Luke shifted in the saddle, putting his gun closer to his right hand. A thickness filled her throat, trapping the air in her chest. She had to think of some way to stop this. But what could she say to men who'd stopped listening?

Sam's face hardened into a mask. He added deadly steel to his sharp words. "You're under arrest. Hand over your weapon, or I'll shoot you where you sit. Take your pick."

Afraid to blink, she glanced from one to the other. Two men, and only one would win.

With narrowed eyes and a squared jaw, Sam waited. Sierra knew it wouldn't take much for him to pull the trigger. Long seconds ticked by.

Luke Weston suddenly smiled and leaned forward, propping his arm on the pommel. "You've been drinking mescal, my friend. Think you're tougher because of your damn name? But then, maybe that's why *you're* a Legend."

Why couldn't Luke realize the folly of needling Sam? Dangerous currents swirled about her. She seemed to be standing in the middle of a deadly whirlwind, ready to catch her up in the twister.

Before Sam could reply, gunshots burst from the

thick brush next to the shack. One bullet struck Weston in the shoulder.

Horror-stricken, Sierra watched blood turn his black coat even darker. But he was thinking of her even now. "Go!" Luke shouted at her.

She turned her mare's head to ride for cover, only to find herself staring into the twin guns of Isaac Ford and three of his men. She froze.

They were trapped in the crosshairs.

Sam aimed at the outlaws huddled next to the dwelling, Luke Weston taking Ford and the rest. The blistering volley of hot lead they released sent the gang diving for cover.

Keeping a sharp eye on Sam and Luke, Sierra tensed. The instant both men dug their heels into the sides of their mounts, so did she. They rode single file with her in the middle, Sam leading the escape and Luke bringing up the rear. Sierra glanced back—as Luke went past Ford, one of the gang leaped and yanked him from his horse.

Her piercing scream alerted Sam. He whirled around and went back. Undecided about what she should do, Sierra stopped a few yards away but had the presence of mind to make a grabbing lunge for the reins of Luke's black gelding as it paused and reared at its owner's sharp cry. Somehow, she caught the reins when the animal came down.

"Let Weston go," Sam barked, pointing his Colt at Luke's captor.

The wild-eyed outlaw jerked Luke up against him, shoving the barrel of a pistol to his head. "Come any closer and he dies."

"Shoot, Ranger," Luke yelled. "Just shoot."

The tense standoff sent fear rippling through Sierra. She wanted to turn away, ride away, only she couldn't stop watching. Praying for a miracle.

Sam's hand was steady, his voice sure. "Put down the gun, you piece of dung. You're not going to get the outcome you want here. Not today."

The skittish buckskin he rode sidestepped. He murmured soothing words and told the gelding to be still. To Sierra's surprise, the animal again settled.

"I told you to fire, Legend," Luke yelled.

Sierra's stomach clenched. Another person was going to die.

Because of her. If they'd stayed on the train instead of helping her, none of this would be taking place.

Running from her problems had only created more. Why hadn't she just stayed in the mountains along with the memories of her cowardice? They'd followed her anyway. At least alone she wouldn't have gotten others killed.

Anger flared in Luke's eyes. "Damn it, just do it! My life isn't worth a damn anyhow."

Please don't, she prayed. *Don't kill him.*

Orange flame burst from the barrel of Sam's Colt. She jerked, even though she'd known in her heart he was going to fire.

One more life snuffed out.

Why couldn't Sam have found another way?

Death followed in her shadow. Why had she thought it would be any different in Texas? How could she bear to watch the light go out in Luke's kind green eyes?

She whimpered, clasping a hand over her mouth to muffle the scream strangling in her throat as the two men toppled and fell.

Eight

THE MINUTE THE LEAD LEFT THE BARREL, SAM SPURRED Trooper forward, leaving smoke and the acrid smell of gunpowder drifting in the air.

He could hear Sierra's strangled cries behind him, but he had no time to comfort her. He had to beat the other outlaws to Weston.

Two horse-lengths away, Weston jerked free from the lifeless outlaw, grabbed his .45, and got to his feet. Sam's aim had been as true as ever. He hadn't lost his touch.

Trooper bolted forward. Reaching down, Sam grabbed Weston's hand. With a fierce yank, he pulled the gunslinger onto the back of his horse.

With a slap of the reins, he urged Trooper into a hard gallop, and they raced for safety.

Sam was satisfied to have Sierra in front on her mare where he could see her. Weston's black gelding trailed the mare as she rode for her life across the uneven terrain, where one misstep could snap a horse's leg.

Though he'd had no choice, he hated leaving the extra horses behind for the Ford gang. Sam couldn't afford to slow for a second or they'd catch them.

His ragged, gasping breath burned his throat and made stars dance in his eyes.

They galloped full-out for a while, dodging juniper, cedar, and mesquite. In an effort to put as much distance between them and their pursuers, Sam hadn't stopped to let Luke off and get onto his black gelding. Sierra proved an excellent horsewoman and had no trouble keeping up. He didn't know how she'd learned to ride so well.

A watering hole lay ahead, hidden by a limestone wall where they could rest the animals. Any farther at this pace would injure the horses. One consolation—Ford would also be forced to stop. Sam figured, prayed, they were a good distance behind. They would've first had to chase their mounts and then settle them down before they could ride.

Luke must've read his mind, because he pointed to the limestone outcropping up ahead that was partially concealed by a tangle of heavy brush.

Riding alongside Sierra, Sam told her the plan. When they halted in the shadow of the rocks, Luke slid off Trooper's back and offered Sierra a hand down from her mare. Blood stained his coat, and agony had carved merciless lines around his mouth.

The way Weston handled his misery told Sam this wasn't his first bullet wound.

Sam dismounted. The sound of trickling water reached him. "Appears the underground stream still feeds this old watering hole."

"That's a relief. Last time I rode by it was real low." Luke staggered, almost falling to his knees.

"I've got you." Sam rushed to grab him. "Lean on me."

Through labored breathing, Luke gasped, "Thanks, Ranger."

Sierra grabbed the horses' reins as Sam put a bracing arm around Luke and half carried him around the rocks.

Near the water's edge, Sam lowered him to a boulder and turned to Sierra. "If you'll get a cup from my saddlebag and bring Weston some water, I'll have a look at this wound."

Nodding, she hurried to the horses.

Luke tried to wave him away. "Just a scratch. Don't need a fuss."

"Save your breath. You're not fooling me." Sam had seen his share of wounds, and this one troubled him. With all the bleeding, the bullet might've gone through more than muscle.

"I didn't ask you to save me again."

"Twice in two days." Sam shook his head, helping Luke out of his coat and shirt. "At the rate we're going, I'm going to run out of fingers keeping score."

The wound sat high on Luke's shoulder. No exit hole in back. Sam stared at the scars on both his chest and back. A dozen or more, some pretty recent. All but one had come from bullets. The exception was from a knife.

A life of violence, told on his skin.

As Sam pressed and prodded, Luke clenched his jaw and broke out in a sweat. "How bad?"

At last Sam raised his head. "The bullet's lodged inside. We won't reach Flatbush until tomorrow afternoon, and even if you make it, they probably won't have a sawbones."

"Take it out here." Luke's firm statement didn't leave any room for discussion.

Though searing pain must be shooting through Weston's shoulder and chest, he didn't allow his face to reflect much. Sam admired a man who didn't bend to his misery, but drew it inside and dealt with it in private. Part of him—a large part, much to his annoyance—respected Luke Weston's grit.

Despite everything, the gunslinger outlaw didn't measure up to what Sam thought he knew about the man. Inside Weston's heart seemed to lurk an honorable man, as shown by his gentleness toward Sierra and how he'd returned to the shack. He was someone who cared about others, who wouldn't leave anyone in danger, and who'd taken a bullet for a sworn enemy when he could've stayed away.

Sierra returned with a cup of water. Murmuring his thanks, Luke gulped it down. Sam removed his bandana, asking her to wet it and fetch one of the bottles of whiskey from the saddlebags. When she gave him a bright smile and turned away, his gaze followed her trim figure for a half second before turning back to his task. If this had happened twenty-four hours ago, he doubted the outcome of their skirmish with Ford's gang. But his finger had been steady on the trigger, his breathing calm. He'd had no doubt in his mind the minute the lead left his Colt that it would hit the right person—and it was thanks to her.

Weston's pain-filled voice broke his trance. "Why didn't you leave me there with Ford?"

"Couldn't." Sam allowed a tight smile.

"Because of the bounty, I suppose."

"Nope, because I want answers. When I came to after the hanging, I saw you bending over me. Don't bother to deny it. Did you have anything to do with that? Were you with the rustlers?"

Luke was silent and still. His voice was quiet when he finally spoke. "No to both questions."

That surprised Sam. "I'm not crazy. I know I saw you."

"I was there, but I was trying to save you." Luke wiped sweat off his forehead with his shirtsleeve.

The confession shocked Sam. He'd have bet even money that Luke Weston would lie. He barked a laugh. "Save me? Is that what you call it?"

"Strange, I know, but it's the truth. I'd been following you and was below the hill in some thick brush. When I saw what those bastards were doing, I started shooting up at the oak tree. Hit one of them, and they lit out. But by then you were swinging. I cut you down, loosened the rope from your neck, and was trying to see if you were still alive when I heard the other rangers. I didn't hang around."

Shocked stillness swept over Sam. The outlaw he'd chased for so long had saved his life? Dare he believe it? But he saw the truth in Weston's eyes.

"I owe you. Thanks." Sam stuck out his hand and Luke shook it. "But why? Us being sworn enemies and all."

"Never like to see a man die that way. Not even a Texas Ranger with a burr under his saddle, bound and determined to catch me. Gives me the shivers."

A moment passed while Sam digested everything. He had trouble processing the fact that if not for Luke

Weston, the man who'd taunted him so long, he'd be dead.

The thought unsettled him. "Weston, tell me this: Why were you on the train?"

"Wanted to make sure you got home. Knew you were still struggling, that you couldn't do your job. In the months of you chasing me and having to use all my wits to stay free… I don't know… I guess a bond of some sort or another formed. The chase became a game."

It certainly hadn't been a game to Sam. But Luke was right about growing close. Something deeper ran between them.

"You noticed it too? The bond, I mean."

"Yep." Luke licked his dry lips.

Sierra returned with the wet bandana and half-empty bottle of whiskey. "Growing up so far from civilization, I learned how to treat whatever might happen. I can help."

"Not this time, *dulce*. Too much blood," Luke insisted gently.

Lifting her chin, she placed her hands on her hips. She was feisty. To go toe to toe with the outlaw showed spirit. He felt a grin tug at his mouth.

"I'm no weak lily, Luke Weston. I've seen my share of blood. Once I had to sew up my brother's leg after a mountain lion ripped it open. By myself. I learned to think fast and do whatever needed doing."

"I'm not questioning your skill," Luke said quietly. "But to me, you're a lady. I don't want my blood ruining that pretty dress."

While Sam listened to the exchange, he washed

Luke's wound with the bandana. He was learning a lot about both, things they didn't suspect they were revealing.

Luke whistled through his teeth when Sam pressed on the wound, trying to get a good idea of the bullet's location. He took in the blood loss—that much would weaken a man fast. Luke soon wouldn't be able to ride.

After Sam removed his knife from his boot, pouring a liberal amount of whiskey on both it and the wound, he gave Luke a big swig of the rotgut.

"Ready? Do you need something to bite down on?"

"Nope, just do it."

Under Sierra's close supervision, Sam set to work. Each time he got close to the piece of metal, the knife slipped. Blood had slickened the implement, making it impossible to hold, and his fingers were too large to get inside and pull out the bullet.

If he couldn't remove it, Luke might not last until they reached a doctor.

Again and again he tried, but couldn't. Finally, he handed Sierra the knife. "Maybe you'll have better luck. At least your fingers are smaller."

Concentration showed in her drawn brows and the tightening of her mouth as she wiped off the blood and bent to the task.

"Easy, lady," Luke growled, muttering a low curse.

"I'm sorry." Sierra bit her bottom lip. "I don't mean to hurt you but—"

"No choice if I want it out, right?" Luke finished for her.

"Exactly."

"Go ahead then. Just try not to maim me for life. Outlaws with a stump can't do much lawbreaking."

"I'm glad you haven't lost your sweet disposition," she replied with a smile. "It helps things tremendously."

"*Humph!*"

Sam admired both her gumption in handling Luke and digging around inside a wound that had already slickened her fingers with blood. The task wasn't for the squeamish. She tackled it as she had everything else—competently and without complaint.

Finally, handing Sam the knife, she stuck her thumb and forefinger into the wound. "I can feel it. I almost have it."

Luke groaned and bit his lip.

The cool morning turned hot as Sam listened for the thunder of horses' hooves, the signal that Ford and his gang had reached them. He prayed for a miracle.

At last Sierra managed to carefully maneuver the spent bullet free, though the digging around had left Luke's shoulder a holy mess.

"You have my thanks, *dulce*. You're a woman of many talents," Luke murmured, dousing himself with a liberal amount of whiskey. As the liquor hit the wound, he barely muffled a yell along with a string of swear words.

"I'm sorry, Luke." She wiped her hands on the wet bandana, then lifted the edge of her skirt.

Sam found himself staring at shapely ankles and the teasing lace edge of bloomers beneath. His mouth went dry.

With a jerk of her wrist, she ripped a long strip from

her petticoat. All too soon, her skirt dropped into place, and the enticing view was gone.

More's the pity. Even so, the image had burned into Sam's brain. In the dead of night he would remember how the sight sent heat rushing to his gut.

Sierra Hunt would be difficult to forget.

After she wrapped the makeshift bandage around the wound, they sat talking, letting Luke recover enough to ride. He was pasty white.

Luke glanced over at Sam. "Next time I tell you to shoot, you'd better not hesitate."

The order rankled Sam more than a little. "Were you so sure I'd miss you?" he spat.

"I've watched you over the years. You always hit what you aim for. You're a crack shot, Legend. I know it, and so does every outlaw in Texas."

The information surprised the hell out of Sam, as did the grudging admiration in Luke's voice. Weston had followed him, watched him—why?

"One thing puzzles me, Weston. Why did you have to murder Judge Percival down in Sonora? A federal judge, for God's sake? Wasn't robbing enough for you?"

Hardness glittered in Luke's eyes. "Didn't kill him. Can't prove it though."

"You expect me to believe you?"

Luke's mouth tightened as though he was used to folks accusing him. "Hell, probably shouldn't."

"Tell me this…were you there?"

"I can't deny it."

"You know I'm going to have to bring you in."

"Expect nothing less." Luke glanced away.

"I want my damn watch back. The one you stole during that stagecoach business."

Weston jammed a hand into an inner pocket, fished out a watch, and slapped it into Sam's palm. "Stopped working a while back."

Sam spared the shiny timepiece a glance, then tucked it away. "Why keep it?"

Luke shrugged. "The inscription. Figured it meant something to you. Always intended to return it."

Surprise at the unexpected thoughtfulness rippled through Sam. The outlaw was an expert at keeping him off balance. He tucked that information away also and turned his thoughts back to the watch. Damn right. The engraving on it did mean a lot. His father had given it to him just after he joined up with the Texas Rangers. The words said everything Stoker Legend seemed unable to say.

Proud of you, son.

It was the only time, before or since, that his father said he was proud of him. The only time his father bent.

And the only time Stoker Legend had let him be his own man.

After Sam told him he was leaving, they'd fought for days leading up to it. Stoker accused him of throwing away his legacy, everything he'd worked for so his sons would inherit the best land in Texas.

To this day, Stoker still didn't understand why Sam had struck out on his own.

In truth, his father's huge shadow suffocated the life from him. It was impossible to know the kind of man he was when Stoker's larger-than-life presence outshone everyone and everything around him.

Trying to live up to the mighty Stoker was a difficult task even now.

For a moment, envy for Luke Weston washed over him. The wily outlaw had freedom to go wherever the path led. Even if that was to jail, which he must've known when he returned to the shack that morning.

Sam took Weston's measure. "If you had it to do over, would you still have returned to the shack?"

With a careless shrug, Weston said, "Knew you were in danger. Couldn't do much else."

"How did you know the Ford gang would come?"

"Because that's what I would've done. They want the girl and that money powerful bad."

Sam still had doubts. Leaving, returning—hell, even getting shot—could be a game to throw him off the scent. Weston could still be involved with Ford.

Weston would bear watching. Still, Sam squeezed out the words he'd give anything to keep from saying. "I didn't thank you for coming back." If Weston hadn't, Sam would be dead, and Ford would have Sierra.

A flicker of a smile twitched at the corners of Weston's mouth. "Sure you did. You didn't shoot me."

There it was again—that thing that made Sam like him despite the thousand reasons why he shouldn't. For God's sake, he'd kept a broken watch he'd stolen because he knew it meant something to Sam.

Hell!

No point trying to figure the man out—it was next to impossible. Sam rose. "The horses haven't had near enough rest, but we can't wait any longer."

"Luke isn't able to ride yet," Sierra protested.

"I'll manage," Luke murmured, slipping on his bloody shirt. The effort brought a groan.

Sierra handed him a cup full of water. "A wagon would sure make it easier."

"I think me and easier parted company quite a ways back."

The outlaw's grim smile didn't fool Sam. Weston was in bad shape. If he could make it to Flatbush, Sam would leave him there. If Luke didn't make it, Sam would be digging his grave. And then, of course, there was concern for Sierra.

He strode to the horses with her. Pausing next to her mare, he lifted a strand of her dark hair and rubbed it between his finger and thumb. He loved the silky feel. In fact, he loved everything about this woman who'd brought him back to life. Sam moved closer, and she leaned into him. "I *am* going to get you to safety at the Lone Star. You can count on that."

"I know you will, of that I'm sure." Lights twinkled in her blue eyes as she smiled. The kiss they'd shared that morning in the coolness of the early dawn crowded the edges of his mind. What he wouldn't give to repeat it.

A low fire still burned inside him. The embers he'd banked that morning seemed intent on flaming up again despite everything. He ran his fingers lightly down the curve of her back and brushed her lips with his mouth, inhaling her fresh scent. "If we only had more time," he murmured against her ear.

"Only we don't."

"More's the pity." He put his hands around her waist and lifted her into the saddle. When he handed her the mare's reins, he held her hand. "The time will come when we'll have all the time in the world. After I find your brother, we'll talk about some things."

Sierra nodded, gently placing her fingers on his lips. "Better go help Luke."

With thoughts of the tangy sweetness of her mouth filling his mind, Sam rushed to brace Luke with an arm, half carrying him to his black gelding.

"It won't be long until dark. You can rest then."

"Don't worry. I'll make it," Luke said, gasping for air.

After anchoring Luke's bloody coat under the bedroll, Sam stuck his foot in the stirrup. The leather creaked when he mounted up. He knew all too well the kind of punishment a well body took from riding over prairie land dotted with low-slung hills and rocky ravines. For one hurting, it would be unbearable.

If Luke Weston had anything left in reserve, he'd have to draw on it before nightfall. Sam prayed he made it.

Not because of any other reason than the outlaw had returned his watch.

If he said that often enough, maybe he'd start to believe it.

Nine

NOT LONG AFTER THEY LEFT THE WATERING HOLE,
Sierra glanced back. Riders were coming up on them
fast. She didn't need Sam's worried gaze to confirm that
it could only be Isaac Ford and his bunch of cutthroats.

With her heart racing, she set her mare into a
gallop, praying they could outrun them.

But could Luke hold on? He leaned forward
in the saddle, his face almost buried in the black
gelding's mane. Luke was a lost soul who'd evidently made some bad choices. Despite their strange
relationship, Sam and Luke had risked their lives to
protect each other, and that bond of loyalty they
shared brought a lump to her throat. She noticed
Sam's sharp eye on Luke even now as they raced for
their lives.

She rode next to Luke and fought to hold him in
the saddle. He'd lost so much blood—he had to be
weak. Pain dulled his eyes and deepened the lines
bracketing his mouth.

Even though Luke was wounded, she knew he and
Sam would face death to protect her. They already

had. But for one of them to die because of her would destroy her.

Ranger Sam Legend with the horrible scar around his neck.

Luke Weston with the high price on his head.

Sudden hotness scalded the back of her eyes. She'd never had anyone give their all for her.

Oh God, I am so unworthy of the sacrifice.

Whitney had trusted her, died waiting for her to lend a hand. Instead, Sierra had stood rooted in fear while her twin perished.

A large rabbit darted across the trail in front of her. Panic-stricken, her mare reared up. Sierra gripped the mane with everything she had to keep from being unseated.

"Whoa!" She plastered herself against the horse and prayed. "It's all right. Nothing's going to get you." The nervous little roan landed on all fours only to rise again on her back legs. The horse's muscles quivered beneath Sierra. "Whoa!" She laid against the mare's neck, crooning softly.

Sam rode up alongside and grabbed the headstall, holding it until the roan settled. "Are you all right?" Sam patted the horse's withers.

"I'm fine." She hoped he didn't notice the violent tremble of her hands. She could scarcely grip the reins. "Thanks."

He quickly scanned the distance behind them, his gray eyes darkening.

She swiveled in the saddle, her breath strangling in her throat.

Isaac Ford leads the pack, and they are coming for me.

Sam's sharp growl split the air, "Move out. Don't stop, no matter what. I'll drop back and draw their fire. If they get me, keep riding hell for leather."

"You're not doing this alone," Luke rasped. "We'll stand together. No other way."

"Weston, you can barely stay in the saddle."

"I'll manage," Luke snapped.

"Ride west, Sierra. Don't look back. We'll catch up." With those orders, Sam slapped her mare's rump with his hat, and she held tight as the little horse sprang forward.

Though myriad gunshots fractured the spring day, she didn't slow, nor did she glance back. She kept her gaze glued on the rugged terrain in front of her and prayed.

That she rode alone didn't frighten her. She was used to that. What froze her heart was Sam and Luke facing danger. For her. Useless prayers to a God who had long since stopped listening repeated over and over inside her head.

Please don't let anyone else die.

Her father's stony features crossed her mind as he'd put her into a stagecoach in Billings, Montana, two months ago. She still felt his scorn.

He was right. She brought death to all who touched her life.

Whitney. Her mother. Even now, her brother Rocky could lie rotting in a grave somewhere. All because she'd not done enough.

Why did she keep living when they'd perished? Why?

She'd even brought her curse to Luke Weston.

A sob caught in Sierra's throat as she raced across dangerous land dotted by gullies and ravines. The cactus, horse nettle, and clumps of juniper she sped past barely drew a notice, so intent was she on watching for drop-offs.

Once the gunshots became sporadic, she chanced a quick glance back to reassure herself that bodies didn't litter the trail.

Thank God! Sam and Luke were only a few lengths behind. More heartening was the fact that the gang had fallen back. Sadness washed over her to see one of their horses lying on the ground.

As she slowed to a trot, Sam rode alongside her and Luke. "Horses gave out," he said. "They never stopped to rest them like we did."

"Poor animals," she murmured.

"They're not going anywhere till morning. We can rest our mounts and give them fresh water at a place I know a little farther down the trail."

Sierra nodded and turned to Luke. "How are you?"

"I won't lie." Luke's lips were white. "I think some wild varmint's gnawing on my shoulder."

"How far to this place where we can stop, Sam?"

"Panther Creek Gap is probably three hours away, I'm guessing. We'll most likely camp there for the night. Our horses need the rest, and it's too dangerous to cross this country at night."

Three hours? She didn't know if Luke would make it.

Pain had dulled Luke's green eyes. "Never bet against me, *dulce*."

"Am I that obvious?"

"I've run across lots of folks who bet the wrong way. I'm hard to kill."

"Seems we have that in common, Weston." The gritty rasp of Sam's voice made her wonder if he referred to the ones who'd tried to hang him.

She met his glance, those eyes that could be so hard one minute and soft the next. "You're both made of granite. I'm sure you can do whatever you set your mind to."

"Always have. Always will," Sam assured her. "We're safe for now. They won't follow until they can get some horseflesh under them. It'll probably take all night to let their animals recover enough to ride." He grinned at Luke. "We make a pretty good team."

Even though she knew more about the pair than she had yesterday, their quixotic relationship kept her baffled. Would she ever understand why they kept putting their lives on the line for each other? And what effect would this have on the tough decision Sam had to make?

His face revealed how he wrestled with the complex issue, how torn he was between duty and his obligation to Luke for saving his life. Faces told so much, and Sierra prayed hers didn't betray the secrets she hid. She'd wasted so much of her life letting her father set the rules and determine her fate.

But she was free at last, and it gave her a heady feeling. She finally had freedom to put down roots, fall in love, get married, start a family if it wasn't too late—to thrive.

Texas Ranger Sam Legend had made her dream again.

Made her hope.

Made her feel like a woman for the very first time. At twenty years old, that seemed wrong. Her father, William Hunt, had taken so much from her.

"I'm glad they can't come after us," Sierra admitted. "I'm looking forward to camping for the night without having to worry. We can all use a restful night's sleep."

"Amen," Sam said. "We'll need our strength for the river crossing tomorrow. With the heavy rain, the Brazos will be swollen out of its banks."

Sudden fear twisted her into a mass of knotted nerves.

"Can we take another route and miss the river?" Her voice quivered, giving away the worry she tried desperately to hide.

"Nope," Sam said. "Afraid we have no choice. I'll make sure nothing happens to you. You'll do fine." His hand covered hers.

The warmth of his touch did little to banish the icy chill that seeped down into her bones. She didn't think she'd ever be warm again.

Leather creaked as Luke shifted in the saddle. "You have me too, *dulce*. Trust Sam and me to keep you safe. Once across, Flatbush lies on the other side. They'll have anything you might need."

Except she'd have to swim the Brazos first.

She couldn't. She just couldn't force herself.

Even if by some miracle she reached Flatbush, she doubted the mercantile would stock the courage she'd lost a long time ago.

"Thank you both." She tried to force a smile, but it

balked, refusing to come. The comforting squeeze of Sam's hand told her he'd noticed her struggle.

Soon he would know she was a coward.

Sierra wouldn't be able to bear the disgust on his face or in those gray eyes—eyes that could grow cold and hard at a moment's notice. Eyes she so wanted to keep looking at her with gentle respect.

Ten

THE PURPLE AND ORANGE HUES OF TWILIGHT BLED together into a beautiful tapestry as they made camp a little while later. Panther Creek Gap, with rippling water alongside its abundant trees, offered everything they needed.

Sam tended the horses, but his attention kept moving to Sierra. He found it most difficult to keep his mind on work whenever she was anywhere near. His senses instantly honed in on her. He grinned. No complaints from him.

She gathered wood for a fire, seemingly oblivious to his scrutiny. He could picture her in the mountains, doing her chores just as she was doing now.

Exhausted and in pain, Luke lay on a bedroll Sam had laid out for him, unable to do more. Sam knew that kind of pain.

His thoughts went back to last month when the rustlers surrounded him. Each time he closed his eyes, he could still see the sneer on the bearded outlaw's face. That cold wash of fear when the noose tightened around his neck seemed a constant part of him now.

The strangling panic as the horse bolted and left him dangling.

One day he would cross paths again with the lynch man who sported the spider on his hand. And when he did...

Sam shoved the nightmare back into its hole and turned his attention back to Sierra. The calm that surrounded her lay around his shoulders. A warmth settled over him. He didn't know exactly why or how, but she always grounded him, brought him back to a safe place.

But what would happen when he found her brother and she left—would he return to that darkness? Without her, maybe he'd stay lost inside his mind. Sam pushed that frightening thought out of his head.

His gaze moved lazily over those lush curves that made him ache with desire. A light radiated from her beautiful face. It should be a sin for a woman to arouse such yearning. He took in the last warm rays of daylight kissing her hair, so dark that it gave off a bluish cast at times. He recalled the silky feel between his fingers and the fresh fragrance that now drifted around him.

She was the woman he wished he'd met before he'd become hard and suspicious of everyone. Before his dreams shriveled and died beneath the Texas sun. He was right back there at the springs. They had things to talk about when all of this was over.

With her arms full of wood, she strode toward him in that easy way she had of moving. Her hips swayed in rhythm to a song that was probably as old as time.

"What else can I help you do, Sam?" Sierra's soft

voice did things to him as she dropped the wood near a circle of rocks she'd arranged as a fire pit. She'd likely learned the art of fire making, plus many other useful things, from her vagabond lifestyle. Something troubled her though, and it had to do with swimming the Brazos. Had to, or she wouldn't keep mentioning it.

"Just watch after Luke while I hunt for game."

Sierra's lips curved in a smile. "That's easy enough." Worry replaced the smile. "He's in bad shape, Sam. His wound has soaked the wrapping."

"Little we can do until we reach town."

"I noticed some yarrow while I was gathering wood. That would help the fever and pain some. In the mountains, we used comfrey for bleeding, but I haven't noticed any here. Maybe I can find some spiderwebs."

Sam nodded. "Never heard of comfrey, but I recall my father once making a poultice using gunpowder one time. We might try that."

"Did you see all the scars on Luke's body?"

"Yep. A good many. Not surprised though." He glanced at the outlaw, whose toughness came unequaled. He sorrowed for the man who'd made so many wrong choices.

"Clearly, he's had a hard life. Too hard." With a light hand on his arm, Sierra told him to get their supper and she'd do her best for Luke.

After staking Sierra's, and Luke's horses within reach of the water and good grass, Sam got his rifle and rode out. The last of the jerky and apples he and Sierra had shared that morning had long disappeared. They all needed meat, or they wouldn't be able to keep going. With luck, he wouldn't have to go far. It bothered him to leave Sierra alone to care for Luke. She was tough, he'd give her that, but he asked too much of her.

A little ways from camp, he saw a doe, but he passed her up. It was too much meat and would be difficult to take back. A turkey caught his attention, and he quickly took aim and hit it. That would feed them tonight and in the morning.

Sierra came to greet him when he strode into camp. "That'll make us a nice meal. I found a patch of wild onions to go along with it."

"You've been busy." He glanced toward Luke and saw he was sleeping.

She followed his gaze. "Luke's worse. I found some spiderwebs to put on his wound later and cover it with a poultice. I didn't have the heart to wake him now though."

The sight of her took his breath. Her blue eyes glistened like stars. That she could know so much at her age astounded him. She had the grit and heart of a survivor. Most women would complain about the grueling pace he'd set, but Sierra quietly did whatever was required with never a word. She was the kind of woman he wanted at his side. A fighter.

The struggle to speak took great effort. "Sleep helps a person heal. Did you gather the yarrow?"

"Yes. Look what else I found." She gently freed some speckled eggs from her pocket.

"Looks like prairie chicken eggs."

"I thought so. We used to eat similar ones in the mountains." She laid the eggs aside where they wouldn't get broken and sat next to him on a rock to help pluck the bird.

He loved having her near. "I'll wager you learned a lot of survival skills."

"Had to or I'd starve." She frowned, her face darkening. "My father was forgetful. The next adventure, next important discovery crowded out our names from his mind. He especially had trouble remembering that we needed to eat, so Mama and us kids became adept at managing."

"Sounds like a rough life."

"My brothers seemed to love it, though."

"And you?" Sam asked softly.

A distant light came into Sierra's sad eyes. "The conditions were too harsh. After a while, it became something I prayed to survive. Only, that didn't quite work out either. I...I disappointed everyone." Her voice broke. She glanced away, whispering, "I was my father's biggest failure."

Something had happened, something so terrifying she couldn't bear to think about it. Trembles shook her body in the silence that spun between them.

Sam wiped his hands and put his arms around her. It was so easy, centering her the way she centered him. Natural. "What's bothering you, Sierra?"

She gave her hair an impatient shove. "It's no use talking about it."

Tightening his embrace, Sam said, "Let me help. Are you worried about your brother?"

"If I just knew he was all right. You know?" She rested her head on his shoulder, sweetly trusting. "If he's cold. If he's still alive. If he's hurt. This waiting is killing me."

"It's tough not knowing, and I wish I could start

my search so you could have some answers." He splayed his hand across her back. "But Rocky's not all that's bothering you. I sense more." A lot more. The beauty held so much sorrow inside.

Sierra's voice simmered with rage. "No one can fix me."

Whoever said silence was golden didn't know beans from squash. This eerie quiet was loud and angry and black as sin.

"I can try," Sam murmured against her temple.

She suddenly pushed away, all business. "Too much work to do. If I don't lay the fire, we can't cook this plump bird."

Shadows had begun to fall around them. He watched her arrange the kindling and place smaller pieces of wood on top. With a strike of the match, she breathed life into the spark, coaxing barely a flicker into flames capable of withstanding the breeze.

His heart ached for her.

Who would breathe life into *her*, banish the memories keeping her in a stranglehold?

Anger shook him—seeing for the first time how truly alone she was.

Except for the sounds of the creek and birds chirping, silence filled the air around them. Sam studied the woman who bore secrets. At last he spoke. "Where did you learn to ride like that?"

"My brothers." She gave him a sad smile. "It was the only way I could keep up with Rocky and Teton. They never eased up because I was a girl and younger. I had to prove I was every bit as tough."

"And?"

"I did, and loved it. But it was even more fun making them admit it."

Sam could picture her outrunning her brothers and making them concede. "You haven't mentioned Teton before. Is he with your father?"

She shrugged, turning away. "Who knows where my oldest brother is."

"Will he be worried about you?"

"No." Now that the fire had caught, she rose, added a larger piece of wood, and changed the subject. "I love horses. I admired your buckskin from the moment I saw him."

Her curt answer about Teton told Sam there was no love lost between Sierra and her brother. In fact, with the exception of Rocky, her family appeared to have forsaken her.

"He's the perfect friend for a lawman. I raised Trooper from a foal and trained him to come when I whistle. Sure helped me out of a lot of tight situations."

"Money can't buy a horse like that. Excuse me." Sierra moved to check on Luke.

Once he'd readied the turkey and got it onto the fire, Sam walked down to the murmuring brook.

The creek ran like a dark thread, reflecting the shadows of the trees growing near the banks. The horses stopped nibbling on the lush grass nearby and raised their heads, as though sensing his frustration.

A month ago, Sam had been content with his calling, his horse, the freedom to simply be who he wanted. Then everything changed. He'd realized how quickly his heartbeats could stop.

His father had been on his mind in those final

seconds, regret that Sam hadn't tried harder to mend their relationship. Remorse for not telling Stoker he loved him had weighed heavy. A person should never put off important things. He took out the silver watch and stared at the inscription. *Proud of you, son.*

Seemed strange that in the seven years since, Stoker had never once said it aloud. Maybe the hardest things were easier to write. Except Sam hadn't even done that.

He shook his head, scattering the unwelcome memory.

With the soft ground muffling Sierra's footsteps, he didn't know she was close until she bumped his elbow.

"Luke's burning up and mumbling something I can't make out," she said.

Sam met her worried blue eyes, wishing he could offer hope. "He'd probably be dead now if not for you. I still don't know how you got that bullet out, buried deep the way it was. The depth of your compassion for Luke amazes me."

"Everyone deserves a second chance." Her face hardened. "Some get it, some don't."

An owl hooted nearby, seeming to mock him. Probably was.

Memory of another regret that day swept his mind—that he'd never known the real love of a woman. He'd wandered Texas over for seven of his twenty-seven years without finding one—until now. Her kindness had changed his life. She made him trust himself, brought color back into his life. She made his heart sing.

Sierra was the woman he'd searched for.

Cupping her face, he traced the line of her jaw,

down the slender column of her neck, and brushed the cut at her throat. Her slightly parted lips drew him.

Placing his hands under each ear, he brought her mouth closer. Their breaths mingled with desire. Their lips almost touched when Luke rasped his name. The outlaw's timing couldn't have been worse.

Sam sighed and pulled back. "Our patient is awake."

"Yes." If her deep exhale bore any indication, she shared his frustration. "We'd better go."

Luke was struggling to sit by the time they got to him. "How are you feeling? Did you want something?" Sam asked.

"Whiskey," Luke rasped.

Sierra knelt and placed her hand on his forehead. "Luke, please eat something first. Sam shot a turkey, and it'll be ready soon."

While Sam agreed with her, he knew a man like Luke needed his alcohol. "If I give you one drink, do you promise to eat?"

Luke shot him a black glare. "What is this? Are we back in school, making deals to get what we want? If so, you make a lousy teacher. Never mind, I'll get it myself."

When he struggled to stand only to fall back, Sam gave in. "Sit still. You're only going to bleed more. I'll get the damn whiskey," Sam growled. "But you're going to eat if I have to sit on you and stuff it into your mouth."

"Fine." Luke's answer was sour.

"Not sure how much is left, but I'll bring what we have."

"*And*, as long as you're awake, I'm going to doctor your wound, mister," Sierra said, setting her jaw.

"Gang up on a sick man, will you?" Luke breathed hard.

While Sierra got the spiderwebs and poultice made of horsemint leaves, Sam rummaged in the saddlebags. Luke's bottle was almost empty, but his only had a little gone. He grabbed a cup and poured a good portion, handing it to Luke.

Sam took charge of the turkey while Sierra cooked the eggs and wild onions in a small skillet from the saddlebags. They made a good team, working in tandem to prepare the meal.

By the time the feast was ready, Luke sported a fresh bandage and appeared more alert. Thankfully, he accepted the food without any fuss.

Sam shared a large, flat rock with Sierra. He loved how her shoulder brushed his. They were like magnets. Every time they got close, they couldn't help but bump against each other. They ate in silence, listening to the croaking frogs, owl hoots, and the gurgle of the water.

Worry deepened on her face. "Sam, about tomorrow…"

He set down his plate and reached for her hand. "Are you worried about Luke? I'm going to make sure he gets there."

Biting her lip, she rubbed her arms. "On second thought, forget I said anything."

"Please, tell me what you were going to say."

"It's not important." She stood. "Are you finished with your plate?" At his nod, she took it along with Luke's down to the creek and knelt to wash them. She was afraid. Of crossing the water? Or something else? Either way, she seemed determined to face that fear alone.

One thing about Sierra—she didn't shirk from difficulties or unpleasant tasks. But at what cost?

No one can fix me, she'd said.

"I can damn sure try," Sam murmured.

❧

Night had long since closed around them as Sam sat with Sierra. Luke, lulled by a special tea she'd made from the yarrow, lay on his bedroll, staring into the darkness. Since his fever had broken, though far from being on the mend, he seemed to feel better. He'd slipped on his shirt that Sierra had washed out in the stream. They all seemed locked in their private thoughts.

Studying Sierra, Sam couldn't help but wonder what she had stopped herself from saying earlier.

He found it impossible to pull his eyes away from her. The flickering light from the fire played across her pretty features, softening the lines at her mouth and forehead.

Her face interested him. High cheekbones, dark coloring, and beautiful eyes bestowed some natural kind of refinement and spoke of possibly a smattering of Native American. Wasn't much though, if any. Her full, lush lips added a hint of mystery, filling him with yearning. But it was the tiny scar above her mouth that added character and spoke of a life of hardship. Scrounging for food, no home, constantly on the move.

"Mind if I ask a question, Sierra?"

Her gaze swung to him. "Depends."

"How did you get the little scar above your lip?"

"A clumsy moment. The tale is quite boring. Not worth a mention." She glanced away and covered the scar with her hand.

Luke rolled toward her. "I'd like to hear it, *dulce*. It'll take my mind off my misery."

Hearing Luke call her that still brought irritation, even though something told Sam it was as natural to the man as breathing. Sam had heard from several sources that the outlaw's mother was Mexican. The white half had to come from his father, though Sam had never learned the man's name.

That Luke always spoke to Sierra in a quiet, respectful manner made Sam wish he had a bit of the outlaw's easy charm. When he realized he was a little jealous of the man he still intended to arrest, he mentally kicked himself.

"That makes two of us," Sam prodded. "I can't imagine you being clumsy for a second. Please, tell us how you got the scar."

"Very well. I slipped in the snow, and my mouth struck the shovel handle. It bled something fierce and loosened a tooth in the bargain."

Sam wondered why she'd been digging in the snow.

Before he could ask, she turned to him. "I'm sure you're anxious to get home to your family. They're worried sick, I imagine. At least your mother."

"My mother died when I was ten." Memories of standing by the fresh mound of her grave washed over him. "It's just my father and brother now."

At the time, he hadn't fully understood things, but

something in him had known that his life was changed forever. And it was. Stoker became more driven to acquire things. Land, cattle, money. Became moody and snapped at everyone. His father became someone Sam didn't know.

"I'm sorry," Sierra murmured, covering his hand.

"A long time ago." He brushed the top of her fingers. "But I'm sure Pa and Houston are pretty worried after meeting the train in Fort Worth and I wasn't on it."

Luke stared into the rising flames. "Let me guess. Houston's the steadier, calmer brother."

"As a matter of fact, he is, though it beats the heck out of me how you would know." Sam wasted the glare he shot him because Weston had laid back on the bedroll, staring up at the stars.

The man wore an odd look—a little wistful and a lot sad. "Family—who needs 'em? They only mess with your head and bring bitter disappointment."

From the corner of his eye, Sam watched Sierra swallow hard and knot the fabric of her skirt, wishing he could take her burden. "Do you have any brothers or sisters, Weston? Someone to go to in times of trouble?"

"Nope."

Hoping to relieve Sierra's unease, Sam barked a laugh. "Fess up, Luke. Don't you ever long for someone to yell at?"

"Nope. I'm all by my lonesome, and I like it that way." A strange light glittered in Luke's eyes. "I'll bet you must have just about everything you want, Ranger. A big spread that covers six counties, horses, cattle, money. Why, I'll bet you even have one of those fancy water closets I've seen in the Brightford Hotel down San Antone way. Heard your pa rode a train to New York City to buy special cigars."

Whether it was the whiskey talking or not, the sarcasm in Luke's voice got under Sam's skin. "You appear to know an awful lot about my family. Why's that?" Maybe Weston was planning on robbing them when he got there. He'd get a rude awakening. Sam was tying the outlaw's hands the moment he was better. A sharp edge filled Sam's voice. "I'm waiting, Weston. Why is it you know so much about the Legend family and the Lone Star Ranch?"

A hood dropped over Luke's eyes, preventing Sam from reading them. "Even outlaws sometimes know how to read, *amigo*. That daddy of yours takes a notion to spit out his window and it makes every newspaper in the state. Must be *real* nice having a powerful man like that for a pa."

Sierra broke the tension. "It's a pity we don't get to choose our family. I always wished I could."

Sadness in her tone bruised something deep inside Sam, tempering the irritation Luke had stirred in him. Secrets lurked behind her eyes, haunting her thoughts. One day he'd figure it out. He was good at puzzles. The lady had pulled his dream from the ashes and single-handedly fixed his head. He hadn't imagined one thing out of the ordinary since he'd met her.

Maybe the cure was immersing himself in her problems and forgetting his own.

Eleven

SIERRA LAY AWAKE LISTENING TO THE SOFT SNORES AND crackling fire that she could barely hear over the hammering of her heart. Thoughts of what lay in wait for her in a few hours trapped her breath inside her chest.

Everything seemed trapped except for her fear, and that spilled everywhere.

Bile rose, choking her.

She freed herself from the bedroll and rushed behind a big clump of cedar, out of earshot of the men. Luckily she made it before releasing the contents of her stomach as quietly as she could. When nothing else remained, she moved a few yards away and sank to the damp ground, burying her face in her arms.

Her father's voice sounded inside her head. *"There are no excuses. You're weak. Water is nothing to be terrified of."*

"I know," she whispered into the gentle breeze. "I know."

Yet the fear remained, all the same. Tenacious roots burrowed into her heart, cracking the layer of protection around it.

Tomorrow Sam would see her yellow streak. He had a spine of steel. No complaining. Just quietly living and doing what had to be done. A whimper escaped. In a few hours, the Texas Ranger who lived with honor and courage would see the kind of woman for whom he'd risked his life.

She despised her weakness. A silent tear trickled down her cheek.

A twig suddenly snapped.

Quickly wiping away the traces of her shame, she turned to find Sam.

He squatted beside her. "Are you ill?"

Sierra shook her head. "I'm worried about my brother."

The ease with which the lie popped out startled her. Maybe she should take up lying as a profession. Probably lots of call for it, though at the moment she couldn't think of any except snake oil salesman. Yet, her confession wasn't a total fib. She *was* worried about Rocky, she mentally defended herself. She was worried about a lot of things—her brother, the Ford gang, and how to hide her fear from Sam.

"I'll find him. I'm pretty good at tracking."

"I'm sorry I woke you."

"I'm a light sleeper. Often my life has depended on sharp hearing. I heard when you rose." Sam gave her a tight smile. "It's dangerous to be away from the fire at night. There's a reason they call this place Panther Creek Gap."

Being eaten by a panther might be preferable to the fear nibbling away inside.

"I hate that I disturbed you, and probably Luke also."

Sam stood, took her hand, and pulled her up. "I'm used to frettin' about folks. One of the rangers used to say I'm like an old mother hen with only one chick and a fox on the loose. We need to get a few winks. It'll be daylight soon."

"How far to the river crossing?"

"Is that what this is about?" He put his arm around her waist as they picked their way through the inky blackness.

"No," she lied again. "I'm only curious."

"It's about an hour's ride." He leaned close to whisper, "There's nothing wrong with being afraid. Swimming the Brazos challenges even the toughest cowboy."

One hour from our camp. Her knees nearly buckled.

"How do you handle fear, Sam?"

"The trick is to never let anyone see it."

"I try, but as you can see, I'm lousy at it."

"Every time you feel cold sweat inching up your back, close your eyes and recite something."

"Such as what?"

"On the ranch, the cowboys like to play this game. They memorize labels on canned foods. I still remember this one from playing with them when I was younger. *Diamond Milk as you like it. Sterilized, unsweetened evaporated milk. Registered U.S. Patent office. So close to fresh it fools old Bessie. Satisfaction guaranteed— the finest quality or your money cheerfully refunded. D. W. Quigley and Company.*

"Of course, a fine lady such as you might want to recite something a tad more refined," he added. "Maybe scripture?"

Sierra smiled in spite of herself, imagining him

passing time in such a way. "My mother made us kids memorize the books of the Bible."

"That'll do. Say them over and over when fear strangles you."

"Thank you, Sam." She loved the feel of his hand on her waist, leading her to safety.

Moments later, she reached the light of the campfire to find Luke sitting up. Her conscience scolded her. The outlaw needed every bit of rest he could get for the grueling miles ahead.

"Are you all right, *dulce*?"

Finally drawing a line at her growing pile of lies, she neatly sidestepped the question. "I'm sorry I disturbed your sleep, Luke. Lie back down."

He yawned, stretched out on his blanket, and began snoring almost instantly.

After getting her a cup of water, Sam drew her down on his bedroll and put his arm around her. Sierra melted against him, laying her head on his broad chest.

"Trust me. Tell me why you're so scared." He covered her hand that must feel like ice.

She sighed in defeat. "You'll learn soon enough, I guess."

"About what?"

His soothing touch on her hair was so gentle. For so long, she'd yearned to have someone care about her. Sierra closed her eyes, soaking it up.

Was this real, or was he merely feeling sorry for the poor, frightened little girl?

How could anyone ever care about her? She'd sent Whitney to her death. Then their poor, sweet mother. Dear God! She couldn't swallow past the lump wedged in her throat.

Sierra opened her eyes and glanced up at his shadowed face. "I was eight the year my ornery brothers decided to play their prank. Sneaking from behind, they picked me up. Swinging me by my feet, they hurled me into Bear Creek Lake. The water was still part ice, and I couldn't swim. My heavy clothes dragged me down. I struggled to get to the surface but the water was so cold, it numbed my arms and legs."

She shuddered, remembering the blackness that closed around, holding her in a watery grave. Feeling the hopeless despair, the terror, knowing she was about to die in those hated mountains that had already stolen so much from her.

Regret, too, had filled her mind of never having been kissed or held in tender arms. Those thoughts had made her fight harder but her stupid dress had wrapped around her legs, dragging her down just as her father had done each time she'd tried to find her way out from under his stifling heavy hand. Recalling the incident brought a rising sob that she tried desperately to silence.

"When I came to, I was on dry land with my father kneeling over me. He dove in and saved me." She lifted her trembling hands to her face and found wet cheeks.

William Hunt had set aside his preoccupation with his work and jumped to the rescue only a handful of times. Mostly he'd been too self-absorbed to spare his frightened little girl a thought. The only attention he'd paid her was in making sure he kept her hidden away…from people, and from life. Then when he did notice her, he'd seen her as nothing but an object of scorn. Whatever affection he might have felt for his daughter turned to ice.

"Everything is clear now." Sam's soft breath ruffled the hair at her temples as he pressed his lips to her forehead. "Fear can eat at a person until there's nothing left."

Except she hadn't told him the rest. She couldn't, for it would be hardest to understand.

"It's silly, I know. I'm a grown woman, and yet I act like a foolish child."

Sam brushed her face with his fingertips. "There's nothing foolish about you." His voice became husky. "And you're far from being a child."

"I wish I had your strength. You always seem calm and sure, even when facing danger."

"You would be wrong, pretty lady." A layer of velvet wrapped the hardness of Sam's words. "Back at the cabin, facing Ford and his men, my hands trembled so bad I thought I'd drop my gun. And on the day of my hanging, until they slapped my horse's flank, I had hope of escape. Once I had nothing but air beneath me and was…" His voice broke.

"I'm so sorry, Sam." Sierra laid her hand on the side of his face. "I can't imagine."

How could she have made him relive that terrible time, and how could she have forgotten the horror he lived with? She needed to have her head examined. Maybe she'd spent too many years roaming the wilderness to ever be civilized. She was like some wild animal that had to be taught not to bite.

The angry words her father had flung at her haunted her mind. *You should've been the one to die.*

Tears pricked the back of her eyes. Yes, it should've been her.

"Why did you stay so long in the mountains, Sierra? You were miserable."

"I got stuck with no way out, and no place to go even if I had the freedom."

"We do tend to get stuck." Sam's arm tightened around her. "Do you mind if I kiss you? I seem to have a great need for the taste of your lips."

His hoarse voice held a strange longing, almost as if he thought he didn't have a right to ask.

"I'd like that." Her words came out breathless and quiet. She wasn't about to admit that her own needs made the yearning for him unbearable.

A smile curved his mouth. He gently cupped her jaw and brought her face toward him. Sierra held her breath as his lips touched hers.

The slow kiss was like a caress, reminding her of the way the wind sighed through the tall pines—gentle and scented with nature's fragrance. Sam's lips, his tender touch, his gray eyes that saw past her failings, all blended, mixing with the night.

Warmth rushed over her, settling into the cold, frigid parts of her body where terror and despair dwelled. The heated flush swimming through her veins thawed a little of the ice gripping her. A quickening lurched in her stomach as the kiss sent jolts through her. Her heart fluttered wildly.

This kiss was different from those they'd briefly shared. This one shook her to her toes and seared into her memory. Excited tingles swept along each nerve ending as his scent mingled with wild sage, saddle leather...and the desperate hope in her heart.

She'd dreamed of finding such a man, but had long given up. Sam's tender touch made her feel beautiful and desired. With him, she wasn't the sad little girl with an absent father and a mother so locked in grief she would rather die than live.

With him, she was welcomed, embraced as someone of value. And with him, she'd never be forgotten.

Surrounded by the whispers of animals scurrying in the predawn hours, Sierra slid her hand around Sam's neck. The soft strands of his dark brown hair wound around her fingers.

"I've been looking for you all my life," Sam murmured against her mouth. "Where have you been?"

Waiting for him, despairing of him ever coming along.

Sierra laid her hand on his chest, feeling the beat of his heart beneath her small palm. So strong. So sure.

Sam Legend was scarred. So was she. But he was everything she wanted.

He seemed to need her. And she for sure needed him. Never could she imagine going back to the shambles of her pitiful life without him.

Closing her eyes, she soaked up his feathery touch as his hand slid down the column of her throat to the collar of her dress. If this was a dream, please let her not wake up.

Nothing would bring greater joy than spending the rest of her life wrapped in Sam's strong arms. Yet her heart told her the odds were stacked against her.

"You make me feel safe for the first time in my life," she whispered.

"My plan's working then."

Sierra heard a smile in his voice. She glanced up, and by the flickering light of the fire, saw the twinkle in his eyes. For a split second she could almost picture herself by his side forever.

Almost, but not quite.

She was smart enough to know that could never be. Too many things stood in the way. She had nothing, no home, no belongings, no family who claimed her. Except maybe Rocky, but he'd disappeared and was most likely dead. From what little she knew, Sam came from wealth and circumstance. He was a dedicated lawman.

She was probably just a woman he felt obligated to save. She was merely part of his job. Still, she savored the strength of his arms and the kiss that made her glad to be alive, to have survived those horrible, hopeless years.

But in a few hours this, too, would end. It would have to, when she refused to cross the Brazos River.

It's there they would part. She intended to stay behind. It was the only way.

"Have you ever wondered what you might've been if you weren't a lawman, Sam?" Her whispered question brought a scowl.

"Nope." He lifted her hand to his lips and kissed the tips of her fingers. "Joining the Texas Rangers is all I ever wanted. What about you, pretty lady? What dreams filled your head?"

"I wanted to be a schoolteacher, write a book one

day about the real American West, and tell folks back East that it's not exciting or a place of adventure—misconceptions all."

Have a good friend—maybe two—who would accept her as she was. A house she'd never have to leave. These secret wishes she didn't mention.

She paused then went on, "Run my own newspaper, and not just work for my brother. Then of course, I'd love to be a mother with children of my own and a husband who adores me."

In her dream, she'd cherish each child and show them they were loved, not simply tell them. Words so often failed.

Sam tucked a loose strand of hair behind her ear. "You have no idea how beautiful you are by moonlight."

She shook her head. She was a mess to be sure with her uncombed hair, layers of dirt, torn dress, and a jagged scrape down one arm. Memories of the mountain men's wives she encountered during her travels came to mind. She probably looked like some unkempt mountain woman with manners to match.

Sierra opened her mouth to remind Sam of the sleep he needed, but she never got the words out. He slanted another kiss across her lips, and she forgot everything except her racing pulse and the heat that crashed over her in waves.

When his palm slid to her waist, she sank against the hard wall of his chest, praying…

That these predawn hours would never end.

That she wasn't dreaming.

That Sam could be the man she hungered for.

She desperately needed permanence and love. Only...when Sam learned the rest of her secrets, how fast would he run?

Twelve

THE HUGE ORANGE BALL OF THE SUN HUNG MIDWAY across the sky by the time the three of them reached the Brazos. It had taken longer because of stopping often to let Weston rest.

Sam heard the mighty roar of rushing water long before he saw it. He shot Sierra and Weston a glance, wishing they didn't have Isaac Ford breathing down their necks. Sam had noticed the outlaws coming fast a few miles back, which prevented them from making camp until the floodwaters receded.

Fear had drained the color from Sierra's face, turning her lips white. He'd give anything if he didn't have to force her to do this. She stared transfixed at the water, as though the angry river was a ferocious beast that would swallow her whole.

The sight of the raging current shook Sam too. Moving Trooper closer, he touched Sierra's arm. "Don't be afraid. I'm not going to let anything happen to you." But she appeared locked in her terror, not flicking a muscle or acknowledging that he'd uttered a word. How was he going to get her, and Weston, across?

Men who rode the trail knew to look upstream for a lower water level to make an easier crossing.

Except he didn't have time to look. Ford would be on them. Sam swung to Luke and told him about Isaac Ford, then added, "Between you and me, I haven't seen the river this bad in a few years."

"Makes two of us. You just take care of Miss Sierra. I'll manage myself."

Sam shot Luke a worried glance. He could barely sit on the horse, much less do something sure to challenge a whole man. "With luck, we should be across by the time the outlaws get here," Sam said. Why had he spoken of luck? That word shied away from Sam faster than a bunch of wall-eyed buffalo in a stampede.

"Sierra's terrified," Luke said, low. "We may have trouble."

"Me, you mean. You'll be doing good to get yourself across. If you get into trouble, I might not be able to help." With Luke looking like death warmed over, Sam wouldn't want to place bets.

"Just worry about her."

Sam clasped his hand. "If we get separated, we'll meet up in Flatbush."

That was the best he could offer. He watched Luke inch out into the current.

One look behind showed Ford almost within rifle range.

Sam's brain screamed to go. *Now!*

With a gentle touch on her arm, he focused on Sierra now. "I need your help, pretty lady." Her frigid skin told of the severe grip of her fear. When she didn't move, he asked again a little louder, then added, "I know how terrified you are, Sierra, but do you think you can help me?"

At last she turned her blanched face to him. "Did you say something?"

"I need you to start reciting those Bible books," he said quietly. "It's time. You can do this. I'm going to make sure you get across."

A glance behind showed the outlaws gaining. Two minutes more and it would be too late.

When she raised her glance to him, panic filled her blue eyes. "No, I can't do this, Sam. I just can't."

Sam silently cursed Isaac Ford for not leaving him time to take her in his arms and offer comfort. "I believe in you. I know you're made of strong stuff."

"You're wrong. I'm a coward. You can pretend I'm some noble woman, but it won't change the facts."

"Pretty lady, I've got you." He brushed the tears from her cheeks with his fingertips. "I'd give anything to change what happened. But I can't. I can promise that I *will* get you safely across this river, and you can count on that."

With terror-stricken eyes, Sierra shook her head. "Our ways part here. I'm staying behind. I'm sorry, Sam."

Damn, he was afraid of this.

Sam leaned to kiss her forehead and rubbed his hand up and down her back, praying he could make her see reason. "Ford is almost on us. Do you want him to get you?"

"No, but it's what has to be." A sob escaped.

"We have no other choice. They've pinned our backs to the wall. I'm not leaving you behind for that sorry outlaw to torture," he growled. "If you stay, so am I."

A quick scan of the area didn't reveal many hiding places. It would be difficult to make a stand here among the thin branches of salt cedar, but for this woman, he would try.

"Don't you see that I'm only going to get you killed? Everyone I touch dies. My father said so."

"Get that crazy talk out of your head right now." Sam didn't know why her father would say such a thing to his daughter. If he ever met up with the man, he'd damn sure find out—right after he gave him a thrashing.

"It's true. Look how many close calls you've already had."

"Close doesn't count…except maybe in pitching horseshoes. I'm still alive. So is Luke." He smoothed back her hair. "We're going to get through this."

"Too many people have died because I couldn't save them," she cried. "Please, don't make me do this."

What in hell did she mean?

"You'll never find Rocky. You'll never save him if you stay here." He gently wiped her tears. She was mentally fragile, and no way in hell was he going to let her go. More than ever, he vowed to keep her safe. To take her fear as his own so she would be free of its grip. He leaned to brush his lips across hers.

Hoof beats pounded the ground. This was do-or-die time.

"You need to start reciting now. Genesis, Leviticus… uh…you know what comes next."

"Sam, don't make me do this." She whimpered like a hurt animal.

The sound pierced Sam's heart. "Try not to hate me, pretty lady."

Making a last-minute decision, he lifted her into the saddle in front of him where he could protect her. Giving a yell, Sam slapped her mare on the rear with his hat, sending the little horse ahead. A second later, he and Sierra plunged into the cold, rushing water of the Brazos.

Sierra screamed, "No! No! Don't make me do this, Whitney!"

Trooper trembled violently as the swift current swept his legs out from under him. The screams of both horses matched Sierra's.

A barrage of gunshots sounded as bullets peppered the surface of the water.

Sam uttered an oath, trying to shield Sierra from the gunfire, praying the shots would miss her, as he tried to settle the horse enough to swim. He cursed the haste that hadn't allowed him to lash her to him by rope. *Damn you, Ford! Damn you to hell!* Once their mount battled the current with strong legs, he took his first breath, but there was no relaxing.

More gunshots sent hot lead around them. He didn't care about himself, just let his pretty lady be spared. That's all he asked.

Now that Trooper was over his initial panic, the buckskin would carry them across.

His arm tightened around Sierra as he yelled over the roaring water, "Hold on to the mane! Trooper will do the work! I'm right here. I won't let you drown."

Her terrified eyes were the only spots of color in her ashen face. Fear had frozen her delicate features into a mask. Her shock was obvious—in this state, she couldn't hear anything.

The loud rush of the water gobbled up the string of cusswords as they left his mouth and flung them back.

Damn it to hell!

"You can't have her, you monster!" Sam shouted.

No matter the risk, he intended to get her safely across. He'd promised. And that was a promise he'd keep. Somehow.

He ground his teeth and renewed a tight grip on the reins. The mighty river taunted him for his brave words. Halfway across, where the current was swifter and deadlier, his worst fears were realized. The powerful force stripped her mare's reins from his fingers.

At the same time, the horrendous energy grabbed at Sierra. He fought in desperation to hold onto her but found emptiness as the water ripped her from his arms.

Sam's heart froze. He dove in after her. But in that split second, the river carried her out of reach.

He had to save her. Not because of a promise he'd made or that he was duty bound. He'd save her because she'd saved him first.

Giving a shuddering breath, he kicked his feet and made powerful sweeps with his arms, praying to catch her.

A few yards away her head bobbed, barely visible due to the waves and spray. He gave a prayer of thanks that she'd somehow managed the miracle of staying on the surface. She wouldn't for long if he couldn't reach her.

A little more. He was close.

But the Brazos seemed in a devilish mood. Each time he reached out to grab Sierra, the monster snatched her away.

Sam knew he had to get to her soon, or it would be too late. His arms and legs became chunks of lead. It was all he could do to lift them.

Soon he wouldn't even be able to save himself.

Soon the mighty Brazos would claim them both.

Thirteen

DESPAIR SWEPT OVER SAM. HE SLAPPED ANGRILY AT THE current. He'd given nothing but another empty promise and delivered Sierra to a watery grave.

In the predawn hours she'd said he made her feel safe.

She'd trusted him, believed in him.

Sam had no right to the pride he'd claimed all these years. A Legend didn't back down from a fight. A Legend would face the Brazos River. A Legend never gave up.

With a sudden spurt of determination, he swam like a man possessed. Within a few seconds, he'd closed the gap separating him from the woman who floated facedown in the water. She'd borne unimaginable sorrow and was far braver than she believed. She would not die here.

Stretching, he grasped her clothes, first with his fingertips then his whole hand, refusing to let the river claim her. When she came within reach, he grabbed her shoulders and pulled her against him.

"I've got you. You're safe," he breathed into her ear.

Her closed eyes and gray color froze his heart. He couldn't tell if she was alive or dead. He had to get the water out of her lungs in time. She'd regain consciousness. She had to!

With a prayer on his lips, he swam for dry land.

Once his feet touched bottom, he pulled her from the water. Gasping for air, he rolled Sierra onto her back and tenderly brushed wet strands of hair from her eyes. Kneeling over her, he pumped her rib cage. He'd seen this done a few times, and once, the person had lived.

Please, God…

It seemed minutes had passed, but he didn't stop. This was her only chance.

Please let her live.

But still he saw no sign of life. Pain filled his chest until it hurt to breathe.

He'd try just once more. Then he'd have done all he could.

Almost ready to abandon hope, he pumped her chest. Tears ran down his face.

Then he gave a cry as water gushed from her mouth. When she started to choke, Sam quickly rolled her onto her side. He patted her back as coughs wracked her body.

When they eased, he sat and pulled her into his arms, burying his face in her wet hair. He had to clear his throat before he could speak. "Oh God, I thought I'd lost you."

Sierra spluttered and coughed for a good while before she could finally speak. "Where are we? Why are we soaked?"

Evidently her shock had blocked out the battle with the river monster. That was a good thing. He would hate for her to relive that nightmare.

"We made the crossing and got a little bit wet," he said, making light of the ordeal that still left him shaken.

"Where's Luke?" she asked, looking around.

"We got separated."

Sam prayed Luke made it across. It wouldn't seem right if the man he'd chased for so long perished now. The toughest rawhide tethered them together. Sam didn't fully understand their baffling relationship, but it seemed more than lawman and outlaw. Putting that aside for the moment, he wondered how far down-river they'd gone. Possibly two or three miles, maybe more. He doubted Ford's gang would be able to find them so far downriver. But he was unwilling to risk Sierra's life on such an assumption.

A glance at the sky told him it was around one o'clock in the afternoon. He told her they needed to move deeper into the cottonwood and oak that grew along the Brazos. "I'll carry you."

Sierra shook her head. "I'd like to walk."

"All right." He put an arm around her in case she fell, and they moved away from the bank and the river that had almost claimed her.

"Do you think the river got Luke?"

"Nope. Weston is a survivor." Despite his assurance, he was anything but confident. Loss of a life always bothered him, but for Weston to drown would cause an ache deep inside. The outlaw mattered. Weston's words at the old shack echoed inside Sam's head. *Just shoot. My life isn't worth a damn anyhow.*

He'd long considered Luke Weston a selfish, arrogant scoundrel. Maybe he was, in part, but Sam had seen another side, one filled with honor and caring, no matter how useless Weston thought himself.

"I'll see you in Flatbush, my friend," Sam muttered, praying it would be so.

They reached cover in the trees, and Sam heard Sierra's chattering teeth. Her blue lips spoke of her need for a fire. With no way of making one, he sat on a cushion of grass with his back to the trunk of a tree and pulled her against him, rubbing her arms to warm her.

Where were the horses? Were they close? The oilskin-wrapped matches were in the saddlebags, along with everything else. Including the outlaw loot, but he couldn't be concerned about that at the moment.

"Put your hands over your ears, Sierra. I don't want to burst your eardrums."

Once she did, Sam put two fingers into his mouth and let out a shrill whistle. If Trooper was anywhere near, he'd come. Sam had trained the buckskin well. He waited a minute then whistled again. A crash in the brush was music to Sam's ears. He grinned when the big buckskin trotted up to him with his ears perked. The little mare trailed right behind.

"Good boy, Trooper!" He apologized to Sierra for having to take away the warmth and stood.

Rummaging around in the saddlebags, he located the matches, in addition to the beat-up pot and coffee. Close by, a rocky ledge jutted out, leaving a protected area beneath with room enough to stand. That overhang would conceal the smoke from a fire should anyone come looking. In no time, he had coffee boiling.

Sierra roused from her daze to scrounge two tin cups and a couple of slightly damp blankets. A short time later, Sam sat by the fire with his arms around her. He'd wrapped her in both blankets to take the chill from her bones while they watched the coffee boil. He was cold also, but her body next to his brought warmth.

They were alive. He grinned.

His Colt had gotten wet and wouldn't fire, his clothes were stuck to him, and he and Sierra were lost, but he was happier than he'd been in a while.

"You wanted to know what *amiga* means."

"I do wonder," Sierra murmured.

"A female friend."

"And *dulce*?"

"Sweet. What Luke called you is certainly true."

"That's real nice. I like it."

"Don't know of anyone more deserving of the compliment." Sam's voice roughened.

Sitting on a patch of wild grass with her back against his chest, Sam folded his arms around her. After what they'd been through, he didn't want any space between them. If she objected, she didn't voice it.

With a brush of his lips to her temple, he inhaled the river air and let peace drift over him. "Back there before we forded, what did you mean about too many people had died and you couldn't save them? After you said that, you called to someone named Whitney."

She jerked as though he'd shot her. "Whitney?"

"You yelled the name as we plunged into the river and told her not to make you do it."

Her breathing stilled. "Why do you want to know?"

"Curious. Never heard you mention the name. I'm not sure if it's a man or a woman." Seeing how upset it made her, Sam shrugged. "Just forget it. It's not important. You getting warmer?"

Her tense muscles relaxed. "I am, thanks to the fire and blankets. Don't you need one of these? I feel guilty for taking both."

"You shouldn't. I'm fine." The coffee had probably finished boiling and he could let the grounds settle, but he didn't want to move. Having her where he could touch her didn't happen near enough.

Turned out, he didn't have to get up. Sierra rose and used the hem of her wet dress to take the pot from the fire. After adding more wood, she resumed her place against his chest.

Sam inhaled her fragrance and counted himself a very lucky man.

"Coffee will be ready soon," she said. "Being out in the open is familiar to me. Not the city with its constant noise and horrible smells. This quiet place beneath the Texas sky." She swiveled and glanced up at him. "With you."

Sam lowered his head and gently pressed his mouth to hers. The kiss was the kind of smoldering heat that joined metals, and sent a fierce hunger through him. Need pooled low in his gut. He'd known plenty of women but never anyone like Sierra.

Sure, she was pretty and smart. But what drew him was her sweet vulnerability. Someone had hurt her, and the wound still festered. He knew for sure her father had, but there could be others. Whoever they were, they'd shredded her self-worth.

With a low moan scraping his throat, he turned himself over to the sweetness of her lips. Coaxing them open, he slipped his tongue into the velvet warmth.

Lingering.

Savoring.

Surrendering.

Despite being fully clothed, he seduced her with his touch, teased with soft words, branded her with his lips until she responded with a mewling cry against his mouth.

When she lifted her hand to Sam's face, he caressed the lines of her arm, starting at her fingertips, lazily sliding down to her shoulder. He worshiped everything about this woman who'd not only been tossed aside by her father but life as well.

He wanted to prove Sierra wrong. He could save her. With time, he could give her back everything she'd lost.

The scent of the fire mixed with the earthy, wild river swirled around, driving him on.

His gentle touch followed the long sweep of her neck, down her soft curves to her shapely waist and farther, until his hand rested at the flare of her hips. His breath hitched. Sierra excited him, made him feel every inch a man.

Sierra made him dream again and forget the ghosts that haunted him. Only she had the power to turn him from revenge.

He took his lips from hers long enough to feather

tiny kisses slowly across her mouth to one shell-like ear before finding the pulsing hollow of her throat. With his breath thundering in his ears, he kissed her wild heartbeat. An aching need for her burst inside him and spread. She was everything he'd sought but never found. Sierra Hunt made him lose all reason.

Captain O'Reilly was right. He *was* mad, mad with hunger for this woman.

"Tell me if you want to stop," he murmured against her mouth.

"Please don't stop. Make me feel all the things I've missed."

He brushed the swell of her breasts with a light palm and felt the raised peaks strain against the confines of her bodice. A light flick of his fingers across the hard nub brought Sierra's muffled cry. Her breath came in gasps as she thrust her hand into his hair.

"Sam!"

The depth of the passion and hunger shaking him was something he'd never known.

His fingers worked at the buttons of her dress. Quickly releasing the first three, he touched her skin and pressed his lips to the silky smoothness.

A familiar dance began inside as his muscles quivered and contracted. He loved this beginning buildup for what was to come, the change in the rhythms of his body. It reminded him of how he felt when facing down danger. Breathing became harsher and more rapid. His heart hammered against his ribs. Time slowed.

"Pretty lady, you make me forget things I shouldn't," he whispered against her ear. "I want you."

Sierra Hunt wasn't some passing fancy. What he felt for her shook him to the very core.

From the blue, her words pounded in his head like a gong. *I need permanence, roots.*

The voice of reason spoke. This was wrong. He had to think of her. Not himself for once.

Though he yearned to take what she offered with every fiber of his being, he couldn't. He couldn't take from her without giving her the one thing she needed most—permanence. Roots. A house. A garden…a husband home every night. Endless routine.

The ache in his chest wouldn't let him promise those things. He couldn't. She wanted everything he didn't. He could never be happy in one place like his brother. The monotony, the boredom would cripple him.

With great effort, he removed his hand and buttoned her dress. Dropping feathery kisses along her mouth, he brushed a tendril of hair from her eyes. "I'm sorry. I can't…"

Bright color stained her cheeks, and she turned away. "I understand."

Hell! She thought he didn't want her. That he did think her a coward and weak. She didn't understand—the unworthy one was he.

He didn't deserve someone good and kind like Sierra.

Fourteen

WITH A FINGER UNDER HER CHIN, SAM BROUGHT Sierra's face around. "No, you don't understand. You don't need someone like me. You can do so much better. I'm all jagged edges and holes and driven by revenge. I'd make your life miserable. You've had more than your share of misery already, and I won't add to that. All your life people have taken from you, giving nothing in return. I won't add myself to that list."

"You're different from everyone else."

God, what he wouldn't give to change himself into the man she needed.

He gazed into her blue eyes, and seeing the hurt there made it hard to breathe. He ran the pad of a thumb across her cheek. He'd never find another like her. "Sierra, I'm all wrong. I can't be someone I'm not, no more than you."

Confusion and misery swam in her eyes. "How can you say that after what we shared?"

"People should always carry love for a partner. Can you honestly say you love me?"

The question seemed to catch her off guard. She wrinkled her forehead in thought. "I…I don't know."

"Never give yourself to anyone until you're sure."

She glanced down at her tightly clenched hands, trying to still her trembling lip.

A bastard. He was a bastard. He silently cursed himself.

"I'd give anything to be able to offer what you want—anything. But my feet have to keep moving, and this need has caused rifts between me and my family for years. I'm a loner. I love my job because I'm always in a different town, seeing different people, sleeping in a different bed." He softened his voice even more, because he knew the next words would sting. "I can't think of anything more stifling than waking up in the same house with each endless day merely a repeat of the last."

The inescapable, sobering truth struck him. He was too much like her father. The same thought had to have also hit her.

She glanced away and said stiffly, "You don't have to explain. We're just not right for each other." Her lip trembled as she paused before asking, "Friends?"

Sam knew by the husky pitch of her voice he'd deeply wounded her. Damn it.

Forcing a smile, he said, "Absolutely. Friends always."

The taste of the word *friend* soured on his tongue. He wanted so much more, and he cursed the differences that stood between them.

She stared toward the river, as though struggling to gather herself.

"I need some of that coffee. How about you?" he said quietly.

"I'll get it." She stood, poured some of the hot brew, and handed it to him.

"Thanks."

Wrapping her hands around her cup, she sat on the log. The quiet was punctured only by bird calls and rushing water.

Finally, she spoke. "This tastes good."

"Most women aren't fond of the stuff," he remarked. "I believe you're the first I've known who had a liking for it."

A sad smile formed. "I grew up drinking worse than this. Thanks to my father, I developed quite an appreciation for a strong brew. From the Indians we learned about berries, leaves, and bark. Then, sometimes, we traded things to the mountain men for their version of coffee. Most of it was bitter."

"I can't imagine the things you've seen. Done. I envy you." Sam took a sip. "I've always been a wanderer, which is why the Texas Rangers are perfect. It doesn't sit well with my father though. He wanted to tie his sons to the ranch."

Sam's broken promise grated across his mind. He'd promised his father he would only be a ranger for two years. He'd gone back on his word. He'd have to explain to Stoker sooner or later that he'd been unable to stop, that this job gave him everything he'd been unable to find in ranching.

"Tell me about the Lone Star."

"It's huge, embarrassing really. Like Weston said the other night, the thing covers six counties. My father, Stoker Legend, bought five hundred acres in 1836 for mere pennies with money he'd saved following the Texas war for independence. Everyone told him this land was pretty worthless. But Stoker was a twenty-year-old with a dream and stars in his eyes. He saw what it could be."

"Your father must've worked awfully hard."

"That's a fact. He's obsessed with acquiring land. Last I heard we have four hundred and eighty thousand acres." Sam took another drink of coffee. "He's had to fight hard to keep it though. Comanche, Apache, outlaws, floods, drought. Says it's mine and Houston's legacy. He endured it all for his sons."

"Stoker sounds like a special man."

"Long as he isn't your father. Don't get me wrong. I love and admire him like no other person. But he can be hard." After a moment's lull, he added, "He wasn't always, mind you."

Memories of Stoker taking him fishing and hunting as a youngster flashed through his mind. Sam loved being with him back then, learning about cattle and life. His father had millions of stories to tell about those early days and, even now, Sam never tired of listening to them.

He sighed and continued, "After my mother died, he started drinking. Became bitter."

Sorrow filled her eyes. "In grief, people change, become someone you don't know."

"Sometimes they certainly do."

Sierra gave herself a little shake, and he watched the sorrow vanish. He wondered who had disappointed her. He wanted to ask, but this wasn't the time to push her.

"How long since you've been home?" she asked.

"Been a while."

Memories of the words he'd had with Houston sneaked into his head. His brother had complained of having to stay behind, tied to the ranch and their father.

"Haven't you thought that I might want to see other things, long for adventure of my own?" Houston had yelled.

"This is what you chose," Sam hollered back. "I thought you liked taking care of the Lone Star and riding herd on things."

"I do, but that's beside the point. I don't want it to be the whole sum of my life. I can count on one hand the times I've been off this land."

"Then go. You don't have to stay."

"Like you? Then Pa sure won't have anyone to depend on. The ranch is too big for one person."

"You have a foreman and over a hundred men at your disposal," Sam snapped. "What is really stuck in your craw?"

"He wants you. He tolerates me, but it's you he stands looking for every sunrise and sunset. You don't know the pain you leave behind each time you ride off to chase your dream, your next outlaw, your big thrill. Nor do you give a damn. Whatever little brother wants, little brother gets. Go to hell."

Sam wiped his eyes, wincing at the memory that left a big knot in his gut. He couldn't forget the angry words. Nor how Houston had thrown his glass at his head, barely missing.

How would it be this time? He looked up, realizing he'd been silent too long. "Sorry."

"What is the plan?" Sierra tossed another piece of wood on the fire.

He glanced at the sky and the waning sun. "We'll stay put for the night. Maybe Luke will find us."

Or Isaac Ford? Definite possibility, though Sam figured they were too far downriver and shielded by thick growth and the rocky ledge above them.

"I pray Luke's all right."

"Don't worry too much on that score. Weston knows how to survive." Though Sam's words came easy, his thoughts did not. Luke was too hurt.

"If he doesn't show up, we're supposed to meet in Flatbush," he added.

"That's good." She got to her feet and reached for his empty cup. "Want a refill?"

"Not right now." He rose to unsaddle the horses.

The crackle of the fire reminded him how lucky they were for the heat. Though it was spring and the days heated up in fine fashion, the Texas nights carried a chill. If Weston had survived, he couldn't make a fire. They had the matches.

Maybe Luke would find them before dark, he told himself. But fear that the outlaw lay dying somewhere wouldn't leave his mind.

Maybe because he knew how great the odds truly were. He and Sierra had barely made it out of the river alive, and they were healthy and fit. For someone living on a prayer… Sam didn't want to consider that. Things had gone south so fast he wouldn't have cared to place a bet on their survival.

He allowed a wry smile. It just paid to never give up.

A warm fire, some hot coffee, breath in his lungs—Sierra beside him. That was all he could ask.

His eyes caressed the beautiful woman who'd gotten

into his blood, and he cursed fate for the rotten trick. Hunger still coursed through his heart, impossible to silence. He wouldn't have missed kissing her for all the stars in Texas.

Why did he have to have a conscience?

❧

Darkness settled over them with still no sign of Luke Weston. Sam stared into the flames and tried not to worry. They'd eaten, and Sierra was next to him, quiet and motionless. Her profile didn't show the hurt he'd inflicted. The lady had drawn it inside as she'd probably done throughout her life. One more thing for him to regret.

She'd gone fishing earlier—took a piece of heavy string from her mare's saddle blanket, fashioned a hook from a piece of bone she found on the ground, and caught two fish for supper. He'd watched her in amazement while he took apart his Colt and dried the inside as best he could.

The pretty woman knew about grit. Truth be told, probably more than Sam did. She'd turned out to be quite ingenious.

Fascinated, he'd watched her select some good-sized stones and lay them close together. Then she'd built a second fire on top of them. Once that had burned down, she'd brushed away the embers and ash with a tree branch and laid the fish on the hot stones.

Maybe he was just hungry, but Sam had never eaten such flaky morsels of fish.

He made a mental note of the process in case he needed to use it sometime. A ranger never knew what life would throw at him next. Out on the frontier, every new thing learned often made the difference between enduring and death.

Sometimes a man didn't get a second chance.

With his wet gun belt drying by the fire, his attention shifted to his Colt resting beside him within easy reach. His business with Isaac Ford wasn't done. Not by a long shot. The man was out there searching for them even now. They wouldn't give up without the money and Sierra.

A rustle in the brush made Sierra edge closer.

"Just a wild varmint," he said quietly.

"How do you know?"

"Heard the whispering, scurrying sound. Men sneaking up snap twigs, or their boots strike the rocky ground no matter how careful they walk. Hunting men, a lawman learns the difference. I'm guessing this is a ground squirrel or other small creature."

She stared at her hand and ran her fingers across the palm. "How long have you been a Texas Ranger?"

"Seven years. Joined up the day I turned twenty." Cook had made a cake for his birthday, but his father spent the entire day riding the range, avoiding him. Then as Sam stepped into the stirrup to leave, Stoker rode up and dismounted. He'd taken a small box from his pocket and handed it to Sam without a word. Inside was a watch. Sam took out his watch, staring at the inscription as memories swirled.

It had taken great effort to choke back the tears that day, but Sam somehow held them in check until he made it off Lone Star land. Stoker had spent all day in the saddle, riding to town and back…just to purchase the watch.

Now, following their brush with death and with the night pressing close, he felt that same tightening in his throat.

His dread of going home had eased. He couldn't wait to see his father and brother. They'd get him fixed up.

God, he was so tired—body and soul.

Sam slid the watch back in its pocket. "I'm ready to call it a day. How about you, Sierra?"

"Past ready." She stood and laid out the blankets.

Hurt lined her face. Sam watched her make a bed, trying to get up the courage to point out certain facts. But Sierra probably wasn't of a mind to listen to anything he said.

If the situation was reversed, he wouldn't be either. Hell!

"It's going to be cold, and with our clothes still damp... Sharing the blankets might be the only way to keep from freezing." He quickly added, "I'll understand if you object and let you have both."

"No, I'll share," she murmured softly.

Bleakness filled her eyes, creating an ache inside him. Clearly, she believed her father's spiteful words. And Sam's rejection had made things even worse. Damn! He'd do his best to make her feel safe and cared for—without giving false hope—in the few hours they would share the blankets.

But how in the hell was he going to tamp down the desire that still burned inside?

Few men had that much willpower. Sam sure didn't. Somehow he'd have to find the strength, because he wouldn't destroy her. A little while later, he lay on his side and pulled Sierra against him. As she settled into the curve of his body, he drew the blanket over her.

Even though it was wrong and he had no right, even though she could never be anything more to him than a friend, Sam soaked up the feel of her beside him. He didn't know what lay ahead, but he was going to grab hold of a few happy moments in the present. Sometimes those were all a man could hope for.

The slight rise and fall of her chest, the brush of her gentle breath on the arm she used for a pillow—they were everything he'd yearned for since she'd landed in his lap on the train.

He called himself every name in the book.

No matter, Sierra Hunt had stolen into his dead heart and brought him back to life, just as he'd done to her after pulling her from the cold floodwaters.

He told himself he was only making sure she was comfortable and warm. She had been through a lot. But as he inhaled the scents of the river and listened to fish flopping in the water, Sam laid a protective arm across her stomach.

Deep wounds had left craters inside her. Something bad had happened to her to scar her. He made a silent vow that no one else would, especially the outlaw Isaac Ford. If the jackal laid another hand on her…

Sam clenched his back teeth together so hard he thought he'd chipped them. He'd unleash a hell like Ford had never seen before.

Fifteen

SIERRA WOKE JUST AS DAWN'S HUSHED PINK LIGHT spread across the dark sky. Being here with Sam brought contentment. In all the darkness, with the raging water so near, she was safe and warm in his arms.

Only he didn't want her. He needed more than she could give. She was too damaged, too battered by life, too easy to forget.

Her lip trembled. What he said was true. She could never be happy in his world, or he in hers. She was done living from campfire to campfire. Sam was done staying in one place. He needed adventure. She would settle for nothing short of deep roots that would offer her a chance to heal. Best she found out now before he broke her heart.

Except it was too late for that.

A scalding lump sat in her throat as she remembered the gentle kisses that still burned on her lips. His touch had awakened desires and a hunger for more. Her heart would never forget what she'd almost had. A crushing ache filled her chest. She didn't know how she would be able to return to the lonely, scarred woman she had been.

Being with Sam had changed her. She wouldn't be content with half measures or making do. Just as well, she supposed. He'd have turned away once he learned the truth. This was really a blessing. It was.

Very carefully, she lifted his arm that lay across her and stood. But when she glanced down, she noticed he was awake.

"Good morning. Did I wake you?"

Sam's lazy smile showed rows of white teeth. "Nope."

Sierra sucked in her breath at the sudden transformation of his somber features. Instant searing heat raced along her nerve endings and spread out, leaving her heart in a hopeless tangle.

"I'll get coffee on." Sierra rushed to put space between them before she did something stupid. With her pulse racing, she snatched the beat-up coffeepot. "I'm sure you want to load up and ride out soon."

Sam stood and stretched. "I wish we could stay here for a few days, but it's safer if we keep moving. Besides, I want to get to Flatbush. Hopefully, Luke will be there. I can't wait to buy some new clothes. These make my skin crawl."

Stooping beside the swift current, Sierra filled the pot. "I'm going to buy a comb. My hair drives me crazy. I want to braid it, but it's a rat's nest." The breeze caught the sound of her laughter, carrying it to a bird perched on a cedar branch. Their feathered friend squawked back as though scolding her for disturbing its sleep.

"Shush, you silly bird." She carried the pot to the

fire before realizing she hadn't yet stoked it. Good heavens. What was wrong with her?

When Sam turned toward the horses, she called, "Sam?"

"Yeah?"

"I never thanked you for saving my life…again. Seems all you've been doing."

"No thanks needed."

Sierra chewed her bottom lip. "Do you think your gun dried enough? Will it shoot?"

"The Colt will fire." The grim statement eased her worries. "It needs a thorough cleaning and oiling, which I'll do at the first opportunity, but for now, it'll do what I ask."

The words brought hardness to his gray stare. Sierra pitied Ford if he should cross Sam's path again. For a moment, she wished Rocky could see this man he idolized. She pictured him scribbling away in the little notebook he always carried. Would she ever see him again?

Clearing her throat, she said, "I'll have coffee ready by the time you saddle the horses."

With a nod, he stroked the thick neck of his buckskin.

She watched for a moment. He was a man who loved his horse and his family. Sadness had filled his voice when he'd spoken of his father. Yet there had been a great deal of pride there as well. Though he said differently, she'd heard longing in his voice and knew he looked forward to being home.

Her father might as well be dead. Without a doubt, she knew she was to him. William Hunt had washed his hands of her, never to see her again.

In a different way, so had Sam. Pain swept through her again with the power and fury of the Brazos. She watched him with the horses, tall and lean and capable. The holster hung at his side within reach. No doubt he had skill at using it. He was capable of so many things.

Except loving her.

Her lips still burned with his kisses. How was she going to pretend that her heart hadn't broken into a thousand aching pieces? With a heavy sigh, she turned her attention to the fire, and when the flames died, she set the coffee amid the hot coals.

An hour later, they were in the saddle and heading toward the town where they would hopefully meet up with Luke. Sierra worried about him. Had Ford and his gang killed the wanted man? A prayer rose in her heart. Despite what they said he'd done, she'd seen how much he cared for Sam and for her.

This land, this Texas, had forged two very strong men.

Though they butted heads like two billy goats, she knew that beneath everything lay admiration and respect. They were alike in so many ways, though she knew each would deny it.

The coolness of the morning soon gave way to the sun's power. Under the hot rays, Sierra grew drowsy. She hadn't slept well. She'd spent much of the night lying awake, listening to Sam's breathing, feeling the tiny quivers of his muscles.

A sidelong glance showed his handsome features grim, his mouth set. He'd climbed into his own thoughts, leaving no room for her.

After miles of nothing, Sierra broke the silence. "Tell me about Flatbush."

"Not much more than a mercantile and saloon."

"Is that all?"

"Let's just say it's a one-horse town without the horse."

She'd seen plenty of those. They weren't much different from her… Empty. Desolate. Dying inside.

❧

Sam didn't lie about the size. Flatbush reminded Sierra of some towns she'd seen tucked away in remote, forgotten areas of the West.

A handful of businesses lined only one side of the street, with vacant land opposite. In fact, the thoroughfare was no more than a goat trail through weeds that sprouted everywhere. Odd why the residents had made the town lopsided.

They came to the saloon first. She noticed how Sam's gaze sharpened, taking in the solitary horse at the hitching rail as they went past. She also saw the flicker of disappointment at the absence of the familiar black gelding.

Folks came out to stare, as though she and Sam had sprouted antlers. Some of the men sported coonskin caps like some of the mountain men she'd met.

Sierra smiled and called good day.

Next came a tiny barbershop and telegraph office, with the mercantile the very last building. Sam halted at the hitching rail and dismounted, then came to help her. With his hand resting on the small of her back, they went inside. Despite the friendship she'd settled for, his warm touch sharpened the longings and made her heart flutter.

The proprietor had watched their arrival through the window and spoke the second they crossed the threshold. "May I help you?"

"Point me toward the clothes," Sam said. "Also, whatever foodstuffs you got."

They moved toward the back while Sierra gravitated to the women's section and selected a comb and brush. She was admiring the hair ribbons when the bell over the door tinkled. She glanced up to see Luke Weston and sucked in a horrified breath. His clothes were ripped, and he staggered, clutching the doorframe.

"Good Lord, what happened?" She ran toward him before he fell, leading him to a cane-bottom chair at the end of the long counter.

"Which time?" Luke tried to grin but never made it.

Sierra hurried to a shelf, grabbed a roll of gauze and other supplies. In the moments it took her to return, he'd sagged in the chair and would have fallen if she hadn't caught him.

"At the river? You've reinjured your arm."

"Don't fuss, *dulce*. Such happens when you wrestle with the devil."

"Stop calling me that. My name is Sierra."

"Anything else before I die here?"

Tears pricked her eyes, and that made her furious. She blinked rapidly. "You worried Sam."

"The ranger's a big boy." He rubbed a hand across his eyes. "Where is he?"

"In back, picking out new clothes. I need water to do a proper job of cleaning your wound."

"Wrap it up. I'll be fine."

She did as he asked. "When are you going to tell me what happened?"

Luke raised his eyes. "Go get Sam. Gotta hurry."

Relief, then concern, showed on Sam's face when he spied the outlaw. He turned to the wide-eyed clerk. "Do you have a doctor in town?"

"Afraid not, mister. Got a barber, an' he fixes up whatever you need, does dentistry and coffin makin'. The best around."

"No thanks," Luke muttered. "I'll take my chances. Let's go, Legend."

With an arm bracing Luke, Sam helped him to a bench outside. "I'm not letting you on that horse until you tell me what happened."

Luke gave a weary sigh. "Ford. That's what. They caught me after I forded the Brazos. I held 'em off until I emptied my gun. They pinned me down, and I couldn't get to my horse for more shot. Luckily, they ran out too. They surrounded me, and it turned into one deadly brawl. I used whatever I could for a weapon. One of the bastards bashed in my head. Guess they figured I was done for, so they threw me in the river to drown. The icy water woke me."

Sierra shivered as his eyes turned to bits of green glass.

"They should've killed me." Cold steel laced Luke's words. "Their mistake will cost them."

Sam got to his feet. "From what you said, they're not behind, they're in front. Have to be, because there's no sign of them here."

Luke wiped sweat from his forehead. "Damn my throbbing skull. My thinking's all messed up."

"Don't worry." Sam laid a hand on his shoulder. "We'll figure stuff out."

Against Luke's insistence that he was fine, Sierra put a new bandage over his angry red wound, and Sam went back into the store to buy laudanum. After stowing some of their purchases in the saddlebags and strapping the larger things onto their horses' backs, they made a quick detour to the saloon for a bottle of whiskey and left the dead town of Flatbush behind.

They rode for about an hour at a leisurely pace before Sam halted under the shade of a sycamore to let Luke rest. The horses drank from a stream and nibbled on wild rye.

Sierra got her patient to drink a bit more of the laudanum, and that helped Luke's pain. She prayed they would find a way to make the gunslinger comfortable, or he wasn't going to make it. They needed a wagon. She took Sam aside. "What are we going to do? He's not able to keep riding, and I think his wound is infected. His fever is back."

"Not surprised. I'll try to figure something out." Sam's hand accidentally brushed hers and sent a jolt up her arm. His gray stare loosened a slew of tingles, telling her he'd felt it too.

She tried to quiet her heart and quickly turned away. Calling herself a fool, she jerked the paper from around the new comb and brush. While Luke regained a bit of strength, she braided her hair. It was strange how putting her hair to rights and getting it out of her face improved her outlook. She tied the end with the pretty ribbon Luke had given her at the shack.

Sure, Sam hadn't meant to touch her, she told herself angrily. Still, it had felt nice. No, that wasn't quite right. The brush of those long fingers made her hot and achy and filled with such longing she couldn't bear it. That was the problem. Yet, she couldn't stand for him to treat her with indifference either. She hated this turmoil inside and no clear direction.

The fact he appeared just as torn only made it worse.

A little while later, the men stood. She climbed back onto her horse and welcomed the easy trot.

Though neither Sam nor Luke mentioned Ford, she noticed their wariness and didn't miss the fact that they rode with the narrow strip of leather off the hammers of their revolvers.

They expected trouble. Uneasiness gripped her as though it were a band of steel.

Once Ford figured out they were behind him, he'd double back. She knew that was why they rode in front of her.

Always protecting her, always seeing to her comfort.

Sierra maneuvered her mare beside Sam. "How long before we reach your ranch?"

His gray eyes moved over her. "Maybe six days to headquarters, barring more setbacks."

What he *wasn't* saying came through loud and clear. If they kept to this pace. If Luke's wound didn't slow them any further. If they avoided the Ford gang. So many ifs. She knew unless a miracle happened they'd not make it all the way.

"We don't have six days at this rate."

"I know. Bad as I want to, we can't hole up somewhere for a day or two."

"We won't have to if we can find a wagon."

Sam quirked an eyebrow, glancing at the desolate landscape. "Might as well wish for a pot of gold at the end of the rainbow while you're at it."

Sierra shook her head at his sarcasm. "We'll see."

Sam lifted his hat and ran his hands through his hair. "Sorry. We'll keep pressing forward and hope for the best." He adjusted his black Stetson back on his head. His gaze met hers and softened. She fidgeted under his scrutiny. "How are you holding up, Sierra?"

"I'm fine." *Almost*, she added silently, hoping he didn't notice her breaking voice or the pain in her eyes.

"We haven't spoken much since this morning."

"Nothing to talk about," Sierra murmured, trying to keep her face from showing the hurt inside.

"I'm sorry about last night. First I kiss you, then tell you nothing can ever come from it. I wish I could be more like you, content to settle down."

"Sam, don't apologize." If he kept on, the tears she'd held back since morning would spill. "You and I are different. Our paths crossed, and that's all. I never expected anything more."

Just a few hot kisses under the moonlight, and his arms around her while she slept.

She was used to being alone, used to being forgotten, used to yearning for things she couldn't have. She turned away to hide her trembling lip.

"You know I'd never hurt you." Sam started to touch her, gave a sigh, then dropped his hand.

"I know," she murmured past the lump blocking her throat.

Only, unwittingly or not, he had. Swallowing hard, Sierra fell back behind the unlikely pair.

Sam's kisses, the way his lips had pressed to hers, burned in her memory no matter how hard she tried to forget. So gentle, with so much passion.

His touch had sent a raging firestorm through her. One moment of happiness. Forgetting Sam Legend would take the rest of her life. Even then, she knew she couldn't. It would never be possible to forget that once under a star-dotted midnight sky she'd truly been desired.

Sixteen

How could he make a six-day ride go any faster? Sam mulled it over in his mind the following morning as they trotted toward the town of Potters Valley. Even that was still a day's ride away.

Luke had worsened, and that worried him.

This morning, Sierra had found a large spiderweb beside a rock, and Sam had showed her how to make a poultice using gunpowder. Hopefully, those would help.

The previous night, they'd camped beside a small stream holding barely a trickle of water. He'd lain awake, listening to Sierra's soft breathing, watching her sleep. He hated that she braided her hair now. He'd loved the black strands hanging unbound down her back.

The lady's beauty stole his breath. He'd been captivated by her dark coloring and those blue eyes the first moment he'd seen her.

Only now, she seemed to look at him with cold regard, and that wounded him. Not that he blamed her.

Someone should kick his rump all the way to the Gulf of Mexico and back.

Still, the truth was far kinder than dishonesty, and he'd vowed to himself to always be aboveboard with her. Sam wouldn't have been able to live with a lie. He stared now at her stiff back in front of him. Sierra's easy way was gone, and so was the warmth of her smile. He'd do well to remember that he had a job to do. Ensure her safety, take care of Ford and his bunch, find her brother, and then they would part ways.

Already he could barely stand the thought of never seeing her again. A constant ache to touch her, hold her, kiss her, crowded around his heart. What would it be like when she was no longer near?

What got him worse was the way she'd turned to Weston. Luke was the one she worried about now, the one she talked to. Sam watched her lean closer to say something to the outlaw. Watched the bond grow. Watched everything slip away.

Well, Weston did have permanence in his future. Too bad it'd be behind bars.

Full of misery, Sam shifted his gaze to a caravan of oxcarts and wagons parked off the trail. A yoke of oxen and some mules pulled two conveyances. But three larger wagons were pulled by fancy horses. Five or six children chased each other, evidently taking advantage of the lull.

Some of the men who walked toward them were dressed in fine clothes. Those who hung back wore wide sombreros and colorful serapes. Sam speculated that these were servants and wondered where the group was headed. Being this far north of the border told Sam they were escaping something. Back in Waco, he'd heard mention of the revolt in Mexico and gathered that these people were in search of a piece of ground that didn't run red with blood. He didn't blame them for that.

Texas had always had a large population of immigrants. For the most part, they seemed respectful of the law and the rangers. More than he could say about a good many other folk.

Sam frowned when Sierra turned her mare and raced toward them. He chased after her.

A man with a neatly trimmed beard, somewhere in his early thirties, stepped in front of the children, staring curiously. He was flanked by three others of various ages. All wore heavy scowls. Their angry expressions didn't appear to slow Sierra. She drew to a halt and dismounted.

"Pardon me, gentlemen, may I trouble you for a word?"

"No *problemas!*" the bearded man shouted. "Go."

Sam kept a sharp eye, ready to draw his weapon at the first sign that they might hurt her.

"Help," Sierra said. "My friend is injured."

They stared at Sam through distrustful eyes, then moved to Weston beside him on the black gelding. They took in his bloody bandage.

"What you need, señorita?" The speaker was a younger man in a short black jacket with silver buttons.

The bearded one gentled his voice. "No food. *Enfermos.*"

Sam dismounted and stood beside Sierra. Before he

could open his mouth to reply, Luke leaned heavily on the saddle horn and spoke in fluent Spanish.

With Weston's mother being of Mexican descent, it stood to reason he'd have full command of the language. Still, it caught Sam off guard. Luke would likely enlist their help when he got well enough to run. Run he would; that was a given. Outlaws always did.

Finally, Luke swung to them. "They got caught in the revolt. Porfirio Diaz has seized control. These people have been traveling for a month. They're out of food, and two of their women are sick."

Sierra smiled at the men. "We have food to exchange for a ride north. My friend here is in too much pain to ride horseback. We must get to the Lone Star Ranch near the Red River. Might you be going that way?"

"I already offered all that, *dulce*," Luke said softly. "They've agreed. Tell them *gracias*. That means thank you."

"*Gracias*." Sierra gave them another smile.

Having seen how fiercely new immigrants kept to themselves, Sam knew taking the three of them in wasn't an easy decision.

Though the men didn't return Sierra's smile, one who wore long, shaggy hair motioned them forward. "Come."

"Splendid!" Sierra turned to Sam. "See? They'll take us the rest of the way."

"I'll never doubt you again." He allowed a grin.

The thing to seal the deal seemed to be the mention of food. Sharing the provisions they'd stocked up on at the mercantile in Flatbush was little enough in exchange for getting Weston a ride.

Sam shot a glance at the man who'd saved his life. Weston had slipped sideways in the saddle now, too weak to hold on. Sam helped him from the black gelding. He put an arm around the outlaw and half carried him to the nearest wagon, where he laid him on a bed of hay. "Just rest now. You don't have to fight to be strong."

Sierra had followed and touched Luke's forehead. Worry lining her face told Sam all he needed to know.

"Sleep and rest, Luke," she murmured. "You have a nice place to lie while we're moving."

They'd move, all right. But at a crawl—sitting ducks. Unease shimmied up Sam's spine. He knew Isaac Ford was out there somewhere. But would he waste a second glance at a wagon of immigrants? Not likely.

"I hate to ask, but can you unstrap some of our provisions, *dulce*?" Luke's words were weak, and he winced when he moved his head too fast. "They need to eat."

"Most certainly."

Sam laid a hand on her shoulder. "I'll take care of that. You stay."

"Please, let me help. I can start preparing a meal so we can get moving." At his nod, Sierra fell into step beside him.

A small boy broke away from the others and shyly came forward. "*Gracias*," Sam said. Drawing on his Spanish, which was just enough to get by, he asked the boy his name.

"Hector."

That unleashed a flood. Hector rattled off words so fast Sam's head spun.

"Whoa! Slow down, Hector." He wiped a bead of sweat from his brow.

It took a bit for Sam to figure out that the boy's mother, the last of his family, died a few days ago, and they had buried her beside the trail. Now the boy had no one. He laid an arm across Hector's thin shoulders that shook with sobs. Kneeling, he wiped away the tears, trying his best to soothe the hurt.

Sierra knelt and rubbed the boy's small back. "What's wrong, Sam?"

After he told her, she said, "Poor thing. Does he have anyone to look out for him?"

"Only a neighbor. He's the one wearing the short black jacket and speaks the best English."

As she folded her arms around the boy, Hector threw his arms around her neck. Sam knew how the boy felt. Losing his mother was the worst pain Sam had ever suffered. His youth and the fact that he'd been so terrified only sharpened the loss. His mother's loving arms had comforted him when nightmares came, when he was sick…and when he'd found at age nine that being a man was too hard.

Those joys were gone for him at ten, gone now for Hector too.

Dragging his thoughts back, he admired Sierra's gentle way with Hector. Before long, she finally coaxed a tiny smile out of him.

"You have a knack for fixing broken hearts," Sam said.

Except her own, it seemed. He tried to swallow around the lump suddenly blocking his throat.

"He's a sweet child." She gave Hector a hug and rose. He tugged her hand, and she went with him to a tuft of wild grass, where she showed great interest in something the boy showed her.

Sam finished unloading the foodstuffs, and before he knew it, Sierra, with the help of one of the older women who spoke a smattering of English, soon had the group eating. Her quiet, efficient movements reminded him of his mother. Both knew how to put everyone at ease. Laying a hand here, giving a smile there, with plenty of laughter along the way, Sierra was amazing to watch.

It appeared they ate in order, with the children first, then the men, and finally the women. Judging by the wide smiles and shy glances, all seemed appreciative.

While everyone else fed their stomachs, the woman—whose name was Sofia—took Sierra to the wagon where the sick lay. From where Sam sat, he saw that she tended to them with care and gentle kindness, following Sofia's instructions with growing confidence. She seemed to excel in so many areas. Sierra Hunt was like a blossoming rose. With each beautiful petal exposed, surprises popped out.

More reasons not to hold her back.

When she strolled toward him, Hector followed. Sam made room on the end of the wagon where he sat. "What's ailing them?"

"I'm not sure. They have a fever and chills. Could be the grippe. I'll mix up some herbs and roots when we stop for the night."

Sam lifted her hand. "You have the hands of a healer."

"My mother was the best teacher."

Back to mothers. They were indispensable. He noticed how Hector snuggled up beside Sierra.

It appeared the boy might've found a substitute. At least for the time being.

~∞~

Though Hector cried to ride with Sierra, one of the women made him go with her. After Sierra checked Luke's wound and climbed in beside him, Sam tied their horses to the back of another wagon. He couldn't explain why. Simply following his gut, heeding the warning.

He intended to ride Trooper and do some scouting, but she called him over.

She chewed her bottom lip. "Sam, will you ride with us a ways? Luke has a favor to ask. I think it's important."

"Sure." He tied the buckskin with the others and sat beside them on the fresh hay.

With a jerk, the wheels turned, and they rolled across the plains. Sam leaned back, staring up at the blue sky. "I could go to sleep without half trying. The sun's warmth, the motion… I feel like a fat cat curled on a windowsill."

"It's heavenly." Sierra lay between him and Luke.

Luke sighed. "*Dulce*, I could kiss you."

"Try it, and you'll find a piece of cold steel in your face," Sam growled. "And I'll thank you to use her name."

The outlaw wasn't too sick to shoot him a glare. "Is there some law against either?"

There is where I am concerned.

"I've got plenty of charges against you. Don't have

to make up more." Secretly, it thrilled Sam that Luke felt well enough to argue. Meant the rest had already made some difference.

"So we're back to that?"

Pulling his hat over his eyes, Sam said, "Yep."

Idly, he wondered who would win in a fight if it ever came to that. Luke was built solid and matched Sam in size. Something said it would be hard to beat a healthy Luke Weston either with fists or gun. Rumor had it he was quicker than greased lightning with his revolver. Facing him in a duel would be suicide.

"What did you want to talk to me about, Weston?"

"A favor. If I die, promise you'll take me down to San Antone and bury me beside my mother."

Sierra gasped. "Luke, don't talk this way! You have to remain positive."

"I will die, one way or another. If not by this damn bullet, then another…or by the hangman's noose. The minutes are ticking down." His stare met Sam's. "Promise me."

"I promise to do what you ask. But you have to do something in return."

"What's that, Ranger?"

"Satisfy my curiosity. Tell me why you take only fifty dollars in any robbery and leave the rest."

Before Luke could answer, gunshots rang out. Sierra's fingernails dug into Sam's arm.

He muttered a low curse as his hand went to his Colt. He slowly rose for a quick look.

"Please tell me it's not Ford," Sierra said.

He wasn't up for lying on this fine day. "It's him

all right, but only three of his men. They're trying to stop the caravan."

"What do you want to do, Legend?" Luke asked. "I can't run, but I can still shoot straight."

Sam's gut clenched. He couldn't let these people who had fled from violence get hurt in a gun battle. "Quick, get under this hay."

Digging frantically, he created a hole for Sierra and shoved her into the space. Luke managed to burrow down by himself. Sam joined them in the nick of time, pulling the mound back over them.

Luke slid his Colt from the holster. "These folks'll play dumb, pretend they don't understand. But if they see our horses…"

"Glad I removed the saddles." Sam gripped his Colt. "Even at that, they still stand out like a red bird in a flock of crows."

Sierra lay with her nose almost touching Sam's. He wouldn't have to move to kiss her, just press his lips gently to hers. God how he wanted to have one last taste of her! Her breasts pressed against his chest, her hips to his thighs. She overloaded his senses. He had to keep a clear head, but she made it impossible.

"We can't let the gang kill our friends," she whispered. "The children. Hector."

Isaac Ford shouted, "Stop, *amigos*! Stop or we'll shoot."

Frightened children began to wail while the adults spoke rapid Spanish. So far, they hadn't lapsed into broken English. Sam prayed they wouldn't. If they continued, Ford might give up and leave.

"Shut up," Ford shouted in frustration. "We want the three *gringos*, and we want them now."

Their wagon driver yelled, "No *comprende*."

"Come on, Ford," Sam murmured, "ride on."

"I'll bet you understand a bullet to the head, Mes'can," Ford yelled. "I know you're hidin' 'em. Think I'm stupid? I see their horses tied to the back. Frenchie and John, start searching."

Sam turned to Sierra and whispered, "Draw up your legs. Make yourself as small as you can." She quickly followed his instructions.

Gripping his weapon and knowing Luke did the same, Sam readied. His breathing slowed, and calm washed over him as it always did when danger called.

The minute Ford's man began spearing the hay with a long stick, Sam reached up and yanked him down on top of them.

He jabbed his Colt into the man's forehead at the same time Luke pressed his to the outlaw's chest. "Do as I say, and we might let you live."

Seventeen

THE OUTLAW'S EYES WIDENED AS HE TRIED TO SWALLOW. He shook so hard he could barely nod. Someone had broken his nose—several times, by the looks of the crooked beak that hooked at the end.

Sam put his mouth next to the man's ear. "Which one are you?"

"John."

"I'm Texas Ranger Sam Legend."

"Reckon I've seen you before."

"Then you know I mean what I say. I'm sure you've heard of Luke Weston too. He's wanted for murder. Gotta warn you, he has an itchy trigger finger."

John's Adam's apple slid slowly down his throat.

"Legend's taking me to jail," Luke rasped. "One more murder won't make any difference."

Sam brought John's attention back to him. "Don't make a sound until I give the word. Then, you're going to tell Ford that the wagons are clear. Can you do that?"

"Yes."

"If you breathe, if you whisper, hell, if you scratch an itch before then, we'll fill you with holes. Understand?"

John tried to swallow, only the spit appeared to get stuck in his throat. He made several attempts, coughed then nodded.

"Say a word later, and I'll see you dead before I die." Sam relaxed his hold a bit.

"I won't," John promised.

Minutes dragged as Sam waited. Cries of the frightened women and children circled around him as the others searched their wagons and carts. No one else was going to be hurt under his watch.

Though a bee buzzed around Sam's nose, he didn't swat at it. He lay perfectly still with nothing showing except his face and arms. Thank goodness they couldn't see Sierra.

Finally, the wait ended.

"John, get the hell out here," Ford hollered. "Where are you? Frenchie didn't find any sign of 'em."

Sam moved into John's face. "Tell him the wagons are clear and you're coming. Do it!"

"Coming, Ford! Ain't hide nor hair of 'em in these here wagons," John yelled at the top of his lungs.

"That's good. That's real good." Weston breathed the words.

"Now, I want you to go out there and climb on your horse," Sam ordered. "Tell your boss that you found a woman who speaks some English, and she told you we boarded the stagecoach at the relay station twenty miles to the south and gave them our horses. If we see a glimpse of anyone from your gang following, I'll pick you off one by one."

Luke put his mouth next to John's ear. "You know what a crack shot Legend is, don't you?"

"I—I heard," John stammered.

"Then I think we're done." Luke patted the man's face before Sam shoved him from the wagon.

Sam rose enough to peer through the cracks in the side of the wagon and watched John stumble to his horse and mount up.

"They caught the stage at the relay station, boss. The Mes'cans said Legend gave 'em the horses."

"What are you waitin' for? We gotta catch that stage." Ford spurred his horse, and the group galloped off in a cloud of dust.

As the hoof beats faded, Sam crawled from the hay. After a moment, he called softly, "You can come out now, Sierra."

"Do you think John will keep his word?" She accepted Sam's help from the wagon and stretched out the kinks.

The stretching and bending pulled her dress tight around her curves. When she drew back her arms, tightening the fabric across her breasts, Sam had trouble swallowing. It was getting harder and harder to remember why he'd pushed her away.

Finally, he managed to get his thick tongue to form words. "Anyone's guess. I gave up trying to read outlaws' minds a while ago. We'll change course. Go where they won't think of looking."

Even then, it might not be enough.

"Tell Carlos," Luke said.

Sam frowned. "Who's Carlos?"

"Our driver." Though breathing heavily, Weston grinned.

Irritated that the man knew things he didn't, Sam

whirled and walked away. When he returned from working out a new route with Carlos, he found Sierra sitting on the end of the wagon, her legs dangling off the end. He took her cold, trembling hands, wishing he could pull her against him.

"Sorry for the scare."

The weary smile she gave him spoke of her struggle to hold on to cheer. "I only hope we're finally rid of them now."

Sam knew outlaws, and he knew Isaac Ford. They weren't through with him by a long shot.

He rubbed her hands to warm them. "Makes two of us. Thank you."

"What for?"

"For not raising a fuss. For taking everything in stride in your calm, quiet way." She was so much more than what he'd always thought women could be.

"How else would I be? You're in this pickle because of me."

Tired of fighting the need to hold her, even though it was wrong, Sam gave in and slipped his arm around her. "We have this wagon to ride in—because your instincts said we could trust this group."

"It was a small thing," she murmured.

"Not to me. Or Luke."

Inhaling her fresh fragrance was his second mistake. Good Lord, how would he be able to let her go? But he had no choice. To watch the constant travel demands of his job kill the light in her eyes would drive a knife into his heart.

Sam released her while he still had strength. He prayed she would find someone to make a life with who could give her everything she needed. After he rid her of Ford and she could return to her life, he planned to watch over her. If she married someone who hurt her, he'd make the man very, very sorry. Even though he couldn't have her in his arms, she would always belong to him in his heart.

"I simply kept my eyes open for anyone traveling in a wagon," Sierra explained. "Initially, I planned to find something in the next town and was just as surprised as you to run across help out here on the prairie."

He chuckled. "Can you pull any other rabbits out of your hat, Miss Magician?"

Sierra's brow wrinkled. "I'm fresh out of rabbits and hats."

"You're an amazing woman, you know that?" He brushed her cheek with a knuckle. "I wish…"

"Me too," she said softly. "But I learned a long time ago that a bear can't be a horse, and sometimes the wind carries wishes far beyond reach."

"What will you do after I find your brother and take care of Ford?"

"Go back to Waco and my life." Her voice lowered to a whisper. "It's all I have."

"What about your parents?"

Sierra straightened. "We should probably get going."

Her abrupt change puzzled Sam. Again he remembered her statement that he couldn't fix her. Until she opened up, whatever had happened would remain a mystery. Besides, knowing her secrets didn't mean he could make whatever it was right.

"Yes, we should. I'll saddle my horse and ride for now." Being close to her was much too dangerous.

Sam quickly had Trooper ready, and they moved out. He rode ahead, keeping a sharp eye out for problems of any sort. As the wagons and carts lumbered along behind, he thought about Sierra. What if her brother, Rocky, was dead? He hated to think of her all alone.

How could he let her go back to Waco to manage by herself? He had to think of a way to keep her on the ranch. Not that he didn't think she could manage on her own. Sierra Hunt had proved very adept at taking care of herself—as long as it didn't involve fording a river.

Each time he recalled how close he'd come to losing her, his heart pounded.

The need to keep her near and safe grew deep inside him.

❧

Sierra was glad when they stopped for the night. She was tired of riding and anxious about the sick. Her conscience said she should've ridden with them. But she was glad she'd been with the men when Isaac Ford came.

The minute she climbed from the back of the wagon, Hector came running on his skinny little legs. The boy had to be around seven or eight, and from all appearances had lived a life of hardship. She could relate so well.

"*Hola*, señorita," he said, slipping his hand inside hers.

She gathered he was saying hello. At least she hoped. "*Hola*, Hector."

That must've encouraged him, because he began speaking very fast in Spanish. She stared at him blankly.

Luke pulled to a sitting position and chuckled. "He's telling you that he's never seen anyone so beautiful and kind. I do think the boy is smitten. You have quite an admirer."

One of the few Spanish words Sierra knew curled around her tongue. "*Gracias*."

"Very nice, *dulce*. You'll pick up Spanish in no time." Luke stared after Sam.

She could feel the need to be up and around biting into him. The need to be vital was something men seemed to be born with. His returning color heartened her though.

Accompanied by Hector, Sierra checked in on their patients—doing well under Sofia's gentle care—then went to find Sam. She located him at the stream, letting his horse drink. He smiled at the motherless boy and ruffled his hair as he spoke to her. "How are your patients? I saw you checking on them."

"Both still have a fever and chills. I'm convinced it's the grippe. I hate to ask, but can you point me toward some yarrow?"

"I'm sure there's plenty around. Texas is full of that stuff. I'm heading out to hunt. I'll bring some back."

The fading sunlight brushed his hair like strokes of an artist's brush. She steeled herself against the remembrance of the soft texture. No sooner had she shaken the recollection from her head than the memory of his passionate kisses bombarded her. The feel of his mouth on hers, his hands doing things to her body that sent exquisite pleasure sweeping through her was nothing she could erase from her mind.

He wants someone I can never be.

And I can't force him into someone he isn't.

Still, the reminders refused to stick in her head. Her gaze settled on his firm mouth and a tiny scar she'd never noticed before just below his bottom lip. She'd intended to ask about some other herbs, but their names escaped her. With a nod, she turned and hurried from the man who had reminded her with his quiet strength that she was a woman with needs and desires of her own.

Sierra struggled to breathe past the pain. To know such hunger left her weak and achy. There would never be any more warm touches that set her on fire. No more gasps of pleasure as he lit a blaze inside her. Dear God, no more nights in his arms, trying to understand this unseen force that drew her to him.

She was with the women, thinking about Rocky and wishing her brother were there, alive and happy, when Sam Legend returned to camp, dragging a mule deer. Despite everything, her heart leaped at the sight of him. She suspected it would always be this way.

The excited men ran to help with the deer. Sam strode toward Sierra, carrying a burlap sack holding yarrow and willow bark.

"Thank you for taking time to gather these."

Sam's gaze went to Luke sitting by the fire. A growl rumbled in his chest. "What's he doing up? He needs to be lying down."

"That's what I told him. As you can see, he does what he wants."

"Brew some of that tea, and I'll see that he drinks every last drop." He stalked away to care for his horse.

A little while later, Sierra walked past one of the wagons and heard sobs. She glanced inside to find it empty. Bending, she saw Hector stretched out face-down on the ground. She crawled next to him and gently rubbed his thin back. Her heart broke in pieces for this homeless child who had no family to claim him, to comfort him, to love him. She lay down, putting her arms around him, holding him until he spent his tears.

She didn't know Spanish, but she understood the language of a broken heart.

Darkness had fallen by the time supper was ready. Sierra filled a plate for Hector, then one for herself, and sat with the boy on her bedroll, along with the other children. Luke talked with the men, and Sam stretched out beside her.

"Tired?" She glanced over the top of Hector's head, since the boy had scooted into her lap.

Firelight flickered over Sam's face, smoothing the deep lines around his firm mouth. The dancing flames brought out the raised veins on the backs of his strong hands. His hands could make her body sing, swim the current of a mighty river to save her, or take her face between them as he gently kissed her.

His gaze met hers. "It's been a long day. How was the tea?"

"The women drank every bit. Did you have any luck?"

A small grin curved Sam's lips for only a moment then was gone. "Yep. Luke drank it."

It sounded like it had been under protest.

"What do you think he and the men are discussing?"

"Hard telling. I can understand Spanish if it's spoken slower. But lightning fast like they're doing hurts my brain. Luke seems right at home."

That he did. At night it was difficult to pick him out from the others. Though he wasn't well yet, his improvement pleased her. But what would happen once he was? Sierra had overheard him and Sam talking right after the shoot-out at the shack and knew Luke had been the one to cut Sam down from that tree.

How could Sam arrest the man who'd saved his life? But she knew he wasn't the kind of man who turned his back on his duty.

Her heart ached for both men. They were as scarred as she.

Hector lay down and put his head in her lap. She smoothed back his hair, wondering what events, choices, decisions would shape his life. Though only eight years old, he already bore scars from his family's deaths.

"The boy's exhausted," Sam said. "Want me to carry him to his blanket?"

"Not yet, but thanks." Sierra cherished the feel of the child next to her. Hector cared nothing about what she'd done. He simply needed love. She could give him that.

Their wagon driver, Carlos, reached behind him for a banged-up guitar and began to strum. Wonderful sound burst forth, wrapping her in soft warmth.

After a time, listening and enjoying the music, Sam sat up. "Would you mind, *por favor*?"

"*Muy bien.*" Carlos handed him the guitar.

Taking it, Sam skillfully plucked the strings and gazed into her eyes. "Any requests, pretty lady?"

"Once in the mountains, a passing stranger played a beautiful song on his banjo called 'Lorena.' Might you know it?"

With a nod, he filled the night with the haunting melody. The clear, sweet notes resonated with such yearning deep inside her, and brought a mist to her eyes.

The stranger had said the song told of a soldier's love for the woman he'd left behind, and his fear that he'd never see her again. The sadness had made Sierra weepy then and again now. She and the lonely soldier had much in common.

Both loved the ones they couldn't have. And oh how she loved Sam, whether she wanted to or not. His touch was branded on her skin. With him, she truly did feel safe, no matter what danger she faced.

The song, the guitar, the man playing it held her spellbound. She was unable to move even after the last soft note floated away on the whisper of a breeze.

Sam leaned forward and brushed her fingers, breaking her trance. "I've made you sad. Sorry."

"No, don't be. It was beautiful. You create magic."

"I doubt that. I have a long ways to go. One of our ranch hands taught me to play when I was young, and I usually carry a guitar around with me." He gave her a wry smile. "Right now, it's probably sitting at the Fort Worth train station."

"You're constantly full of surprises, Sam."

"That's me all right. Here's one called 'The Yellow Rose of Texas.' It's become a state anthem of sorts."

He began playing such a lively tune that she couldn't help but keep time with her foot.

Sam's stare never left her throughout the entire song.

For a few moments, she'd felt as though she mattered more than a friend to him.

Eighteen

STRUMMING THE GUITAR AND SINGING AROUND THE campfire after nightfall became the most pleasurable part of the day for Sam. This night marked the sixth day they'd been traveling with the small caravan, and they inched closer to the end of their journey.

Tomorrow, they should reach headquarters. In fact, they'd been on Lone Star land for a while now. Soon Sierra would be safe.

Except for a few small parcels to the west, the entire ranch was comprised of sections to the east that ran almost to Fort Worth and to the south from the direction they came. Stoker still claimed the man he'd lost the western acreage to had cheated at cards. Pa just couldn't accept that he'd gotten drunk and made huge, rash bets.

Maybe poor judgment ran in the family. His father had lost land, and Sam had lost the woman he ached to have.

Sam had ridden horseback ever since Isaac Ford surprised them shortly after they'd joined the caravan. He thought putting distance between him and Sierra would lessen the ache in his heart. That he'd stop wanting her so much. What a fool. His eyes searched for her every minute of the day. He rose to check on her at night long after they turned in. Most times he found Hector curled up next to her. Two people who needed the other. He was glad she had the boy.

At least she had someone.

One painful thing Sam had come to know: he needed to see Sierra's smile and beautiful eyes as much as he needed air and sunshine. Now, sitting around the campfire with the others after supper, he watched her get up from her place beside Luke and walk toward a wagon with a younger woman named Maria.

One of the women who had been sick came to sit with the man named Miguel. Smiling, Miguel put his arm around her. Two days ago, both of the women had risen from their sickbeds. Sam knew that, in addition to Luke's recovery, pleased Sierra.

Carlos ran his fingers lightly across the guitar strings. He could play really well and had given Sam some pointers. Music calmed him. He couldn't wait to get home and collect his guitar along with the rest of his gear from the Fort Worth train depot. Unless Houston or his father had already fetched them.

Letting out a long sigh, he shoved his thoughts from his mind and turned to the conversation between Carlos, Miguel, and a man called Pablo. He understood enough to know they spoke about the sad fact that they had no money, no home. No place to go.

Carlos sadly shook his head as the others murmured low.

Sam laid a hand on the man's shoulder and asked in his limited way what work he did.

"*Todo*, Señor Ranger. All."

"Cows? Horses?"

"*Sí*," Carlos said, adding that before the soldiers came he had land and cattle.

"You can work for me." He pointed to Carlos and then to himself.

"*Gracias*, señor."

Sam shot the others a glance. "How about your compadres?"

Carlos nodded. "*Sí*, they work."

"I'll give you a good place to live. Safe for *los niños*."

"*Gracias*, señor."

Suddenly the ground shifted under him.

Sierra strolled from one of the wagons, and his tongue stuck to the roof of his mouth. She wore one of the colorful skirts worn by the women and a low-scooped white blouse that hung off her golden shoulders.

Though he'd felt and even briefly tasted her smooth skin at the river, he'd never seen it. With her dark hair and blue eyes, she took his breath. He stared, unable to move.

What a fool he'd been to let her get away.

When she dropped down beside him on the blanket and tucked her bare feet beneath her, the fragrance of wild flowers kissed by the scented night swirled around him.

She was too close.

He wanted her much closer.

An ache inside throbbed, sending heat rushing through his veins. His heartbeat pounded in his ears, drowning out everything except an overwhelming desire to hold her in his arms. Unable to resist touching her, he brushed her cheek with his fingertips. "I like your new clothes. You seem different wearing them. More free."

"I feel…daring, liberated." Her smile warmed him. "Texas is such a contrast from where I came from. Everyone here is open and welcoming. With the exception of Isaac Ford, that is." She wet her lips. "Trust doesn't come easy in the mountains. Everyone eyes one another with suspicion."

"Any reason why?"

"Harsh climate. Harsh life. Food, shelter…happiness…all are very hard to come by."

A shadow crossed her eyes. What had that lifestyle done to her? He had no right to know, but it bothered him. He had a feeling the happiness part was the hardest to bear.

The moonlight caressed Sierra's bared shoulders and drew Sam's envy. How he wished it were him touching all that satiny skin. He dropped his hand before it could drift downward.

"Barring problems, we'll reach ranch headquarters tomorrow. You'll be safe, and I can start looking for Rocky." Still, Sam couldn't look away. She'd cast a spell on him.

"I hope you find him, Sam. Like me, Rocky has his own demons to fight."

"We employ a lot of men, and each is ready to give his life for the brand for which they ride. An outsider steps foot under the crossbar, and he's not fit for buzzard bait."

She grinned. "I'm familiar with buzzards—both taloned and two legged."

"By tomorrow afternoon, you'll know what I'm talking about. Our men grab outsiders so fast it makes their heads swim." Firelight reflected in her blue eyes, turning them dark and mysterious. It was hard to keep his thoughts on the subject. "My father's created a small town on the Lone Star, complete with a school. I'm sure you'll find plenty to do."

"Just until I find my brother, and Ford meets his end, whether dead or in jail," she reminded him. "Then I'll return to Waco."

Sam frowned. "You don't have anything waiting there."

"Rocky's business—the newspaper. If he's dead, I'll carry on what he started."

The stubborn tilt of her chin warned him that she had her mind set and there was no changing it. Sam studied her, wondering at this need to keep her from leaving. Why couldn't he just let her go? Dammit, why did he have to be so selfish? He'd said he only wanted her happiness. And he meant it. But could he really accept seeing her walk away?

The answer to all these questions was like a mustang he couldn't rope—dodging, fighting, rearing.

With her eyes shining in the firelight, Sierra leaned forward. Her blouse gaped, allowing him to see the top swell of her breasts. All that bare skin teased him. His mouth dried.

"Will you play something, Sam?"

How could he refuse those sparkling eyes? Those lips that seemed to beg for a kiss? That body he couldn't forget? Sam reached for Carlos's guitar. This time he chose one of the traditional Mexican songs that street musicians played in San Antonio. Sierra's dress, the moonlight, and her new sensual freedom called to him like the next hill to his wandering feet.

At the first strum of the chords, several of the women began to dance. One was a very pretty señorita, probably in her early twenties.

He didn't know if it was the men vigorously clapping in time with the music or Sierra's sudden shift in mood that made her rise and join the dancers.

Though she was a little shy at first, her confidence grew. Soon, her skirt swirled about her slender ankles as she whirled, moving to the rhythm. Raising her arms high above her head like the other women, she clapped, keeping time while her bare feet stomped the ground.

The flickering firelight, with dust circling in a sudden gust of air, made the dance…made *Sierra* seem more like a beautiful dream.

Unable to take his eyes from her, Sam didn't realize how fast he was strumming until an older woman sitting near nudged him, jerking him from the trance. He forced his fingers to slow.

When Luke Weston got to his feet, Sierra took his hand, pulling him into the circle.

A hot flush crawled up Sam's neck at the way the outlaw drew Sierra against him. The silver conchas on Luke's trousers flashed in the light as he tucked one hand behind his back and twirled her around in a flash of movement. His hand grazed her bare shoulders with each turn, then slid down the length of her arms to rest at the small of her back.

Weston was doing everything Sam wanted to do.

And no telling what the scoundrel was murmuring in her ear. Just then Sierra threw back her head in laughter.

Anger washed over Sam. What did he expect? He'd sent her into Weston's arms.

He quit strumming midsong, thrusting the guitar to Carlos, who quickly picked up the chords. Sam strode into the darkness without a backward glance, leaving the laughter, the music, and the heartbreak behind.

Trooper raised his head and whinnied.

"At least you're still happy to see me." Sam smoothed the long neck of his faithful friend. "I've made a real mess of things. What kind of fool turns away love? She's everything I want, everything I need, and a whole lot more than I deserve."

The worst part of all was that he'd sent her into a wanted outlaw's arms.

Weston could never make her happy, because he was going to jail for a very long time. Sierra would waste her life waiting for the likes of him. Weston might even be hanged for the murder of Judge Percival. And then what? She might be left with a babe to care for.

Damn. Sam raked his fingers through his hair.

A rustle made him reach for his Colt and whirl. Sierra silently stood there. "Go back," he warned low, returning his gun to the holster. "It's dangerous here."

Her head jerked up. "Is it Ford? Has he found us?"

"*I'm* the danger." Damn, didn't she understand? Isaac Ford only wanted to inflict physical pain. Sam would destroy her heart. "Go back to your friends."

She crossed her arms protectively over her chest. "I had to see if you're all right. I was worried."

That tremble in her voice and knowing he caused it made him wince. "You shouldn't be here. I'm no good for you. Run as hard as you can away from me." Run before he destroyed her.

"Are you angry at me?"

"Nope." Never at her.

Sam tried not to notice how beautiful she was, standing there with one foot poised to run and the other planted firmly. She was scared but trying very hard not to show it.

"What then? Is it Luke?"

"It's nobody, all right? It's me. I'm the problem."

Him and the damn frustration of wanting what would never be his.

Texas Rangers were loners. The hard fact was, what he did was dangerous. Death rode in his saddle, hunkered in his shadow, waiting for him.

Sierra should never have to share that.

Bathed in the moonlight, she looked a sight in the clothes that were so out of character. Those and her bare feet reminded him of a newborn foal wobbling around on its spindly legs, just learning to walk.

The desire to kiss her witless came over him. How he yearned to trace every curve, every hill and valley of her body with his hands. Run his fingers through that dark hair that hung unbound. But it was her slightly parted lips that drew the most attention.

Sierra Hunt had a bit of the untamed in her. She awoke a fierce hunger that shook him to the core, and he couldn't think of anything past this moment.

He fought the overpowering temptation to crush her against his chest, feel her heart beating wildly next to his.

Why didn't she go before he lost control? Before
he hurt her more than he already had. "Run, Sierra.
Leave me to my misery."

"I can't." She spoke the words so low he barely
heard them.

"Out of curiosity, do you mind if I ask what your
feelings are for Weston?" he asked tightly.

"He's a friend, Sam. Same as he is to you. The same
as *you* decided I would be to you." Anger laced the
words she flung at him.

If only friendship would be enough. It wasn't. It
never would be. He saw that plainly now. That left
him with exactly one choice—to walk away.

"Were you having fun dancing tonight?"

Her eyes sparkled. "Oh yes. That music made me
do and feel things I never have."

He could only imagine what else had taken place
between her and Weston and didn't want to know.
He was out of his mind enough.

"Surely you didn't dance like that in the mountains."

"No, Maria, the young woman in the caravan,
taught me. Over the miles, we developed a friendship.
Tonight she loaned me the clothes." Her face took on
a wistfulness. "After I mentioned days ago how much
I love the music of her people, she showed me the
dance. A strange longing came over me when I put on
these clothes tonight. I felt so beautiful."

"That's because you are," he said gruffly. "You
don't need the clothes to transform you."

She moved closer until her bare shoulder touched
his. He couldn't resist her pull any longer. He surren-
dered to desire. With a gentle brush of his fingertips

across the curve of her shoulder and down her arm, he decided it was like touching heaven. He closed his eyes, soaking up the velvety sensation.

He wished someone would tell him how in the hell he'd manage to keep breathing after they parted ways. He'd have to relearn.

Relearn a lot of things—how to sleep, how to banish the dreams, how to keep from remembering and looking for her at every turn.

His eyes flew open when he felt her lips on his cheek. The soft kiss was his undoing. With a hoarse cry, he clasped her against him, crushing his mouth to hers. If he was going to go to hell, he wanted it to be for more than lustful thoughts.

His palms grazed the smooth curve of her shoulder, then moved down her shapely arms to her waist and finally the flare of her hips.

Hunger for her consumed him. Sierra was a powerful storm that swirled, rearranging everything he knew and felt about life and love. No other woman came close to her. She'd ruined him. Walk away from her, and he'd leave his heart behind.

The fire raging inside resisted all his efforts to put it out, and it had become impossible to ignore.

Dear God! He was caught in a living hell.

Gripping his shirt, Sierra removed the last little bit of space between them. Knowing she welcomed his touch made his heart hammer.

Sam's lips left hers to nibble at her earlobes, then drifted down her long, elegant neck to her teasingly bare shoulders. They were being kissed by the moonlight.

Damn that moonlight! He was as jealous of it as he'd been of Luke and his roving hands.

Doing his best to tamp down the eagerness that exploded like his frenzied strum of the guitar earlier, Sam lost the battle. Releasing a ragged groan, he trailed kisses over every inch of warm, exposed skin. Sierra slid an arm around his neck as low moans slipped from her throat.

She was temptation, but to deny himself would kill him as much as any bullet.

With a cry, she threw back her head, allowing him greater access to what he sought. Breathing hard, he pushed aside the fabric that covered those plump breasts. They weren't overly large, nor were they small. Spilling into his palms, they seemed exactly right. He bent his head and captured a dusky, swollen peak.

A hot ache swept over him like the floodwaters of the Brazos—rushing, roaring, pushing him faster, harder, as though he were lost, alone in the swift current of the river. Raw desire surged with the honeyed taste of her silky skin. The heat in his groin made him swell, tightening his trousers. He had to have her, had to feel her beneath him.

His hands slid to her firm bottom, cupping the rounded flesh.

Voices from nearby penetrated the lust. Others could stumble upon them any minute. Frustration bit into him. He cursed himself and his damnable need. Again, struggling to push his raging hunger aside, he reminded himself that he would destroy every good thing inside her. If he took what he shouldn't, she'd one day curse him for stripping her of the chance at her dream.

Using every last shred of willpower, he raised his head and growled, "You're going to be the death of me, Sierra Hunt."

"I want you, Sam. Can't you see?"

With an aching sigh of regret, he drew her blouse up over her, covering that lush softness. "Go, darlin', while you still can. Or else I won't be able to restrain the beast…"

Her arms fell to her side. "I'm not asking you to."

"No, but I'll not take advantage of something you know little about." He lifted her palm to his lips and kissed the tender skin. "Nothing has changed between us. I can't offer you a life. I won't promise what I can't give."

"Maybe—"

"I found out a long time ago that maybe is simply another word for no," he said softly. "Cut your losses while you can, pretty lady."

"What if you decide that you've made a mistake?"

"That will never happen. What we have is wrong. Steel your heart against me."

"It's too late," she whispered.

Pressing a kiss on the scar around his neck, she turned and walked toward the campfire. Sam watched those gently swaying hips and her dark hair rippling to her waist.

How many more times would he be able to turn her away before he took what she ached to give? His heart felt parched and full of ugly craters. He touched his scar where her kiss still burned. One kiss, one caress, a thousand memories.

Sam knew this night with the woman who'd bared her shoulders and danced with passion would linger in his heart forever. These were the kind of memories that never faded.

Blinking rapidly, he swallowed the lump blocking his throat and turned away from the temptation. He turned away from everything that could've been. He had to be strong for them both.

"Good-bye, my one and only love," he whispered brokenly into the night.

Nineteen

MIDAFTERNOON THE NEXT DAY, WITH THE SUN BEATING down, Sam rode beside the wagons. In the distance he could make out the entrance to the ranch. They were almost there.

The hair on his neck stood as he scanned the rugged terrain through narrowed eyes. His gut told him Ford wasn't done with them. From the corner of his vision something moved. Then he saw them—riders galloping up from a ravine on his right. Even from where he was, he knew they weren't ranch hands from the Lone Star, and he could make a pretty good guess who they were. The gang must've hidden in the gully, waiting for one last chance to inflict damage and hopefully get the loot and Sierra.

"Make a run for it!" he yelled to the drivers. "Go!"

"Let me on your horse," Luke hollered, firing his pistol at the group.

"Stay with Sierra. I'll hold them off." Sam aimed, hitting the closest attacker.

A blistering barrage of gunshots told of Ford's desperation. One bullet barely missed, stirring the air next to his ear. He had to keep drawing their fire and give the caravan time to make it inside the gate.

"Dammit, Sam! Come get me."

Hell, all he needed was for Luke to get shot again.

Giving in, he rode up next to the trailing wagon, and Luke jumped on behind him. Wasting no time, Sam spurred the horse directly into the ambush, shooting left and right. Luke did the same from behind.

The men scattered, not brave enough to stand and be caught by one of their straight-flying bullets.

Once through them, Sam whirled to make another pass.

"I'm reloading, Sam," Luke hollered. "Are you out?"

"Close to it."

"Take mine and let me reload yours."

It seemed like a good plan. He knew cowboys would hear the shooting and gallop from the ranch soon. All he and Luke needed to do was keep the attackers away from the caravan until help arrived.

Sam took Luke's Colt while Luke reloaded the other. Sam took aim and fired at one of the shooters, striking him in the chest. He yelled and fell from his horse. The man looked up as Sam went by. He recognized John, the man they'd threatened from the hay wagon, confirming Sam's suspicions.

As he pondered that, a sudden bullet tore into his upper arm. Stinging pain shot through his body. He sucked in a quick breath, steeling himself against the fire.

Though he felt blood running down his arm, he had no time to look. He had to protect Sierra and the others. All else could wait.

From his seat behind, Luke released rapid fire at the remaining riders, managing to hit two. Instead of Ford and his bunch giving up, a group of new riders joined him. Sam prayed the cowboys would soon come, or he'd have to think of a new plan.

"Are you all right back there, Luke?"

"I'm fine. You hurt bad?"

"A scratch." Sam kept one eye on the slow caravan. They approached the entrance.

And then he saw what he'd been waiting on. Men on horseback poured from beneath the crossbar. Had to be fifteen or twenty at least. A grin formed.

Stoker Legend led the charge.

With the outlaws in capable hands, Sam turned toward home.

He drew alongside the caravan that had stopped beneath the huge crossbar. Above them was emblazoned the words *Lone Star Ranch*.

A lump rose in Sam's throat the size of a peach pit.

Legend land run by Legend men.

Down the road, he glimpsed the immense white stone structure and the tall flagpole at one corner with the Texas flag unfurled in the breeze. He blinked hard to clear the mist in his eyes. Three colors—red, white, and blue. One big star. Men had fought and died for the star, for God, state, and country.

Next to the flag, though he was too far away to see clearly, a large bronze star hung between two heavy iron poles.

He was home.

Luke slid from the horse and looked up at him. "We did it again. You and me make a good team."

"That we do." The decision Sam had wrestled with the whole way brought an ache to his chest. He couldn't put it off any longer.

"If you ever find the straight and narrow too rigid, look me up." Luke winked. "I'll show you the ropes. It's been fun."

"I wouldn't exactly call it that."

With a laugh, Luke patted Trooper's rump. "Thanks for taking care of my ornery hide."

Sam watched him stride to the black gelding and sling his saddle onto the horse's back.

Sierra climbed from the wagon. Fingers of sunlight brushed her face and caressed her hair, paying homage to her dark beauty. Sam watched her glance at Luke then at Sam. Indecision rippled in her blue eyes, rooting her to the spot for a second. He didn't have to wonder long who she'd choose. She ran to him.

"You're bleeding! I thought…" Her quivering lip was more than Sam could bear. "They could've killed you."

He dismounted. "I'm fine."

"But they shot you." A sob escaped despite her attempt to smother it.

Against his better judgment, he put his arms around her. She laid her head on his chest. He yearned to keep her there, to give in to the hunger that gnawed on him night and day now. But *his* life wasn't the life she wanted. True, she was mixed-up and confused and sorting through her own problems, but one thing he knew she would never budge on—roots and permanence.

"I've bled more shaving." He chuckled. Maybe joking would ease the stabbing pain in his arm. Nothing would work for his heart. "One more scar to add to the others on my body."

She stepped out of his arms. "This isn't funny."

"I've been hurt lots worse." Sam's gaze went to Luke where he was finishing with the saddle. "Can you excuse me for a moment?"

"What are you going to do, Sam? You can't arrest Luke. You just can't."

Without answering, Sam took Trooper's reins and strode to Luke. For the first time in his life, he cursed his job. He owed Luke Weston, and no amount of money could ever repay the debt. The outlaw had proven worthy of trust. Sam even considered him a friend. They made a formidable team.

"I can't let you leave, Weston."

Sierra gave a strangled cry. "Please don't do this."

"It's all right, *dulce*," Luke rasped. His cold eyes hardened when he turned to Sam. "Figured this was the way it'd end. At least I'll get to see the grand Lone Star. Maybe if the cards fall right, I'll meet the big man himself—Stoker Legend. Now that would surely be something."

The thick sarcasm wasn't lost on Sam. He had a feeling the showdown with Luke he'd been expecting was twisting and whirling toward him in the form of a black storm cloud.

"You might want to save all that until after you let me finish. I'm not arresting you. I'm going to hold you while I help you get out of this mess you're in. I'll help you clear your name."

"It's too late for that, *amigo*. It won't change who I am. And maybe I don't want anything different.

Maybe I like exacting my own brand of justice, having men fear me. Having power."

The Mexican families in the caravan watched silently. The children were wide-eyed, and a few shed tears. Sam hadn't wanted to do this in front of them, but hadn't had a choice.

"Whether you want my help or not, you're getting it."

With his green eyes flashing, Luke stood there proud and arrogant. "Gonna make me walk, Ranger, or do I get to ride up to the castle?"

"Don't be stupid and mount up," Sam snapped, sliding into the saddle.

"*Gracias, Patron*," Luke jeered, sticking his foot in the stirrup.

Sam felt the hairs on his neck bristle as he evaded the angry scowls of the travelers. Luke was one of them the way Sam never could be. The caravan slowly moved toward headquarters and he toward the face-to-face with Stoker and Houston.

"This may not turn out the way you expect, Legend," Luke growled.

"Warning me you'll try to leave?"

"If I'm not under arrest, why would I need to escape?"

"Exactly."

The wheels rumbled and bounced over the rough road. At last the caravan stopped in front of the stone headquarters.

Sam dismounted and turned to Luke. "This is the best deal you'll ever get."

"Save your empty words, Ranger. No one cared about me before. No reason to start now."

By the time Sam moved to help Sierra from the wagon, she was already out and lifting Hector down.

"Thank you, Sam, for not arresting Luke." A tendril of hair blew across her eyes. He fought the urge to brush it away.

"I'm not an ogre. He still has to face the charges. But I think what I have to say will carry a lot of weight."

Stoker Legend galloped up in a cloud of dust. He was out of the saddle almost before the magnificent white horse stopped. His customary hand-tooled gun belt and holster slapped his leg as long strides carried him to Sam.

"It's about damn time, son." He glanced at Sierra, lifting his hat. "Pardon the rough language, miss. Sometimes out here I forget my manners."

Sam introduced her. She smiled and accepted his outstretched hand. "No apology necessary. It's nice to meet Sam's father. He's told me a great deal about you."

"Not everything, I hope."

She laughed. "Only the best part, I assure you."

Stoker swung back to Sam. "It's great to have you home."

"Thanks, Pa. It feels good."

Houston galloped into the yard, reining up sharply. Sam took in his older brother, who cast almost as long a shadow as their pa. How long would it be before they were trading angry words? Or worse yet, blows.

"You're a sad sight, little brother." Houston grabbed Sam, lifting him off the ground.

"Whoa! Put me down," Sam protested. "I have to get Luke Weston settled somewhere."

Stoker pretended to only now notice Luke standing beside Sierra, but Sam had seen his father's eyes shift to the outlaw the first second. His father didn't miss a single detail. Of anything. He'd bet Stoker knew how many buttons lined Sierra's bodice and how many pairs of children's eyes peered from beneath the tattered blanket in their wagon.

And Sam for damn sure knew Stoker had already seen the scar around his neck. Hell! He tugged his shirt collar higher, wishing for the bandana that had come off during the fight.

"Can't you put aside your job long enough to let Doc Jenkins tend to that gunshot?" Stoker's eyes flashed like glittering green stones. For a second they reminded him of Luke's.

Sam swallowed the angry words he ached to say. "This won't take long, Pa. Then I'm all yours."

"Tell me what you need, son. I'll help." Surprisingly, Stoker's rough edges softened a bit.

"Need somewhere to put Weston."

"I'll take care of it. Who were those attackers out there?"

"Part was Isaac Ford's gang. Don't know yet who the others were that joined him." But you could bet Sam was going to find out. "Thanks for the help. I was hoping you'd hear."

"They hightailed it when they saw us. My men were chasing after them when I turned around. Didn't get a good look at any. They didn't even stop to gather their dead. I'll see to their burial."

"Post guards at the gate, Pa. They'll be back."

"What do they want?" Houston asked.

Sierra stepped forward. "Me."

"And some outlaw loot I have in my saddlebags," Sam added. "They chased us all the way. They shot Weston, and he nearly died."

Stoker's eyes hardened, turning to green stones. "They'll go through me to get you, Miss Sierra. You're safe here."

"Thank you, sir." She seemed to relax some.

"Enough of this unpleasant business. We'll discuss it later." Stoker's gaze flicked to the rest of the party. "Introduce your friends."

Starting with Luke, Sam went around the group. When he finished, Stoker boomed, "Welcome to the Lone Star. Thank you for bringing my son home. If you need anything, let me know." He turned to their housekeeper. "Mrs. Ross, take this lovely young woman to the prettiest room."

Smiling, Mrs. Ross nodded. "Of course, sir."

Stoker stepped toward Sam and took the side opposite Houston. Sandwiched between them, Sam gave a frustrated sigh and let them pick him up and carry him into the house. His father was doing it again. Taking charge, pushing Sam's thoughts and wishes aside as though he was a child too young to know his own mind.

Only this time, Houston had joined him. Now Sam had two to battle to be heard. Hell and be damned!

The prodigal has returned, Sam thought sourly.

Twenty

ONCE INSIDE THE COOLNESS OF THE HOUSE, SAM expected them to put him down or deposit him in a chair, but Stoker and Houston didn't slow. They continued right up the curved mahogany staircase that glistened in the light spilling in from outside and kicked open the door to Sam's old room.

"My arm's shot, not my damn leg. I can walk." Sam grunted when they dropped him on the quilted coverlet. "And don't be so rough."

Houston grinned. "Getting soft, little brother?"

"Nope. Just been through hell."

Stoker's piercing green gaze made Sam fidget. "I sent out a search party, but they came back empty-handed. Didn't know what had happened to you. Thought you might be dead. One son's already died in my arms. I don't need another." His fingers combed through his shock of gray hair. "Dammit, this is why I didn't want you to be a Texas Ranger. Still don't."

When had his father gotten so old? Two years ago, he still had plenty of brown in his hair. And the lines around his mouth were deeper now. Maybe Sam had stayed away too long this time.

"I could die here on the ranch, Pa," he reminded softly. "Being here can't keep me safe."

"No, but at least I'd know and have a place to visit when I took a notion. Your mother would want you beside her. Looks like you'd consider her."

Sam shot Houston a questioning glance. Standing slightly behind their father, Houston shrugged. A talk seemed to be long overdue.

"Back to bringing me upstairs. It's the middle of the afternoon, for God's sake."

"You would've preferred for Doc Jenkins to undress you downstairs in front of God and everybody?" his father blustered.

"I don't need undressing. Even if I did, I can do it myself. It's my damn arm that's shot. Can either of you hear that?" He held it up. "My arm."

"We've got eyes. You stink, son. Before you crawl between these clean sheets, you're gettin' a bath. Same goes for coming to the supper table. Being already undressed, you can bring down two calves with the same rope." Stoker laid a gentle hand on Sam. "I've ordered Jenkins to check you out. I doubt you've seen a doctor in all this time away."

Houston rolled his eyes, hiding a grin. Hell!

Sam softened his voice. "Pa, I'm not a two-year-old."

"Don't get smart with me." Stoker strode to the door, turning back before he left. "I also want to know who tried to hang my son, and I want to know if the mangy coyote is still breathing. If so, why.

Doc Jenkins will be right up. Houston, make sure he doesn't sneak down the back stairs. Hog-tie him if you have to. I've got guests to see about."

Sam stared at the slamming door. "Damn! Not much has changed."

"You didn't expect it to, did you?"

"Nope."

"Then you weren't disappointed." Houston pulled a knife from inside his boot. "You want me to cut off your pants or start with your shirt?"

"Neither. These are brand new." Sam gave his brother a warning glare.

"You're never going to get all the trail dust out. Might as well burn 'em."

"Put the knife away, or I'll do it for you." Sam removed his gun belt and hung it on the bedstead. "Pa's a lot grayer and has deeper lines in his face. Noticed a new scar below his eye. Is he all right?"

"Fit as a fiddle, according to Doc."

"What was that about dying and me not considering Mother?"

Houston's brown eyes met his. "That's what I was trying to tell you last time you came home. He's worried that someone's bullet will find you, and he'll never know where your bones rest. A year ago he erected his own telegraph line and hired a man to do nothing but sit in that office, manning it."

That obsession seemed a little odd, even for Stoker Legend.

"When you weren't on the train," Houston continued, "he burned up the lines, contacting everyone he could think of." He paused for a moment, then added, "Pa didn't tell you, but he already has your grave marked next to Mother."

Sam scowled. "Well, I ain't ready to kick the bucket."

"Makes two of us."

"What about you? Where will you be in the plot lineup?"

"Said he wants me next to William. So I can watch over him."

The crack in Houston's voice at mention of their baby brother, who'd lived less than a year, bruised something deep inside of Sam. Pa would only entrust William's care to the best.

Sam frowned. Giving Houston that special responsibility didn't match the angry words Houston had flung at him last time he was home. *He tolerates me, but it's you he stands looking for every sunrise and sunset. You don't know the pain you leave behind each time you ride off, chasing your dream.*

It sounded like Pa did a sight more than tolerate his oldest son.

After clearing his throat, Sam could speak. "That's because you're the strongest, and Pa knows it. Can't think of anyone I'd rather stand, or lay, beside. When the time comes, of course."

"I often wonder how our baby brother would've turned out."

"Like us, probably," Sam said quietly, unbuttoning his shirt. "Ready to ride into hell at a moment's notice. Regardless of what you think, I do give a damn. About you and about Pa."

"What is it then that makes you always leave?"

"I'm different. I don't know why. I just know I

am. It's something I can't explain or control. I don't feel really alive unless I'm facing danger. Maybe something's broken inside."

Houston dropped the shirt Sam took off onto the floor and sat next to him. "I'm glad you're home, brother. For however long this time."

"I'm tired, Houston. Down-to-the-bone tired." His brother's hand on his shoulder settled some of the weariness. He left out the part about his boss sending him home. Houston already thought he was crazy as a bedbug anyway.

"The Lone Star is a good place to rest up."

Sam took in the familiar room that had always been his refuge as long as he could recall. It was exactly as he'd left it. "Do I really stink?"

Hearing his brother roar with laughter filled his soul. He'd missed that sound. No matter what, they were brothers and always would be. Just the two of them.

"Pa wasn't lying," Houston said when he sobered. "You smell like a pigsty."

"Thanks a lot. You always side with him. Do you ever miss not having a sister?" Sam asked.

"Yeah. A sister would've been nice. She'd know how to gentle Pa the way Mother did. Too bad we didn't get one. Then I could've teased her too."

"Guess we'll have to wait until you take a wife," Sam said.

"Me? What about you? That Sierra Hunt is a pretty thing."

"Only friends. Rescued her from the Ford gang, which I'll tell you more about later. You got any prospects?"

Houston grinned. "Been seeing Becky Golden over at the Triple R."

Sam walloped his brother's arm. "Sweet little Becky?"

"Not so little anymore. Grew up in all the right places."

"Sounds serious. Does her pa need to get his shotgun out?"

A knock sounded at the door, interrupting them.

"Come in," Sam called.

Portly Doc Jenkins hurried into the room, carrying his black bag. Dressed in a three-piece suit, he thought himself a dapper man. He carried a bowler hat and never went anywhere without a cane hanging on his arm, though no one had ever seen him use it.

"Mr. Sam, I hear someone put a bullet in you." Doc laid down his hat and cane. "Houston, start a warm bath."

"He thinks you stink too, brother." Houston moved to the door, grinning. He paused and turned. "About being different… I think they dropped you on your head when you were born. You haven't been right since."

Sam grabbed a pillow and lobbed it, thinking it was too bad it wasn't a cannonball.

The sound of laughter drifted back into the bedroom, filling Sam with contentment. Things were good. So far.

"Find out where they put Weston," he hollered, though he doubted Houston heard him. "And bring me my saddlebags!"

He hoped the outlaw stunk too. Really, really bad.

❧

After seeing that Hector was settled with Sofia and Carlos, Sierra followed Mrs. Ross inside the immense stone headquarters that had taken her breath at first glance. While a bit overcome, she already loved the place where Sam had grown up.

Immediately, the glaring differences between Sierra's and Sam's upbringings struck home. It was very obvious that she'd never fit into his world, no matter how hard she tried.

They climbed a wide staircase to the second floor. From the outside, the house appeared a mighty fortress. The interior was just as beautiful. She was afraid to touch anything, sure she might break it or else leave fingerprints on the surface.

Once she'd put her mind to rest about Hector, Sierra let Mrs. Ross take her arm and lead her into the cool interior. The gracious housekeeper, with her dark brown hair arranged in a loose twist pinned to the top of her head, appeared somewhere in her forties and was close to six feet tall. A quick glance around showed the kind woman appeared to run the household very capably. Sam had told her before they arrived that Mrs. Ross oversaw a score of women and girls who kept the place in tip-top shape.

"Here we are." Mrs. Ross opened the door to a sunlit room.

Sierra gasped, taking in the large bed covered with a beautiful rose-colored counterpane, and a sitting area in one sunny corner. Her admiring gaze swept to a rather large piece of furniture that probably towered a good foot above Mrs. Ross and was at least six feet wider. She'd heard that these were where people hung their clothes, but she didn't know what to call it. A dresser with an oval mirror and a washstand caught her eye when she finished gawking.

"I've never seen anything so fine."

"You can come in, Miss Sierra." The housekeeper swung the doors to the tall monstrosity wide. "Once they bring in your trunk and you find there aren't enough hangers, let me know."

"I don't have a trunk."

"Then I'll ask them to bring up your bags."

"I don't have any of those either. I left home quite…unexpectedly. Sam bought me a comb and brush in a small town we passed through."

"No worries, dear." Mrs. Ross patted her arm. "We have a mercantile right here on the Lone Star. While you bathe, I'll hurry over and pick up everything you need to get you through the night. Tomorrow you can go and select everything else."

"I…I have no money," she whispered.

"My dear, Stoker Legend wouldn't let you pay if you did. Come, I'll show you to the water closet. We have one at each end of this hallway."

Excitement replaced Sierra's weariness. She wanted to see how hot water could come at the mere turn of a knob. She'd heard of such things but never thought to witness it.

When they moved into the hallway, a noise made her turn. Houston was helping a shirtless Sam toward the other end, presumably where the second bathing room that Mrs. Ross mentioned lay.

Seeming to sense her, Sam turned with a piercing stare, his legs apart as though bracing for a storm. From this distance, she couldn't judge the temperature of his changeable eyes, but she had no question about the deep sadness and longing dripping from him.

This thing between them, that Sam kept pushing away, burned with the intensity of a blacksmith's forge, and the fire threatened to consume them both.

Sierra lifted her fingers to her lips that he'd kissed with such burning passion, vividly remembering his mouth on other places as well.

Hunger for him weakened her knees. But there would never be any more. All she had left were memories and regret and the stark truth that he'd told her good-bye in his heart.

She'd lost him for good.

"Come, dear," Mrs. Ross said, gently touching her arm.

With tears stinging her eyes, Sierra stumbled to her waiting bath.

Twenty-one

HOT WATER FLOWING FROM OF THE PIPES IN THE bathing room was simply amazing. Pure luxury, just as Luke had said. Sierra quickly undressed and sank into the inviting, decadent warmth. The pure pleasure dulled the ache in her heart for a moment.

The water slid over her skin as Sam's sensuous mouth had done the previous night. Only his caress had left smoldering, raw passion in its wake. Passion he'd locked away somewhere in the hardness of his broad chest and gray stare.

Sierra cupped her hand, catching the water, but like the feelings Sam once had for her, the liquid seeped between her fingers, just as elusive.

Whatever they had was gone.

She gave a heavy sigh. The days of travel had taken a toll, both mentally and physically.

Sinking beneath the water, she let the warmth relieve her sore arms and legs and thought about their arrival. The place was overwhelming. Sam's father reminded her of a prickly cactus. All thorns on the outside, but inside lay lifesaving pulp. As evidenced by the small town he'd created for his workers and the deep respect the ranch hands had for him, he had a caring, kind heart, even if he tried to hide it.

With his booming voice and piercing stare, Stoker Legend intimidated her more than a little. The sense of power swirling around him was an undeniable force. Beyond a doubt, he was accustomed to giving orders and having them obeyed. The difference couldn't have been more pronounced between *her* father, William Hunt, and Stoker Legend. She imagined that Sam's father never forgot anyone, or anything. He would take care of his family and fight for them.

Stoker Legend was a fierce protector, like his son.

Then there was Sam's brother. Houston had put her at ease from the first moment. He and Sam bore a lot of similarities. Both were tall and lean, and they had the same strong jaw and high cheekbones. But Houston's ready grin was nothing like Sam's permanent scowl and piercing stare.

Two brothers who were as different as a mule from a horse.

And then there was Luke. Her heart ached for him. She was relieved that Sam hadn't arrested him. Maybe with Sam's help, Luke wouldn't have to stay on the run. Where had the men taken him? She and Sam were getting clean and would soon put on new clothes. Luke deserved the same. As soon as she finished, she was going to find out where he was and sneak him what he needed.

And she meant to check on Hector again. The boy would be lost, as she was here in this unfamiliar place. She needed to know that he and the others had settled in.

With that decision made, she scrubbed away the filth of the trail and washed her hair. She was rinsing the soap from her hair when Mrs. Ross bustled into the tiny room, her arms full of clothing.

"I don't know if these will fit." The housekeeper laid a robin's-egg-blue dress along with pretty underthings on a chair and set new shoes on the floor. "Your waist is so tiny."

"My mother told me to never look a gift horse in the mouth. They'll be fine."

"If not, you can make do tonight and get others tomorrow."

"Thank you for all you're doing. I truly appreciate it." Sierra met Mrs. Ross's friendly brown stare. "Do you perhaps know where the people in our caravan were taken—the Spanish families…and Luke Weston?"

"Each were given a small house of their own. I understand Mr. Stoker has hired them."

That was a relief. Now they could find peace and put down roots in the Texas soil.

"And Mr. Weston?"

The housekeeper's brow furrowed. "I haven't heard."

Sierra stood, taking the towel the housekeeper handed her. "Thank you, Mrs. Ross."

"I'll take your dirty things down to be washed."

At least she'd have a change of clothes if accepting more charity became simply too hard. "You're a godsend."

"Supper will be at five o'clock downstairs, dear."

Left to the quiet, Sierra finished drying and dressed. She opened the door and saw the hallway empty.

Hurrying back to her room, she towel-dried her hair at the window, staring openmouthed at the bustling scene below.

A conversation with Sam a few days ago entered her mind. Each time she referred to the dwelling where he lived as a house, Sam had laughed and told her it was the headquarters. She didn't know how someone could live in headquarters. Strange. In a fort, headquarters meant offices. This Texas jargon might be difficult to rope, but she would adapt.

The row of whitewashed buildings sitting opposite where she was comprised the Lone Star's town. Her gaze moved from one storefront to another. She had no trouble making out the mercantile and small bank, even without signs. With some doing, she spotted a telegraph and doctor's office, as well as a blacksmith and school.

Sam had explained that the nearest town with stores and medical help—Squaw Valley—was a full day's ride, and often the busy hands and their families couldn't go that far. Besides, accidents seemed to be the way of life on a ranch. She could see how having a doctor near could often mean the difference between life and death.

It must take an awful lot of money to run a spread this size.

Her gaze shifted to the tall pole and the Texas flag fluttering in the breeze at the corner of the house. These Texans were quite patriotic about their state, she'd discovered. Except for the windmill, the pole towered above everything, which allowed the impressive flag to be seen from quite a distance.

Deep yearning for Rocky to see this rose up, strangling her. He'd love it here. But would he get the chance to come? Hot tears lurked behind her eyes, blinding her for a moment. She blinked them back, refusing to let them fall, and brought her attention back to the view.

Everything appeared huge and magnificent where the Legend family was concerned.

Only…she'd learned from Sam that such outward signs of wealth hid secrets. Things weren't as they seemed.

She swiveled a bit and released a delighted gasp.

Next to the flag stood a large metal frame. A thick iron chain attached it to two poles that held it high off the ground. In the center of the frame hung a huge bronze star, the points of which were notched, allowing light to come through. The delicate, lacy design the shadows made on the ground brought a soft cry of wonder to her lips.

A hushed sniff made her whirl in alarm. Her thoughts instantly flew to Isaac Ford. Had he somehow managed to get onto the ranch? Sierra laid down her brush and picked up a fireplace poker. Movement in the far corner on the other side of the bed caught her eye. No grown man could make himself that small.

"Hello? Who's there?"

The sniffling grew louder.

When she rounded the bed, there, squeezed tightly in the corner with his head on his knees, sat Hector. The eight-year-old glanced up with a tearstained face.

"*Hola*, what's the matter, little one?" She took his hand and sat on the end of the bed, pulling him into her lap. "What's wrong?" Remembering the language barrier, she put her fingers to her eyes and moved them slowly down.

Hector began to chatter as fast as he could, stopping once to take a deep breath. Unable to understand why he was so upset, she took his hand. They'd reached the stairs and were about to go down when Sam strode from what had to be his room.

"Please help me, Sam. I need someone to tell me what Hector is saying. I found the child hiding by my bed, weeping, and I don't know what's wrong."

"I'll try. Come with me."

She and Hector followed him down the hall and into a room that was decidedly masculine, with heavy mahogany furnishings. Though she tried to stop herself, her eyes swept to the bed. It was huge and very fitting for a tall man like Sam.

A large needlepoint with the word *Mother* hung on the wall above the bed.

A thickening formed in Sierra's throat.

Sam motioned them to a grouping of chairs, green-and-rose tapestry fabric lining the back and seat of each. While she didn't know much about such things, it surprised her to find something that seemed more feminine amidst the heavy wood. She would never have guessed a tough Texas Ranger as the type who would choose these.

But yet he must have, or he'd have wasted no time tossing them from the room.

"How is your arm?" She couldn't tell through the shirt if he wore a bandage. Surely he did, though.

"It's fine. Only a flesh wound. Doc fixed me up."

She turned away from the sad longing in his eyes. "Good."

"Come." He gently lifted Hector onto his knee and spoke a few halting words in Spanish. Deep caring filled Sam's eyes and showed in the way he rubbed the boy's slender back.

How different this scene was from her childhood. She fought back sudden tears.

After a few minutes of talking back and forth, Sam turned. "He cries because he misses his mother, and he thought he'd lost you too when he couldn't find you. For whatever reason, he's latched on to you."

"Because he needs desperately to belong some-where. We all yearn to have someone who loves us," Sierra whispered. "I love this child. He's all alone in the world now. No matter how complicated, I'll keep Hector with me. I'll care for him."

Her heart broke for the boy. She knew what it was to ache so badly for someone to care and find no one wanted you. While she hadn't quite figured it out yet, she'd make sure Hector knew he was wanted. He was already hers in her heart.

While Sam drew Hector out of his shell with fool-ish magic tricks, she moved to the window. As she looked out, her thoughts drifted to the moment she had found her mother's broken body.

That vivid blue sky following days of snow had brought her hope. Mired in the depths of deep grief, Daisy Hunt had stopped eating, couldn't sleep, and wouldn't acknowledge Sierra. But that morning her mother had smiled. She rose and got dressed for the first time in weeks, ate a biscuit, then went for a walk.

When Daisy didn't return, Sierra went in search of her. She found her mother lying on jagged rocks twenty feet below a cliff. She'd leaped to her death, her spirit broken.

Sierra's paralyzing fear of water, her inability to act, and each wrong, terrible choice had broken her mother.

Her father was right.

A sob rose into her throat. Swallowing hard and clasping a hand over her mouth failed to keep it quiet.

At the strangled cry, Sam glanced up. "What's wrong?"

She met his worried gaze. "Nothing. Why?"

"You made a strange sound."

"I tried to hold back a sneeze. That's all."

Nodding, he turned back to the boy who desperately needed his own mother. Sierra knew his pain, the loneliness ahead, endless nights when it seemed dawn would never come.

She straightened as though struck by a bolt from the blue. She needed a purpose, something that gave her a reason to wake in the mornings. Hector would be her purpose for starters.

If they needed a schoolteacher, she could do that too, until Ford was caught and her brother found. Or she might start a small newspaper for the people on the ranch. Her entire life, she'd never had a purpose. Here in Texas, she planned to find not just one, but as many as she could.

Excitement swept through her. "Is there an opening for a schoolteacher here?" she asked.

"I'm not sure. I'll find out. Any reason?"

"Twiddling my thumbs isn't very fulfilling." She

wrinkled her nose. "I've done too much of that in my life. I want a job, some reason to crawl out of bed. For however long I'm here. You may find Rocky very soon, or it might take a while."

Surprise flickered across his face. "That's a good attitude. I never considered how hard this is for you. I plunked you down here with never a thought. Don't worry. I'll find something. On a ranch this size, there's no shortage of work."

"I could start a small newspaper maybe. Just something small and handwritten that can be tacked to the window of the mercantile."

"I'll help any way I can." Sam ruffled Hector's hair affectionately as he spoke to her. "I'll find your brother. Not knowing what happened to him must prey on your mind."

"More than anyone knows. I can't stop thinking about what he's going through. If he's hurt and suffering. If he's alive." If he simply disappeared in search of a story and hadn't been taken. She paused to swallow the lump blocking her throat and changed the subject. "Can you tell me what happened to Luke?"

"Nope, but I intend to find out." He sighed. "My father took charge as usual."

"He seems to have a good heart. I think he only tries to do what's best."

"That's the problem. What's best for Stoker might not be right for me. Or Luke."

Hector looked up and said something in Spanish.

Sam grinned. "The boy needs to take care of personal needs. I'll show him where to go, then bring him to your room. How's that?"

Those rows of white teeth set off in his tanned face made her stomach flutter wildly. Unable to speak, she simply nodded.

Throwing his arms around Sierra, Hector smiled up at her and said something. She glanced at Sam.

"I think he said not to go anywhere."

As though she could. She bent to kiss the boy's forehead.

In the hallway, Sam and Hector headed to the water closet at the end. Sierra stood for a moment, watching the man with a horrible scar around his neck take the hand of the frightened little orphan. The way Sam held those small fingers spoke of great tenderness. Her eyes misted.

For a moment, she wasn't sure who was helping whom.

❧

Sam searched all the obvious places but found no sign of Luke. Nor could anyone shed light on who had taken charge of the outlaw, or where they'd taken him.

Luke Weston seemed to have vanished. Hell and be damned!

The outlaw's words echoed in Sam's head. *This may not turn out the way you expect, Legend.* It appeared he'd made good on the thinly veiled warning. Sam muttered an oath. He must've walked several miles, scouring the buildings around the compound.

Just dandy! What else?

The talk with his father loomed. They had things to get out into the open. Sam's broken promise to only serve as a ranger for two years for starters. How could he make his father finally see that he could never, ever be the rancher son Stoker wanted? That being a Texas Ranger was the only thing that fulfilled him and brought peace to his soul?

Then, the hanging. Dear God, how was he supposed to tell his father about that?

With a knot in his gut, he swung toward the house. When he spied Sierra coming from one of the group's new lodgings, he stopped in his tracks. Hector skipped happily beside her. Sam stepped into the deep shadows.

Caught in the sun's dying rays, the white light arcing around her, she looked like an angel in blue.

An angel with a broken wing.

Though she'd claimed to have been holding back a sneeze, he recognized a sob when he heard one. She'd been a million miles away. Back in the mountains, he'd guess, reliving a horror of some sort. Over their days on the trail, he'd seen something powerful bad eating at her. Whatever it was went beyond fear of water. The mention of her father saying that everyone she touched died...

A woman wouldn't get that sort of thing out of her head.

Sierra's angry response that no one could fix her had come from a deep, dark place inside.

His admiring gaze followed her trim figure and the easy motion in which she strolled. He'd forgotten to tell her earlier how pretty she looked in the new blue dress. Or how her hair shone all clean, smelling of a field of daisies in the morning dew.

Her lips and the memory of kisses he still hungered for had erased the words from his head. Just as well, because no words had yet been thought of that could do justice to her.

Once she went inside the big house, Sam moved from the shadows. He might as well give up. It was only thirty minutes until supper, and Stoker would expect him at the table whether he wished to be or not.

Houston caught him minutes later as he went through the door. "How about a drink before supper? You can tell me about this Ford gang."

"I can use a shot of something strong." Sam followed his brother into their father's study and lowered himself onto a sofa upholstered in cowhide.

"How's your arm?" Houston flung over his shoulder.

"Sore. It's nothing."

Houston filled a tumbler with two fingers of whiskey and handed it to Sam. "How long has this Ford bunch been trailing you?"

"From the moment we got off the train." Sam took a sip, hoping the liquid fire would burn away the ache inside.

"They seem mighty determined to get Sierra."

"Yep. But then they also have six hundred and fifty other reasons. Something tells me if they don't get that loot back, they're dead." Sam told him about the telegram they found with the money. Ford was a desperate man, and he was out there waiting for them to make a mistake.

Houston poured a generous amount in another glass and sat next to Sam. "Why do they want Sierra so badly?"

"The crazy fools think she has some sort of map that doesn't exist. It's only a matter of time before they try to take her from here."

"Let 'em come. Be the biggest mistake they ever made." Houston tossed back his drink. "Who the hell tried to hang you?"

"Rather not talk about it." Sam turned his glass up and didn't flinch as the amber liquid burned all the way down. "Having enough nightmares."

Some so strong they strangled him just like that rope. He hadn't gotten a full night's sleep since it happened. He'd jerk awake, drenched with sweat, fighting the vomit in his throat. No, he didn't want to talk about that.

"You know Pa will force the issue."

Sam glanced up. "Time enough then to do the telling."

Standing, Houston walked to the huge oak desk and slammed down his glass. "Damn it, Sam. I can't imagine what that was like." He turned. "You're a lot tougher than me. Always were."

Forcing a careless shrug, Sam said quietly, "You taught me everything I know, big brother."

Stoker stuck his head in the doorway. "Thought I'd find you two in here. Time to eat. I feel like celebrating."

Sam didn't rise until his father's footsteps continued on to the dining room. Maybe it was out of rebellion, to prove to himself he wasn't at his father's beck and call. He was too tired to figure it out.

Finally he glanced at Houston. "The prodigal has returned. Eat, drink, and be merry, for tomorrow we may die."

"Yep."

Shoulder to shoulder, they strode from the room—two brothers who'd fought hard side by side all their lives. And would do so again. No matter what trouble the wind blew their way, they'd face it as they always had—head-on and warning it to take its best shot.

Sam froze when he stepped through the double doors. Shock, then anger swept through him.

Looking spit-shined and very pleased with himself sat Luke Weston.

Twenty-two

WHEN SAM PRIED HIS BACK TEETH LOOSE, HE ROARED, "What the hell, Weston? When I said you couldn't leave, I wasn't inviting you to our table. Why are you sitting there like you belong?"

Luke lifted one eyebrow and gave him a lazy grin.

"I invited him," Stoker's voice boomed as he rose from his seat, daring Sam to usurp his authority.

That piercing stare sharpened to a jagged knife-point, and meeting it took everything Sam had. But he didn't back down. Not this time. This concerned his job, his livelihood, *his* right to arrest lawbreakers and hold them accountable. "Do you know the price he has on his head?"

"I do. Take a seat, son. In this house, we behave in a civilized manner." Stoker dropped into his chair and took a large platter of meat from Cook. "For tonight, Mr. Weston is a guest. My thanks for helping you get here. And from what I heard, it took you both."

Houston leaned closer. "Smile, it won't be *that* bad."

His brother sat down at the end while Sam took the place directly opposite the wanted man. He propped his elbows on the table and met Luke's glare. No telling what he'd told Stoker. Anything to gain his father's favor, he was sure.

"Luke was shot trying to protect us, sir," Sierra said. "He almost died."

For the first time, Sam realized she sat at his right. Still seething, he swung his attention her way and immediately forgot about Weston. His heart leaped at the sight. Her upswept hair lent quiet elegance and left her slender neck bare. A neck he'd nuzzled and left a trail of kisses down while on his way to other places.

The blue of her dress provided a contrast to her dark beauty. The woman who'd come from the mountains with nothing could easily fit into high society if she chose. Or beside a campfire next to the swollen Brazos.

She could fit anywhere but in his heart.

No—he rephrased that. She already occupied that place. It was his life that seemed to be the problem.

"You're quite a sight, Miss Sierra. Don't think I've seen a prettier woman." He lifted her hand to his mouth.

With the scent of her brushing against him like a whispered caress, he had trouble getting words to his brain. It was all he could do to keep from scooping her into his arms and carrying her upstairs to his bed.

A pretty blush colored her cheeks. "Thank you, Sam. You look quite different as well."

"You mean clothes free of blood?"

"That too, but what I meant was how they fit... so well."

When he released her hand, she folded it in her lap

and sent an anxious glance around. He realized she didn't know what to do. She'd probably never dined in such a setting with so much silverware.

He leaned close to whisper, "Watch me." He put his napkin in his lap.

Color crawled up her neck. "Thanks."

Stoker forked a slab of meat onto his plate and held the platter while Luke got a piece.

The help made sense with the injury limiting the weight the outlaw could lift, but the way Stoker treated the common criminal like royalty ate at Sam. He seemed intent to throw Luke Weston in Sam's face.

Stoker handed the platter off to Sierra on his left. "Doc Jenkins looked at Weston's wound. He reports you did an excellent job of getting that bullet out and keeping the wound clean, Miss Sierra."

"Thank you, sir." She laughed. "He wasn't the easiest patient. Sam helped, of course, and told me about the gunpowder for a poultice. I think that might've saved Luke."

"I'd vouch for you any day, *dulce*," Luke said with a grin.

Houston drank from his wine glass. "You can't beat a ringing testament. We're glad to have you with us, Miss Sierra. My Becky would love to meet you. I'll bet you two will become fast friends."

Sierra smiled. "I'm not sure how long I'll be here, but I'd love to meet her."

"Weston, is that steak to your liking?" Stoker leaned forward. "If not, Cook can char up another one."

"It's perfect." The gloating look Luke shot Sam made his blood boil.

The meal seemed to be turning into a welcome for the outlaw hero. And if Stoker were to learn that Luke Weston saved Sam's life at the hanging, no telling how big of an affair he'd throw. Sam spied a glass of dark wine in front of him, lifted it, and came near to draining the thing before he realized the spectacle he made.

Lost in reflection, Sam glanced up when silverware tapped the side of a glass. Stoker stood, lifting his glass high. "To my son. You make me proud. The name Legend stands for toughness, loyalty, and cussed stubbornness. You have all three in spades, Sam." His father's voice broke. "Everyone eat up."

"Before you do, I second everything Pa said." Houston lifted his glass. "To Sam, the best brother I could ever have."

Overcome, Sam couldn't swallow. When his eyes met his brother's, Houston nodded. Damn, he was glad to be home.

When he set down his glass, he noticed Luke's grim expression. The outlaw wore a look of deep sadness and longing. Sam wondered if he was thinking about his family, maybe missing them. He was ashamed that he hadn't taken time to find out more about Weston's mother or where his father was. Maybe he had uncles and aunts somewhere. He realized he knew very little about the man he'd chased for so long.

"That was real nice, Sam," Sierra said softly, covering his hand with hers. "Your father loves you, no doubt about that."

Sam looked up to see Stoker disappearing with Cook—some matter in the kitchen no doubt.

"So it does appear." He took the platter of meat, stabbed his fork into a thick steak, and selected a smaller one for Sierra. "You got your wish, Weston."

"Not by a long shot. But you'll have to tell me which one you're talking about."

"You got to meet the king. What do you think of Stoker Legend?"

"Is this a trick question, Ranger? Off to the dungeon if I answer wrong?"

"Nope."

"He's big. Powerful. I can see why some might get tongue-tied coming face-to-face with him."

"You'd be surprised how many do," Houston said, laughing.

Sam reached for a bowl of potatoes. "But not you, I take it, Weston?"

Weston's eyes became hooded, blocking Sam from seeing his thoughts. "He might have more than most by half, but he's just a man. He bleeds like the rest of us."

The door opened, and Stoker reemerged with a bottle of his best bourbon that he reserved for special occasions. He started around the table, filling glasses.

A glance at the baffling man—a constant surprise these days—filled Sam with pride. "Yes, he does. What about your father, Weston?"

Luke forked a bite of meat into his mouth. "Never knew him. Didn't even know his name until two years ago. I always figured I was a spawn of the devil. At least that's what folks *used* to claim."

"How mean," Sierra exclaimed. "Your life apparently wasn't easy either."

With a shrug, Luke took a sip of wine. "It is what

it is. No changing the hand you're dealt. Just have to limit your wagers."

"A gambling man, Weston?" Houston asked.

"Always." The outlaw's face hardened.

"Me too," Sam said. He was betting Weston would find his bed extremely hard. He turned to Sierra. "Is your room to your liking?"

The tiny scar above her lip disappeared with her wide smile. "I've never seen anything so beautiful."

"Quite different from a bedroll on the ground," he agreed. "I'll ask around tomorrow about that job."

"Thank you. I have to find something to busy myself with, or I'll go out of my mind with worry about Rocky."

"About that—I'll set the wheels in motion come morning."

She clutched at his arm, and the warmth of her hand burned through his shirt. "Please don't ride out again so soon."

Her concern for him brought a smile. "Pa would send men after me with orders to kill if I tried to leave this soon."

Stoker pointed his fork at Sam. "That's for damn sure, son. I'm thinking of hiding your horse. But then, you'd just find another. Miss Sierra, apologies again for the strong language. I think what my son meant was that he'd start burning up this telegraph line I put in and see what he can learn."

Blinking hard, she murmured, "That would be wonderful, sir. I'm very afraid for my brother. I hope we can find him."

"If anyone can track him down, it will be Sam." Pride filled Stoker's voice.

"Thanks, Pa." Sam reached for his glass newly filled with bourbon. "I'll do my best. If he's in Texas, someone knows something. A reward might sweeten the deal and pry some tongues loose."

"Only I don't have a cent to my name," Sierra murmured.

"Nope, but Pa does."

"Great idea, son." Stoker shot Sam a glance. "Just tell me what the going rate is."

"I don't deserve all this," Sierra murmured. "My life changed when I fell into your lap on the train."

So did mine, Sam realized. Even though they would part when they left the Lone Star, he'd never forget the sweetness of her kisses after walking around dead for so long.

"I had to be there so I could help you." He tipped up his glass and drained it. "Would you like more potatoes or green beans? There's plenty."

"No thanks. I'll do well to eat what I have."

Sam studied her. No one would guess that her blue dress and fancy hair hid an untamed woman who'd danced in the firelight to the strum of a guitar. "After supper, we usually sit on the porch. Would you care to join us?"

"If you're sure I'm welcome." Uncertainty lined her face.

"You're always welcome." Sam winced at his husky tone.

Across the table, Luke Weston wiped his mouth on his napkin and sat back, nursing his glass of whiskey. His eyes glittered as he shot daggers at Stoker. Sam could feel the anger strangling him. Words an old ranger once told him came back: *"If you really want to know a man, find out what makes him mad."* Weston seemed to hold a grudge of some sort against Stoker. Sam recalled their conversation at the shack and then after and Weston's sarcastic comments about the ranch.

Until Sam knew what had brought about the angry words, he would never truly know the outlaw.

Why did he care so much about learning what made Luke tick? Maybe because of all the life-and-death moments they'd shared. Like it or not, an unbreakable bond had formed between them. He just hadn't considered fully how deep it ran.

The rest of the meal passed with only the clank of the silverware and the ticking of a tall grandfather clock in the corner.

At last Stoker pushed back his chair and rose. "I trust you will all sleep well."

Sadly, Sam watched his father collect another bottle of bourbon and head upstairs. Damn. It was going to be another one of those nights when Stoker would fight his demons the only way he knew how.

Houston got to his feet to leave but stopped when Sam asked him to stay.

Sam stood and pulled out Sierra's seat. "I'll join you on the porch in about thirty minutes."

"Certainly," she murmured and slipped from the room.

He leaned across the table and met Luke's eyes. "We need to talk."

Weston released a low oath. "I can't imagine what about."

"Can't you? Come with me."

"And if I don't?"

"My brother would love to make our fight very uneven."

With a sardonic lift of his brow, Luke pushed back his chair. "Lead the way, *amigo*."

Sam pointed Weston to a small room containing a sofa and two chairs. Houston moved to a decanter, poured three glasses, and handed Weston one.

"What do you have against my father?" Sam said.

Luke pressed the glass to his cheek before slowly taking a sip. "Who says I have anything?"

"You did," Sam snapped. "The things you said on the trail. I can refresh your memory if you want. And I saw the way you stared at him tonight."

"Some have nothing, go to bed hungry and sick." Luke's eyes grew cold and hard. "Your father sits on his big fancy horse, surveying his kingdom with never a care for others."

"Shows how little you know. He gives anyone a job who wants to work, provides a doctor when they're sick, and grieves over them when they die. He cares for their children and gives them an education. The people on this ranch are family. So before you judge him, you need to get your damn facts straight." Sam downed the amber liquid that burned his throat and set down the glass. "Tonight, he invited a wanted man to sit at his table and fed him steak."

Houston dropped onto a chair, silently listening to the exchange. He glanced at Sam, lifting an eyebrow. Sam knew he thought he was crazy. Maybe he was.

Luke sauntered to the window, staring into the black night. "Did you mean what you said about helping me?"

"I've taken your measure and seen the kind of man you are. I wouldn't stick my neck out for you if I didn't think you were worth the risk."

"You're a strange lawman, Sam Legend."

"Maybe. But I've always tried to be fair. A few times I lived to regret it."

"No one's put much stock in anything I said before. This'll take some getting used to." Luke turned to face him. "I swear on my mother's grave that I didn't kill Judge Percival."

"I believe you."

"I can't prove it."

"Someone has to know who did. If they exist, I'll find them." The stress of the day suddenly dropped over Sam. "I'm sure you're beat. I'll walk you to your quarters."

A short distance from the headquarters, Sam opened the door to a one-room dwelling and lit a lamp. "It's not much, but it's clean. You'll find blankets in the trunk at the end of the bed. You'll eat in the cook shack with the hired hands."

"It'll do." Luke flashed a quick grin. "Lots better than the one we took shelter in from the rain."

"Weston, I haven't said as much, but I owe you my life. By all rights I shouldn't be here."

"Goes both ways. Get some rest." Luke stuck out his hand.

Sam clasped it, giving a nod. The man who'd never known his father, who'd spent years being called a spawn of the devil, had become a friend. It would make his job harder; that was for damn sure. But trusting Luke Weston felt like it had cleansed a piece of Sam's soul.

Twenty-three

SAM FOUND SIERRA WAITING WHEN HE STROLLED ONTO the porch. He dropped heavily into the rocker next to her, relieved after his talk with Luke. Somehow, someway, he'd give Luke back his life, just as the outlaw had done for Sam. And then they would be even.

"Sorry about the delay. Needed to talk to Luke."

"I hope everything's all right. He's a good man, Sam."

"Everything's fine. I agree that he's a good man. He just irritates me at times. I don't know how to explain. It's a thing between men."

Her brow wrinkled in thought. "Sort of like trying to prove who's better?"

"Exactly."

"I saw that in my brothers." She smiled and leaned her head against the high-backed rocker. "Sam, it's lovely here. If I owned this ranch, I'd never leave."

Moonlight bathed her beautiful face. Memories swirled like autumn leaves, bringing an ache that almost doubled Sam over. Firelight flickering on her hair—her shoulders bare. Their last kiss. When would he stop yearning for her? With great effort, he finally dragged his attention from her blue eyes and honeyed lips.

"This land is in my blood, but not the same way it is for Houston or my father," Sam admitted softly.

Perhaps for the first time, he realized the words held truth. For Sam it was the beauty and the calm that he loved. Not cattle or turning a profit or the power that came with owning so much land.

It was finding contentment after a trying time…or peace after a hanging that nearly took his life.

The moon was just rising, and the fragrant smell of sage drifted in the breeze around him. Nowhere in all the state of Texas did the air smell so fresh and pure. The faint lowing of cattle blended with the tranquil night.

"I'm glad you're here, Sierra. I regret what happened between us last night. I was an ass. You didn't deserve that."

"You're a hard, complicated man, Sam Legend." She stared into the darkness.

Sam winced at the pain in her voice. "All the same, I'm truly sorry." He was silent a moment, then added, "I'd like to send to Waco for your things."

Her eyes reminded him of the Texas sky, bright blue and filled with mystery.

"No need. I intend to go back there to live. I just hope Mrs. Jones at the boardinghouse hasn't thrown them out. I'm sure she's wondering what's happened to me."

"I'll send her a telegraph and ask her to hold them."

"Thank you, Sam. What I have isn't much, but I'd hate to lose it."

An awkward silence dragged as he searched for a way to change the conversation. Finally, he said, "Houston will be out shortly."

"You and he have lots to catch up on." Sierra turned to face him, and he found hard lines around her set mouth. "I'm tired, and I have to collect Hector from Sofia. The boy asked to sleep in my room for a few days until he can get used to the strange sounds and people. Mrs. Ross brought in a small bed for him."

"Your soft spot for him shows the depth of your heart."

"He's lonely and grieves for his mother—his family. Something I relate to."

Back to mothers. It's where all roads seemed to lead.

"You haven't mentioned your mother. Is she with your father?"

"No," Sierra whispered. "She took her own life, and I'm to blame. Mama was unable to live with the pain of losing her daughter."

Funny, she'd never mentioned having a sister before. Curiosity made him want to ask, but he kept silent. He wasn't certain she wanted to say more. Sam started to reach for her hand, only to think better of it. "Whatever happened, I'm sure it's not your fault."

"You're wrong. But nothing I can say or do now will bring them back."

"You might feel better getting it out. Despite being a donkey's behind, I am a good listener." Sam took a gamble. "At the river you said your father told you that everyone you touched died. Is this what you meant? Was Whitney your mother?"

Sierra was silent for such a long time, and it was then that Sam knew silence could be a speech.

What she didn't say filled volumes. He was beginning to understand her angry declaration that he couldn't fix her. Clearly, terrible secrets weighed on her. He felt the ache of her pain in his bones. Blame, self-loathing, fear. You name it.

"No. You may as well know—Whitney was my twin sister. What I did was so shameful I can't bear to think of it." She raised her eyes to his. "The night before we reached the Brazos, I wasn't entirely truthful."

"About your fear of water?"

"I didn't tell you how deep my cowardice goes. Whitney drowned two years ago…while I watched, helplessly frozen on the shore. She begged me to save her, but I stood rooted in fear. I had a rope in my hand, but I couldn't throw it to her. I got the scar above my lip digging her grave. Father made me do it…alone. He said it was my punishment."

Anger at the horrible cruelty shook Sam. There were gaping wounds inside Sierra that hadn't even begun to scab over. He didn't trust himself to speak, his fury was so great.

Sierra went on, "She was my father's favorite and more like him than any of us. Where he went, she tagged right behind. He will never forgive me for taking Whitney from him."

Sam interrupted. "That wasn't your fault. It was a horrible accident."

Sierra flung herself from the chair and leaned against the porch support. "And now Mama. *I* put her in that deep grief. I took beautiful, loving Whitney from her."

Unable to bear her misery, he went to her. Thinking only of comforting her, he folded his arms around her. Rubbing her slender back, he held her while she cried.

Raw pain spilled from her wounded heart.

Minutes passed before she was able to speak. "I never wanted you to see how…broken I am."

As his arms tightened around her, he brushed her temple with his lips. "There's no shame in being human. We all fail in some way or another. And that's okay. We don't have to be perfect. We only have to try our best."

"Rocky's the only family I have left who'll claim me. If I lose him…"

"You won't. I'm going to find him. I promise that." Sam's jaw clenched. One way or another, she was not going to have reason to blame herself for one more devastating loss.

Sierra raised her face. Droplets lingered on the tips of her long, dark lashes. Sam brushed them away with the pad of his thumb. He couldn't deny the strong magnetic pull drawing him to her. He couldn't control the hunger that burned inside. He only knew he had to taste her lips or die.

"Do you mind if I kiss you?" he whispered.

Without a reply, she rose on tiptoe and pressed her mouth to his. There was nothing shy about the need appearing to drive her. She seemed sure of what she wanted, bold even, despite the differences standing between them. Or maybe it was the fierce need for the warmth of a touch. It had been a long while since she'd had that.

The minute their lips met, Sam was lost.

The wild stampede of his heart sent an explosion bursting through him. Heat collected in his stomach and seared into his brain, branding her there forever.

Why had he thought it a good idea to meet her out here?

The torment of seeing her was bad enough, but holding and kissing her ripped away his last shred of willpower.

His hand splayed across her back, holding her near. Whether right or wrong, he wanted her more than anything on earth.

Shifting, he deepened the kiss and let his hand slide along the soft lines of her body. In the back of his mind he knew he had to let her go, but he couldn't pry his hands loose.

What he felt was primal and savage, as though he stood in the midst of a thousand thundering buffalo. His heart pounded in his ears. His breath became ragged and harsh. His blood pumped through his veins with a force he'd never felt.

She needed him.

And even if he was about to get trampled to death, he'd give everything within his power to make her whole and happy. Yet he knew she had to find that within herself. She'd been right in saying he couldn't fix her.

But he could damn sure help.

Before she left the Lone Star, he vowed Sierra Hunt would know more than the pain and heartache that had walked in her shadow all her life.

Twenty-four

SIERRA LEANED INTO SAM, LOST IN HIS PASSION. THE kiss ignited sleeping embers that had started at the shack, and later banked at the river with no chance of ever fanning back to life.

Now, the blazing fire burned a path through her.

In the mountains when a wildfire broke out, you raced ahead and lit another one in hopes of stopping it. Maybe that's what this was. A secondary fire that would burn up the fuel of the first and snuff it out.

A sob tore from her heart and hung in her throat. She couldn't bear for this fragile love to die. But last night in the moonlight, she'd realized once and for all that Sam didn't love her, at least not in the way she yearned for.

This man, this Texas Ranger, was everything she'd dreamed of finding. Often during lonely, endless nights she'd dared to hope for someone who could see past what she'd done and not judge.

Yet even though Sam Legend didn't love her, she knew he cared. Just now, he hadn't turned away in disgust when she finally, for the first time, bared her soul.

She'd trusted him with her secrets and her failures.

Shivers of delight followed his touch as he moved along her body. She quivered under the tenderness of his mouth as it drifted down the column of her throat to the fabric of her collar.

Sierra laid her palm on the side of his face.

All they'd ever had were stolen moments. An ache for something lasting swept along her nerve endings. But maybe this was all there would ever be. If so, she'd settle for what she could get if he would only stay. Except in her heart she knew he wouldn't.

Sam had an insatiable need to keep moving, just like her father. Restless feet had ruined her family, and it would destroy her and Sam. He'd not been home in two long years. She couldn't tie herself to such a man.

The whole sum of her life would be more than standing at a window, watching the road, waiting for him to remember that he had a wife, a home, possibly a child.

Wondering if he might be hurt or dead.

Waiting for a few stolen moments when he would notice her.

No. Her thoughts returned to the mountains and the aftermath of a fire that had left everything scorched and desolate, the landscape unrecognizable.

She wouldn't want to live with nothing but charred piles of ash inside.

Sometimes love couldn't save two people.

Maybe it was best to saddle a horse and leave while she had enough strength.

Trembling at thoughts of leaving, she leaned back to look up into those gray eyes she loved. "Why did you invite me out here, Sam?"

He wore a puzzled expression. "I miss sharing a campfire and listening to the sounds of the night with you. I loved those nights on the trail. I don't want that to end."

"Everything has to end." She meant both the words and the hardness that sneaked into her tone as a reminder for herself.

Sam tucked a strand of hair behind her ear and kissed her cheek. Sadness filled his eyes. "You're right, pretty lady."

When the screen door creaked behind them and boots struck the porch, they jerked apart.

"Pardon me, ma'am," Houston said. "I didn't know you were out here. I need to talk to you, Sam."

Sam shoved a hand through his hair. "It's all right, Houston. We were finished."

"I need to collect Hector and head to bed anyway," Sierra said. "I'm sure you brothers have lots to discuss. It was nice meeting you, Houston."

"Same here."

Sierra stepped into the dark shadows. At least she knew what to do for needy little boys. Grown-up ones were far too complicated.

Pausing under low, overhanging branches of a solitary elm tree, she glanced back. Her gaze searched for the Texas Ranger, whose warm kisses had given her frozen soul a place to thaw. If only for a moment.

The brief pleasure of their passion would have to last a lifetime. "I love you, Sam," she whispered brokenly from deep in the cool shadows. "I wish you loved me back."

◦⊱✦⊰◦

Sam stared after her for a moment, then plopped down into a chair, feeling spent. "What's this about?"

"Luke Weston." Houston took the chair next to Sam. "Knowing he has a price on his head makes me nervous. Even without his gun belt and pistol, that man looks lethal. The rage in those eyes makes me want to run for cover, and I'm not a fainthearted man. What are we dealing with?"

"He's nothing to worry about." Sam glanced toward the dwelling that housed Luke. The windows were dark. Probably already went to bed. "I got to know him pretty well during the trip. He has guts and then some."

Houston bristled. "That's not what I'm asking. How dangerous is he? Will I wake up to find him standing over me?"

"Nope."

"How can you be sure?"

"Weston gave his word."

"That's it? A wanted man gave you his word?"

"I trust him. Houston, I owe him my life. If he hadn't cut me down after the hanging, I wouldn't be here." Sam touched his scar, recalling those pale-green eyes of the man kneeling over him.

Houston let out a whistle. "That's a mighty big debt."

"I feel sorry for him. He grew up poor. Never knew his father, though I gather he was white. Luke's mother, a woman of Mexican descent, died a couple of years ago. He had plenty of opportunity to shoot me. But he didn't."

"So why bring him here?"

"I'm going to help clear his name. I owe him that

much. He's not as bad as he wants everyone to believe. I've seen his honor and the depth of his heart. He put his life on the line for me more than once."

"I'd feel better if you took his gun," Houston complained.

"He's not under arrest. I'm only holding him here until I figure out how to proceed."

"What are his crimes?"

"Robbery and murder."

"And you think he's just misunderstood?" Houston raised his hands to his head. "My God, Sam. Have you lost your mind?"

Maybe so. Or had he finally found it?

"Luke admits to each of the robberies in which he only took fifty dollars, but he swears he didn't kill that judge. I believe him."

Houston laid a hand on Sam's shoulder. "Don't you think you're taking this need to repay a debt a bit far? What if someone finds out Weston's here on the Lone Star?"

"No one will." If he, Houston, and his father kept quiet, who would know?

"Just say someone did. Are you willing to risk your job and your reputation for an outlaw with a price on his head? It could land your butt in jail along with him. Think about it."

Would Sam give up the life he loved, that he'd fought tooth and nail for? Why for Luke Weston and not for Sierra? Maybe because Luke's was a blood debt. That carried a heavy price, and not paying it would destroy the fabric of his soul.

"Sam, other lawmen can get away with picking

and choosing which lawbreakers to lock up. But not you."

"Not when our name is Legend," Sam agreed quietly. "Like it or not, we stand for toughness and getting the job done. Everything to the letter. Thanks to Pa." He felt the burning urge to steer the conversation away from his duty and Luke Weston. "What did you want to talk to me about?"

"Pa. I don't know what to do." Houston sat down and leaned back with his hands behind his head.

"I was hoping he'd slowed down on the bourbon."

Houston's deep sigh caught on the breeze. "The demons he fights won't leave him alone. Drowning their voices is all he knows to do."

"Too much of that stuff can put you in an early grave. Or is that what he's hoping for?"

Houston let out a huff. "Who can see into the mind of Stoker Legend?"

Sam sat beside him. "Our pa is a man of excess. A little is never enough."

"Maybe we should try to find him a woman."

Sam snorted. "That's a dumb idea, Houston. What woman in her right mind would find Pa a good catch for anything other than his money?" Picturing his father making love was not a sight he wanted stuck in his head.

"Well, let's see you come up with something." Houston paused a moment and lowered his voice. "I saw Mrs. Ross sneaking from his room very early one morning. Have a feeling she wasn't there to change the sheets."

"Mrs. Ross? Surely you're pulling my leg." Sam

had always liked the kind housekeeper, and until now, always thought she showed a lot of good sense.

"Nope. If you'd come home once in a while, you could see these things for yourself." Houston rose and propped himself against the porch railing. His voice became soft and low. "Tell me about the hanging."

"Do we have to talk about this now?"

"No better time. You know you'll have to tell Pa tomorrow."

Sam sighed. "Happened a month ago. Rustlers surrounded me after I got separated from the other rangers. Too many of 'em."

"From the looks of the scar, you barely survived."

"Thought I was dead. Would've been if they'd done it right. And if Weston hadn't been following me. Don't know the name of the man who put the noose around my neck, but he had a black widow spider drawn on his hand between the thumb and forefinger."

Houston swung around. His brown eyes grew hard. "I'll kill him if I find him."

Sam's mouth tightened. "You'll have to beat me to it."

"I can't imagine what that must've been like. The fear, the pain."

"My last thought before losing consciousness was regret for not telling Pa I loved him. I still dream about the hanging and wake up drenched with sweat."

"Appears you get a second chance."

"Yep." Sam dragged in a lungful of fresh air. Second chances at a lot of things. Only one question still haunted him. Was he man enough to grow and learn from it? "When were you last over to Lost Point?"

"Been a while. Why?"

"Captain O'Reilly received some reports that out-laws moved in and asked me to check it out."

Houston was quiet for a long moment. When he spoke, his voice held anger. "So you just came home to work? Not because you wanted to see us?"

"Don't be ridiculous." Sam had thought to hide the real reason for his visit, but now he didn't have any choice. Damn! "I have something to tell you, and I'll break your neck if you breathe a word of this to anyone—especially Pa."

After his brother gave the blood oath, Sam told how the hanging had messed up his head, and about the captain sending him home to find his marbles. He thought Houston would laugh, but he didn't even crack a smile.

"I can imagine." Houston rubbed the back of his neck. "Going through something like that would make you a little crazy. You almost died. Your secret is safe."

"Thanks. I was lost, more dead than alive when I ran into Sierra. Her calm ways brought peace, anchoring me. Somehow, she settled the chaos in my head and helped me find myself."

Suddenly that missing grin appeared as Houston changed the subject. "I thought you said Sierra was just a friend."

"She is."

"What you were just doing, I've never done with a friend." Houston chuckled. "Looked like a whole lot more to me."

Sam shot his grinning fool of a brother a glare. "For

your information, I was comforting the lady. She was upset. Worried for her brother, fearing he may be already dead."

Houston raised his hands. "Hey, merely making an observation."

"Yeah? Well, you're grinning."

"Not my problem if you make it too easy for me."

Silence stretched as Sam thought about Sierra's painful secrets. How awful to watch a sister die while you stood frozen. No wonder she'd had such fear of crossing the Brazos. It made sense now. He knew what it was to blame yourself.

If Sam didn't save Rocky…

"I'd like your help, Houston. As soon as I get information on where Sierra's brother might be, I'd be obliged if you'd ride with me. I have to save him."

"Say the word, and I'm beside you. We'll ride straight into hell if we have to."

The grit in Houston's words meant far more than he was saying. For all their fighting, his brother would lay his life on the line anytime, anywhere for Sam. And vice versa.

They were blood. They were brothers…

They were Legends.

Twenty-five

A NOISE DOWNSTAIRS AWAKENED SAM A LITTLE BEFORE dawn, dragging him from the horror of his usual nightmare. For a second he couldn't place where he was. Sitting up, he lit the lamp, spilling light over the now-familiar surroundings.

The sound came again. Grabbing his Colt from the holster hanging above his head, he threw back the covers and jerked on his trousers, not bothering with a shirt.

He crept into the hallway and leaned over the banister. A ribbon of light under the door of his father's study didn't seem all that strange. Maybe Stoker had run out of liquor and went down for another bottle. Sam was about to go back to bed when he heard a muttered oath.

Curiosity got the best of him. If it was Stoker, maybe he needed something. Sam moved downstairs and opened the door of the study.

A tall, lean man stood over the desk, staring at something.

"You better have a good explanation for being in here," Sam grated, pointing his weapon.

The man whirled.

Luke Weston.

Disappointment washed over Sam. "You gave your word. I trusted you, Weston."

"And I haven't broken it."

Fire shooting from the outlaw's eyes would've made Sam back down, if not for the fact that he backed down for no man. Friend or foe. At the moment he didn't know which hat Luke wore.

"Why would you steal from us? I was willing to risk everything to help you." Keeping his Colt leveled at Luke's chest, he crossed the space between them. "Hand over what you have in your hand."

Luke's mouth tightened. "Or what? You'll shoot me?"

Sam's eyes narrowed. "In a heartbeat. I caught you red-handed. Give it to me."

With a low curse, Luke slapped a gold locket into Sam's outstretched palm. Before he spared it a glance, Stoker and Houston burst into the study. While Houston wore only long johns, Stoker was fully dressed, complete with his gun belt around a waist that was still lean and firm despite his fifty years of living.

"What's going on?" Stoker demanded.

"Seems I caught a bandit," Sam answered without turning.

Stoker marched to within inches of Luke. He pinned him with a steely stare that could make men quake in their shoes and look for a hole to climb into. Sam was gratified to see the feared outlaw shift uneasily.

"You repay our kindness by stealing?" Stoker barked.

"No, sir."

Houston strode to Sam's side. "You'd best start talking. What are you doing in here?"

"Keeping a deathbed promise." Luke's green eyes narrowed to slits. "I was putting something *in* the desk, not taking anything out."

"Let me see what you caught him with, Sam," Stoker said.

"It's a locket of some kind." Sam passed it to his father.

Houston crowded close to see. "That pins on a woman's dress. Did it belong to Mother?"

The minute Stoker opened it, his face drained of color. "No, it's not your mother's." He stumbled to the desk and dropped into the chair.

"Whose then?" Sam asked impatiently. He needed answers, and the sooner the better. He'd never seen his father this upset and white.

Stoker stared up at Luke. "How did you get this?"

Luke Weston shifted again. "The locket belonged to my mother. She made me promise to return it to you. Said you'd know what it meant."

With a nod, Stoker murmured, "That she's dead."

"Yes, sir," Luke said quietly.

"What is this about, Pa?" It seemed foolish for Sam to hold a gun on Weston if he hadn't stolen anything—yet he didn't want to lower it until he knew what was going on.

A faraway look shadowed Stoker's eyes. "I always wondered if my time with Elena had resulted in a child. I loved her, you know. I thought…how old are you, Weston?"

"Twenty-nine. Be thirty in a few months."

"You know, don't you?" Stoker gazed up at him.

Luke's fixed stare hardened along with his voice. "Yes."

Whatever they were talking about, Sam wished they'd tell him. Glancing from one to the other, he could see some kind of terrible secret hanging between them. "Who are you really, Weston?"

Luke stood in stony silence, his face as though carved from granite.

Sam's question jarred Stoker from his stupor. "This is your brother."

A brother? *Luke Weston* was his brother?

The words refused to sink into Sam's brain. His brother was a wanted man with a price on his head, an outlaw? And *he* was responsible for bringing Luke to their door?

Hell and be damned!

"When did this happen, Pa?" Houston looked as shocked as Sam and just as clearly in need of answers.

"August 1846, down in Galveston." Stoker's voice was distant as he ran his finger across the likeness of the beautiful woman who must have been Luke's mother.

Sam was relieved to find a bit of color returning to his father's face.

"I was born the following year," Houston ground out. "August. Unless my figuring is off, that means…" He turned to Luke. "When were you born?"

"End of May 1847."

Hurt crawled across Houston's face. Sam would do anything to take it from him. Secrets brought such awful pain when they came out.

Houston pinned Stoker with a glare. "Did Mother know you'd been unfaithful?"

Their pa flushed at the insult to his character. "I was never a philanderer, son. I hadn't met your mother yet. I went to Galveston to buy some horses. I'd gotten wind of a shipment of prime Spanish horseflesh. I met Elena Montoya." Stoker grew wistful with remembrance. "My, she was a beautiful woman. Such kind and gentle ways. Lord, how she loved to laugh and dance. She loved life."

"You had your fun, and you left her," Luke spat.

"You're dead wrong!" Stoker thundered. "I wanted to marry her and make her lady of the Lone Star. I loved her."

Luke snorted. "You had a funny way of showing it, *Pa*."

Sam watched Luke's hands clench tightly at his sides. If he made one move toward Stoker, Sam would have to stop him, however he could. Ever since he'd recognized Weston at the shack, he'd had the feeling that one day he'd be forced to fight him. Maybe this was the day. How it would end would be anyone's guess. Luke was lethal even without a gun. His half brother would fight to the last breath.

But then, so would he.

"Show him some respect," Sam growled a warning at Luke.

"Like he showed my mother?"

Stoker jumped to his feet and towered over Luke by a good two inches. "I don't know what your mother told you about that time, son, but I asked her to marry me before leaving that morning to make arrangements for the horses I bought. When I returned, she was gone. Disappeared along with her belongings. No one knew where she went. I searched and searched for weeks. Finally, I was forced to think the only thing I could—that she'd left me. That maybe she'd decided I wasn't good enough for her. Or that she loved someone else. I never knew what happened to her."

Luke's spine straightened. "I'm not your son. You're not my father. I belonged to Elena Montoya. No one else."

"I understand your anger—"

"You understand nothing, Legend," Luke interrupted Stoker.

Sadness filled Stoker's eyes that so resembled Luke's. "Why did you come? What did you hope to gain? Money?"

"I promised my mother before she took her final breath that I would find this man who hadn't cared to look for her. Her brothers came that morning, forced her into a carriage, and took her to San Antonio. After six months, she finally escaped and came here. To tell you about me. But you had taken another wife. You broke her heart, her soul."

"I'm sorry. If I had known—"

"No, I'm not buying that," Sam said, jabbing his finger into Luke's chest. "There's more. I've felt your anger and resentment from the beginning. I think you wanted to see what you'd missed out on. You wanted to snub your nose at us, but smearing our faces in a big pile of horse apples tempted you even more."

With anger darkening Luke's face, he stood nose to nose with Sam. "Hell yeah, it did."

Sam stood his ground. "We had everything, and you wanted it."

"You're dead wrong about that, *hermano*. I don't

want any part of you or this ranch. You can keep it and all go straight to hell."

Houston had evidently kept silent too long. "Then why did you risk capture by coming all this way? From what Sam tells me, you could've left as soon as you'd recovered enough."

Luke swung to Houston. "I wanted to make sure Sam got home and got Sierra safe. When those rustlers hanged him, they did more than put a rope around his neck. They messed with his mind. He was sent home and told not to return until he got his head on straight and could do his job."

"Is that true, Sam?" Stoker's hand rose as though to touch Luke's shoulder. Before it got halfway, he let it fall.

"I can't deny it." Though Sam dearly wished he could, wished he could've hidden that he'd lost his sanity for a bit. He wasn't proud of that. "We'll discuss it later."

"I guess you want this back to remember your mother by," Stoker said, holding out the locket.

"Keep it. I have memories that no one can take."

"I'd like to do right by you, son."

"Keep your name, your money, and your big, fancy ranch. You've got nothing I want."

Sam watched him turn and lazily saunter out the door. A lot of questions about Luke Weston just got answered. Despite everything, his heart ached for his lawless brother who was alone now, with no one to care whether he lived or died.

But Sam knew that was a lie. Part of him already cared about Luke—not as an outlaw to help, but much deeper where it counted...as a brother.

He'd sensed that bond even when he hadn't known why. His heart must've somehow recognized that he and Luke shared the same blood. Now it all made sense, why their paths always crossed. Luke had watched over him as an older brother. Saved him.

Despite everything, like it or not, Luke Weston or Legend or whatever the hell he wanted to be called had at least one person on his side.

Sam wouldn't stop until he saved him back.

Twenty-six

TENSION SO THICK IT CLOGGED SAM'S THROAT FILLED the study. In the wake of the slamming door, he stared at his father and Houston. "What do we do now? Are we just going to let him go like that?"

"You heard him. Luke hates me. Hates the Legend name." Stoker ran his fingers through his thick gray hair. In the last ten minutes, he seemed to have aged ten years.

"Are you sure you're his father?" Houston asked quietly. "He could have stolen that locket for all we know."

"He didn't. He's my son as much as you and Sam are. He knows too much, things that only Elena would know to tell. This locket is proof enough. She said if I ever got it back, it would mean that she's dead."

Houston blew out a deep breath. "How did he turn out to be an outlaw, I wonder? What are you going to do now, Sam?"

"Good question." On both counts. Sam's gut twisted into a knot. Whatever choice he made, he was going to lose. But no one was going to call Luke the devil's spawn again.

"You're not going to arrest my son, even if he hates me," Stoker declared. "Law or no law, you're letting him be. He's suffered enough by my hand."

While Sam agreed, his conscience had already begun to prick. Everyone made their own choices, good, bad, or indifferent, and they had to live with those. Putting aside the murder charge for the moment, Luke had chosen to rob. No one made him turn thief.

Yet he truly seemed to want to fix his mess.

"I told him yesterday that I'd help clear his name, and I mean to do that. If he still wants me to. Although after this, I'm not sure he's willing to give up that life." He was hurt and full of rage. Men with nothing to live for would wind up alone and bitter.

"Thanks, Sam." Stoker put his hand on Sam's shoulder. "Whatever you need, I'll provide. Money, influence, anything."

"What he needs worse than anything is a father," Houston said quietly, reflecting Sam's thoughts.

"If he'll let me." Stoker turned.

"Myself, I need coffee." Sam started for the door. "How about you two?"

"Sounds good. Get dressed, and we'll meet in the kitchen," his father said. "I always think better on a full stomach."

"Me too. I'm hungry," Houston declared.

"You're always hungry." Though Sam didn't feel playful in the least, he desperately needed to lighten the dark mood that had enveloped him. He jabbed his brother's arm. "It's because you were raised by a pack of mangy coyotes who found you in the desert. Heard they left you on the doorstep one night, and Mother took pity on you. At least that's what she claimed when you weren't around."

"Ha, ha. Very funny."

"Just paying you back for saying I stunk like a pigsty yesterday." Sam watched his father head outside and make for the small dwelling across the way.

He hoped Luke took it easy on him. The old man was hurting and blaming himself. Sam could already tell this would be a two-bottle night.

Exchanging silent glances, he and Houston turned to the stairs. At the top, Houston hurried to his room. Deep in thought, Sam collided with Sierra. Suddenly, he was acutely aware of his bare chest. And the fact that she could be going for a Sunday stroll in another pretty dress. He wanted to cover himself with his hands, but decided that would look silly, especially since he still held his Colt.

Instead, Sam straightened to his full height and smiled. "Good morning, Sierra. I trust you slept well."

Her brow knitted. "The bed was heavenly. Hector had nightmares, though, so sleep was spotty. According to Mrs. Ross, who happened to hear the cries and came in, the boy kept thinking he was still in Mexico and soldiers were trying to kill him." She leaned close. "Once he rubbed his hands in a panic, thinking they were covered with blood. I was afraid he'd wake the rest of the household."

He found the fragrance of her and her kissable mouth extremely distracting. Her words buzzed like busy bees in his head.

Finally, he murmured, "I didn't hear him."

"I'm glad. If he's a bother, I'll find other sleeping arrangements."

Sam laid his hand on her shoulder. The thought of not having her near almost put him in a panic. He needed her close.

"The boy is no bother. I won't hear of you looking for other quarters. What are you doing up so early?"

"I heard a commotion and angry voices. Sounded like trouble." She glanced down at his pistol. "I assume I was right, since you have your Colt."

"Thought we might have a thief in the house, but I was mistaken." He hastily hid the Colt behind him. "You don't have to worry. Isaac Ford won't get in."

Sierra tilted her head to the side and squinted. "I sense trouble lurking behind that charm of yours. You're upset and trying to hide something. I can tell."

"Family stuff. Nothing to bother you with."

"Then I'll leave you to it."

She spun to go, and her foot slipped over the edge of the landing. Sam grabbed for her. Her palms flattened against the wall of his chest. The contact was like a hot brand. His muscles quivered, almost as though she was inflicting pain. But then, she was. The misery seared past the sinew and bone, down into the fiber of his being.

This pain had only one cure and one price.

"Be careful, Sierra," he growled low. One hand fell to her shining hair.

She jerked her hands away, and he let his drop. "You kissed me last night," Sierra said, her eyes blazing. "You say you don't want me, but your lips lie. You tell me to find someone else, but you bind me to you with strong rawhide. You say one thing and do the complete opposite. Make up your mind, Sam. Keep me or let me go. I won't wait. I'm not some long-suffering martyr."

Before he could form a reply, she whirled and marched back to her room. He could only watch her go.

And take his heart with her.

⁓

With Sierra's ultimatum still ringing in his ears, Sam joined Houston and his father at the breakfast table.

Could he truly let her go? Was he that strong…or that weak?

Did he have the strength to watch the woman who had his heart leave?

He tried to put her out of his mind and focus on the other looming problem. He was surprised at Luke's absence from the table—he knew from experience how persuasive Stoker could be.

His father glanced up as Sam poured some coffee and took his seat. "I went to invite your brother to join us, but I couldn't find him. I want you and Houston to track him down—if he's still on the Lone Star."

"And then what? Do you plan to use force to keep him here?" Arrest his brother? That was something he'd promised not to do. Too many broken promises weighed a man down.

Stoker slammed his hand on the table. "I'll not have any of my sons locked up."

"One of us likely will be, if he goes on a tear," Sam said quietly. "Which one do you prefer?"

His plan had unraveled before he'd even started. If Luke went on the rampage, Sam would have no choice but to hunt him down. And if the authorities found out the Legends were harboring a felon, Sam's butt would be the one in a sling.

"I only want to talk some sense into him," Stoker snapped. "I want a chance to be a father. But I won't hold him here if he wishes to go. You won't either."

"Who knows what he'll do in the state he's in. Right now, Luke doesn't see that he has much to live for," Houston pointed out.

"I know, son." Stoker pushed back his chair. "I know too well."

Houston lifted his cup. "Luke and I are the same age, Pa. When exactly did you meet Mother? It had to be within a month or two of leaving Galveston. Did you love Mother at all? Or was she simply a woman to run the ranch? A substitute to handle your needs."

Stoker's fierce gaze pierced Sam as well as Houston. "I don't expect you to understand. I loved them both, but Elena owned a bigger piece of my heart. She was an amazing woman, so full of fiery passion. If I'd known where she was, and in the family way, I would never have married your mother."

And Sam and Houston would never have been born. A knot twisted in Sam's stomach.

Houston cleared his throat. "What about the ranch? How will you split it up, Pa?"

"Each of you will share equally," Stoker replied without hesitation.

Sam admired his father for taking the shock that had shaken him to the core and doing the right thing.

No doubts. No questions. No discussion. He wished he could be more like his father where Sierra Hunt was concerned. Wished he could take her in his arms and keep her there forever, give up everything he'd worked so hard for…for her. Dammit to hell!

Taking a sip of coffee that Sam suddenly wished was whiskey, he said, "Luke and Houston can split my portion. The Lone Star isn't in my blood, not like it should be. I don't intend to settle down and live here."

Even if he lost his job as a Texas Ranger, Sam wouldn't stay. He'd load a packhorse and ride until he found a woman with a cloud of dark hair who loved dancing in the moonlight to the strum of a guitar. One whose spirit was as restless as his.

Anger flushed Stoker's face. "I'll hear no talk of giving up what I've scratched and clawed all my life to build. I've fought and bled for this land, this piece of Texas. And you're not throwing your share away."

His father was doing it again—overruling Sam. Treating him as though his thoughts, desires, dreams were nothing.

Doing that was bad enough, but refusing to respect his job brought Sam's dander to the surface faster than swollen floodwaters. "I've fought and bled, too. Trying to make Texas a safe place to live, where folks can settle without fear," he said angrily. Then his voice softened. "I'm not saying I don't appreciate what you've built, Pa. I just want a chance to blaze my own trail."

Silence dropped over them like ominous clouds blocking the sun. Sam concentrated on the plate of eggs and bacon that Cook had placed in front of him. He was tired of arguing. Maybe he should leave before it got really ugly.

Finally, Stoker said, "I know you've faced far worse than I ever did, and that kills me. A father doesn't want his sons to hurt, to bleed...to die. When I saw that scar around your throat, I wanted to ride out right then and hunt down the ones who did it. I wanted to feel my hands around their necks while they begged for mercy. I wanted to spill their blood. Still do." He slammed his palm down on the table. "I will before this is over; you can bet your hat on that."

"When they strung me up, and I had nothing but air under my feet, my biggest regret was I never told you I love you. I regret that we argue, that I broke my promise to only ride with the Texas Rangers two years." Sam's voice broke. "Pa, I do love you. I have more respect for you than anyone on earth."

Having said the words lifted weight off Sam's shoulders. What surprised him was it hadn't been difficult at all. Sam glanced up and met his father's gaze. The glimmer of wetness shocked him. Maybe Stoker was simply being a typical father. Sam filed that away to think about later.

"I'm proud of the man you've become, Sam, and, damn it, I've done a sorry job of showing it."

"Pa, I'm tired of fighting. Let me do the things I'm good at without trying to put me in some box that stifles the life from me."

"No more fighting, son. I promise." Stoker put his head in his hands. "You're a damn good Texas Ranger. I see what you've accomplished, the name you've built for yourself. I was wrong to try to take that from you."

Relief washed over Sam. He finally heard the words he'd waited so long for. "Everything carries danger. You can't always protect us."

Stoker rubbed his eyes. "I see that now. These men who hanged you—give me their names, Sam. Are they alive?"

"Last I knew, but I have no names to put to them. The ringleader had a black widow spider drawn on the back of his hand. One day I'll cross paths with him again."

"He's a dead man if I do," Stoker vowed. "The bastard best pray I don't find him."

"Or me." Houston's tone was hard and brittle. "We'll show them how Legends handle their kind. But back to Luke. He said he doesn't want this ranch or anything to do with us."

"A man's pride makes him say a lot of things." Stoker refilled his cup from the pot Cook had left on the table. "I'll add him to the will. It'll be here when he's ready for it."

Hell might freeze over first, Sam thought. Luke wasn't one to say things lightly. He meant what he said, and seemed pretty determined. He'd done without his whole life, while they'd had everything. Men growing up that way had a hard time forgetting. Resentment was deep in the marrow of his bones.

While Sam didn't condone Luke's lawbreaking ways, he was beginning to understand why his brother had turned to crime.

He pushed back his plate and stood. It was time

to have a chat with his half brother. Assuming Luke hadn't done anything foolish. If he'd saddled his gelding and ridden out to continue his life of crime, Sam would have no choice but to go after him.

Hell!

How did a man go about arresting his own damn brother?

❧

Sam checked the corral first. No sign of a gelding the color of midnight. His gut wrenched. He might've known.

The parting words Luke had flung at them before storming out came back. *Keep your name, your money, and your big, fancy ranch. You've got nothing I want.*

Sam winced. Anger was eating his brother alive. But if he stood in Luke's shoes, he'd probably feel the same. Not feeling good enough could destroy any man.

One of the ranch hands told him Luke had saddled the gelding. "He asked how to get to the closest creek, so I told him. Saw him riding that way," the man said.

That seemed funny. What did Luke have in mind?

Sam thanked him and saddled Trooper. Within a short time, Sam galloped toward the creek that lay to the north.

Was Luke meeting someone there? Or looking for a place to die?

A stand of cottonwood and oak lined the stream that broke off the Red River. The glistening offshoot furnished plenty of fresh water for nearby cattle—or at least it did when they weren't in a drought. The last several years had seen a fair amount of rain.

He moved slowly up and down the deep channel

before he finally spied the black gelding tied in the trees. No others were around. He dismounted, leaving Trooper to graze.

Instinct born from years of hunting down bad guys urged Sam to draw his Colt. The gnarled oak trees brought back bad memories he'd do anything to block. With the hair on his neck raised, he crept forward.

"Don't come a step closer." The low warning came from the shadows.

Twenty-seven

Sam froze in his tracks. "That you, Luke?"

"Checking on me, Ranger?" Luke stepped toward him with a gun in his hand, his gun belt slung low around his lean hips. "You think I hightailed it out of here?"

"Crossed my mind." Sam holstered his Colt.

"Still don't trust me to keep my word?"

"I'm trying. What was I to think after you stormed out like that? What are you doing here?"

"Thinking. Any law against that?" Luke slid his gun into leather.

"Don't be insolent. It doesn't suit you."

"What does suit me, Sam? Running from the law? Robbing? Being two seconds faster on the draw than the man who wants to step into my shoes? That's all I know. That's who Luke Weston is." Luke turned and walked down to the babbling creek.

Sam followed. "You can change. I told you I'd help."

"Too late for that." Luke pulled a small book from his shirt pocket and flung it at Sam.

"What's this?" He opened it and saw names and amounts listed on each page.

"I've kept track of everyone I stole from. There are *nine* pages." Luke's voice was hard and flat. "Does that look like I can change? That I can ever truly become Luke Legend?"

"Why did you keep this list?" Sam met Luke's flashing, wounded eyes.

"A foolish thought that one day I could return what I took. Crazy, huh?"

"No, it's exactly what a man who has something to live for would do," Sam said softly. "You have family now. A father and brothers. Though you knew that a while back, I'm guessing."

"My mother told me before she died. I had to think about it first."

Sam picked up a small pebble at his feet and skipped it on top of the water until it sank. "I felt a familiar tug when I saw you on the train, a bond of some kind. That's why I was boiling mad at the shack. You kept denying I knew you."

The corners of Luke's mouth quirked up. "I did it to get under your skin. I didn't want to like you."

"I sure didn't want to like you either." But when Luke got shot, Sam discovered how much he cared. They'd shared a common bond—of cheating death.

"Men like me don't get to belong, have families, own land. Have someone to care."

Deep sorrow lined his lost brother's face. An ache squeezed Sam's heart until he could barely breathe. "Your life can be whatever you choose," Sam insisted.

Luke's cold voice lashed the space between them. "You don't know what I've done, the kind of man I become when the darkness inside takes over. The secrets I hide, and the men I've killed—it's too late. I can't fit into your perfect little world, *hermano*. Not now. Not ever."

He spoke a lot of truth. Righting his wrongs wouldn't be easy. It depended on how much he wanted it. Right now, Sam suspected he didn't want it bad enough to fight for.

Sam returned the black book and sat down on the bank. "This was mine and Houston's favorite place in the summers growing up. We'd peel off our clothes and swim until Pa or Mother sent someone for us." He pointed to one of the trees with branches hanging over the water. "We'd tie a rope around one of those branches, swing out, and turn loose."

Luke dropped down beside him. "I had the San Antonio River to play in."

"Bet that was fun."

"It was." Luke's voice hardened. "Until I learned that such things came with a price."

"I'd like to know what happened. If you want to talk."

"Talk and rotgut are cheap," Luke snapped. He picked up a stick, launching it into the lazy current. "Either won't accomplish much of anything except give you a splitting headache."

Curiosity burned. Sam yearned to understand what had happened to make him the outlaw he became. "Why did you turn—?"

"Bad? It's all right if you say it." Luke slid his

infamous Colt from the holster and spun the cylinder. "I am bad to the core, and don't you ever forget it."

The words slammed into Sam with the force of bullets. "Help me understand why."

"I have my reasons." Luke gave a bark of laughter. "Will it change anything if I spill my guts and confess my sins?"

"I just want to know. Let me help you."

"Too late." The breeze caught Luke's angry snarl and sent it swirling.

Sam's ire rose as well. "This ranch, the perfect lives you think we've had…well, let's just say that me and Houston didn't have it easy either."

Memories of missing his mother, confusion at his father's withdrawal, the long, lonely days, crying himself to sleep at night, swept through his mind. The impossibility of reaching the high bar Stoker set.

"Your charmed life was a smokescreen?"

"Yes. Stoker was Lord Almighty tough. He expected us to earn every last thing we got. Nothing was free. And when we failed to measure up—" Sam's voice broke. "Let's just say hell's fire wasn't as hot as Pa's anger."

"You and your brother were lucky to have a father."

"Though I didn't see it at the time, I reckon so," Sam agreed. "When I got bigger, I realized he was tough because he cared. He wanted to turn us into men he could be proud of. Mother was always sickly. After she died, he turned to stone, worked like a man obsessed. I rarely saw him." Sam shot Luke a hard stare. "You might think he wants to do right by you because of his conscience, but you're dead wrong. Pa is thrilled to have another son. He loved your mother. Probably more than he loved mine. Yours was his first love."

Hell, from what Stoker'd said, maybe his *only* love.

A man never forgot the first time he lost his heart. Sam knew that to be a fact. Sierra was his first…and his last. There would never be another for him.

"I wish I could believe you."

With a long sigh, Sam got to his feet. "Wish you could too, Luke. I'll leave you to your thinking."

"I was married once."

Luke's soft words stopped him before he'd taken two steps. "What happened?"

Self-loathing oozed from each word. "She stepped in front of a bullet that was meant for me. Angelina died to save my worthless ass."

Sam laid a hand on his shoulder. "I'm sorry."

"Save it," Luke spat. "Don't deserve sympathy. Like you said, I made my bed. I'm not laying claim to the Legend name. I'll keep my own. I intend to ride out, and you'll never hear from me."

"Luke, I'll stick my neck out until they chop it off for you. But you'll have to stop the robbing."

"I don't think I can." Luke's words were low, as though saying them louder would seal his fate. "I never took any of that for me."

"Hell, I figured that out. Who are you thieving for?"

Silence stretched before Luke said, "Lives are at stake. I can't say more. I won't put them at risk."

A jolt went through Sam. "Luke, you can work and earn the money you need. You don't have to rob. When you make up your mind, let me know. By the way, Stoker wants to talk to you when you get around to it."

Without a look back, Sam mounted up. All the way back to headquarters, he thought of his brother haunted, driven by his demons, wondering where to begin in fixing things.

He, Luke, and Houston were like branches of an oak. Houston's was straight and tall. Sam's was gnarled and twisted. But Luke's had snapped in half. One part wanted to do right and make amends, but the other part wouldn't let him, and neither was connected to any kind of root. A tree needed roots to grow strong.

Sometimes, he felt the same way. Maybe it *was* too late, both for Luke and for him. With turmoil turning him inside out, his thoughts turned to Sierra as they always seemed to.

Keep me or let me go, she had pleaded that morning. Damn, he wished it was that simple. If so, he'd grab her in a heartbeat and try his best to make her the happiest woman alive. But he'd seen the wives who waited for weeks and sometimes months on end for their husbands to come home. Watching, worrying that he lay dead somewhere. Fearing a rider might bring his lifeless body home slung over a horse. Bringing him home to bury.

No, Sam refused to do that to her. His job was dangerous with deadly consequences. No matter which choice he made, someone would lose. He'd rather it be him. He'd sacrifice anything for her happiness.

To ruin her life would be the biggest sin of all.

❧

He walked straight into the eye of a cyclone when he entered the Lone Star headquarters. Angry mothers were shaking their fists and shouting at his father. Houston stood beside Stoker but couldn't get a word in edgewise to restore calm.

Skirting the women's flying fists, Sam made his way to Houston. "What's the problem?"

"Miss Beecher, the schoolteacher, up and took off last night with Margaret Simpson's husband. There's no one to teach school. It'll take months to find a replacement."

Sam grinned. "I have someone ready to step into the job."

"Did you go to magician school while you were gone so long? Who?"

"Sierra. She can start in the morning. You get these mothers to simmer down, and I'll go tell her."

Houston stopped Sam with a hand on his arm. "Did you find Luke?"

"Yep. He was up at the stream where we used to play when we were kids. He'll stay put for now. We've got to talk, Houston."

"I'm pretty busy now. How about after supper?"

Sam nodded and went in search of Sierra. After trying her room, the rest of the house, and finally the workers' cottages, he found her in the mercantile, shopping with Mrs. Ross.

"There you are." He took long strides toward her. "I've been looking all over."

Sierra turned at the sound of his voice as the housekeeper piled yet another dress on top of the ones in her arms. Sierra's blue eyes silently pleaded for help. "Do you need something?"

"Yep. I have a job for you."

Mrs. Ross scowled at him. "Shoo. That can wait a minute. She can't do anything until she's properly clothed."

Relief crossed Sierra's face. She quickly transferred the clothes to Mrs. Ross. "I'm sorry, but I can't do this. I have enough dresses." Beaming, she took Sam's arm, and they walked to the door. "What kind of job?"

"Teaching these pitiful little ranch children reading, writing, and ciphering."

"A schoolteacher! Oh, Sam, I could hug you."

He could hug her too but for a different reason. The heat of her hand on his arm had brought a flame to the dying embers he worked with all his might to smother.

God help him!

Each time she was near, the desire for her grew stronger. He wished someone would tell him how in Sam Hill he'd be able to do the right thing by her.

Not when the wrong thing felt so good.

Twenty-eight

THEY STEPPED TO THE SIDE WHEN THE MERCANTILE door opened, making room for the patrons to get past, then moved out onto the wooden walk. Sierra's hands trembled with excitement. She had a job. Not only a job, but one she knew she'd excel in—teaching school.

Finally, she had the purpose she'd yearned for while she waited. But make no mistake, when Sam found Rocky, she'd go back to Waco. And leave her heart on the Lone Star.

"I'm so happy. Thank you, Sam! If only I could find my brother, my life would just about be perfect." She gave his rugged profile a sidelong glance.

The pain in her heart nearly buckled her knees.

It was time to move on. She didn't need Sam Legend to make her happy. She had a job and a place to live. And soon she'd have her brother back.

From beneath his black Stetson, Sam's gray eyes seemed to peer into her innermost thoughts. "I got sidetracked this morning. But I'll send out telegrams in a few minutes. I'll find Rocky."

"I appreciate anything you can do." She quickly

removed her hand from his arm to sever the contact. "When will I start my job?"

"First thing in the morning. Is that too soon?"

"It's perfect. I'll have to find out how many students I'll have." Sierra noticed a rider galloping down the road from the entrance. Her heart thumped loudly, praying it wasn't trouble. She forced her attention back to Sam. "Have you seen Luke? I'm worried about him."

"Just came from talking to him." Sam's face darkened. "To my surprise and shock, I found out he's mine and Houston's brother. Stoker is his father."

"Sam, that's wonderful. He needs family." Sierra knew firsthand now what it was to have no one.

"We all have a lot of sorting out to do."

"I'm sure learning you have an outlaw brother wasn't what you expected." She couldn't imagine how difficult this would be for Sam, especially given his job. It was sure to cause big problems.

"That's putting it mildly." His gaze also lit on the approaching rider.

The grim set of his mouth sent unease through Sierra. Something was wrong. "Did Luke know you were family before now?"

"That's the part that sticks in my craw. He knew several years ago. Makes me madder than a locoed steer that he kept it secret. Even at that old shack and along the trail home, he never said a word."

"So much makes sense now. The reason he came all the way with us. I guess he needed to see what he'd missed out on. No wonder he's angry."

"No more than I am. He should've told me."

"When? How? That's not something you mention in normal conversation. Luke Legend has a nice ring."

"Don't get used to it. Says he's keeping his own name."

The red-haired rider reined up hard in front of them, kicking up dust. He lifted his hat to her and murmured "Ma'am" before leaning from the saddle. "Sam, you wanted to know if strangers came," he said, out of breath. "Well, they just did."

Sierra's heart pounded as she listened to the cowboy tell about three riders fitting Isaac Ford and his men's descriptions.

Her heart pounded.

The outlaws are still out there.

"They said they were lost and asked directions to Squaw Valley," the cowboy said, "but I could tell they used that as an excuse to get closer. The one with a broken nose took in every detail."

John—him, she remembered.

"That all they said?" Sam's eyes narrowed to slits as he stared to the south.

"Yep. Then I sent them on their way."

"Thanks, Grady. Be sure to keep guards at the crossbar. We haven't seen the last of them."

"Sure thing, boss." Grady tipped his hat to Sierra and hurried to get more men.

"Why won't they go away?" Sierra whispered.

"Men like them don't give up." His voice was as hard as granite.

"What are we going to do?"

A layer of ice frosted Sam's gray eyes. "Wait for them to return—then I'm going to arrest them...or shoot them. Don't worry. Our men will keep them away from you."

She hoped he was right. But she remembered the old trappers in the mountains speaking of the cunning of cougars. Ambush predators, the men called them. They would lie in wait and spring when they least expected them.

Ford and his gang were ambush predators, stalking their prey, waiting to pounce. And when she and the others let down their guard, they'd grab her.

All for some map that didn't exist. Why did they keep coming? And what had they done to Rocky?

If they wanted her, they'd find a way.

Only there was no if. They *did* want her, and that brought cold sweat trickling down her spine.

The next time, she might not survive.

Twenty-nine

SIERRA PUSHED ASIDE HER FEAR AND PASTED ON A SMILE for Hector, who came from Carlos's house. The minute he spied her with Sam outside the mercantile, he ran as fast as his legs would carry him. "Señorita Sierra!"

She put aside her worry, forcing a smile. "*Hola*, Hector. I have good news. You're going to school."

The boy threw his arms around her waist, staring in confusion.

Sam patted his head. "*La escuela.*"

A grin spread across his face. "Hap-py," he said with eyes shining.

"Very good, Hector," she praised, then swung to Sam. "I'd better see what I can learn from the mothers about the size of my class. I want to be prepared."

Sam laughed. "Then you'd best find a good switch. Some of these kids are little heathens. I know me and Houston were."

It was good to hear Sam laugh. "I'm relieved to know that you're too old for my class."

Good heavens, if he were, she'd have trouble remembering the alphabet or how to do sums. He made thinking impossible. Except how much she wanted to be in his arms.

Stop that, she scolded herself.

Pushing away the hurt, Sierra told Sam good-bye and set off with Hector in tow, wishing she knew how to speak the boy's language. He was slowly learning some English, as evidenced by the word happy, but was nowhere close to understanding enough. How could she teach him the things he needed to know? This was going to be a challenge.

She found some mothers shopping in the mercantile and learned that she'd have fifteen students, not counting Hector and the other Spanish children. The women also told her they ranged in age from thirteen to six.

Her stomach whirled as a million doubts set in. What if she couldn't handle that many? What if she couldn't measure up? Everyone's expectations were so high.

"Thank you," she told them. "You've been most helpful."

One of the mothers, Mrs. Smith, she thought, called, "You'll do fine. The children know what's waiting for them at home if they misbehave."

Waving to the prune-faced woman, Sierra turned her attention to finding Luke. She needed an interpreter.

Failing that, some quick Spanish lessons.

Full of purpose, she marched to the dwelling where she thought she'd seen Sam come from. As she approached, Luke rode up.

"To what do I owe this pleasure?" Luke swung easily from the saddle. Her gaze went to the heavy Colt riding low on his hip, reminding her of his dangerous occupation.

"I have a job as the new schoolteacher and a request of you." She noted his somber face. He didn't appear any happier than Sam. When he didn't reply, she hurried on, "Will you talk to the immigrant families? I want to teach their children also."

"I'll speak to them." He ruffled Hector's hair. "You're doing a good thing, Miss Sierra."

When he turned to go inside, she touched his arm. "Luke, will you teach me some Spanish phrases so I can communicate with the children?"

He tugged his hat lower on his forehead, so low it totally hid his eyes. Though when he spoke, his voice was gentle as always. "You can't learn a whole language in one sitting. Why don't you ask Sam?" He shifted his weight. "The thing is…I may not be here long. Best if I move on."

Hot tears lurked behind her eyes. It seemed to her that he'd be glad to have someone to belong to, a family. Instead, it had made him sullen and troubled. He hadn't even called her *dulce*.

She wanted to ask where he was going, but pain in his eyes stopped her. "Sam told me you're his brother."

"Appears that way. That's the reason I'm leaving."

"I don't understand. He wants to help you."

"Long as I stay here, I'm only going to be trouble for him and the others. I see that." Luke gazed toward headquarters. "I got myself into this mess. It's up to me to get out of it. I won't cost Sam his job."

Hector tugged on her hand, trying to pull her away.

Sierra barely felt the boy. All she could feel was the big lump in her throat. "Please don't leave without saying good-bye. I consider you a friend."

"And I you." He turned and walked into the simple but sturdy dwelling.

Hector pulled on her hand. "Go."

The new English word brought a smile in spite of everything. Sierra put thoughts of Luke out of her mind. "Where do you want to go, Hector?"

Unable to grasp that much English, he gave her a mute stare.

"No worries." She aimed him toward the cool, inviting porch at the house they called headquarters. Today she would begin his English lessons.

Seating him in a chair in the cool shade, she hurried inside and gathered up simple things like a book, pencil, apple, and whatever else she could find. Joining Hector, she held up each item and said the word for it. She repeated them until he could tell her without any prompting.

"That's very good, Hector." She hugged him. "Come."

They went down the steps, and she touched the grass, saying the word. Then went to the tree, the flagpole, and finally pointed up at the huge bronze star hanging between the two poles. "Star."

The long shadows told her hours had passed. She'd been so intent on the lessons, she hadn't realized daylight was fading fast. Hector scampered off to play.

A cough came from behind. She whirled to find Sam standing on the porch.

The waning sunlight touched his hair and softened the lines in his face. "Sierra, I sent some telegrams out. We'll see what comes back."

"Thank you." She noticed his sorrow. "What's wrong?"

"I had a telegram from Fort Worth. The wife of my friend, a former Texas Ranger, died very suddenly."

"I'm so sorry." Sierra touched his arm, wishing she could do more to comfort.

"I promised Pete Walker as he died in my arms that I'd take care of Amy. At least she didn't leave any children." Sam brushed his eyes as though to wipe away memories. "She didn't have anything other than a few personal effects, and the rangers laid her to rest next to Pete." He slammed his hand against the porch railing. "I should've done more to keep my promise."

"I'm sure you did your best," Sierra said. As though he wasn't shaken enough finding out Luke was his brother, now Amy Walker's death had brought even more guilt.

"If you're bothered that you have to put off finding Rocky, please don't give it a thought. I understand. Do what you need to do." She just prayed Rocky could last until help arrived.

"This won't affect my commitment to you, but thanks for understanding." Sam turned and dropped heavily into a chair on the porch.

The violence of Sam's profession slammed into her. He was right. She saw what devastation law work brought. Lawmen died, leaving wives without husbands, children without fathers. And sometimes the kids were left orphaned.

Her gaze swept over the man who held her heart. He lifted a guitar lying beside the chair and began to lightly strum. Music must soothe him.

Dear God, if only she had something to soothe the jagged hurt inside her.

Thirty

As music swirled around her, Sierra's thoughts returned to the night she'd danced with such reckless abandon. The night Sam had tried to warn her of the danger of falling for him.

Her skin tingled with the sudden memory of his lips on hers, on her bare skin, her breasts.

She watched his long fingers gently plucking the guitar strings. Those fingers, his hands, had skimmed over her body so capably, arousing such hunger and desire. But it was the depth of his heart that had sealed her fate. She'd seen how much he cared for his family and Luke, even though Luke was an outlaw. How torn he was over performing his job and duty to family.

The only one he didn't seem to care about was himself.

Sam had selflessly given everything to others and kept nothing for himself, no reserve to fall back on. When those men had placed that rope around his throat, they'd left deep, scarred ruts in his soul. She could help heal him. He needed her, but he kept pushing her away.

No use to keep trying. His mind was set.

But so was hers. She lifted her chin.

Sam's gaze met hers, and his sorrowful smile showed a row of white teeth.

Though she could tell her body what to do and make decisions about where to go, her heart was a different story.

Her heart refused to listen.

Sierra suddenly turned and went inside. She had to move out of the headquarters. To put distance between them.

With Hector eating with Carlos and Sofia, she could talk uninterrupted. Following supper—from which Luke was absent—she caught Sam's attention. "May I have a word?"

He turned to Houston. "Give me a minute."

"I'm sorry," she said as Sam pulled out her chair. "I don't mean to take you from your brother. It's just that this is important. It won't take long."

Across the hall, Sam pointed to a small room that had a sofa and some chairs. "We can talk in here. Have a seat."

Instead, she stood, facing him. "I'm moving out."

He was silent for a long moment. Finally he spoke. "And go where? I can't let you leave the safety of the ranch."

"If one's available, for now I'll move to a small house similar to the immigrants'. My needs are simple."

Sam studied her. "If you're unhappy with your room, we can move you to another."

Sierra fidgeted under his gray stare. "It's not that."

"Then I don't understand."

How could she tell him he was too close and reminded her of everything she needed to forget? How did one go about telling a man she loved that living under the same roof was ripping her heart out?

"It's not the house or the room. I have to start making my own life, Sam." She drew on the strength inside to make him see and not hurt him more. "We've been over this. I'm leaving the ranch as soon as I safely can. Hopefully, I'll have Rocky, but if not, if he's dead, I intend to return to Waco alone."

He strode to the window and looked out into the night.

"It's best this way," she continued. "My mind is made up."

With his stiff back to her, he said, "I'll see what I can find."

His cold tone pierced her. She swallowed hard. "Thank you. It's nothing personal, Sam."

He turned and slowly moved to stand in front of her. "Isn't it? At least be honest. You don't want to be near me."

Sierra squared her shoulders and met his hard gray stare. His eyes burned with such intensity that she took a step back. She had hoped to avoid saying it, but he was going to force her.

"You're right. It's too painful for me here." She lowered her voice to a mere whisper. "I offered you my heart, the sole tally of everything I own. Only you gave it back. It wasn't enough. *I* was never enough for you. I'm walking away, Sam." While she still could. Make a clean break before they grew to hate each other.

He flinched as though she'd struck him. Before he could answer, she turned and fled through the door and out into the night. She ran past Houston and down the steps of the porch.

He called after her, "What's wrong, Sierra? What has that brother of mine done now?"

With a sob, she sought solace in the darkness behind the mercantile. She yearned to saddle a horse and ride out, far away from the Lone Star Ranch and the man who didn't want her. Isaac Ford and his men were all that stopped her. They lurked out there, waiting for her to leave the safety of the ranch, but she wouldn't risk capture again.

Despite everything, she was still a coward.

She was still the daughter William Hunt didn't want. And now she was the woman Sam couldn't love.

❧

Silence deafened Sam as he stared at the open doorway Sierra had run through.

The agony of her angry words echoed in the room. He released a string of cuss words, calling himself every name he could think of. Disgust rippled through him. She'd asked for nothing except for him to love her. Why couldn't he tell her he did, ever since they'd kissed at the shack after the rainstorm?

But she was wrong on two counts.

He hadn't given her heart back. He kept that in a very safe place.

As for saying she wasn't enough for him… Good God, she was everything he wanted and needed. If either of them could—should—change, it was he.

Sam moved to go after her, but stopped. She wasn't of a mind to listen to him now in the state she was in, even if he could find the words to say and get them out in time.

Better wait. Meanwhile, he'd give her what she wanted. He'd give her space. The house the former schoolteacher had occupied was available.

Even as he told himself he needed her close to keep her safe, he recognized the lie.

Already his heart rebelled against not having her down the hall.

Already the house felt cold and empty.

Already he'd lost the most precious thing he had.

With a sigh, he set down the glass before he threw it against the wall, and went to find Houston.

Maybe the night air would cool him.

His big brother turned at the sound of the door. "What's wrong? Miss Sierra flew out like the devil was chasing her."

That description fit all too well. Sam took a chair and propped his leg on a nearby stool. "Wants to move out." The words soured in his stomach worse than a big glass of buttermilk.

"Why? Is something wrong with her room?"

"Nope. Me."

Houston chuckled. "Seems the lady shows uncommon good sense. Tell me why you wanted this powwow."

"It's Luke." Sam put Sierra aside in his mind and shared what he'd learned—about Luke's account book listing all his robberies, about their brother's dead wife, and his refusal—again—to claim the Legend name. "He wants to change, Houston."

"Kinda sounds that way. The list proves it."

Sam shoved his fingers through his hair. "If he was to pay everything back, he might get free of those robberies. The murder charge though…will take more doing. We'd have to find the person who really killed the judge."

"On the robberies, how much money do you estimate he took?" Houston shoved away from the porch rail.

"Less than five hundred dollars. Something else was odd. In each robbery, the dates were exactly four months apart—starting three years ago."

Houston took a seat next to Sam. "He's committing them for a very specific reason."

"When I asked him why he'd turned to crime, he told me he has his reasons, and he didn't want to talk about it."

"I know Pa will give him the money to make restitution."

"I'm sure Pa would. But if Luke won't take our name, he damn sure won't take the money. On the other hand…he might if he worked for it."

"Hey, you might have something there. I'll put his butt to work. Be happy to."

Sam scowled. "You're a tad too eager. Wanting to test our new brother?"

"Damn right. I want to know what he's made of."

"I can tell you right now, Luke is one of the toughest men I've ever seen. He can take anything you throw at him and then some. When we were running, two steps ahead of Isaac Ford, I was proud to have him by my side. The man doesn't quit. Not ever, not even with a bullet in his shoulder." Sam was silent, then added low, "I owe him, Houston."

"Sure sounds like he has Stoker's blood in him."

They had a clear view of Luke's small house from the porch, and Sam saw the door swing open. Sam leaned forward as their father strolled out with his arm around Luke's shoulders. Though Luke had a commanding height, he was still shorter than Stoker.

It surprised Sam that his father hadn't taken a bottle after supper and gone upstairs, as was his custom. Instead, he'd sought the company of his oldest son. Luke didn't look all that happy.

Houston murmured, "It appears they had that talk."

"Yep." Sam softly plucked the guitar strings.

"Probably giving Luke my job," Houston said sourly.

"Settle down. It's reasonable for a father to want to know his son. Luke made himself ample clear. He spurns the ranch and us."

"Probably too damn civilized for him."

Sam muttered oaths to himself. Houston was determined to find fault, no matter what. Thinking he wasn't at the top of the totem pole any longer seemed to have gotten under Houston's skin. For almost thirty years, he'd known his place in the family. Now everything had turned upside down and crossways, starting with not being the oldest anymore, undercut by three months.

Houston's words—that Stoker simply tolerated him—again drifted across Sam's mind. How long had Houston felt second to him? Now his brother saw himself slipping another notch to third. "Stop it, Houston. Listen to yourself. No one's trying to take your place. Not me, and damn sure not Luke. You're Pa's right-hand man. He depends on you. You and he have the deepest bond of all."

"I guess."

"He's turned over the Lone Star to you to run. He's not blind. He knows how capable you are. He trusts you."

"All that can change in a heartbeat."

"Damn, Houston, I feel like I'm talking to a boy in knee pants. Nothing's going to change. You're the only one who knows everything about this ranch. You know stuff Pa doesn't, because you're out there every single day."

"True."

"And you keep him from gambling away more of the land."

They watched Luke go back inside, and their father stride toward them. As always, Sam was struck by the sheer power of the man. Anyone who thought it easy to whip him had better think again. The sudden memory of Stoker Legend once fighting a mountain lion to protect him swam across his mind. Caught without a weapon, his Pa used his bare hands to rip open the beast's throat. The incident left quite an impression on a nine-year-old boy. Though he'd seen his fiftieth birthday, he hadn't lost a bit of muscle or mental toughness.

"Nice night." Stoker strode up the steps and sat down next to Houston. He didn't appear to have taken one drink of liquor. "Your mother always loved sitting out here after supper."

"I remember," Houston said. "She'd sit out here for hours, doing nothing but looking out over the land."

Stoker nodded. "The air feels good. Nothing like it to clear your head."

"Did you get things settled with Luke?" Sam asked.

"Broke the ice is all. I didn't think anyone could be more stubborn than you are, Sam. Luke is hell-bent not to take anything from me. Refuses to even stay over here in the house."

"Give him some time. He'll come around. This is new for all of us." Sam lightly strummed his guitar.

Stoker sighed. "He feels like an outsider."

"I'm sure," Houston said. "The three of us have a history with each other. Luke has nothing, not even one memory to help him relate to us. Sam's right. Give him some space."

"That's just it. He wants to leave. I told him I wouldn't hold him here. That I'd help him if he'll stay." Stoker fixed Sam with a warning stare. "You arrest him, and you'll go over me. I know he broke the law, I know he's a wanted man with a price on his head, and I know all about your job. But you're on Lone Star land, son. I'm in charge here."

Hell, Sam thought, *isn't that the way it has always been?*

Sam bit back rising anger. "We're on the same side, Pa."

"On this land, you're all equal." Stoker rose. "Luke carries deep scars. Some are what I unwittingly put there. Thinking his father didn't want him, wouldn't claim him, dammed up something inside Luke. It'll take time and patience to heal."

"That it will," Houston agreed, then told him what Sam had learned during his talk with Luke.

Some of the worry left Stoker's face. "Get me that

list, and I'll pay back every cent to those people. That's easy to fix."

"It doesn't smooth over the murder charge, Pa," Sam reminded him. "And what good will paying back this money do if Luke keeps right on robbing? I told him that if I stick my neck out, he has to stop. He doesn't know if he can."

"Hell, this is a fine mess. I'll need to have another talk with him. Good night, boys."

After their pa went inside, Sam sat in silence, listening to the distant bawling of a calf probably looking for his mother, and the clank of the heavy chains securing the huge bronze star. A glance at the star revealed moonlight shining through the cutouts in each point. The shadow on the ground was eerily beautiful.

Sam thought of the legend of the ranch he'd always heard. *The man who sleeps under the star will learn his true worth.* Somehow, he'd always thought it meant sleeping on the ranch. But maybe it wasn't that at all.

"Houston, have you ever slept under that star?"

"Nope. Why in the hell would I want to?"

"The legend."

Houston laughed. "Someone made that up to tell around the campfire. We sleep under the Lone Star every night."

"What if it's talking about under the hanging star?"

"Go ahead, but I'm sleeping in a bed."

"Maybe I will before I ride out."

"It'll probably fall on you." Houston chuckled, then sobered. "Sam, you already know you're the best lawman in the state. Don't let Pa mess with your head."

"It's always a battle when I come home. I wanted

this time to be different. I thought he might have mellowed a tad."

"Nope. Hell hasn't quite frozen over yet."

Sam laid down his guitar. "We've got trouble of another sort to discuss."

He told Houston about Ford and his men riding up to the crossbar. "They're biding their time. Sooner or later, they'll find a way in. They're like a bunch of rats, always gnawing, searching for the smallest opening. Sierra is terrified. I hurt her real bad, Houston. I'm afraid she's going to saddle up and ride out some night after we all go to bed."

"Damn! She might. And if she does, I know your shirttail won't hit your backside before you go after her."

"You know me well, brother."

"Because we're two of a kind, and that's what I'd do. She means a lot to you."

"More than anyone knows, even her."

"Then you'd better do something fast," Houston warned.

Sierra was wrong. She was more than enough for him. Even if he could never become settled enough for her or as much as he knew he should, he didn't have it in him to let her go.

He couldn't.

Thirty-one

SAM STOOD AT HIS BEDROOM WINDOW, WATCHING DAWN break the following morning. The Texas flag fluttering proudly in the air was a welcome sight and, though not enough, brought a bit of peace to his ragged soul.

He hadn't slept a wink. Too much thinking to do. He'd gone looking for Sierra last night after everyone turned in and had found her at the corral, watching the horses. He'd stood in the shadows a good bit. After a while, he'd finally approached and quietly suggested she return to the house. She'd jerked away from his touch and silently did as he asked.

And then he'd discovered that Luke was gone. Sam had waited in the darkness and seen his brother ride in again about three a.m.

Now in the early morning, his attention caught on another sight that brought an ache to his chest. Pink light from the rosy dawn brushed Sierra's face as she slipped from the house for her first day teaching school. It was awfully early. She was either anxious to get a look at the small school…or else trying to avoid Sam. He'd bet on the latter.

The blue dress she wore was another new one. The bodice hugged those curves he'd run his hands over more than once. How he longed to do it again. With passion knotting inside him, arousing unbridled hunger, he leaned forward to get a better view.

God, how he wanted her!

Just one night. One night in her arms was all he asked. Then maybe he could finally get her out of his blood. He could set her free to find the kind of man she really needed.

Damn! He cursed the memories that refused to let him rest.

He could tell by her jaunty step she was happier than she'd been last night. He'd bet anything that she was humming. Satisfaction washed over him that he could give her what she wanted—a job. At least he could do this much.

He felt her need to have a purpose. Everyone needed one. Even him.

And he listed several. Find Rocky, talk to Luke, and get rid of Isaac Ford and his bunch.

A tall order. He'd take some men and scout around to see if Ford was still lurking about.

He'd ask about the schoolteacher's house over breakfast and kill two birds with one stone.

"That'll make her happy," he grumbled, buckling his gun belt.

Once she took her things from headquarters, he'd probably see very little of her. His heart throbbed painfully.

Best get the day started. Picking up his hat, Sam went downstairs.

But already he looked forward to school letting out.

After finding out the little house Sierra wanted was available for occupancy, Sam sat on the porch with his third cup of coffee, watching the sun finally edge above the horizon. He stood, intending to saddle Trooper for a ride over the land, when he spied the man who minded the telegraph hurrying toward him.

Jim Wheeler reminded him of a little bantam rooster. The short man stared at the ground and walked on tiptoes as though he wore women's high-heeled shoes. Looking for a soft landing spot in case he fell face-first, Sam supposed. Wheeler's fingers on the telegraph reminded him of a rooster pecking, always pecking.

"Mr. Sam, I have news," Wheeler said, out of breath, falling into a nearby chair.

"I could sure use some. What do you have?"

"Captain O'Reilly sent this." Wheeler handed Sam a piece of paper.

MAN MATCHING DESCRIPTION OF ROCKY HUNT SEEN IN FORT WORTH STOP CONTACT SHERIFF HOLMAN

Sam glanced up. "Telegraph Sheriff Holman in Fort Worth. Tell him I need details of the sighting of Rocky Hunt. Wheeler, I'm obliged for your help. You have my thanks."

"You're welcome, sir. Glad to be doing something. With you at home now, my days are endlessly boring. Oh, I also got this second one."

Sam reached for the paper and saw it was from a U.S. Marshal in San Antonio.

FLATBUSH STORE PROPRIETOR REPORTED LUKE
WESTON IN YOUR COMPANY STOP DID YOU
ARREST HIM QUERY

Guilt perched on Sam's shoulder. Hell! Was everything going to come crashing down before he ever started clearing his brother?

Jim Wheeler cleared his throat, the sound reminding Sam he was waiting.

Wadding up the telegram, Sam said, "As far as anyone knows, you didn't get this."

The man didn't blink an eye. "Understood. Do you need anything else, Mr. Sam?"

"That'll be all."

With a curt nod, Jim Wheeler tiptoed down the steps and rushed on raised heels toward his small cubbyhole.

Sam jammed his hat onto his head. His second morning at the ranch, and a tidal wave had washed his feet from under him.

Mired in the quandary, Sam glanced up to see Luke sauntering onto the porch.

"Ranger, I'm leaving."

The bold declaration and the fact that the outlaw didn't use Sam's name poked him like a sharp stick. "I'm your brother, not Ranger. When are you thinking of hitting the trail?"

"Today. It's best. Just wanted to give you fair warning."

"I'm aware of the agreement Stoker made with you, but once you leave this ranch, all bets are off. You have a price on your head. Stoker can't protect you."

"I don't need his…protection. I have somewhere I need to be." Luke's piercing eyes held sadness.

"Don't we all?"

"I feel your bite of frustration, and I'm sorry I caused it. Thank you for trying to help me. Wish I could say I'm worth it." Luke pushed back from the porch railing. "I'm glad we're brothers, even though we're on opposite sides of the law. You have a good thing here, Sam. Don't take it for granted."

"This could be yours also," Sam reminded him softly.

"It's half past too late. I can't turn back time."

A rider sped from around the house and reined up. Sam recognized Grady, one of the ranch hands, and stood as he dismounted. Alarm skittered along Sam's nerve endings.

"Boss sent me. Said he needs you to check some cut fences in the south corner of the west pasture, and he and Houston are tied up." Grady mopped his forehead with a neckerchief.

So much for his plans. Sam turned to Luke. "Want to take a ride out there with me?"

"I'll saddle the horses." Luke turned toward the corral without giving Sam time to reply.

Sam thanked Grady and sent him back to report to Stoker. Adjusting his hat, he met up with Luke at the corral and finished saddling the horses.

They set out at a gallop. Even Sam knew the haste a cut fence called for.

By the time they reached the remote section, the sun was high. As they rode up, Sam spotted the cut fence and nearby the carcass of a cow. The hide was black with flies. Sam and Luke dismounted and stood over the animal.

Luke hunkered down on his heels to get a better look. "Someone shot it."

With a grunt, Sam said, "This is a good spot to kill one."

He scanned the ground for signs. Hoofprints indicated several horses. He put the number at three or four, though it was hard to be sure with the packed earth.

An odd arrangement of rocks caught his eye. He strode over to see. The stones crudely spelled something out. He turned his head sideways and squinted. The breath caught in his throat.

I'm coming.

"Luke, come over here a minute."

"What did you find?"

"A message."

Luke's boots crunched on the rocky ground. "What the hell?"

"Both the location and the threat have Isaac Ford's name written all over this." The rat had found his way onto the Lone Star.

The sunlight caught on something metallic. Sam walked over to see what it was and found a concha like the ones that went down each leg of Luke's black trousers—the ones he still wore. A muscle worked in Sam's jaw. He picked up the concha and flicked it to Weston.

Luke caught it and glared. "I didn't do this. I noticed one missing after we joined the caravan. Maybe Ford found it."

"Maybe." Sam's eyes narrowed. "But I know you went somewhere last night."

"I did, but not here. What reason would I have to

kill this animal? My mother scrubbed her fingers to the bone and died from overwork. Still, she never said one harsh word about Stoker Legend. I wouldn't sully her memory by doing this. If I wanted to destroy the great Legend Empire, I would go for the jugular, attack the money source, not kill one cow. Keep attacking until I'd bled your family dry, then take all you have." Luke whirled and stalked to his horse.

Sam watched him ride off as Houston rode up. Luke didn't return the hello.

"What's wrong with him?" Houston asked, dismounting.

He was quiet as Sam told him. Finally, he spoke. "He didn't do this, Sam. Everything he said is true. Losing one cow isn't going to break us."

"I know." Sam's heart ached as he stared at Luke's back getting smaller and smaller.

"The buzzards will eat well for a few days. Some of the boys are bringing wire to mend the fence. Let's see what else these varmints might've left behind." Houston stuck a foot in the stirrup.

"Reckon so." Sam gave a shrill whistle, and Trooper came running around a mesquite tree.

Over the next two hours, they tracked the thieves, finding a small cave where they'd spent the night. They'd cooked the beef over a fire and left the remains. Sam still had nothing to go on. He didn't have proof it was Ford, but his gut told him it was.

His gut was always right.

Sam pulled out the telegram from the U.S. Marshal and showed it to Houston.

"What are you going to do?"

"For now, nothing." But if the marshal followed up with a visit…

"I think we're about to get our tails in a crack."

That Houston had said "we" instead of "you" brought a lump to Sam's throat. His brother wouldn't let him bear the brunt alone.

Even if their tails were to land behind bars, Sam wouldn't go back on his word.

∽⌀

Satisfaction filled Sierra as she closed the door of the small schoolhouse. Teaching the children had given her a degree of self-worth and contentment she'd never felt.

When she turned, she jumped at Sam standing there. "You startled me."

"Didn't mean to. Can we talk?"

She glanced down at Hector, who'd become her shadow, with his hand never far from her dress. Even now he clutched a handful of material as though she'd disappear if he let go. "Is it important?"

The low brim of Sam's black Stetson shielded his eyes, but she knew they would be as somber as his voice. "There have been developments."

A frisson of fear danced up her spine. Her first thought was of Rocky. Had they found him? And if so, was he alive or dead? A lump formed in her throat, blocking her ability to swallow.

"Let me take Hector to Carlos."

"He'll probably be working. But I'm sure some-one will keep him for a bit." Sam gave her a crooked smile that vanished the minute it formed, leaving her to wonder if it had been there at all. "I'll wait for you at headquarters."

After finding out Sam had been right about Carlos, she left Hector with Maria.

Sierra's legs trembled so badly she could barely walk as she rushed to the big house. She stumbled up the wide steps. "Please tell me you found Rocky."

"The sheriff in Fort Worth saw him. I wired him back for more information."

Hope surged. "This is good. Isn't it?"

"It's a start. Hopefully, we'll know more soon."

Sierra listened as he related finding the butchered cow and the stone message. She inhaled sharply. "Ford."

"Looks like it. Also, I found a silver concha there with it, like the ones on Luke's trousers. Someone made a pitiful attempt to frame him."

"Why?"

"Who knows? Maybe they banked that it would put us at odds. Probably figured we'd start fighting amongst ourselves and let down our guard."

"He needs a friend, Sam. I think it's been a long while since he had one."

"Gunslingers and outlaws don't have friends," Sam said quietly.

Thinking of all Luke had missed out on made Sierra's heart ache. "You'll let me know the minute you hear more about Rocky?"

Sam dropped a hand to his side, brushing her fingers. A tingling jolt ran up her arm.

"You know I will." His voice was husky. He cleared his throat. "I have other news. Everything is arranged for you to move into the former schoolteacher's house."

"That's wonderful!" In her excitement, she threw her arms around him. It was only when his tightened around her, and she smelled the wild scent of Texas that clung to him, that she remembered their heated words and stepped back. "I'm sorry. I'm always doing that."

"You don't hear me complaining. Gather your things, and I'll help you move."

When she turned to go for them, she heard him speak under his breath. "You're enough. Always have been enough."

Her heart constricted, but she kept her eyes ahead and pretended not to hear. He couldn't mean it, no matter how much she wished he did.

Thirty-two

SAM GLANCED AT SIERRA'S PITIFUL BELONGINGS FIFTEEN minutes later. They were all she'd accumulated since arriving. One trip would do it.

He picked up a burlap bag she'd hastily stuffed full. "Let's get you moved so you can settle in while it's still daylight. It'll be dark before you know it. I hope you'll continue to take supper with us. You'll make Pa happy. I think he fancies you the daughter he never had."

With a nod, she moved onto the porch.

They covered the ground between headquarters and the schoolteacher's house in silence. She gave a soft gasp when she noticed the pretty flowers along the front. He held the door and followed her inside.

Though only one room with a small loft above, the house was surprisingly cheery. A colorful quilt on the bed and rugs scattered around gave it a homey atmosphere.

A closer look at the quilt brought a grin. In each square, the quilters had stitched short Bible verses that called for chastity, purity, remaining virtuous, and others. But a larger square in the center bore the Ten Commandments.

The women had wasted their efforts on the former schoolteacher, who had absconded with Margaret Simpson's husband.

He set down the burlap bag, watching her. Beaming, Sierra clasped her hands to her chest as though someone had bestowed a great treasure.

"This suits you," he said. "I think you'll be happy here."

Sierra turned. "Sam, you don't know what this means."

"It's just a house. A very small one," he pointed out.

"No, it's just the right size. The room you gave me at headquarters was too overwhelming. I got lost in it. Don't get me wrong, it was breathtaking. Probably the most beautiful room I'll ever see. But it intimidated me. I was afraid I'd do something wrong, mess something up, or break some valuable decoration. I like this one. This is me. Comfortable. Neat."

Sam allowed a flicker of a smile. "I understand now. Headquarters will be empty without you. I took comfort in having you within reach down the hall."

"You'll ride out before long, off to find another hill to climb, another road to go down, another outlaw to chase."

Though Sierra's reminder was soft, the words pricked him. He shifted uneasily. "Probably right."

With a sad smile, she turned away and removed some items from the burlap bag.

"I need you to know, Sierra—you're enough. For me. For any man. The problem isn't you at all. I'm the one lacking, and I curse my inability to give you what you need. If I could change, I would, and in a heartbeat. Because you're everything I want."

Sierra laid down the hand mirror she'd gotten from the mercantile and came to him. She placed a gentle hand on his jaw. "You and I are two lost souls, Sam. Maybe this is all we'll ever have. A few stolen moments will have to carry us through the dark nights when our heartbeat is so loud it's the only sound we can hear."

"I'm no stranger to those nights," he said in a hushed voice. Only just the midnight hours didn't cover it. Right now his heartbeat resembled a war drum in his ears.

She dragged her fingertips along the scar circling his throat. "You've suffered so much."

"No more than you, pretty lady." He wanted to kiss her so badly it burned. When he looked in her eyes, he saw permission there—a longing that matched his own. "One more stolen moment," he murmured. Sam lowered his head and slanted a soft kiss across her moist lips. His arms tightened around her. When she didn't pull back, he deepened the kiss, inhaling her sweet fragrance, the scent that reminded him of the flowers outside the house.

One kiss to tuck away to remember later when he lay alone beneath the stars on a cold night.

Each time she was near, he couldn't keep his hands or his lips off her. The intense hunger for more left his knees weak. If the world stopped revolving, spinning slowly down to die, he'd wrap his arms around her and spend the ending minutes with her—the two of them lost in a glorious, dizzying whirl, holding her tight.

Yesterday was gone. Tomorrow they couldn't count on. All they really had was the here and now.

"Sam, I can't fight this thing between us anymore. It's too strong," she murmured against his mouth.

"I'm tired of fighting too. You're all I think about. Your face is all I see. This pull is stronger than both of us. But I have to be honest. I can't see beyond tonight. I don't know what the future holds."

Sierra leaned back and met his eyes. "I've always played this game I call If Tomorrow Never Comes. I won't lose this moment in time. I have to grab what I can, because this may be it. Make love to me, Sam. I want to know how it feels. At least we'll have this if the world ends before dawn."

He stilled, wondering if she truly meant what she said. As if in answer, she quickly undid his shirt. Pushing the fabric aside, she rested her palms on his broad chest. The heat of her touch seared like a brand. He'd just grown accustomed to the sensation when she slid her arms under the shirt, encircling him.

Shrugging out of his shirt, he unbuttoned her dress, praying she wouldn't have a change of heart before he released the last pearly disc in the very long line.

Why did women have so many darn buttons anyway? And why so small? His large fingers had a devil of a time slipping them through the holes. For two cents he'd give up and rip the darn things free. But he didn't. He took another stab. Finally, he was able to draw her arms from the sleeves, letting the dress puddle around his boots.

A single row of lace around the neck of the chemise, tied with a rose-colored ribbon, did nothing to hide the swell of Sierra's enticing bosom. A flick of his wrist untied the ribbon, and the fine cotton fabric fell open. His breath hitched at all that bared velvety skin.

With a hand under her jaw, he hungrily covered her lips, while his other released her hair from the knot at the nape of her neck. The dark strands spilled over his hand in a silky waterfall.

If he couldn't have this woman now, he'd die.

Sweeping her against his naked chest, he carried her to the bed and sat her down on the quilt. Kneeling, he drew each stocking slowly down her shapely legs.

Tossing them aside, he raised her small toes to his mouth and kissed each one. He loved everything about this woman who stole his breath.

Finally, he stood. Kissing the nape of her neck, he removed her chemise and laid her back on the bed. Her beautiful dark hair spread in wild abandon around her.

Quickly disposing of his gun belt and boots, he shed his trousers and propped himself on his elbow beside her. "Are you sure about this, Sierra?"

Tears sparkled in her blue eyes as she placed her small palm on the side of his face. "I've never been surer of anything."

"I've wanted to make love to you from the moment we met on the train. You're so beautiful and kind, and you make me crazy with want. This hunger for you has taken over, and I don't have the power to squelch it."

He nibbled her mouth and ran his tongue along the seam, then captured her lips in a soul-shattering kiss. It had to have totally and fully swept all doubts from her mind about Sam finding her enough.

If she was any more, he wouldn't be able to stand it.

With the gentlest touch, he outlined the curves of her body with his hands before returning to her soft, pliable breasts. He loved the weight, the feel, the sight of them.

He kissed each one and watched them seem to yearn for more. Despite the fact that women were mysterious creatures, they fascinated him. Take, for instance, Sierra's response to the slightest caress. Her spirit held a bit of the wanton—a hint of the wildness of the mountains that he loved.

She gasped when his mouth closed around her nipple and he began to gently tug on it. A moan slipped from her as she sank her hands into his hair.

"I need you, Sam. Get rid of this achy feeling inside me. I can't bear it."

Sam lifted his head and laid a palm on the dark curls that guarded the juncture of her thighs. He slipped his fingers inside and stroked as Sierra arched her back, pressing herself harder against his hand.

Each stroke brought her higher and higher to the top of the wave.

At last she gave a cry and, as shudders ran through her body, he took a swollen, hard nub of her breast into his mouth.

She lay spent, her body covered with a thin sheen of perspiration. Sam snuggled beside her, drawing her into the hollows of his long form. He took her hand and kissed each fingertip while she caught her breath.

"Sam, I've never known anything like that." Sierra turned to face him. "I rode cresting waves of pure pleasure."

"I'm happy I could introduce you to that part of yourself, darlin'." He grinned. "There are other delights to come."

"I don't think I can beat that."

"You will," he murmured. He had lots more to teach her. After a few minutes' rest, he slowly mounted another sweet assault on her beautiful body, beginning with the soft curve of her ear. He left a trail of kisses from there to her cheek before settling on her mouth.

The eagerness with which she welcomed his kiss stoked the fire inside him. She laid her hand on his jaw. Without breaking the kiss, he rolled on top of her. A surprised gasp rushed into his mouth when her bosom met the hard planes of his chest.

One thing he could say with certainty: Sierra Hunt was a very fast learner. She locked her arms around him, pulling him tight against her.

A grin formed as he ended the kiss. He maneuvered his hand between them to explore. First the wetness that bore proof of her desire, then the entrance to the center of her being.

A low moan slipped from her mouth. "Please, Sam. I need you inside me."

That was all he needed—her assent.

Pain was inevitable. With a prayer that she would forgive him, he thrust into the warmth. He stilled immediately so she could grow accustomed to him, kissing her eyes and mouth in silent apology.

When Sam felt her relax, he began a rhythmic dance. With an instinct older than time, she matched his movements.

This dance appeared to be inborn within Sierra, a part of her she didn't know existed. Sam had been taught by the best and knew how to bring her to the release she sought.

Making little mewling sounds and gasps of pleasure, she ran her hands up and down his back. She caressed, stroked, and nibbled.

Sam rose to dizzying heights and hung there suspended while he waited for her. They would reach the crest and ride the swirling passion together.

When he felt her muscles clench him tightly in release, he took his pleasure. Blinding light burst around and inside him. He hurtled from the confines of his body to float on waves that carried him up beyond the planes of earth.

With ragged breath, he rolled to the side, exhausted and quivering. He'd never experienced passion this deep, this all-consuming. This magnificent.

When he was able, he glanced at Sierra. She lay with eyes closed, her lips gently parted. Instantly, he felt remorse. What had he done? Though he knew she wouldn't blame him, the fact was he'd ruined her. A woman's sullied reputation made her life hell. She could never regain good standing. People had long memories.

It had to be this house. Miss Beecher had abandoned her students, her reputation, and her self-worth to run off with another woman's husband. He glanced at the Bible verse quilt. The square beside him read "Flee Fornication."

A glimpse of the other side said, "Abstain."

Sam grinned. Nope. They weren't about to make him feel guilty. He'd waited too long for this.

Sierra, looking drugged and very happy, rose and gave him a smile that sent heat pooling again into his belly. When she slowly dragged one finger down his chest and belly, all thoughts of scripture and sinning vanished in an instant.

"I've never felt so alive, Sam. Do you think we might possibly…?"

Voices outside reminded Sam of the daylight beyond the windows and that he must do whatever he had to in order to protect Sierra. That meant leaving with no time to waste. He'd give no one reason to talk about this woman who'd been spurned by her family.

He tweaked the tip of her nose and gave her luscious body one last, longing glance. "It's getting late. You have to go for Hector, and I need to get out of here before someone sees and the tongues start wagging fit to beat all."

"You're right, of course."

Rolling off the bed, Sam grabbed his trousers and slipped them on. He located Sierra's petticoats and dress and helped her into them before putting on the rest of his clothes.

"That should wipe away the notion that I gave your heart back. It's right here. Safe." He patted his shirt, then picked up his gun belt and buckled it on.

Sierra stood in front of him, clutching his arm. "But will you feel the same way tomorrow?"

Sam took her face between his large hands, "Tomorrow and every day after that. Don't ever, ever think you're not enough. And I will fight to become the kind of man you need." He lowered his head and gave her a kiss that probably singed every Bible verse on that quilt.

Thirty-three

ALL THROUGH SUPPER, SAM COULDN'T TAKE HIS EYES off Sierra. He remembered every minute, every stroke of the passion they'd shared. When he rose from the table, he saddled his buckskin. He had some thinking to do, to make sense of the turmoil inside. Lots of thinking—not only the way Sierra had changed his life, but also the telegram from the marshal.

Not that the latter would matter much with Luke determined to ride out. Might have already, since he wasn't at supper and his gelding was gone from the corral.

He galloped to the place he'd always gone to sort through things in his mind—a high bluff that overlooked the Red River snaking below. He rode along the bluff a ways before reining up. Dismounting, he stood looking down at the rushing current. The powerful river struck fear in the hearts of anyone trying to ford it. Drovers taking large herds up the cattle trail to Kansas called it the Mighty Red.

That river wasn't what troubled Sam now.

Sierra Hunt and what choosing her meant to him, and his job, did.

Just when he'd managed to convince his heart that loving her would only destroy her, he'd swept everything right back to the beginning. Hope blossomed that he'd somehow, someway find a way to have a life with her. For if not, he would shrivel and become a shell of a man.

She made love like she'd danced that night by the light of the campfire—free and full of wild abandon. His skin still burned with her silken touch, caresses that had lit such a fire inside him. He'd thrown caution to the wind and taken pleasure, forgetting everything that lay at stake.

A troubled sigh escaped as he hunkered down on his heels.

No way in hell was he going to let her go. The lady was his.

Some said he was a fair man. Honest and loyal to a fault. He would argue that he was a son of a biscuit eater for not seeing what was in front of him.

At the sound of hooves striking the ground, Sam stood, pulled his Colt, and whirled all in one motion.

"Gonna shoot me, little brother?" Houston said.

Sam holstered his sidearm. "Can't be too careful, with trespassers running around."

Houston swung down. "Saw you ride out. Knew you'd head here. This is where I always come when I need to sort things out."

"Then you know such a task is best done alone," Sam growled.

"I wanted to bring some late telegrams Jim Wheeler brought over. Better read these." Houston handed him two slips of paper.

By the light of a match, Sam read Captain O'Reilly's

message. The sheriff of Bridger, Texas, had spotted a man fitting Rocky Hunt's description riding toward Lost Point. He was in the company of Felix Bardo, an outlaw as ruthless as they came.

This was the break he'd searched for. But would Sierra leave when he found Rocky? No way could he let her go now.

Dragging his thoughts back, he read O'Reilly's second telegram.

ANOTHER STAGE HOLDUP NEAR YOUR RANCH STOP FOLKS SAY IT WAS WESTON

Doubts circled in Sam's head. Fact was, Luke rode out late at night, and not only had he refused to say where he'd gone, he'd admitted he couldn't give up outlawing. Hell!

"Appears we might have a storm brewing," Houston said.

"Yep."

"Do you think Luke is back to robbing stages?"

"I'd be lying if I said no. Where does he go these nights when he rides out and doesn't return until early morning? I can't really trust him, Houston. And that tears me up inside."

"Does me too." Houston threw a rock into the river below. "The other about Sierra's brother is good news though."

"Not if she still plans on leaving afterward. I can't lose her, Houston."

"Sorta thought it might be that way. She means a lot to you."

Sam nodded. "It's serious."

Houston hunkered down. "She's what you need."

Sam stared up at the sky and the millions of stars. "Are you ready to ride to Lost Point, Houston?"

"Say the word. Pa can handle things here."

"How about now?" Sam slanted a look at him. "The night would give us cover."

"Or we could walk blind into a hornet's nest. I say leave at first light. Two men innocently passing through would get us closer, and we could get more information from the people who live there." Houston stood next to Sam with their shoulders touching.

"You have a point. Dawn it is." Sam folded the telegrams and stuck them in his pocket. "After that, I'll have to straighten out this mess with Luke."

"Yep."

"Luke's just like us in a lot of ways, Houston. He wants to be alone until he can figure stuff out in his head. He shares a lot of Legend traits. Maybe he rode off to think."

"Maybe. I hope so. He's growing on me."

Sam wasn't ready for a showdown with his brother. To have to put Luke in jail would rip their family apart at the seams.

⊸∽⊷

When Sam and Houston rode up to the corral, surprise rushed through Sam. The dwelling they'd given Luke, since he still refused to stay at head-quarters, had a light inside. It had be early—around nine o'clock, which told him Luke hadn't gone anywhere.

Sam didn't know why that filled him with happiness, but it did.

Houston also noticed the light. "Go talk to him. I'll unsaddle the horses," he said.

Giving his brother a nod, Sam covered the distance in long strides. He knocked on the door.

Seconds passed before Luke came. Sam took in his brother's tousled hair, bare feet and chest, noting that even in a state of relaxation, Luke wore his gun belt. When Luke had fought for his life, he'd kept that Colt within easy reach. Sam had only seen him without it once—that first night at the Lone Star at the dining table.

"What?" Luke growled. "Checking on me?"

"Concerned is all. Gonna let me in?"

Luke finally opened the door wider, and Sam stepped in. The rumpled bed called his attention.

"Can't a man get some sleep around here?" Luke barked.

"This will only take a minute." Sam leaned against the doorframe. "You informed me you were leaving, so imagine my surprise to see your lamp."

Luke let out a troubled sigh, rubbing the back of his neck. "Decided to wait a few days." He glanced out the open door. "This land casts a spell over a man. My mother would've loved it here. But for a quirk of fate, I'd be running the ranch, and...you and Houston might've been the outlaws. Deep stuff to think about."

He was right, and the different viewpoint gave Sam quite a lot to ponder. "Strange, isn't it? I wish you could've grown up here with Stoker."

Luke barked a laugh and waved his arm wide. "I

wasn't prepared for this—to be taken in and treated as an equal. Thought you'd throw me out on my rear." He laughed again. "Or shoot me."

"Well, you didn't know us very well," Sam said.

"I rode this way often, you know." Luke's voice was wistful. "I'd hide and watch all of you, wondering what it would be like to live here. It troubled me that you were always gone. So I followed you, doing my best to keep you alive…for them."

The ache for his brother was almost unbearable. "If not for you, I would be dead. Probably many times over."

Luke jerked from his thoughts. "You didn't come to hear all this. Why the visit?"

"Got a telegram telling of a stage holdup near here."

Anger darkened his brother's eyes. "I wondered how long it would take before doubts set in and the trust faded. I didn't rob any stage recently. Do I need to put my hand on a damn Bible and repeat it?"

Relief flooded over Sam. "Nope. Your word is good enough." He pushed away from the doorframe.

"One day soon I'll show you proof of where I go and put your doubts to rest."

Sam welcomed that. "Me and Houston are riding to Lost Point tomorrow. Join us."

"Sure. I'm glad you want to include me. Thanks."

The lump in his throat prevented him from saying another word. With a curt nod, Sam left. Tonight he'd looked into Luke's heart and saw his brother's pain clearer than ever.

⁂

Before daylight, Sierra stood at her window, thinking about Sam—about making love to him and hearing him say she was more than enough. Those words had finally put to rest every doubt that he cared. Her lips tingled as she remembered his kisses and his gentle touch.

A few minutes ago, in keeping with her custom of looking at the Texas flag flying so proud, she'd opened her door. There, lying on her stoop, was a note from Sam, saying he might have an idea where Rocky was. Her breath caught in her chest. Was it possible she was going to get him back? Her brother was all the family she had. Hope that Sam would find him alive burst inside her.

Movement outside caught her attention. She pressed closer to the window in time to see Sam riding out, sandwiched between Houston and Luke.

Her breath caught at the sight of the man who'd made such passionate love to her. His black Stetson rode low on his forehead, and though she couldn't see his eyes, she knew they were cold and hard. The way he sat in the saddle, his tight grip on the reins, and the stiffness of his spine told her he meant business. Her gaze shot to the sight of his deadly Colt hanging at his side. All three brothers wore grim expressions.

For a moment, she stared, struck by the powerful sight. Three men riding as one with a singular purpose.

Each rode tall and proud in the saddle. Brothers. Legends.

They didn't know the sight they made. If she saw that line galloping toward her, she'd run for cover.

She didn't know how she'd keep her thoughts on

the children's lessons. The hours would be hard with the low hum of worry in her head.

Releasing a troubled sigh, she turned to organize her day, hoping to fill it with so much work she wouldn't have time to think about the danger Sam would face. She had so many plans for her students. Yesterday, for the first time in her life, she'd found true purpose that filled the empty hole inside. She meant to make the most of what she'd found.

When she arrived with Hector at the school promptly at eight o'clock, a few children already perched on the steps. Soon the routine of getting ready to teach swept the worry and fear from her mind.

By noon, Sierra still hadn't been able to shake the worry from her mind. She had the children gather their lunch pails, and they walked to the elm tree for lunch under the wide branches. She couldn't help glance at the corral in hopes of seeing Sam's buckskin. When the animal wasn't there, worry set in. *Please don't let a bullet find him.*

Doubts rose to nag her, to make her question her decisions. How could she live as the wife of a lawman? Fear that he'd not return alive would rise each time he left.

And yet it was already death for her now without him.

❧

Sam and his brothers were on edge crossing the land Stoker had lost gambling. The new owner had threatened to shoot them if they stepped foot on his property. The relationship between Stoker and Newt

Granger was beyond prickly. Fair to say the two hated each other, and Stoker had put a bullet in Granger's leg already during an argument over the land. The fact that headquarters, which once sat in the middle, was now on the western edge still stuck in Stoker's craw.

They reached Lost Point without incident a little before noon. The town was as quiet as a tomb. Everyone probably still slept after being up all night doing whatever outlaws did.

He glanced at Luke. His brother would know. It had surprised Sam when he'd agreed to come with them. Sam had expected him to say no. Or expected him to be gone come daylight.

The thought ran through his mind that Luke was more than likely at home in dangerous places like this. His outlaw brother was one of them. They'd accept him, no questions asked.

They paused at the edge of town. Sam turned to Luke. "You ride in ahead. I don't want anyone to know we're together. We'll split up and meet back here."

"I'll blend in. You stick out like a whore in church, Ranger."

Though it bore truth, the image drew Sam's frown. They waited until Luke tied up at the saloon before Sam led the way slowly to the mercantile halfway down the street. He and Houston dismounted at the hitching rail, glancing around. Without speaking, Sam opened the door, and they stepped inside.

The dim interior made it difficult to see clearly, but Sam made out an old woman hobbling painfully toward them on a pair of homemade crutches.

"Howdy, strangers," she greeted them. "Are you lost?"

"No, ma'am." Sam swallowed hard when he glanced down and spotted only one shoe below her dress. "I'm Sam Legend. This is my brother, Houston. I'm looking for someone."

She cackled. "Ain't we all?"

"He's young, dark hair and eyes, comes to about my chin." Sam tried to remember what Sierra said. "Rocky Hunt is a slight man with a thick black beard." Sierra had said her brother never liked to be clean shaven. Of course, the outlaws might've done that to disguise him.

"Cain't say as I recall. 'Course the way men come an' go around here, I ain't surprised. I'm Sally."

Houston glanced around the dim store. "How about Felix Bardo, ma'am?"

Fear rippled across her wrinkled face. "Don't mess with that one. He'll cut out your gizzard an' feed it to you faster 'n you can spit. He bears the blame for these crutches."

Sam studied the terror darkening her eyes. Whatever her infraction had been, nothing was bad enough for the cruel punishment. "Mind if I ask what happened, ma'am?"

Sally licked her lips. "I burnt the bread. Got busy an' forgot about it. I tried to run. He said he was gonna teach me a lesson."

"Why do you stay, ma'am?" Sam asked quietly.

"No one leaves this place. No one escapes alive. No one." She rested her hand on the counter. "Might I interest you in some homemade bread, Sam?"

Glancing at the wooden countertop that bore enough dirt to plant a garden, Sam almost shook his head. But he knew how much a few coins would mean to her.

Sam gave her a wink. "I'd love a loaf, ma'am. Fresh bread will be mighty tasty on the ride back to the Lone Star."

Houston's look said Sam had lost his mind. But as the woman hurried after it, he called, "Make that two, Miss Sally. My brother doesn't share."

The woman's cackle echoed in the shabby store. Sam knew the money they'd pay her would make a lot of difference in her day.

They each walked out with a loaf of bread under their arms.

After stashing them in a saddlebag, Sam glanced toward the saloon. Luke's horse was still at the hitching rail.

"What do you want to do now?" Houston asked.

"Let's leave our horses here and see if we can find someone else in town to talk to us."

At his brother's nod, Sam moved toward a hotel that tilted to one side at a precarious angle. Except for the handful of nails holding it together, the thing would probably fall into a dust heap.

"What are you going to do with your bread, Sam? You'll get lockjaw if you eat it."

Sam shrugged. "Feed the birds, most likely."

"I thought you'd lost your mind back there."

"Never know when I might need a friend. She's had a hard life and faces a bleak future." Sam's eyes narrowed at a flash in the grimy window of the barbershop.

"My thoughts exactly. She could come in handy."

"Don't look, but someone's watching from the

barbershop," Sam warned. "The way the hair on my neck is twitching, whoever it is has a gun pointed at us."

"I won't make any sudden moves."

At the hotel, Houston opened the door. Sam sauntered to the registration book. He was flipping through the pages when the sound of a rifle cocking reached him. When he glanced up, the barrel of a rifle poked through the curtains behind the counter.

"We don't want any trouble." Sam let his hand rest on the grip of his Colt.

"Then you'd best move on before I count to ten."

"We only want to talk," Houston said quietly.

"Not in the mood for shootin' the breeze," the voice behind the curtain snapped. "If Bardo catches you here, he'll kill you. And then he'll put a bullet between *my* eyes."

"Don't mean to cause problems. We'll be going." Sam backed to the door with Houston, turning only after they'd reached the street. "These people are terrified of Felix Bardo."

"With good reason, it seems," Houston agreed. "Now what?"

"Let's get back to the horses." On the way, Sam told his brother about the hotel register. "Only the first ten pages contained names, with the last entry a year ago. Everything after that was blank. I'm guessing that's when Bardo came and took over the town."

"Even though we didn't find Miss Sierra's brother, we seem to have come to the right place." Houston's leather chaps slapped against his legs with the long strides.

Sam nodded. "This town holds some powerful secrets."

Houston pushed back his hat. "Do you think Rocky could've joined up with Felix Bardo?"

"The thought crossed my mind. Sierra mentioned that he fought demons." If he did find that to be true, Sam didn't know how he'd tell Sierra. It would finish her, and she'd already borne enough heartache and sorrow to last a lifetime. Hopefully, they were wrong. "Let's see what Luke learned. That will decide our next move."

Back at the mercantile, they mounted their horses and headed toward the edge of town to wait for their brother, hoping he'd gotten more than they had.

Though it went against the grain for Sam to pretend Luke was a stranger and not with them, he had no choice if they meant to come back.

Their return to Lost Point was a given. Rocky had to be here. Even without him as an incentive, Sam intended to clean out the nest of outlaws—for Sally, the man in the hotel, and any other law-abiding citizens.

He'd do it even if he wasn't a Texas Ranger and Captain O'Reilly hadn't asked him. Some men didn't need to be asked to give decent folk back a safe place to live and work and raise their kids.

While they waited, Sam and Houston discussed how odd it was that they hadn't seen any children.

"Maybe they were in school?" Houston said.

"I didn't see any sign of a school," Sam answered. "I think the parents are scared spitless to let their sons and daughters out of the house."

"Could be right."

Luke arrived, and they discussed what he'd found out. The barkeep told him Felix Bardo lived in the hotel and that Luke wouldn't want to cross him. Seemed the mean outlaw kept a place somewhere outside of town and made two trips a day out to it.

"The barkeep once overheard the outlaws talking about Rocky Hunt but didn't know where they kept him," Luke said. "Bardo has gathered an army here. We're going to need a lot more men to root out the evil from this place. It'll take a lot more than the three of us."

"Sounds like you crawled into bed with the guy, Luke." Houston rested his elbow on the pommel. "Didn't he get suspicious of all the questions?"

"I told him I was looking to join up with Bardo." Luke grinned. "Said I had information about a shipment of gold. I'm guessing that will make the outlaw sit up and take notice."

Sam chuckled. "You definitely know how to get someone's attention." He sent Luke a narrowed glance. "You'd better have made that up."

"Stop worrying so much, *hermano*. Bet you didn't know having a black sheep in the Legend family would come in handy."

Houston drawled, "At least you don't appear to have been dropped on your head like Sam. And you're a whole bunch better looking."

The way they joked put a lump the size of a river rock in Sam's throat. He needed them, probably more than they needed him. Slowly, one day at a time, he was putting his life back together. He'd come awfully close to missing out on this deep bond between brothers. On meeting Sierra too.

"Let's do some more scouting and see what else we can dig up before we go put together our own army. We need to get back here quick."

"Lead the way, brother," Houston said.

Thirty-four

AFTER A LONG DAY, SIERRA CLOSED AND LOCKED THE schoolhouse door. As she and Hector turned to go, she caught sight of a riderless horse galloping away. A little girl stood at the foot of the steps with her hands on her hips, staring forlornly after the animal.

Alice Graham awoke her motherly instincts. The girl was in the third grade and small for her age. She was far too young for the large red roan she had to ride to school. Sierra had learned that Alice's mother had died, and her father worked as a ranch hand, which explained the girl's appearance—uncombed hair, dirty clothes, and no lunch.

Sierra had shared hers, or Alice would've gone hungry. She longed to give the child's father a piece of her mind. Except she knew how early the cowboys went to work and how late they got home. The man probably did his best.

Fat tears rolled down Alice's face. Sierra hurried down the steps and put her arms around the girl. "It's all right, sweetheart. I'll borrow a wagon and take you home."

"Thank you, Miss Hunt," Alice whispered.

"Don't worry." She bent to gently wipe Alice's face, then she kissed her forehead. "I know how it feels to try to be more grown-up than you are."

Alice pressed tightly to Sierra, as though seeking a bit of warmth. The wind whistled through the elm tree, rustling the leaves while she let Alice gather herself.

"I don't know where you live, so you'll have to show me. Is it close?"

"No, ma'am. We live across the creek and over a ways."

"I'll find it. Come along, children." She pointed Hector and Alice toward the stables.

The man there loaned her a wagon, and they soon rolled toward the Graham dwelling. The afternoon was pleasant, with puffy clouds resembling big snow-banks in the sapphire sky.

Neither child spoke. She was used to Hector's silence, thanks to the language barrier. But shyness, she guessed, kept Alice's lips sealed. The girl seemed more akin to a sorrowful old woman instead of a child. She was far too old for her tender years.

"Are you all right, Alice?"

"Yes, ma'am."

"I'll have you home before you know it."

Following the girl's directions, they moved farther and farther from headquarters. There was nothing but waves of tall grass and prairie dotted with mesquite. Sierra spied not one house anywhere upon the rolling landlocked sea.

"Are we getting close?"

"No, ma'am," Alice said quietly. "Not much."

Anger rose. What was her father thinking, taking her so far off from people? An eight-year-old needed playmates and laughter. Not having to ride a large horse she couldn't handle, from such a distance in all kinds of weather. The man either didn't think about what it was doing to his daughter or didn't care.

Memories of her own father swept across her mind, and the days and nights when she yearned just to be a carefree little girl.

Lost in her thoughts, she didn't see the water until the traces stopped jingling and the horses stopped. Panic raced through her, and her palms grew cold and clammy.

"Did we come the wrong way, Alice?" She hated the tremble in her voice.

"No, ma'am. This is the creek I told you about."

A creek? It was more like a river. A deep river. She had to turn around and go back. They couldn't get across in the wagon. They wouldn't make it. Panic rose.

The face of her sister, Whitney, surfaced on the water, silently pleading. Sierra swallowed hard, but fear blocked her passageway. "You cross this each day on your horse?" she asked nervously.

"Yes, ma'am. It's not so bad. He just swims across. Aren't you going to go to my house now? You promised." Alice's eyes bubbled with tears, and her chin quivered. "The water isn't so high. The wagon will make it."

Sierra took a deep breath, trying to calm herself. She couldn't allow her fear to show in front of these children.

"Go," Hector said, then followed with a quick spurt of Spanish. Even he was getting impatient and wondering about her.

Everyone you touch dies. Her father's words echoed in her head.

She could do this. She had no choice. She was all Alice had. Sweat trickled down between her breasts. Taking a shaky breath, she flicked the reins and inched forward. It was deeper than she'd thought. Sheer terror gripped her as the water swirled around them and rose up through the cracks in the wood, wetting her shoes and dress.

God in heaven, please help me do this.

As they began to float, Hector jumped to his feet, flailing his skinny arms. Sierra didn't know what the Spanish words meant, what he was trying to tell her.

"Sit down!" she yelled, panic-stricken. She tried to grab onto him but couldn't reach him with Alice between them. Alice screamed, gripping Sierra's hand with every bit of strength she had. This was the Brazos crossing all over again. Only this time she didn't have Sam. There was no one to come to the rescue, and the river meant to claim them.

Suddenly, the wagon tipped at a sickening angle, tossing Hector into the rushing current. As he sank beneath the surface, fear squeezed around her heart as though it were a band of steel. She couldn't breathe, couldn't think, couldn't move. She was frozen in place, just like with Whitney.

Everything moved in slow motion. Finally, Hector's face earlier as he'd stared up at her with trusting eyes released her from the icy nightmare's grip. She was his whole world. He needed her.

"Hector!" She clutched the side of the wagon box, staring at the paralyzing sight. "Hector!"

The boy's dark head surfaced. "*Ayuda!*" he cried. "Help!"

Terror-stricken, she watched him vanish again from sight.

"Get him, Miss Hunt! Don't let him die," Alice yelled.

Sierra licked her dry lips. Her heart hammered so loudly she could barely hear. She tore at her shoes and the laces that held them. Kicking them off, she jumped in.

"I'm coming, Hector!"

She flailed her arms and kicked her feet like her brothers had instructed her so long ago. But her heavy skirts tangled about her legs. She slipped under the water. Her mouth filled as her hair floated across her eyes.

That this was just like Whitney's last moments raced through her mind. Soon she would join her sister. In minutes, she would die. But she desperately wanted to live. She had to look into Sam's eyes once more and see the love he had yet to voice.

Using the last of her strength, she began kicking and clawing at her watery tomb.

Suddenly arms lifted her up, and she breathed in great gulps of air.

"I've got you, Sierra," said a man's voice in her ear. "Put your arms around my neck."

When she could focus, she stared into Sam's face and those gray eyes she loved. He knelt over her. Maybe it was a dream she'd conjured up. He couldn't possibly be there. He'd ridden off with his brothers.

She jerked, clutching his shirt. "Hector! I've got to save him. I can't fail again."

"Hector is fine. Houston has him, and Luke is with the little girl in the wagon." He set her on dry ground and brushed wet tendrils of hair from her eyes.

"Sam, are you really real?"

He laughed. "I sure hope so. This water is too cold to be a dream."

Tears sprang up as she sobbed, "I couldn't get to Hector."

"You tried so hard though. Lord, I'm very glad we happened along." He slanted his lips on hers in a searing kiss.

Warmth sped through Sierra's body as his arms tightened around her. Her shivering stopped. She didn't know how or why he'd ridden upon them. She only knew if she was dead, she wanted to stay that way. They hadn't spoken of love, and maybe they never would. What they had was enough. She would take Sam Legend without any promises, fancy words of commitment, or changed dreams.

She would live in her little house alone, and when Sam passed by, they'd make passionate love until he had to move on.

She would take him as he was with all his scars and hurt, for to change him would alter the very things that had drawn her to him—his honor, sense of duty, and loyalty to family. She would never ask him to give up the things that made him whole.

"Thank God you're all right," Sam murmured against her mouth. "If I lost you, I wouldn't want to live."

Sierra became aware of the children and the fact that she was their teacher. What they were doing was not acceptable for an unmarried woman, never mind a teacher. "Sam, the children."

"Oh, right. Sorry." He took a step back.

With the taste of him on her tongue, she rushed to Hector and Houston, who bent over him. The boy smiled up at her.

"*Hola*," he murmured.

Smoothing back his hair, she blinked away her tears. "*Hola*, Hector."

"He'll be fine, Miss Sierra." Houston stood like some tall mountain of a man. Becky Golden—whom Sierra hadn't yet met—would be lucky to have him. "If we'd arrived another minute later..." His words trailed off.

"Except you didn't. Thank you, Houston, Luke. Thank all of you." She sent Sam a special glance that said more than words.

Luke stepped forward. "I'll take this little girl on home."

"Appreciate it," Sam said. "Houston and I will get the wagon out and take care of these two. Meet you back at headquarters."

Luke nodded, plucking Alice from the wagon. Sierra's eyes misted as he settled the girl in the saddle in front of him. Those two had a lot in common. Loneliness dogged their shadows.

Sam turned to Sierra. "Wait here with Hector until we get the wagon on solid ground."

"We're fine. Do what you need to." She put an arm around Hector, pulling him close.

While she watched the two brothers work, she wondered why Hector had stood, causing the wagon to lurch to the side. She wished she could ask him. Hopefully, he would tell Sam.

Had she done something to cause it? Perhaps the boy had sensed her terror. Or maybe he shared the same fear of water.

One thing was very clear—she'd failed again. Had the men not ridden by, they both would've drowned, and maybe Alice too.

How could she live with the knowledge that no one would be able to depend on her? That she'd always let them down?

Laying a hand on top of Hector's head, she thought of how precious life was, how fleeting. This child had already suffered the sting and came awful close to joining his mother.

"I'm sorry, Hector," she murmured.

When he glanced up at her, she saw tears in his eyes. "Love you," he said in halting English.

"I love you too," she whispered, kissing his forehead.

Even so, she wasn't fit to raise him. She wasn't fit to raise any child.

❧

Sam pulled the wagon to a stop in front of Sierra's small dwelling. Setting the brake, he glanced over at her. She'd been very quiet on the drive. He'd felt the heavy pall over her.

"Here we are." He jumped to the ground and turned for Hector, setting him down. Then, putting his hands on Sierra's slight waist, he swung her easily from the wagon. She didn't weigh anything. He held her against him for a long moment, fighting the need to kiss her. Finally, he couldn't bear the torture and set her on her feet.

"I wish I knew what to say to make you feel better." He tucked a tendril of hair behind her ear.

Her hair had dried during their return, as had their clothes, and she'd put on her shoes.

Sierra's eyes meeting his showed her misery. "There is nothing, Sam. I failed—once again."

"Maybe in saving Hector, but that's understandable. You had so many things working against you. Your long dress hampered you, for one. It was too heavy and dragged you down. You were swimming as well as you were able when we rode up, and had almost reached Hector."

Tears shimmered in her blue eyes. "I couldn't save anyone. I let my sister, Whitney, drown, and my mother jumped off a cliff to her death."

Sam took her frigid hands in his. "You couldn't have saved your sister. Don't you see? If you'd jumped in, you would've died also. Her death is not your fault. Nor is your mother's." He brushed her cheek with his lips. "I'm so very proud of you."

"I froze. I was so scared."

Her words were so quiet he could barely hear them. "But you jumped in anyway. That took a lot of guts. You were willing to risk your life for this little boy."

Her face brightened. "I never thought about what might happen to me. He was my only concern."

"That's the mark of a hero, darlin'." His glance swept the busy place. "I wish I could come in, but there are too many people watching. I need to talk to you though. Can you come to the house after you do whatever you need to?"

"Is this about your mysterious ride this morning?"

"Yes. We're making a plan to go back."

She curled her hand inside his. "I can't wait to hear about it. Before you go, Sam, will you ask Hector why he stood, tipping the wagon over? I want to know what made him do a foolish thing like that."

"Sure." After speaking Spanish to the boy, Sam met her eyes. "He saw us in the distance, but he thought we were Ford and his men. He tried to warn you."

Sierra hugged Hector close. "You're a sweet boy with a gentle heart. Thanks for saving us, Sam. I'll see you in a while."

With a reluctant sigh, Sam climbed back into the wagon and drove to the stables. He glanced back at Sierra. Pride swelled in his chest. She'd made great headway toward overcoming her fear. He prayed that today had relieved her at last of the blame she'd carried for so long.

Sierra Hunt could do anything she set her mind to. The tiny steps she'd taken would get bigger. With each one, she'd grow stronger and more confident.

One thing he knew—she was a keeper.

And she was the only one who could stoke a fire inside him.

Thirty-five

WHILE SAM WAITED FOR SIERRA IN THE SHADOWS OF the porch, Wheeler hurried toward him from the telegraph office.

"What is it, Wheeler?" Sam asked when the man drew close.

The man huffed and puffed up the steps. "I heard back from Captain O'Reilly." He handed Sam a slip of paper.

O'Reilly's telegram said the sheriff at Bridger, Texas, was shot and killed by a group of masked riders this morning. Sounded like Felix Bardo's work. The outlaw must've sensed the sheriff had seen him. O'Reilly warned Sam to be careful.

"Wheeler, I don't need to send a reply." Sam stuck the telegram in his vest pocket, thanking the man. He happened to glance toward the mercantile, and his breath hitched at the sight of Sierra strolling toward the house. Fingers of dying light lingered on her hair and brushed the soft curve of her jaw.

If he was a painter, he'd try to capture that picture just the way he filed it away in his mind. Her softly parted lips reminded him of the night she'd danced to the guitar music with her shoulders bared and slender arms raised over her head.

Damn, he couldn't get that image out of his mind!

The opening door caught his attention. He turned to see his father and Houston. Earlier, his brother mentioned riding over to the Golden place—something about needing to talk to Becky's father about one of their bulls that showed up on the Lone Star, but it appeared he'd changed his mind. That was good, because what they had to discuss couldn't wait.

It wouldn't be too many more days though before Houston would be with Becky Golden, stealing kisses. Or maybe making plans for their future.

Sam envied him. Houston knew exactly how to go after what he wanted. While Sam knew he wanted to spend his life with Sierra, they had many, many things to work out.

Sierra slowed when she saw them, and he watched indecision cross her face. He hurried down the steps to meet her and put her at ease. At times, Legend men seemed to intimidate her. Hell, they did him too.

With women and children, she was so confident and sure. It was men she had trouble with. Her father had caused this.

Sam caught her hand. "Pa wants to hear about our visit to Lost Point today, and you'll be a big help."

"I don't know what I can contribute, but I'll try." A smile wiped the worry from her eyes.

Sam put his arm around her waist. "Luke might join us. But I hesitate to say."

His black-sheep brother was moody and unpredictable.

Houston strode forward to kiss Sierra's cheek, saying he was anxious for her to meet his Becky, and promised to have his lady friend come soon.

"I'd like that. I'm sure she's a lovely woman."

Her words were genuine and true, just like the woman she was. Sam gave her his attention and ushered her up the wide porch steps with a hand on her waist.

"Come into the parlor, my dear," Stoker said, taking her arm. "If I had been fortunate enough to have a daughter, I'd have wanted her to be exactly like you. You're a beautiful young lady."

Sierra blushed. "Thank you, sir."

"Not sir. I'm Stoker," his father insisted.

With a scowl, Sierra said, "It seems rude and irreverent, though."

"I'm not a reverend, dear. I'm just a plain old rancher who knows what he wants. And I want you to call me Stoker."

Sam grinned. His pa could charm the horns right off a billy goat when he wanted to. Sam followed, but as he and Houston reached the screen door, it slammed shut in their faces. He frowned. Their father was ever one to keep a man humble, and he knew a hundred ways to do it.

By the time Sam and Houston reached the parlor, Sierra was seated on the cowhide sofa with Stoker beside her.

"I tell you, Sam was a sight after I pulled him from that big pile of manure." Stoker roared. "He had it in his mouth, hair, and even up his nose."

"You really get a kick out of telling that story, don't you, Pa?" Sam fought the urge to laugh, even though the memory of that event wasn't one he enjoyed dredging up. Cow shit was all he'd smelled and tasted for a month. "Anything to embarrass me."

"You sure learned fast to leave those bulls alone, son, and limit your riding to horses."

Houston strode to the window and stared into the evening shadows. "Keep any stories about me to yourself, Pa."

"Can I join your powwow?" Luke spoke from the doorway.

Sam glanced up. "I thought you were too busy with whatever it was you needed to do."

"I'm never too busy for *dulce*." Luke's eyes seemed to issue a challenge.

Stoker waved his arm. "Come on in, son. I'd like to get your thoughts on this."

Luke's face darkened, and for a moment, Sam thought he'd spin around and leave. Clearly the word *son* hadn't set well. But with that lazy saunter of his, Luke entered and took a chair.

"Now that we're all here, did you have any trouble riding across Granger's land?" Stoker asked.

"Nope. Never saw a soul." Sam watched relief show on his father's face.

"I'd still have that land if the cayuse hadn't cheated me out of it. Hell and be damned!"

"Pa, that horse is dead enough. You don't have to keep beating it." Houston glowered. "The land is gone. Done."

Sam sat down beside Sierra and stretched out his legs. "We have other things to talk about. Trouble's afoot over at Lost Point, but where do we go from here?"

Sierra leaned forward. "First, I'd like to hear what you found, if you don't mind."

After filling in her and their father about Sally and the state of affairs in the small town, Sam said, "It's a surefire bet that Rocky's there. I just have to find him."

A scowl darkened Luke's face. "*We*, you mean."

His brother's insistence brought a grin to Sam's face. "Of course. Wouldn't have it any other way."

Houston turned from the window. "If there's no map, what the heck is that bunch after?"

"Someone had to have led them to believe there is a map, and that Sierra has it," Sam growled. "And when I find out who, they'll be very sorry."

"Luke and I will let you go first, but we'll be right behind, waiting for our turn to whip the daylights out of him." Houston's eyes hardened.

Stoker patted Sierra's hand. "You can bet I'll be there too."

"Thank you all." She blinked hard. "Until I met the four of you, I never had anyone stand up for me."

Sam cleared his throat. "You've got us now, and no getting rid of us." He'd ride through hell for her if that's what his lady needed. She didn't even have to ask.

This woman whose quiet strength had fixed his head meant more to him than anything on earth.

More than his life. She was the woman he'd waited so long to find.

"Say that a map exists—what would it lead to?" Houston stalked back and forth in front of the window.

"Chances rank high of it being ill-gotten gain."

Luke's quiet words echoed Sam's thoughts. "Could be stolen army payroll, outlaw loot…hell, it could be Mexican gold from the War of Independence. Or Confederate gold, for all we know."

Her face drained. "I don't see how my father could be a party to anything such as that. Or Rocky."

"Pure speculation, my dear." Stoker shot Sam and his brothers a warning glare. "What we should discuss is a plan. We'll gather the ranch hands and ride to Lost Point at first light. Legends united—a strong force to reckon with. We'll ride in with guns blazing."

"You do that, Pa, and Bardo and his bunch will kill Sally and everyone in sight. It'll be a bloodbath." Sam could see the woman lying dead in the street with those damn crutches next to her.

Houston leaned forward to weigh in. "I say we ride in from four directions at once and hit 'em hard. Confuse the heck out of 'em. They won't know where to shoot."

"Hold it." Sam glared. "These are crazy plans. We first have to find out for sure if Rocky's even in the town and not out at that place Sally spoke about. We ride in willy-nilly with guns blazing, and they'll kill him before we can get close."

Sierra spoke up. "I should go. He's my brother. A woman can get—"

All four men yelled at once, "You're not going!"

"Sam's got the right idea," Luke said, "and I'm the best one for that job—I can fit in amongst them. I'll go tonight, join in some card games. Drink some whiskey. Liquor loosens men's tongues. I'll gain their trust. If possible, I'll even talk with Felix

Bardo. Then I can meet you at the edge of town at daybreak."

"Too dangerous, Luke. I won't send you in alone," Stoker objected.

Sam watched Luke's hard gaze tangle with his father's.

"It has to be this way," Luke said quietly. "No one better knows the outlaw ways. Any one of you go in, and they'll shoot you on the spot. I've lived my life with outlaws. I know how to act, what to say, and what *not* to do."

"Makes me madder than hell," Stoker thundered. "A nest of outlaws wouldn't have taken over if I still had that land."

"Enough, Pa!" Houston yelled. "Good grief!"

"I'll get ready to ride." Luke moved to the door.

"Luke." Sierra hurried and kissed his cheek. "Thank you."

He turned. "Anything for you, *dulce*. Once I couldn't save someone very precious to me. Maybe I can save your brother."

The break in Luke's voice thickened Sam's throat. "Be careful, brother."

"Always am. No other way for me."

If anything happened, there would be no one there to help him. And if Luke should die… Sam was unable to finish the thought.

Though Sierra covered her mouth with a fist, a sob escaped. "Sam, I couldn't bear it if Luke should die beside a dark road somewhere with no one beside him."

Sam drew her closer. "If my brother vanishes, I'll not stop until I find him. I promise." Though Luke hadn't fully embraced his family yet, he belonged to them all the same. A fierce love filled him for the brother some had called the devil's spawn.

‌❧

At the little house she loved, Sierra brushed by Sam and went inside. Stoker's insistence that Hector stay with him tonight seemed a bit odd. The gruff man had cleared his throat, saying he wanted to get to know the orphaned boy. Sam had chuckled, telling him he'd get on Sierra's bad side if he even thought about teaching Hector to play cards and drink whiskey.

Sierra smiled at the memory, grateful for precious time alone with Sam.

She removed her shawl and turned, studying him. Bright moonlight outlined his handsome features. Power coiled inside him. He was tough and lean and could strike fear into any lawbreaker.

Without bothering to light the lamp that might invite visitors, Sam undressed Sierra in the dark. Trembling, she felt his sure fingers release the last button, then caress her skin. The dress slid down her legs to puddle around her feet.

"Sam, in case something happens to you tomorrow..." Her voice cracked.

"It won't. I'm going to be back here—with you."

He placed his lips on hers, smothering her reply. Flutters whipped up a froth in her stomach as she melted into his strong arms.

Their breaths mingled in a searing kiss that went all the way to her toes. That kiss cemented their feelings for each other—the love that curled inside her heart.

A love she'd never spoken aloud. Maybe it was time. His heart and soul seemed to have overridden all his fears. They still had things to sort out, but she hoped they could come to an agreement that satisfied both.

Tingles at the thought of spending the rest of her life with Sam swept over her.

The slight pressure of his hand below her jaw made her feel cherished, as though he thought her a treasure of some kind.

Warmth flooded over her as her heart beat wildly. The excitement and hunger racing through her blood was like a thundering herd of buffalo.

She needed Sam. She had to feel him inside her. She had to know he wanted this too.

He broke the kiss and murmured against her skin, "Lady, you light a fire inside me like no one ever has. You're all I want, all I can think about. With you, I have everything I need. You make life worth living again."

His large hands drifted down her back and cupped her bottom. Sierra could feel the hardness of his jutting need pressing against her.

As a woman possessed, she worked at the buttons of his shirt and flung it aside. When she fumbled with his gun belt, his hands replaced hers.

Sam chuckled. "Let me help, darlin'."

After he laid the belt and holster on a chair, she aimed him toward the bed. "Sit down."

Darn all these clothes. She had a bonfire blazing inside her and couldn't get to what would put it out fast enough.

"I like a bossy woman." Again came a soft chuckle.

She didn't care. She knew he wanted what she did. Straddling first one leg and then the other, she pulled off his tight boots. But it probably was his hand on her rear that helped.

Quickly, they shed the rest of the bothersome barriers.

"Come here, pretty lady." Sam picked her up and laid her on the Bible verse quilt, then curled beside her.

He nuzzled her neck and trailed kisses between her breasts, then down to her flat stomach, where he placed his lips.

Sierra wound her fingers in his hair. "I love you, Sam. I think I always have, even before you kissed me."

Sam stilled for a moment and Sierra held her breath. She shouldn't have spoken the words aloud. She could tell by his silence he wasn't ready to hear the talk of love.

Finally, his lips brushed the hair at her temple. His voice was raspy. "I didn't know exactly how bone deep I cared until I faced losing you. 'Keep me or let me go,' you said. That scared ten years off my life. I knew you were ready to walk away."

"I was. I'd come to the end."

"It was the kick in the pants I needed." He pressed kisses to the insides of her thighs.

A moan slipped from her throat. "Make love to me, Sam. Take me to heaven as only you can. Let me dance among the stars. I'm already barefoot."

She would enjoy this night to the fullest and pray he met no harm in a few hours as he did the job he was born to do.

With a loving touch, she ran her hands across his broad back and felt the muscles quiver beneath her fingers.

Now Sam Legend belonged to her forever—even if he couldn't say the words she longed to hear.

Thirty-six

SAM DIDN'T KNOW IF HE COULD CONTAIN THE HUNGER driving him. Having Sierra beneath him, his body pressed to hers, was still like a dream he feared would end.

As he slipped inside her warmth, he marveled at the love that swept over him for this beautiful, sensitive woman.

She had changed his life and given him hope again. For the first time in a while, he'd not had any nightmares about the hanging, or thought about drawings of black widow spiders. His captain had ordered him to get his head on straight. It was straighter and clearer than it had ever been.

He loved the feel of her body around him, the little quivers of her muscles with each thrust.

Her moans and gasps told him she was getting close. The waves were building and would soon crest. He maneuvered one hand between them and found her breast. With his thumb and forefinger, he rolled the hard nub of her nipple.

With a cry and an arch of her body, Sierra found her bliss that relieved the burning hunger. Sam gave in at the same time, exploding in wave after wave of ecstasy that hung him suspended, until at last he fell back to earth.

His shuddering release had never been deeper. Or as full of passion for her.

Sam fell to the side, gasping for air, wondering what had just happened. In all his experience over the years, he'd never felt this way, as though he'd died and been reborn.

He reached for Sierra and pulled her against him. A thin sheen of perspiration covered her body. He curled around her curves, loving the warmth of her back pressing to his chest.

"I'm not sure how or when, but some day I'm going to show you what you mean to me."

"Sam, this thing we have is special, and I'm not going away. Even if you can't voice the words, I know how you feel."

Moving her hair aside, he kissed the back of her neck. "You're a special woman, Sierra Hunt."

Truth was he didn't deserve her. He fell far short of being worthy of the love she'd freely confessed to. Why couldn't he just say the words? Why couldn't he just admit that he loved her?

Maybe because it meant he'd have to choose either her or his job.

She chewed her lip. "I know how dangerous those men are. If something happens tomorrow...if you don't make it..." Her trembling voice trailed off.

"Darlin', please don't worry," he murmured into her ear. "I'll be okay."

Sierra stroked the hair on Sam's arm. "If you're not...I

TO LOVE A TEXAS RANGER   353

think I'll stay here with your father. It'll be like having you with me."

He turned her to face him. Moonlight spilling through the window let him see the tears shimmering in her beautiful blue eyes. He kissed her long and deep.

"Nothing's going to happen. But if it does, I know Stoker and Houston will take care of you. I'm glad you're staying."

"Me too." She pressed a kiss to his throat before laying her head on his shoulder.

The soothing fragrance of her washed over him. Nothing would happen. He'd have his father and brothers with him. Legends were unbeatable when they fought side by side.

Sam let the night settle around him and waited for the dawn.

About an hour later, gunshots startled him.

He jumped up and hurriedly dressed. He could see Sierra's eyes wide with worry. "Darlin', lock the door, and don't open it for anyone but me," he said, strapping on his gun belt.

"I will. Please be careful."

"Don't worry. I won't leave you for long." He pulled her naked body to him for one last kiss. Then, without looking back, he raced to join whatever hell had broken loose.

༄

Sam found Luke's house ablaze. Thank goodness his brother rode out earlier. Houston and his father had taken cover next to the mercantile. "What's happening?" Sam barked.

"We're under attack," Stoker yelled. "Don't know who or why yet."

Houston reloaded. "Someone tossed a lit torch into Luke's house to start this mess, then began shooting. The attackers are keeping us from fighting the fire."

"It's no huge loss. At least Luke's not in it," Sam said. "Where are the ranch hands? I don't want to hit one of them."

"They're scattered behind us." Stoker quickly pushed fresh cartridges into the chamber of his Colt. "I told them to call out if they come forward beyond this store."

"Good." Relief filled Sam.

A flash of orange spat from the dark shadows of the elm tree, and a half second later, a bullet splintered the wood next to him. A lucky shot, or had the shooter seen them? He took aim and returned fire. In the blackness, he couldn't tell if he hit anyone.

"Cover me," he told Houston. "I'm going to work over to that tree."

"Be careful, brother."

Using the blistering firepower to his advantage, Sam sprinted from one building to another like a silent shadow. He constantly scanned around him as he ran.

The attackers blended in with the thick darkness. Evil always chose to hide, to curl and strike on a moonless night.

Sam's gut clenched. Whoever they were, they'd made the wrong move. They'd find the Legends were hard to kill. He crept noiselessly along the side of the telegraph office.

Silent.

Deadly.

Focused.

Root out the scourge that had attacked and kill them. They'd find no mercy in him. Sam hunkered low, waiting. At last he saw the flash of orange fire. He had him. He raised his Colt and squeezed the trigger.

Through the smoke, he watched the man tumble. Sam ran to him. Kicking the gun away, he turned him over.

No mistaking that hooked nose. The dead eyes of Ford's man John stared up at him. This confirmed it. These shooters were outlaws. Some belonged to Ford's gang, but there were far too many to be just them. Ford had to have joined forces with others. Probably the same bunch he and Luke fought the day they arrived. Sam itched to know who they were.

Felix Bardo?

Suddenly, he remembered the initials on the telegram that had been with the outlaw loot. FB. Felix Bardo.

Maybe this attack was an attempt to get that money back. He stared toward headquarters and saw a man going up the steps. Sam fired and dropped him, then quickly swung to three horsemen galloping toward him.

Flames from the burning structure lit the face of the nearest one. Shock ran through Sam.

Luke Weston!

Hell and be damned! Aching heaviness filled Sam's chest. His brother. He rode in this attack, fighting the only people in world who gave a damn about him.

Luke's words the morning after the revelation that he was Sam's brother filled his head. *"I am bad to the core, and don't you ever forget it."*

That had been a warning to Sam to never trust him.

Only Sam had forgotten. Hope that he could save his outlaw brother had wiped out those words. Now Luke had turned on them, just like he'd tried to tell him.

Out of choices, Sam set his jaw and aimed his pistol at his brother's forehead. Putting a bullet there would be quick. No suffering. Tears blurred his vision.

He loved Luke Weston as a brother. They shared the same blood—Legend blood.

They'd been too late to save him.

Gritting his teeth, Sam tightened his finger on the trigger. All he had to do was pull it. He'd just be doing his job. One more outlaw sent to hell.

One second passed, then two. Sweat trickled into Sam's eyes, and his palms grew sweaty.

He couldn't make himself do it.

Instead, he shifted aim to the rider next to Luke, and fired. The man slumped in the saddle. His partner on the other side grabbed the reins of his horse and headed back toward the ranch entrance.

Luke's hard eyes met Sam's for an instant before he turned to follow the others. "Retreat!" he yelled.

As Sam stared after his brother, a woman's blood-curdling scream brought shivers up his spine.

"Sam!" she cried. "Sam!"

He ran toward the sound as a horse galloped away from the little schoolteacher's house. The light picked out a woman's dress rippling in the wind.

Sierra!

The rider anchored the woman Sam loved in front of him.

With his aching heart pounding, he raced toward

the horse. Neither bullets nor getting trampled entered his mind.

Desperation to save Sierra filled his brain. She was his reason for living.

He'd vowed to keep her safe, assured that no one could get her inside the compound. They employed a hundred men. His promise had been worthless.

Hell had opened up, and the devil snatched her. The diversion, chaos, catching them off guard, and now they had her.

He had to stop the bastards. Just give him one more chance. He'd tell her he loved her and shout it to the world. His job meant nothing if she wasn't by his side. Life meant nothing without her. He was nothing. And evil hands had plucked her from him.

Please let him stop me.

His heart thudded painfully against his ribs. Thick fear clogged his throat as desperation crawled up his spine.

When the horse Sierra rode neared, Sam lunged and grabbed the stirrup, holding on for dear life. The animal dragged him past headquarters and toward the huge crossbar marking the ranch entrance.

Rocks and brush tore into him, the rough ground peeling away skin. He clenched his jaw against the blinding pain. His arms burned, stretched beyond their limit.

Finally, with the horse's thundering hooves barely missing him, and unable to bear any more of the brutal punishment, he lost his grip.

Lying hurt and bleeding, Sam watched her vanish from sight.

They'd taken the woman he loved.

And Luke had helped.

Thirty-seven

STOKER TOUCHED SAM. "SON, DON'T MOVE. YOU'RE probably hurt bad. The doctor's coming."

How had his father gotten there so fast?

Sam groaned in pain. He'd probably left all the hide from his face on the dirt road.

But he was alive.

Another rider arrived, and Houston's face joined his father's above him.

"They got Sierra. I couldn't stop them." Her screams still echoed in Sam's head. "She called my name, and I couldn't save her. I couldn't do anything." He tried to jerk to his feet, but Houston held him down.

"Damn it, Houston, let me go, or I'll mop up this road with you."

Stoker touched his shoulder. "Stop, son. Doc needs to look at you."

Sam glared at his father. "No one is going to keep me from riding after her. Not even you, Pa." He'd fight them all if they didn't let him go.

Houston finally helped him stand. "We'll get her back. They haven't won."

"Did you see Luke?" Sam asked, striding toward headquarters and the corral. He had to get Trooper saddled and ride. Precious minutes ticked by in his head.

"Yes." Houston let out a curse. "The traitor."

A growl rumbled in Stoker's chest. "Don't be hasty. It doesn't mean he's joined them."

"Doesn't it?" Sam glared. "What else could it mean?"

"We have to give him the benefit of the doubt," Stoker insisted. "They may have forced him to attack us."

Small chance. Luke Weston was a killer, an expert one. He'd have drawn his Colt in a split second and killed again before letting anyone force him to fight against them if he didn't want to.

No, his brother was there because he wanted to be. Luke had finally taken his vengeance.

Sam closed his eyes a moment, and her terrified face stared back. God, she was so scared and in the hands of horrible outlaws who'd stalked her like prey. Trembles shook him. They'd do unimaginable things to her before they took her life. He increased the length of his stride.

Sierra needed him. And he needed her like he needed air.

Those who took her had better find a hole. He'd tear that town apart, board by board, until he found her.

Dear God, please let her be alive.

Sam didn't have time to waste. But the corral was too far away, and his wobbly legs weren't going to make it. Just then a wagon rumbled down the road and stopped. He, his father, and Houston jumped on.

"Hurry!" Sam yelled to the driver.

"You look like hell, little brother," Houston said. "Added a bunch more scars to the mess you already have."

"Thanks for that observation, Houston."

"You gave me a heart attack when I saw that horse dragging you. What gave you the idea that you could stop that horse? I'm beginning to think you really were dropped on your head."

"I used the only thing available," Sam snapped. "You would've done the same if it had been Becky."

"For damn sure," Houston growled.

~

Bound tightly, Sierra found herself in a room in the pitch-dark. Somewhere close by, she heard the rustle of clothing.

"Is anyone in here?" she called softly.

"Sierra, is that you?"

Excitement swept over her. "Oh, Rocky, you're alive! I was so afraid. Are you hurt?"

"Not too bad. How about you?"

"These ropes bite into my wrists, but other than that I'm fine. They attacked the Lone Star Ranch tonight and took me." Her lips quivered. Had they killed Sam? She didn't know how anyone could survive being dragged by a horse that far.

If not dead, he'd be in horrible pain.

Sam wouldn't be coming. Maybe no help would arrive. She took in a shuddering breath. What would these ruthless men do to her? To Rocky?

"I'm relieved they haven't hurt you yet. But then you only got here. Give them time."

Sierra tried to curb the panic racing through her. "Why are we here? Do you know?"

"They think either you or I have a map or know where one is to whatever they want. These people are determined to get it. The trouble is, I don't know what they're talking about. Do you?"

"No. The first time they took me, they…" Sierra forced back the memories. "They like to hurt people. They insisted I turn over this map, but I don't know anything."

What would the outlaws do to them if they didn't have the answers? She didn't want to think about that. They had to find a way to get loose. Except they'd taken her shoes when she got there. She couldn't go far barefoot.

"Are you bound also? And did they take your shoes?"

"Yes to both questions. I've tried to loosen the ropes with no luck," Rocky replied.

Just then, the door swung open. The meanest man she'd ever seen stood there. The lantern in his hand lit his features and made her curl against the wall. His hideous face seemed to have melted at one time, probably in a horrific fire. Even the shadows of his scars terrified her.

"So nice of you to join us, *chica*. It's time to start jogging this memory of yours."

Thirty-eight

SIERRA SHRANK AGAINST THE WALL AS THE OUTLAW stole toward her like a panther. His scarred face terrified her. When a smile curved his mouth, she trembled. Ruthless men smiled right before they hurt you.

Whatever he meant to do, she would show no fear.

He jerked her up by the hair. Though her eyes smarted from the pain, she refused to cry out.

"You call me Bardo." He pulled her face to his. His breath reeked, nearly knocking her down. Then he stuck out his tongue and licked her cheek. "We're going to get acquainted. And before I'm done, you'll give me what I want."

"Leave her alone!" Rocky yelled. "Take me instead."

"Shut up, *gringo*. You don't have the right...smell."

"I'm not going anywhere with you." Though Sierra's legs quaked, she knew she had to stand tall. "I've seen your kind. You're nothing but a bully. I'm not afraid of you."

Bardo's eyes darkened. "You *will* know fear when I'm done."

"You're awfully brave when you're facing a bound

woman. But when it's a man like Sam Legend, you run like a scared child." She didn't back down from him, though he struck such terror into her she could scarcely breathe.

"You know nothing, *chica*." His face darkened with fury. "I hanged Sam Legend once, and I'll do it again. This time I'll make sure he dies."

Stillness washed over her. This was the rustler who'd tried to end Sam's life. And if Sam was alive, he was coming. She had to warn him before it was too late.

"Hanging someone isn't a sign of bravery. I hope he kills you and feeds your rotten body to the buzzards."

The outlaw drew back and slapped her, whipping her head around. He grabbed the front of her dress and ripped it open. Clutching a handful of her chemise, he pulled her out the door and down a hallway to another room and kicked open the door.

"You're going to beg for mercy. And when you do, I'll cut your tongue out." He flung her onto a dirty mattress.

Sierra's heart pounded with sheer terror. She would not get out of this room alive.

When Bardo hovered over her, she spat in his face. It splattered his cheek and ran toward his jaw.

"You're going to be very, very sorry for that," he said softly. "After I'm done with you…if you're still alive…I'm going to let my men have you. You've never seen a woman after they finish with her."

The door squeaked. A throat cleared, and Isaac Ford spoke. "Boss, we have a visitor."

"I'm busy," Bardo growled.

"You're going to want to see this one," the man insisted. "He says he has it."

A gleam shone in Bardo's eyes. He cruelly squeezed Sierra's breasts. It took every bit of willpower not to cry out. He yanked her up and into him, digging his fingers into her buttocks.

Bardo sighed. "We must delay my pleasure, *chica*. A bit of business, and then I'll show you how a real man takes a woman."

He dragged her back to the room where Rocky was, shoving her to the floor so hard her head slammed against the rough boards, and she saw stars. Bardo jerked up the lantern and left with Ford. She heard the padlock on the outside snap shut.

Again in darkness, Sierra trembled. Felix Bardo was ten times worse than Ford. Her cheek was still wet from his tongue, and she hurt all over.

"Sierra?" Rocky said. "Are you okay?"

She didn't answer.

This outlaw loved to inflict pain. It seemed to feed some kind of twisted, demented need inside him.

Dread of his return brought shivers.

No one could help her.

A tear rolled down her cheek. Even if he *had* survived the attack, she'd never see Sam again.

❧

Sam jumped off the wagon before it stopped at the corral and raced to his horse that one of the cowboys had already saddled, with his father and Houston behind.

Ranch hands had mounted up, waiting for orders.

Stoker stuck his foot in the stirrup. "Are you sure you're up to this, Sam?"

"Let's go." Sam bit his tongue to hold back a groan of pain and pulled himself into the saddle, biting his tongue to hold back the groan of pain. He met his brother's and father's eyes and nodded. Silent and grim, they galloped toward the crossbar.

With the three Legends leading about two dozen ranch hands, they rode in pitch black toward Lost Point.

A muscle worked in Sam's jaw. He wouldn't return without Sierra. And for those who hurt her…

This would be a day of reckoning.

His thoughts swept to their lovemaking a few hours ago. He wished he'd said the words that had sat in his heart.

He loved her. He did with all his heart and soul. But dammit, he hadn't told her, and now he might never get a second chance. His eyes filled with tears. If, by some way, they survived this, he'd change.

Whatever he had to do, he'd make it work, even if it meant giving up the Texas Rangers, something he never thought would happen. But she meant far more to him than his damn job. He wouldn't be a part-time husband. Sierra deserved a whole life.

If Bardo or Luke or anyone killed her—God have mercy on their soul.

His eyes narrowed as he tried to see through the black of early morning. He didn't think Luke would harm the woman he called *dulce*. But then, Sam never thought he'd join forces with those against them either.

Luke Weston had more darkness in his soul than

Sam had known. Maybe no one could save an outlaw like him. When that black demon took over, some men couldn't fight it. It was too strong.

The time would come when Sam would kill him. He'd have to.

Maybe that time would come today.

To kill the bad in him, he'd also have to kill the good.

When it came, Sam would will his finger to pull the trigger. It wouldn't mean the brotherly love he felt would die. That would always be there. Even as darkness had taken root in Luke, love for his brother would always be there in Sam's heart.

Sam glanced at Houston riding beside him. Though they'd fought and had words, Sam had always loved him. And Stoker. They were family and blood.

That was something Luke had never known. Or Sierra.

Filled with deep sorrow, Sam shook his head and focused on the task ahead. Today, Sierra would know how it felt to have someone fight for her.

~

Sierra was grateful the outlaws hadn't stuck a gag in her mouth. She and Rocky talked for a while about everything that had happened since Waco.

"The outlaws first took me to Hell's Half Acre in Fort Worth, where we waited for Felix Bardo," Rocky said. "They fed me little, because they stayed drunk. I managed to get away for a short time until they caught me. After that, the beatings started. Things got even worse when Bardo arrived. He thrives on violence. He brought me here to Lost Point."

The picture Rocky painted sent a shudder through her. Bardo had no conscience or soul.

"Sister, I wish I could protect you from him. When he comes back, don't fight, because that only makes him crazier. There's no telling what he'll do. To me or to you."

"Rocky, I can't just lie there and not fight back," she whispered. "It's not in me."

A key worked the lock on the door. When it swung open, shock ran the length of her.

William Hunt filled the space.

Ford shoved her father inside. "Thought you might have family stuff to catch up on, Hunt. Before Bardo kills them, you get to watch your son and daughter suffer." Ford's sinister laugh brought chills.

Before the outlaw left with the light, Sierra took in her father's haggard appearance and the blood oozing from his mouth. No one spoke as Ford removed her father's shoes and checked the ropes binding him. William Hunt stared straight ahead with cold eyes.

Ford gave them a snarl, picked up the lantern, and left.

Why didn't her father speak?

Silence had to mean she was still dead to him. Her heart ached. But still, she had to try. "Father? Are you all right?" she asked.

He was quiet for so long that she thought he wouldn't answer. Then he cleared his throat. "Don't worry about me." William Hunt's low voice grated in the darkness. He sounded tired. "The thing is…I don't know what to say, Sierra. I'm the reason these men took Rocky and you. The reason they've been chasing after you."

His words chilled her. "I don't understand. Do you know them?"

"No, but I set them on your trail." William's voice cracked. "I…uh…" He cleared his throat. "I told them you took the map they want."

"Why?" She wanted to cry, the gut-wrenching sorrow seeping down into her bones. Had he truly hated her so much?

"I tried to save my own skin. When they showed up in my camp, looking for the map, I knew they'd hurt or kill me if I didn't give them something. I told them you and Rocky had taken it." Her father's voice held remorse and pain. Too little, too late. "After I realized what I'd done, I boarded the first train to Texas." William Hunt sobbed. "I'm sorry, Sierra. I never meant to cause this. My anger took over."

Her brother spoke. "How did you know where we were?"

"A woman in Waco came to the newspaper office and said you'd both been taken by a rough bunch of men, but she didn't know anything more." William Hunt took a deep breath. "I went to the saloon, looking for more information, and overheard two men talking about you. Then one told the other that they'd been ordered to hurry here to Lost Point."

"Texas is a big state," Sierra said dryly, not believing. "How did you know which direction to go?"

"I followed the men for a good ways but lost them when I stopped to catch an hour or two of sleep. After that, I asked for directions in the towns I went through."

"I'm glad you came." Her brother's voice held relief. "Maybe now they'll let us go."

"Is it too much to ask for forgiveness?" her father asked.

She hesitated, unsure if she could forgive the hateful words and actions. The way he'd pulled them into this mess. How could a parent do that to his children?

How could a father say those hurtful things that had destroyed his daughter's self-worth? Sierra huddled in the quiet. She would withhold judgment.

At last Rocky spoke up. "I forgive you, Father."

Not trusting herself to speak, Sierra kept silent.

"He seems genuinely sorry, Sierra," Rocky said. "He's suffered."

William Hunt had suffered? That was laughable.

When she spoke, her words were hard, and she offered no apology. "Did you bring the map, Father? Or did you leave it in a safe place to go for later after they've killed me and Rocky?"

She had no kindness left for the man who'd thrown her away like a piece of garbage.

None.

"I deserve that," her father said. "And more. I lost the original map and have been looking for it for a very long time. I realized that these men wouldn't know, so I drew another one and smudged it up to make it look old. That's what I gave them now, hoping to spare your lives."

Nothing would change the minds of their captors. Their fate was sealed. These weren't men who would allow witnesses to live. Bardo, Ford, and the others would do as they wished with them.

"What did the map go to, Father?" Rocky asked. "You never said."

"Confederate gold that a friend sent me to bury thirteen years ago. I dug a hole along Trammel's Trace, not far from Stephenson's Ferry. The heavily wooded area provided the perfect place."

"How much do you think the gold's worth?"

"More than you or I combined will ever see in this lifetime. It would've made such a difference in our lives. I had to struggle to get the box from the mule into the hole. Never saw anything so heavy. Must've weighed a ton."

Sierra searched for some memory. "When did you come back to Texas to do this? I never knew you left the mountains."

"You were only six years old, Sierra. Rocky was ten. I was gone most of the time anyway, so you wouldn't have known. I didn't even tell your mother that month I was away."

His words bore truth. Memories of those years crowded Sierra's mind. Little food except what they could scrounge, a dark cave for a home, cold nights when she huddled next to Whitney and her brothers to keep warm. They'd lived no better than wild animals.

All while her father had a fortune in gold hidden.

Tired of it all, Sierra struggled against the ropes, but they wouldn't give. They cut into her, bringing pain. She felt the blood running down her wrist and pooling in her palm.

Panic made her heart race. Felix Bardo would come soon.

Despite her brother's plea not to fight, Sierra knew she would. She would die fighting, just like Sam would. Looked like she was a ranger's woman after all. "Rocky, try once more to loosen your ropes."

"Mine don't seem to be too awfully tight," her father volunteered.

If only one could get free, they could untie the others, jump anyone who came through the door, and hopefully escape. Only she didn't know how far she could trust her father. He'd betrayed them once to save himself. He'd probably do it again.

Were he to get out from his ropes, he'd escape and leave his children behind.

She tried to stick her bare feet under her dress to warm them.

"Try to get some sleep," William Hunt said. "Save your strength for later."

Right. The only thing she'd save for him would be contempt.

"Do you think your friends might come to rescue us?" her father had the audacity to ask.

She'd seen Luke riding with the outlaws. He hadn't even looked at her, much less tried to intervene on her behalf. It left her with the realization he'd joined them. The intense betrayal and hurt in her heart made her physically ill. This would kill Sam—if he was alive.

She thought of Stoker and Houston. Even if Sam had died trying to save her, they'd come. They had backbones of steel and more heart than she'd ever seen in a family. Nothing but death would stop the men of Legend.

Thirty-nine

An hour west of the Lone Star, Sam and the riders reached Lost Point.

Sam dismounted behind a cluster of scrub oak and mesquite and joined his father and Houston. "They'll put a bullet in Sierra's head the minute they see us. Let me go in alone and see if Bardo has her here or out at his other location. It might save us time and needless spilled blood."

"We're coming with you." Stoker's bullish eyes met his.

Houston planted his feet. "You're not up to doing much fighting. We can help."

"Look, one man can slip in and out quietly. If they hear anything or get suspicious we're near, they'll kill her." The thought of holding her lifeless body in his arms stopped Sam's heart. "Please, I beg you, let me do this alone."

Stoker placed a hand on Sam's shoulder. "All right, son. Do it your way. But if I hear any shooting, I'm coming in with guns blazing."

"If that happens, Pa, I pray you hear it." Sam

allowed his mouth to twitch. "Once I know where she is, I'll make my way back."

"I'll give you twenty minutes." Houston opened his watch and struck a match to check the time. "That's all. I just hope I run into our traitor brother. I'll let my Colt do the talking."

"Hell, if Luke has gone bad, I'll shoot him myself," Stoker said grimly.

Sam gave a nod. "I'd give anything to be wrong about him."

Now he knew where Luke had been going when he rode out at night. No doubt he'd been in cahoots with the low-down bunch the whole damn time.

"One other thing—a big favor, Pa. Hector is all alone in the world. I'm not saying it will, but if something happens to me or Sierra, give him a home. And love."

His father cleared his throat and blinked. "You got it."

Without more, he silently slipped from behind the scrub oak. If Sierra was there, they'd have lookouts posted. No lookouts would mean this wasn't where they kept the captives.

This dry area of Texas had precious little vegetation, so not much to offer in the way of cover. Scrawny clumps of scrub oak, mesquite, and juniper wouldn't hide much.

He tried to avoid the low brush that could scrape his trouser legs and make noise, but the darkness made it difficult.

The rocky ground posed a special problem. Loosen a rock or let his heel scrape one, and his careful approach would be for naught.

Sweat rose on Sam's forehead as he crept along. Daylight would come soon, but he needed every possible second of darkness to cover him.

His sharp focus was all that stood between Sierra and death. He scanned every bush, mesquite, and gully. When a noise came off to the right, he froze and pointed his Colt. A harmless jackrabbit hopped from a thick mass of sagebrush and broomweed. Sam kept moving, silent and deadly.

The buildings rose up on the main street ahead.

He noticed the lookouts just in time. Odd that they hadn't been there the day before. But they didn't have Sierra then. They now knew the Legends were coming to get her.

Sam ducked behind some thick juniper and peered through the branches, paying no mind to the sharp needles sticking him. He'd come to the right place. Sierra was here.

Two guards with rifles and six-shooters at their hip kept watch. Sam skirted them and worked his way to two brightly lit buildings. One was the saloon. A group of well-armed outlaws lounged near the swinging door.

Judging by the noise, those inside were celebrating. Probably playing cards and bragging how they'd bested the Legends. He'd find Luke there. No doubt waiting for them. The outlaw would have something special in store for Stoker, the father Luke hated. Sam clenched his back teeth so hard he thought he heard them crack.

Too bad his rotten brother would soon pay the price of betrayal. As soon as he knew Sierra was safe, he was coming for Luke. Sam moved on to the second building, where only a few low lanterns burned. It was silent. He'd bet a year's pay she was there, but with no windows in the structure, he couldn't make sure.

While he tried to decide whether to try to bust down the door, Sally hobbled from a small dwelling, moving slowly on her crutches. She headed toward the mercantile. Sam snuck around to the building and waited until she arrived.

"Miss Sally, don't be afraid. It's Sam Legend," he called softly from the thick shadows.

She turned toward his voice. "It's too dangerous for ya here, Ranger."

"I only want a quick word. If you'll speak to me, go on in and wait. Don't light a lamp, please. I'd rather no one knows I'm here."

"There's bad doin's goin' on here. I'll do what you ask."

Once she disappeared through the door, Sam followed. He made out her form in a chair by the counter. "Thank you, Miss Sally." He moved toward her. "Bardo raided our ranch tonight and took a woman, Sierra Hunt."

"Not surprised. Heard him braggin' he was gonna." Sally's voice quivered. "Wouldn't know nothin' 'bout no woman bein' here though. I hunker down at dark. But I did see that man you came lookin' for. Felix dragged him into that buildin' over yonder, the one with a small light."

Sierra had to be there too. Relief flooded over him.

"Thanks, Miss Sally. You've been a big help. One more thing before I let you go about your business. Would you know if Bardo stations men in there?"

"Naw, they come 'n' go. I figure only captives in there. I'd offer to try to see for ya, but Felix would chop off my other leg." Her thick fear filled her voice.

"No, ma'am. I wouldn't ask that. I'm obliged to you."

"I hope you hurry an' find that woman. I've seen some of 'em after he gets finished. Not much left." Sally leaned on her crutches. "Now I gotta get some bread bakin' for Bardo an' the others. If'n I don't have any, my goose is cooked."

"Men from the Lone Star are waiting to attack. When you hear shooting, get down, and don't come out until it's over."

"Appreciate the warnin', Ranger."

Sam left with a better feeling. Vowing to check on her after it was over, he silently returned to the place where Sierra likely was. The twenty minutes Houston gave him was ticking by. Even now, they might be mounting up.

Cold fear swept over him. What he did now would determine if Sierra lived or died. One misstep, one glimpse of him, and his world would end.

But no matter the cost to him, he had to get to her.

With his mind made up, he gripped his pistol and burst through the door, splintering the wood.

Ford jumped up from a chair, but before he could pull his weapon, Sam took it. "You won't need this."

"You're a dead man, Ranger. When Bardo finds out you're here, he'll send you to your grave."

"Yeah? I've heard that threat before from tougher outlaws than you." Sam stuck the gun in Ford's ribs and glanced around the small room. Three straight-backed chairs. Dried blood was on the floor around one. In addition to the chairs was a small table. Nothing else. A door had to lead into another part. "Give me the key to the room where you have the woman."

"Who said she's here?" The outlaw whirled, knocking Sam's gun from his grip.

Before Ford could blink, Sam grabbed his arm, twisting it hard behind him.

"The key. Now!"

Hate glittered in the man's cruel eyes as Isaac Ford reached into his pocket. But instead of pulling out a key, he drew a small derringer. Wise to all the tricks bad men played, Sam was prepared. The second he saw the weapon, he grabbed the outlaw's hand and forced it above his head. The derringer clattered to the floor.

In the ensuing struggle, they shattered the chair, then fell back hard into the wall. The wood gave way with a loud crack.

Growling, Ford scrambled for a jagged chair leg and slammed it across Sam's back. Pain shooting through him took his breath. He blinked hard and jabbed his elbow into the man's chest.

A loud grunt filled the space. As Ford brought the length of wood up, Sam grabbed it and forced him against the wall, pinning the chair leg across Ford's throat.

The outlaw gasped for air, but before Sam could finish him, a piece of metal struck the back of his head. He saw stars as rough hands yanked him around.

"*Hola*, *hermano*. Thought you might come to save *dulce*."

Sam turned and stared into the cold green eyes of Luke Weston.

"Good job, Weston." Felix Bardo pushed through his men blocking the door. "I didn't know if I could trust you, but I guess you showed me. You make a good partner. As long as you remember I'm boss."

That voice—the same one that had permanently lodged in Sam's memory. His heartbeat, his breath stilled. He forced his eyes to focus.

There it was—*the black widow spider staring from Bardo's hand.*

"I've never been much for following, but I will for a share of the gold," Luke replied. "Make no mistake, that's the only reason I'm here."

Instead of thirty pieces of silver, Luke Weston had betrayed them for thirty pieces of gold.

"You could've had much more than that, Weston, if you'd stuck with your family," Sam said softly.

Luke drew back and slammed a fist into Sam's jaw. He staggered backward but stayed on his feet. Sam shot him a deadly look as he wiped blood from his mouth.

"I never needed family." Luke grinned, showing his white teeth. "Gold can give me everything I want. Even buy me one."

"That's right, *amigo.*" Bardo slapped Luke's back. "You know, I think you earned the right to be second with our beautiful *chica*…if she's still alive after I'm done."

A growl came from Sam's throat. He prayed to God he'd get one last chance at Weston. This time he wouldn't hesitate at pulling the trigger. Nothing meant anything to his outlaw brother. Not even Sierra, who'd saved his rotten, miserable life.

Turned bad? Weston was in cahoots with the devil. Evil had eaten away all the good.

Bardo stuck his face next to Sam's. "Now I have some unfinished business with you, Ranger. This time I'll make sure you die. And I promise to make it *very* painful."

The stench of whiskey nearly overpowered Sam.

"Ever hear the saying about not counting your chickens?" Sam ground out.

The scarred outlaw leaned close to Sam's ear. "I had a taste of your woman. She likes it rough. Such soft skin and silky hair. I'm afraid I left some marks on her."

"You bastard!"

"Light the lanterns in the barn," Bardo ordered, giving him a gruesome smile, twisting the scars on his face that could only have been made by fire. The outlaw must've been in untold agony. "We're gonna have some fun, boys. Weston, I have something special in store for you."

"Then let's not waste any time." Luke waved his arm. "Come along, all of you. You don't want to miss this. The more the better to watch Sam Legend get what's comin' to him. Too bad we don't have his pa and real brother. But I bet we soon will."

Just like before, Sam listened for help but heard no galloping horses or gunshots.

Come on, Stoker and Houston, don't dillydally.

Whooping and hollering, the outlaws dragged Sam into a barn. Sleepy horses poked their heads from the stalls and nickered.

Weston yanked Sam's hands behind him and tied

them. Only, his brother sure needed lessons in tying knots. The ropes were loose. But getting free was only part of Sam's dilemma. Outlaws surrounded him. Without a weapon, he didn't stand a chance. Still, getting shot was better than hanging.

Sam worked on the ropes, all the while willing Luke into hell's fire.

"One of you climb up to that loft. Throw a rope over that rafter up there," Bardo ordered. "I'm gonna hang Sam Legend good this time."

The fear pumping through Sam was different from the other hanging. Back then, the unknown was what terrified him. This time he knew the pain, the strangling and choking he faced, and that struck far greater terror.

He thought of Sierra. He'd found the genuine love of a good woman too late. If only he could have one last kiss.

Too late. Agonizing seconds ticked by while he waited. He had only one regret this time—that he hadn't taken the shot when he had the chance.

He glanced at Weston, who watched in silence. Sam could expect no help from him. A thought sprang into his head. Maybe he'd had it wrong. Maybe Luke *hadn't* saved him before. Maybe he'd been with Bardo even back then.

But if not Weston, who had cut him down?

Another thought crossed Sam's mind. The reason Luke boarded the train with him was to report to the boss.

Bardo's words a few minutes ago returned. *You make a good partner.*

He wished he could warn his father and brother somehow. It would be just like Luke to return to the ranch and lie his way again into their good graces. Weston had proven to be a master at deception—everything that came out of his mouth was probably a lie, even down to who his mother was.

What a fool Sam had been. Where was the cavalry? Damn it!

With the rope securely tied to the rafter, Felix Bardo fashioned a noose.

Please hurry, Pa.

Luke pushed a chair into place and pulled Sam onto it. "Get up there, *brother*."

Bardo finished with the noose and handed it to Luke. "I give the privilege to you, my friend. Legend's chased you longer than he has any of us."

"And he never caught me," Luke bragged, taking the rope and stepping forward.

Sam longed to slap the cocky grin off the piece of bear scat.

Luke's cold eyes met his as he slipped the noose over Sam's head, adjusting the stiff hemp around his neck. "I've wanted to send you to hell for a long while, *brother*."

"I'll save a spot for you near the hottest fire. Only a matter of time before you join me. We'll settle up down there."

Still no sound of help. In seconds, he was going to die.

He never got to tell Sierra he'd give up his wandering ways and settle down—tell her he loved her.

I'm sorry, darling. In my heart, you're already my wife.

Forty

"KICK THE CHAIR OUT FROM UNDER HIM, WESTON," Felix Bardo ordered.

Sam took a deep breath, steeling himself. This was it. He couldn't get lucky twice. He feverishly worked at the knots.

But instead of kicking the chair, Luke whirled, drawing his pistol at the same time. He put a bullet in Bardo before swinging to the rest of the onlookers, dropping three as they scattered.

One last jerking twist, and the ropes came off. Sam quickly removed the noose, staring in disbelief at the scene, confusion spinning through him. Who the hell was Luke?

"Here, Sam." Luke pitched him a pistol.

The barn door burst open. Stoker, Houston, and the men from the ranch swarmed inside. Sam turned, searching for Felix Bardo. He'd seen Luke's bullet hit Bardo, but the smoke from the weapons made it difficult to follow the outlaw's shadowy movements. Sam jumped from the chair in time to spy the man he was looking for running down the row of stalls.

Go after Bardo, or get to Sierra? Which to choose? Oh God! He couldn't do both.

Luke turned. "I'll get Sierra. Go!"

Fear lodged in Sam's throat as he raced after Bardo. *Please let Luke get to her before someone executes her.*

❧

The sound of gunshots penetrated the room where Sierra huddled with Rocky and their father. It must be pure chaos outside, as told by the yelling, thunder of horse's hooves, and gunfire.

Someone had come.

Stoker and Houston? She could think of none other. And from the noise, they'd brought plenty of help. But did it mean Sam was alive or dead?

Sierra strangled a sob.

The door burst open—Isaac Ford stood there with his gun drawn. Of course. He must have orders to kill them in case of attack. She shrank tighter against the wall.

Ford saw her. "I think I'll start with the woman." He raised his gun.

"I don't think so." William Hunt sprang up, his ropes falling off as he lunged toward the outlaw. Somehow, he'd managed to free himself. Her father lowered his head and rammed Ford.

The gun went off. Smoke and the pungent smell of spent gunpowder filled the air, choking Sierra.

William Hunt slumped to the floor.

"Father!" she cried.

"Don't worry about him." Ford turned the gun on her. "I hate that I shot out of order, but it doesn't matter. You're next, girl." He leveled the pistol at her heart. "Say your prayers."

Another shot sounded.

The snarl froze on Ford's face. Sierra watched him fall, saw the blood soaking his shirt.

Luke Weston stepped over him and came inside, sliding his Colt into the holster. Sierra gave a cry and tried to scramble away. He was one of them. He'd ridden in the attack against the ranch. If Sam was dead, she'd blame no one but Luke. She'd make him pay dearly.

"Get away from me!" she screamed, full of rage. "You're no better than Ford."

"I came to save you, *dulce*." He stopped. "You know I'd never hurt you. We're friends."

"No," she stormed. "You're one of them. I don't trust you. If Sam is dead, I'll make sure you follow him. Even if I have to do it myself."

"Sam's alive." Luke's words were soft. "He's here."

"You lie. I don't believe you. You're a traitor."

"I speak the truth. I'm not with Bardo. I only pretended to join them so I could learn their plans and put myself in a position to help my brother."

"Why should I believe you?" she spat.

Luke moved closer and knelt down. She saw sadness in his eyes, and hardness, as he pulled her dress together in front. "Because I would never lie to a woman who saved my life. Turn around and let me untie you."

His hands were gentle as he cut the ropes. The minute she was free, she ran to her father. He was still alive.

"Sierra," her father said weakly with blood flowing from his mouth.

"Yes, I'm here." She lifted his head. "Thank you for saving me."

"About time I acted like a father."

Mist filled her eyes as she said the words she'd held back. "I forgive you, Father. For all of it."

"I don't deserve it." A gurgle came from deep inside.

William Hunt was right. He didn't deserve it, but she had to live with herself. Though it would take a long while, maybe one day she could look back at her past without pain.

"Don't talk. Save your strength."

"No, child. I'm not going to make it." He touched her face with his fingertips. "I did and said some terrible things. Even in my anger, I always loved you." He gasped for air.

Freed, Rocky scrambled to them. "Father, I'm here."

"I'm proud...of you both. I've been...rotten father. Nothing can make up...for the pain I've...caused." Her father closed his eyes and drew his final breath.

Luke took her hand. "We need to go now. I told Sam I'd get you to safety."

Numb, cold, and barefoot, Sierra let him lead her into the early morning dawn where bedlam reigned.

Bodies lay all around, and men still battled each other. She didn't see Sam.

Dear God, help him make it through this hell.

"Come, I'm taking you to a woman who'll look after you until we whip these bastards." Luke's gaze swept the grisly scene. Sierra felt his body tense, alert for trouble.

The dirt street was rough and hurt her feet. She wished she had her shoes, not only to shield the tender flesh, but also so she could run in case she had to, but who knew where Bardo's men had taken them. Noticing her trouble, Luke scooped her up and strode to the mercantile.

He rattled the door. "Sally, it's Luke Weston—let me in."

An old woman on crutches finally turned the lock and opened the door. "Almost didn't hear ya over the racket."

"This is the young woman I mentioned—Sierra Hunt and her brother."

"Mr. Sam's lady. Well, don't jus' stand there."

"Thank you, ma'am." Luke pushed his way inside and set Sierra down. He turned to her. "You and Rocky stay here until someone comes for you. I've got to help round up this bunch."

"Thank you, Luke. I'm sorry about earlier."

"Nothing to apologize for. I've got to go."

"Please tell Sam where I am."

He kissed her forehead. "You can count on it."

She watched the old woman he'd called Sally shut and lock the door behind him. Her thoughts turned immediately to Sam. "Stay safe, my love," she whispered.

❧

Pain swept through Sam as he followed the loud trail of groans and cuss words Felix Bardo left. The outlaw wasn't going to escape this time.

Today was a day of reckoning.

Sam sprinted after him. Justice demanded that Bardo pay with his blood for the evil things he'd done. He had to be put down like the animal he was.

As Sam passed each stall, he carefully glanced inside. Then he came to the last one. His quarry had to be in there. Not knowing if the man still had a gun, Sam pressed against the side of the wooden slats.

"Come out, Felix Bardo. You're under arrest."

"You want me, come an' get me," snarled the scarred outlaw.

"Men like you are all alike. Nothing but cowards. When the law catches up with you, never do any of you stand and fight like men." Sam peered around the corner. "You hide like rats."

A bullet splintered the wood next to his ear.

Sam didn't waste a second. He flung open the wooden gate, ducked low, and rolled into the stall, returning fire. The horse inside reared, its forelegs kicking the air. Sam quickly got out of the way before the animal trampled him.

Pressed against the side, Sam spied Bardo crouched in a corner, breathing heavily. Sam's gaze swept to the pistol lying in the blood-soaked straw. So Luke did manage to wound him.

"Out of bullets, I reckon. You're trapped and bleeding like a stuck pig. I've got you this time. You have nowhere to go."

"Too bad your woman is dead." Bardo gave him a twisted smile. "I gave orders to kill her before we brought you to this barn. Even now she lies in a pool of blood."

Rage filled Sam. If Sierra was dead, they may as

well kill him too. She filled every inch of his heart and his mind. Even if she somehow lived, what had she suffered at these brutal outlaws' hands?

What would he find?

Sam moved closer. Bardo suddenly stood and lunged with a pitchfork, barely missing him but catching Sam's gun. It flew to the floor as the terrified horse raced from the stall.

Sam sidestepped and spun around, his hands held wide. Bardo's beady eyes darted this way and that in the dim light, just waiting for him to make a mistake. Sam, too, looked for an opening, one chance to grab the pitchfork. Barring that, getting to his Colt lying three feet away.

If he could just reach it. But he knew the second he tried, Bardo would plunge that pitchfork into his back.

From the noise, the fight outside still raged, though Sam was confident his father and brothers would either shoot or round up the rest of the outlaws. When all this was over, he and Luke had some settling to do.

Bardo's eyes glittered, reminding Sam of a rabid dog he'd encountered a few years ago. That old dog went stark raving mad, didn't know what he was doing. Bardo appeared the same.

Wariness crawled up Sam's spine. A cornered man would do most anything.

"You think you got me, don't you?" Bardo snarled.

"You're not getting out alive. We're ending this here and now."

"It ain't over till *I* say." Bardo jabbed at him with the pitchfork, this time catching Sam's arm, drawing blood. The outlaw's thin lips curled into a smile.

Pain swept up his arm as Sam stood back, waiting for the outlaw's next move. "I'm curious. What were you doing in the Hill Country? That's a long way to drive those beeves."

"Didn't drive 'em. I sold 'em right off. Quick money that way, and I don't have to keep the ornery beasts long." Bardo laughed. "It's why no law has caught me."

Sam took note. This bore the earmarks of a racket that had gone on for years. Captain O'Reilly would be interested.

Grunting, Bardo lunged at him again. Sam grabbed one of the sharp prongs, but he couldn't hold on. He drew back bloody fingers.

Streaks of sunlight came through the cracks in the barn walls. Thank goodness. The darkness had lasted an eternity. Looking around, Sam saw a whip hanging on a hook. He hated to think whose backs they must've used that on. In a sudden move, he reached for it.

Now, he'd evened the odds.

He flicked his wrist, and the whip snapped, licking Bardo's boots. The man leaped backward.

"Scared you, didn't it? Your lawless haven is gone. Everything is gone. You got nowhere to run." Sam cracked the whip just above Bardo's head. "Put down the pitchfork or face this lash. I can stand back over here and whip you until I peel every inch of flesh off your rotten carcass and each scar from your ugly face."

"My men will come any minute and string you up."

My God, the man was demented!

"Keep telling yourself that. Surely you can hear?

My father, brothers, and our ranch hands have already rounded up all your men. No one is going to save you."

"You lie."

Sam cracked the whip again, curling the thin leather strip around the pitchfork handle, yanking it from Bardo's hand. He tossed the implement and whip behind him, disarming them both.

Whipping the outlaw with his fists would bring much more satisfaction.

With a mighty yell, Sam rushed forward and grabbed Felix Bardo around the neck. The outlaw delivered a stinging blow to his face. Tasting blood, Sam shook his head and slung Bardo to the dirty straw littered with big piles of horse manure. Before Sam could finish him off, the outlaw scrambled for Sam's gun on the stall floor.

They collided when Sam lunged. Bardo reached the weapon first, but Sam's hand tightened around the man's wrist, forcing his arm upward.

"You're done for, you bastard. Your reign of terror is over. Turn the gun loose."

Suddenly, Bardo's arm came down, bringing the gun between them. Sam felt the hard steel of the barrel against his chest. With his hand closing around the deadly end of the weapon, he flung it away.

Breathing heavily, Sam hauled the outlaw up.

He had to get to Sierra. He had to know that she was all right. Having her in his arms would right this crazy world.

As Sam marched Bardo out of the stall, the man broke free. He quickly stuck out his leg. The outlaw gave a loud grunt, landing on the packed dirt floor.

Scrambling on all fours, Bardo reached for the pitch-fork at the same time Sam dove for his Colt. Grabbing it, Sam whirled, pulling the trigger.

The hot metal slammed into Bardo's chest, ripping open a gaping hole.

Felix Bardo's sightless eyes stared up at him.

Winded, Sam slumped against the wall, wiping blood from his mouth. It was over. An awful end to a cruel man. Gasping for every bit of air he could draw in, he stumbled out. He had to find Sierra.

He had to hold her. She was his anchor.

His one and only love.

Forty-one

SAM RUSHED FROM THE BARN, BUT JUST AS HE STARTED for the mercantile, he saw Sierra sprinting toward him.

She was alive!

Tears filled his eyes. Racing for her, he swept her into his arms. The kiss was one of thankfulness for getting another chance and searing, raw passion.

He crushed her to him and settled his lips on hers with a savage hunger. Blood pounded in his head as he poured all the love he'd denied himself into her. He felt the wild beat of her heart against him. His splayed hand on her back kept her anchored. He'd never let her go. The woman who'd borne such hurt was his for all eternity.

When he raised his head, he stared into her blue eyes so like the Texas sky. "There's something I need to say. Sierra Hunt, I love you. I love your smile, the depth of your heart, the way you look at me. I don't have all the answers yet, but I'm ready to settle down. With you if you'll still have me. God knows you shouldn't—but will you be my wife?"

"Oh, Sam." Looking up at him, Sierra slid her arms

around his neck. "Yes. My answer is yes. But not because you said you intend to settle in one place. I love you and want to marry you no matter where we live or what kind of life we have. I don't ever want to change you. I love you as you are. For now and forever."

Pure happiness washed over Sam. "I don't deserve you."

Sierra gently touched his face he was pretty sure looked like raw meat. "I was so worried about you. I thought they'd either dragged you to your death, or Bardo had killed you here."

"Takes a sight more than they had." He took in her torn clothing, the man's shirt covering her chest, her bare feet. He winced at the dark bruise covering her cheek and wished he could breathe life back into Bardo and kill him again. "I see they hurt you. I failed in my promise."

Sierra glanced away. Her refusal to meet his gaze told him all he needed to know. "You got here in time. You saved me."

A throat cleared behind them. Sierra turned. "Meet my brother, Rocky. I found him."

Sam shook his hand, liking the firm grip and the way Rocky looked him square in the eye. That was the mark of an honest man. He was about Sam's age and a little shorter, with Sierra's black hair and blue eyes. Rocky's dark beard needed a trim.

"It's good to finally meet you. I'm glad you're all right," Sam said.

As though sensing Sam and his sister needed some private words, Rocky moved to speak to Luke, who watched from the barn door.

"My father was here also," she murmured, stroking Sam's face. "He finally did the right thing and came to buy our freedom. Only Isaac Ford shot and killed him before my eyes."

"I'm sorry."

"I forgave him as he died. He did some unforgiveable things, true, but in the end we made peace."

Sam smoothed back her hair and kissed her forehead. He couldn't wait to get this amazing, beautiful woman alone, and he'd shoot the first person who disturbed them. They had a future to discuss.

"Reckon you're lookin' for these, Miss Sierra," Sally said, hobbling to them. She held out Sierra's shoes.

"Oh, there they are. Thank you, Sally. I'd wondered where to start looking." Sierra kissed the woman's cheek. If kindness was measured by the width of a person's smile, then Sally showed how much the gesture meant to her.

She leaned heavily on the crutches. "Thank you for givin' us back our town, Ranger. We's right grateful."

"You'll be safe now, Miss Sally." Until they let someone else take over. They weren't strong enough to stand up to men like Bardo. "Hire a good sheriff. You'll need law here for the town to thrive. The citizens have a lot of work ahead."

"Yep, we do. Jus' wanted to say thanks."

"Yes, ma'am. Can I help you someplace?"

"Nope, I can manage but appreciate the offer." She hobbled off toward the mercantile.

Sam swept Sierra up and sat her on a bale of hay next to the barn. Then he took each slender foot and slipped on her shoes. Rocky had found his also and sat down next to her to put them on.

"Excuse me just a minute." Sam eyed Luke, who stood with Stoker and Houston, loading the remaining outlaws into a wagon. It was settling time. Sam strode over. Without a word, he drew back and drove a fist into Luke's jaw, knocking him back against the barn wall.

"What the hell, Sam?" His father glared.

"Ask him." He turned and walked toward Sierra. She'd likely never speak of what had happened here, but he knew enough to guess it had been torture. "Damn you, Bardo!" he muttered. He felt like slamming his fist into a wall. "Damn you! I hope you rot in hell."

Before he reached her and Rocky, Luke caught him. "You throw a hell of a punch, Sam." Luke rubbed his jaw. "But I reckon I see why you'd be a little upset."

"*Little* upset?" Sam growled. "You could've let me in on your plan. Given me *some* sort of sign. Wiggled your ears or scratched your rear or something. I understand that you wanted Bardo to think you'd joined them, and your reason for making sure as many of them as possible were here in the barn, but did you have to go so far as to put that noose around my damn neck?"

Houston listened to the exchange in silence, his eyes widening.

"I was buying us a bit more time. I knew reinforcements were close by somewhere, and I know how a hanging holds fascination for a good many. I didn't want Bardo's men wandering off. What better than one brother hanging the other?"

"Next time, we'll switch places," Sam snapped. "I'll put the noose around *your* neck, and you'll know how it feels."

Finally, Houston broke his silence. "I think you owe him an apology, Luke."

"You're right," Luke said. "I really am sorry, Sam. If I could've thought of another way, I'd have done it."

Sam's eyes narrowed. "Why did you join the attack on the ranch?"

"Bardo was testing my loyalty. He didn't trust anyone. He said if I went to raid the Lone Star, he'd make me privy to his plans. When he handed me the torch with orders to throw it, I aimed at the house where I lived, knowing no one would be inside." Luke shook his head. "I didn't know they planned to take Sierra. They never let me close enough to help her."

Sam pushed back his hat. "Sounds like Bardo didn't trust anyone."

"None except Ford, who was his cousin," Luke said.

"I see you have the prisoners in the wagons. Can you both take it from here? And give Rocky a ride, if you don't mind. I need to get Sierra home." Sam's gaze went to her. She was about to fall off the bale of hay. "She's dead on her feet."

"Yep, you go ahead," Houston said. "We'll be along. Need to bury the dead first. About Miss Sierra's father—should I bring his body back to the ranch?"

Sam glanced at her. "No. Bury him here. That's all that needs doing."

"I understand," Houston said with a nod.

"I'll owe you." Sam said his good-byes and took Sierra's hand. "Let's get you home." Arm in arm they went in search of his horse.

A crowd marched up the street. A man dressed in overalls with only one side fastened was evidently the spokesman. He stepped forward. "Legend, can we have a moment of your time?"

"Certainly, but there's no need to thank me."

"Words can't say how much we do, but that's not what this is about."

"What do you need?"

"A good sheriff. One who will help us stand up to lawless men like Felix Bardo. Will you take the job, sir?"

"There are a lot of excellent lawmen."

The spokesman stood his ground. "None of your quality. You put the fear of God into rabble-rousers and lawbreakers."

Sam met Sierra's tired blue eyes. Maybe this was the answer they were looking for. "What do you think, darlin'? Can you be the wife of a sheriff?"

Her fingers curled inside his hand. "I can be happy anywhere you are. I don't intend to be separated from you again. These last few days have taught me many things—my priorities have changed. Please don't give up the Texas Rangers for me. I don't want that."

"My priorities have changed too." His arm went around her. "All I want is to put a smile on your beautiful face. If I get that, then I'll be thrilled with whatever life we choose."

"Pardon me." The spokesman cleared his throat. "Is that a yes?"

Sierra nodded as Sam answered, "I believe it is, Mr...."

"Dink Quinby. Thank you, sir." He stuck out his hand.

Sam liked the firm handshake. It said a lot about the man. "Quinby, we've got a lot of work to do. I have some affairs to put in order first, and need to find a nice place to live. My lady has her heart set on a white house with a picket fence around it. I won't disappoint her. Know of one?"

Quinby grinned. "For you, Sheriff Legend, we'll build one. Matter of fact, we'll begin immediately."

Gazing deep into Sierra's eyes, Sam said, "Her happiness is everything. You help me make her happy, and you and I are going to get along just fine."

Dink Quinby smiled. "We'll work hard to assure it."

"My lady is a schoolteacher. Is there an opening?"

A sad look crossed Quinby's eyes. "The school has sat empty for a long while. We'll welcome her with open arms."

"That means more than I can say, Mr. Quinby." Sierra touched his arm.

Sam smiled at how her warm gesture besotted the man. "I'll ride back in a few days to finalize everything."

"Very good, Sheriff."

"Let's go home, darlin'." Sam turned to see a boy leading Trooper. He fished out two bits. Ruffling his hair, Sam pressed the coins into the small hand. "Thank you, son."

With a shy grin, the boy held the reins until Sam

lifted Sierra into the saddle, then mounted behind her. The horse didn't have to be urged. Trooper ambled toward the Lone Star.

Sam loved the feel of her backside against him. Closing his eyes, he laid his cheek against her hair and took a deep breath. She was alive. That was more than enough. He'd make a home for her and be in her bed every night for the rest of his days.

No more wandering for him.

"I can't wait to get back to the ranch." She swiveled to glance up at him. "I am going to make love to you like you've never been loved, mister. Any argument?"

A big grin covered his face. He could barely hear over the pounding of his heart. "No, ma'am."

"Sam, are you sure this job is what you want? You won't regret taking it?"

"Nope. I'm positive." He pushed her hair aside and kissed her neck. "I'm sorry about the poor job of proposing back there."

Her eyes sparkled like blue gems as she laughed. "Sam Legend, you should know by now that people waste a lot of time trying to conform to rules. Don't count me amongst them."

"I love that wild, rebellious streak in you. It's sexy as hell." He nuzzled her neck and behind her ears. "Sierra, I've looked for you my whole life. I promise to make you happy to the best of my abilities, meager though they are."

"How soon do you think we can make it happen?"

"It's a day's ride to the nearest preacher. If we leave in the morning, we can be in Squaw Valley by late afternoon. We'd have one on the ranch, except he left a while back after his wife threatened divorce if he didn't take her back east to her family."

"I only have one simple hard and fast rule."

"What's that, Miss Teacher?"

"To never stop loving me."

He chuckled. "As if I could."

Nope, he'd love her when the world stopped turning and they laid him in the ground. Even then, he didn't think death was strong enough to separate him from the woman who filled every inch of his heart.

Sierra Hunt was both his love and salvation rolled into one.

Forty-two

THE TALL TEXAS FLAG CAME INTO VIEW BEFORE SIERRA realized how much time had passed. The ride from Lost Point had gone fast. With his powerful arms wrapped around her, she leaned against Sam's chest. Despite being exhausted, she embraced the contentment filling her. Their bodies did the only talking that was needed. Inside that safe cocoon, the miles had melted away.

She glanced down at those arms lying lightly across her breasts. The corded veins bulged. She supposed those veins told of his strength, but she knew it went much deeper, beyond mere skin, tissue, and muscle.

Sam's strength was in his heart and mind. Armed with a sharp sense of justice and dogged determination—this man of Legend would be impossible to defeat.

He was a man to cherish, and she meant to spend the rest of her life doing that—and giving him babies. She wanted lots.

"I've never loved you more than I do at this minute." She kissed the bruised, bloody knuckles of his hand. "When faced with death, I didn't fear for myself. What struck sheer terror in my heart was that I'd never see you again. That you'd never hold me in your arms once more, or kiss me like I'm someone to treasure."

Sam's voice was husky. "You're worth more than a pot of gold. I made up my mind if I failed to get there in time, I'd go off alone somewhere to die. I wouldn't live without you. You're my sun and moon, my compass. *You* pointed me in the right direction when I was lost and alone."

A rider galloped through the gate toward them.

"Looks like we have company." Sam shifted his hold around her and tugged the large shirt she wore closer to cover her ripped bodice. That he took such care to preserve her dignity spread warmth through her.

The rider was Grady Wilkerson, a longtime hand at the Lone Star. He slowed and tipped his hat to Sierra. "Howdy, Boss. Ma'am. I'm mighty glad to see you found Miss Sierra and brought her back. Me and the boys were right worried. 'Course, ain't no one can beat the Legends."

Sierra could vouch for that.

What she would have given to have seen the look on Felix Bardo's face when they showed up. She hoped he suffered greatly before he died.

"It wasn't easy, but we got the job done," Sam replied. "The others are dragging up the rear with two wagons full of outlaws. See if you can rig a place up to keep them until rangers arrive."

"Does it have to be comfortable, like with a bed?"

Sam grinned. "I want them to be god-awful

miserable. Cages, if you can arrange it on such short notice. If not, chain them under a tree."

"Yessir! We can sure do that." Grady's grin covered his whole face. "How far back are they?"

"At least an hour. Maybe more. They're coming slow."

Warmth rushed over Sierra when Sam's arm tightened around her. She was anxious to get undressed and lie next to him. They would soon. Home was a stone's throw.

"Welcome back, Boss. Ma'am. Sure wish I could've been there. I'll go tell the boys the good news."

Trooper must've smelled the oats, because his ears perked up, and he stepped into a trot. Sierra was all for that. She meant to scrub Bardo's stench off her first. Then she'd make slow, passionate love to Sheriff Sam Legend.

Maybe he'd make her his deputy. Now, there was a thought.

❧

With a happy yell, Hector ran to her side when they rode in and followed her and Sam to the corral. She kissed and hugged him, letting the boy see she was all right. Then telling him to give her a minute to get her breath, she and Sam locked themselves in the same bathing room she'd used before in the big house.

While the water ran, Sam removed her ruined clothes. His eyes hardened to jagged bits of ice at the sight of her bruises.

"I'm so sorry. I failed you. I didn't protect you." He kissed each mark of violence.

"Mine are nothing compared to yours. The pain you must be in." Sierra tenderly touched his scrapes, some of which were raw and bleeding.

"None of that matters. I can take it," Sam murmured against her temple.

Her chin rose a bit. "Are you saying I can't?"

"Nope." Lifting her hand, he pressed a kiss to her palm. "Good Lord, I know you have taken more than any person should and still can if you have to. You're one tough lady, and you're all mine. I intend to make it legal as soon as I can."

He helped her into the tub and pulled her back against him. Slowly, he began to wash away the dirt and each painful memory. Something told Sierra they'd never speak of this awful time again, and that was fine with her. To keep going over it wouldn't change the horror of the past, and Felix Bardo would win.

What mattered was to keep looking forward—to their bright, shiny future as husband and wife. Partners. Equals.

Sam valued her, and she adored him.

Tired and weary, she rested her head against his chest. His hands moved over her, soaping her breasts. No one had a gentle touch like Sam Legend's.

For a moment she wondered at this magic that filled her life.

"Sam, will it always be this way, this love we share?"

His voice rumbled in his chest the way men's sometimes did, and the sound sent tingles through her. "My love for you will never, ever fade. I'll always and forever be your husband, friend, and lover. After the hanging, I felt shriveled and dead inside, that there was nothing left of me, that I had nothing to give anyone, not even myself. Then you came and poured your amazing love on me." His voice cracked. "You brought me back to life."

He'd once warned her of the dangers of loving him. Such beautiful words now from this tough, rugged man brought tears to Sierra's eyes. They rolled unchecked down her cheeks.

When she could speak, she maneuvered around and put her hands on each side of his face. "I once told you no one could fix me, that I was broken beyond repair. You did, Sam. I'm strong and whole. Your belief in me helped me find it within myself. I can't wait to share this incredible, wonderful life with you."

Sierra pressed her lips to his in a kiss that bound them as surely as a piece of iron. Heat ran through her veins like molten steel, and she felt it in him too.

Unwilling to wait for a bed, she positioned herself over his jutting hardness and lowered onto him. Powerful spasms of tenderness and passion made her gasp. Surrounded by the slickness of the water, her eyes holding his, Sierra began to move.

Sam's eyes darkened with hunger as he kneaded her breasts, worshipping her with his gaze. Fire shot through her when he took each into his mouth.

She buried her hands in his hair, clutching him to her, wanting everything he had to give. He was her champion. He'd risked death to fight for her.

The memory of once wishing for just one person to say she mattered to them, that they'd stand beside her to the end of time, flooded over her. Tears filled her eyes. She had all of that and more in Sam.

She loved the power to make his breathing ragged and his heart race just like he did to her now. Sierra teased his lips, her hands brushing his scarred chest, murmuring words of love in his ear.

"Lord, woman!" he cried hoarsely.

The light tip of a fingernail raked down his chest as she followed the trail of fine hair even lower. His groan, the heat in his half-closed eyes spoke of deep hunger.

Searing desire lay in the long, scorching kiss. She was through teasing.

Sierra wanted him, ached to have him. Her breath came unevenly. Sam Legend had her heart, her body, and her soul.

His fingers drifted down the column of her throat, between her breasts, sliding down to her stomach. Then gripping her hips, he increased the friction of her body on his. Desire for this man she was going to make a life with shook her to the depths of her being. With each stroke, the smoldering flames in his eyes grew higher.

Sierra gasped with pleasure. One after another, she rode the waves toward fulfillment.

Before the water grew cold, they shattered into millions of twinkling, beautiful stars.

She collapsed against Sam's chest, totally spent.

When they recovered, Sam rose and wrapped a towel around his waist. He put Sierra into a thick robe and carried her to his bedroom. The quiet house told her the others hadn't yet arrived.

His bed swallowed her as she knew it would, but that was all right. Sam filled most of it with his large frame. She sank into the softness and reached for the corner of the towel he wore. Her hunger for him was insatiable."

"Love me, Sam," she said.

❧

Those quiet, perfect moments ended way too soon when the prisoners arrived and Sam had to get them settled. He glanced up from checking the ropes binding them when a rider rode toward the house from the gate.

Sam narrowed his gaze. As the lean horseman drew closer, he recognized Texas Ranger Tom Burdine.

"What brings you this way?" Sam called.

"What's going on, Legend?" Chuckling, Tom dismounted. "Did Stoker decide to open up his own jail now?"

"You mean the prisoners?" Sam told him about Felix Bardo's den of snakes. "Any thoughts on how to get the live ones to jail?"

"Gonna have to wire for more rangers to bring a prison wagon." Burdine pushed back his hat. "Heard Stoker put in his own telegraph."

"You heard right. Why the visit, Tom?"

In the long pause, Tom glanced around. "The size of this ranch boggles the mind."

"It's big, all right." Why was the ranger avoiding the question?

"Might as well get right down to it." Burdine removed his hat to wipe his forehead with a sleeve. "U.S. Marshal Henry sent a telegram and never got a reply. Anything you want to tell me?"

Sam had been expecting this. "Let's get you something to drink and talk."

Over the next hour, he came clean about Luke. About everything.

Finally, Tom Burdine wagged his head and set down his whiskey. "I wouldn't be able to arrest mine either. It's a hell of a deal to find out your own brother is an outlaw. I'll think of somethin' to tell Marshal Henry. Hopefully, you can help Luke, but a large part is up to him."

"Thanks for not hauling us both to the calaboose." A sudden thought hit Sam. "Tom, didn't you used to be a preacher before you joined up with the Texas Rangers?"

"Yep. Got tired of savin' my flock every Sunday after they'd been robbin' and lyin' and cheatin' and beatin' their wives during the week. Decided they'd listen better to a gun than sermons. I'm much happier sendin' them to God and lettin' him sort it all out. Why?"

Sam told him about Sierra. "We want to get married. Tomorrow."

Ranger Burdine's eyes narrowed. "Why the rush?"

"It's not what you think, Burdine. Death almost claimed us last night. We don't want to spend a minute longer apart than we have to." Sam's gaze drifted out the window of Stoker's office, and his heart caught at the sight of her coming toward headquarters.

A solemn smile broke across Tom Burdine's whiskered face. "Death can be a motivator all right. When do you want the ceremony?"

"Come with me and ask the lady yourself."

Sierra's smile widened when she saw him. He loved how her smile made her eyes twinkle. Sam introduced her to Burdine and said his friend was a preacher. "He wants to know when you'd like the ceremony to take place tomorrow."

Sierra wrapped her arm around his and gazed into his eyes. "At sundown. I've always thought sunsets to be God's paintings to us."

"Sunset tomorrow it is." Sam gave her a wink.

"Below the bronze star with the Texas flag flying," Sierra added quickly.

❧

A whirlwind descended over the Lone Star as preparations began for the big celebration the following day. Sam sent Captain O'Reilly a telegram to apprise him of the situation with Bardo and his gang and to tell him about the rustling ring. The captain replied that a man had come forward and they'd arrested a wealthy businessman for being the leader of the operation. His former boss told him the rangers would be the worse for losing such a good lawman and wished Sam congratulations and good luck.

Now, Sam sat with Sierra and Rocky on the wide porch, watching Hector play with some toys they'd scrounged from the mercantile.

He glanced up to see Sofia, Carlos, and the other displaced families strolling toward them. They formed a line and came up the steps one by one. Sam held Sierra's hand and stood as each person congratulated them. The group told them their plans for music and dancing after the wedding.

"We take care of everything. *Sí*?" Carlos said, grinning.

"Thank you, *amigo*. You don't know how much work this saves me," Sam said with a chuckle.

Maria took Sierra's hand. "We bring flowers. *Sí?*"

"Oh, Maria, thank you." Sierra gave her young friend a hug. "You're a dear."

Hector jumped up from his toys to throw a spindly arm around both of them and grinned as though giving his blessing. A mist filled Sierra's eyes. The boy had no one. What would become of him?

She took Sam aside. "What do you think about adopting Hector? I'd like to make him our son."

Sam took her hand and kissed her fingertips. "I'm glad you mentioned it, because I've been thinking of doing just that. I love that little boy. My heart aches to see him so alone."

With his arm around her, Sam called Hector over. He and Sierra knelt down beside him. In halting Spanish, he asked the boy if he'd like to belong to them, be their son.

Tears bubbled in Hector's eyes, and his lips quivered. He glanced down at his feet, then at Sierra. He touched her cheek, and a sob escaped. Overcome, the boy swung his gaze to Sam and nodded.

Hector dragged his sleeve across his eyes and whispered, "Hap-py."

A few minutes later, Sam stood behind Sierra and folded his arms around her. "I can't wait to make you mine. This wedding, starting our lives together, will be everything we dared to dream of."

Rocky and Ranger Burdine wandered up onto the porch. The ranger grabbed a chair and leaned back, propping his feet on the railing. Sam grinned, remembering the days of riding with his ranger friend and the narrow scrapes. Burdine had more courage and more heart than any man he'd ever ridden with. Though a part of Sam was sad those days were gone, he had so much more waiting. He kissed Sierra's dainty ear as Hector slipped his hand in hers.

"How did you meet such a nice group of people?" Rocky asked.

Sam told both men how Luke got shot, running into the travelers' caravan, and what a lifesaver the weary travelers had been. "Luke wouldn't have lasted if not for them. I offered the families work here on the ranch, so they stayed," Sam explained. "What will you do now, Rocky?"

"I'll go back to Waco right after the wedding." Rocky rubbed his dark beard. "I'm anxious to open up the newspaper office. I have to get these stories out of my head."

"Can't you wait just a little longer?" Sierra begged.

"I'm afraid not, sis. I've been gone too long already."

Luke trotted up on his black gelding and dismounted at the hitching rail. He sauntered up the steps in that lazy way of his. Sunlight reflected on the silver conchas running up the side of each black trouser leg.

Luke spoke to Sierra and Rocky before turning to Sam. "Got time for a word?"

"Sure." They walked down the steps where they could talk. "What's up?" Sam asked.

Luke seemed even more quiet and withdrawn. Something was bothering him. "How about a ride, little brother?"

"Certainly. When?"

"Daybreak. You wanted answers to your questions. I'll show you so you'll understand."

At last. Relief flooded over Sam. That Luke trusted him meant more than he could say.

"Anything to help me learn more about my brother." Sam paused, then said with a grin, "Just as long as I get back in time for my wedding."

"You will. It'll take the better part of the day, so we'll have to leave very early."

"Then absolutely. I can spare the time."

Finally, Sam would learn what made Luke do what he did. He couldn't imagine what he'd find, but he couldn't wait.

Forty-three

THOUGH THE TALK WAS LIVELY AND LAUGHTER FREE, Sam could hardly sit through his prewedding supper for thinking about his impending ride with Luke. He sensed a turning point in their relationship and welcomed it. His brother was full of contradictions.

Sam put his thoughts aside for now and focused on the celebration. Every seat at the long table was full. Houston's Becky Golden had arrived with her parents and would stay until after the wedding. Despite all that, it was Sierra who stole Sam's attention. She sat next to him in a pretty rose-colored dress he'd never seen before. The bodice dipped low in front, and he had hell keeping his eyes from straying to her enticing cleavage. Anticipation of stripping away the fabric made it difficult to sit still and calmly make conversation.

He draped an arm around her and leaned close. "You certainly know how to torment a man."

Sierra looked at him with wide eyes. "Whatever do you mean, Sheriff Legend?" she drawled.

"You know very good and well what you do to me," Sam growled. "You're asking for trouble."

"Oh my, I do hope so." She grinned and kissed his cheek.

How in the hell had he gotten so lucky? And how could he sit there patiently while he wanted to whisk her away to her little schoolteacher house and bar the door. He watched her tuck a napkin into the neck of Hector's clean shirt before leaning across the table to speak quietly to Becky Golden, looking all pretty with her blond hair and big brown eyes. The two already seemed fast friends. But how could anyone not love Sierra? She was one of those people everyone wanted to be with.

Him most of all.

Stoker cleared his throat behind Sam. "Don't want to interrupt, but I need a few words." He'd pulled his chair over next to Sam and dropped into it. "I love you, Sam. I've been a poor hand at saying that. I apologize for being absent when you most needed a father.

"I'm going to make that up to you, son," Stoker continued. "I'm turning over a new leaf. No more drinking myself blind. I realized today how close I came to losing you and how much time I've wasted." His voice broke. "Besides, I'll soon have a grandson now. I can't have Hector thinking his grandpa is some no-account drunk."

Sam gazed at his father and tried to swallow. He knew how much the words had cost Stoker. "You don't have to apologize, Pa. I always knew if I needed you, you'd come running. I'm glad you're cutting back on the bourbon though. That stuff'll kill you, and I'm not ready to bury you alongside Mother yet."

"I'm not ready either." Stoker laid a hand on Sam's back. "I'm real glad you took the sheriff's job over at Lost Point. I like having you near."

"So you're okay with it?"

His father let out a deep sigh. "Son, I'd rather you live here on the Lone Star, but I want you to do what makes you happy. It's not far if I want to ride over and pay you a visit."

Would wonders never cease? "Thanks, Pa."

"I have a wedding gift, and I want no argument." Stoker's blustery voice softened. "Before you say anything, it's not land or money. Fact of the matter, it doesn't cost one cent, but it's more valuable than all the land and cattle I own."

"You sure know how to be mysterious, Pa."

Stoker handed Sam a large envelope. "I think you'll like it."

Sierra finished talking to Becky and swiveled around to Stoker. "You're always full of surprises, Stoker. Thank you for opening your arms and your heart to me. I've never known anyone like you."

"I'll be your father…if you'll let me," Stoker said gruffly.

Sam watched the woman he loved struggle not to cry.

"I accept. I never had much of a father, and now he's gone." She leaned to kiss his cheek. "Thank you for taking me in."

"It's no hardship to love you, dear." Stoker patted her hand.

Under his father's watchful eye, Sam broke the seal and removed two items, one of which was a letter. His heart stilled at sight of a woman's delicate blue handkerchief. His fingers trembled as he held it to his face. He couldn't stop a tear from trickling down his cheek.

"What is it, Sam?" Sierra asked.

"This belonged to my mother. It still smells like her. God, I miss her so much." He reached for Sierra. "How I wish she was here."

She gently rubbed his back. "She is here in spirit, sweetheart. I know it. Let's see what she says."

With a nod, Sam unfolded the letter from Hannah Legend and read aloud.

Dearest Sam,

If you're reading this letter, then it means that this is your wedding day. I asked your father to give you this. I regret that I cannot be there to welcome your new bride into our family, as I know she will be a very special woman. I already know you love her, because you, my precious son, will never settle for anything less. I would tell her to be patient and gentle with you. I feel a need to warn the poor dear. Of my two boys, you have a stubborn streak a mile wide. Blame it on your father. You didn't get that trait from me.

Sam's mouth curled into a smile. Who was she kidding? Hannah Legend was one of the most stubborn women God ever put on the planet. She certainly gave Stoker a run for his money. He continued to read.

You've always had a restless spirit. Only the love of your life can change that. I suspect my new daughter will.

To both of you. Marriage can be a challenge, but oh, the rewards far outweigh any problems that arise. Always treat each other with respect and love. If you do this, you'll have someone to stand beside and weather the storms with.

To my new daughter, I would say that you're a very lucky woman. You'll find no bigger heart in any man than Sam's. He's a diamond in the rough, though, and needs some corners sanded down. But you couldn't get a better husband.

One of my biggest regrets is that I won't get the pleasure of spoiling my grandchildren rotten. I do foresee many. You'll make a wonderful father, Sam. Teach them how to be men and women you can be proud of. You have a great legacy to pass on—Legend courage, Legend honor, and Legend pride to instill in them.

Be happy always. Never settle for second best, and never compromise your principles. Those are the foundation upon which to build.

Now go kiss your bride, Sam, and spend the rest of your days being the husband I know you will be.

> *Much love and tenderness,*
> *Your mother*

Sam clutched the letter and handkerchief, struggling to swallow past a big lump blocking his airway. His mother's gentle advice, her spirit, and her love, even from heaven, deeply touched him. Her foresight to do this so long ago, just for his special day, staggered him.

A sniffle drew his attention to Sierra. She brushed tears away with her hand, clearly as moved as Sam. He reached into his vest pocket, but Stoker beat him, handing Sierra a handkerchief. Sam put his arm around her, full of love for this woman who'd taught him so much.

"Your mother was an amazing person, Sam," Sierra said with a sniffle. "If only I could've known her."

"I wish you could've too, darlin'." He glanced back at his father waiting behind them. "We'll both treasure this gift forever, Pa. It means a great deal to us. But when did Mother write this?"

"Two months before she died." Stoker cleared his throat. "She made me promise to give them to you and your wife on your wedding day. Left one for Houston too. I'd almost despaired of a reason to save them. You sure took your own sweet time," he ended gruffly.

Sam scowled. "Houston is older than me."

His father sighed again. "I know. But he's also coming around."

"I'll always treasure Mother's handkerchief and words."

"I thought you might." Stoker rose and grabbed his chair. "I'm glad you're adopting Hector. He's a smart boy. Don't worry about him for a few days. I'm going to get acquainted with my grandson. Gotta get started on teaching him about the ranch. Now, let's get back to the celebration. Houston has asked for a moment."

After Sam and his father returned to their seats,

Houston took Becky's hand and stood. "Many of you know that I've been seeing someone very special for a while—"

"You could've knocked me over with a feather," Stoker interrupted with a chuckle. "I'm sorry, go ahead, son."

"Ruin the moment, Pa," Houston joked with a grin. "Tonight, Miss Becky Golden and I are announcing our engagement." Houston gazed deep into his love's eyes. "Becky wants a May wedding, and I just want her. So this is a double celebration, I reckon you might say."

Sam raised his glass high. "To you and Becky. May you find the same happiness and joy that Sierra and I have, brother." He and Sierra hurried around the table to congratulate them.

As Sam moved toward Houston, he stopped short. Luke sat with a sad, strange look on his face, and trying awfully hard to hide it.

Sam sat down next to him. "What's the matter?"

"Don't mind me, Sam. Go on over there."

"Nope, I'm not budging until you talk." He laid a hand on Luke's shoulder. "Something's wrong. Now spill it."

"Thinking about someone is all. I'm not fit company." Luke attempted a smile but didn't make it and pushed back his chair. "Excuse me. I'll congratulate our brother and Becky and get out of here. You and me have an early ride planned come morning."

With his heart aching, Sam watched him say a few words to the happy couple and saunter from the room. If only he could change things for his brother. Luke had no plans for marriage, no letter from his mother reminding him he was cherished.

If the shoe was on the other foot, Sam knew how he'd feel.

Alone.

Unloved.

Probably unwanted as well. Hell!

Across the room, Sierra met his gaze and smiled, sending a silent message. He rose and moved to her side, slipping an arm around her waist. "Let's offer our best wishes and leave. What do you say, soon-to-be Mrs. Legend?"

"I say yes. Do you think Luke will be all right though?" She sent a concerned glance toward the door.

"He'll be fine. Just too much family overload and bad memories."

A few minutes later, after offering their best wishes, Sam drew Sierra close for the short walk to her small house. When they reached the door, he swept her into his arms and carried her over the threshold. With one foot, he kicked the door shut.

"Sam, you were supposed to wait until *after* we're married to carry me inside," Sierra moaned.

"So I'll do it twice. Besides, how do you know about this rule, lady? I thought mountain folk didn't pay attention to this sort of thing."

"It was a custom amongst some of the trappers," she explained. "Their wives told me."

Sam set her down. "Why don't we make it a ritual for every night?"

With a giggle, Sierra kissed the hollow of his throat. "I might get too fat, and you won't be able to lift me."

"Silly woman." Sam couldn't see this slender woman getting fat. Nope.

He didn't light a lamp. Didn't need to. He knew Sierra's body like the back of his hand, and the silver moonbeams streaming through the window provided all the light they'd need. Besides, he'd just have to blow it out in a second anyway, and he was all for saving time.

"Come here." He pulled her against his chest, feeling her wild heartbeat. The kiss Sam pressed to her lips spoke of deep hunger he doubted he could ever satisfy.

"I couldn't wait to get you behind a locked door," he growled, nuzzling her neck while he worked at her buttons. "Where did you get such a scandalous dress? I couldn't keep my eyes off you. I wanted to kiss you, run my hands over your body, make mad, passionate love to you right there in the dining room. And whip every man who stared at you."

"Heavens, I'm sure glad you didn't." Sierra giggled. "Can you imagine the stir we'd have made?"

"Yep." His lips found hers again. "Only thing that curbed my impatience."

As he released the last button, the dress slithered to the floor. The rest took very little time. He kissed her silky shoulders.

"Sam, I felt the same way about you. You're the most handsome man I've ever seen." Sierra ran her fingers through his thick dark hair. "Your tanned skin against that white shirt made me ache with want. So dark and lean. But it was the smoldering flame in those beautiful gray eyes that made me tingle all over. I can't believe I'm going to be your wife. That you would want someone like me when you could have your pick from dozens of others."

"None of them are you. You're the only one who has what I want." Sweeping her up, he carried her to the bed where she propped her head on her arm and watched him undress.

"Are you really sure about this new job, Sam?"

He shed the last of his clothing. "Please stop asking, Miss Worrier. I can't think of anything more fulfilling than helping that town and those people get back on their feet. I have lots of ideas rolling around in my head." He lay on his side next to her and lifted a tendril of her hair, caressing it between his thumb and forefinger. "I want to draw new settlers, set up a stage line, and make Lost Point a thriving community."

"I'm glad." She kissed the hard planes of his chest and licked each nipple, drawing Sam's moan. Sierra raised her head. "I'll help. We'll make it a wonderful place to live."

"No more talking," he growled, rolling on top of her. "I'm going to show you a few tricks I know, and before the night is over, you'll be one *very* happy almost-wife."

"But are you sure you're up to it with all your bruises and scrapes and raw knuckles?"

Sam laughed. "Even if I was half dead, it wouldn't stop me from doing what I'm about to. Are you scared?"

Sierra's fingers tenderly brushed back his hair. "Hush and kiss me."

Forty-four

THE FIRST FRINGES OF DAYLIGHT STOLE THROUGH THE
window like a thief, and already Sam was up and
dressed. He turned to kiss his sleeping beauty, only
to find her awake, watching him. The cast-iron bed
creaked when he sat down on the edge.

"Good morning, darlin'." Sam captured her lips,
tracing the curve of her hip. "Sorry I woke you."

"You didn't." She let her fingers trail down his
chest. "I doubt if either of us slept. You didn't fib. You
definitely made me a *very* happy soon-to-be wife."

The news pleased him. Hearing the smile in her
voice caused his heart to race. She'd come a long way
from the woman he'd met in the pounding rain.

"I hate to leave you, but—"

"You have to see what Luke wants to show you.
It's important. I'll get to know our son and finish our
wedding preparations while you're gone. I have to
find something to wear."

"Have I told you how much I love you?"

Sierra grinned. "At least a hundred times." She
pushed back the covers. "I want to walk you to the

corral. Can you wait a minute while I make myself decent?"

"Darlin', I'll always wait for you."

⚜

Luke had the horses saddled by the time Sam and Sierra reached the corral. The door to headquarters opened. Stoker and Houston came toward them side by side, walking with long strides. They reminded Sam of twin avenging angels in their hand-tooled gun belts with their holsters hanging low. Either man alone would put the fear of God in anyone, but together, they were the epitome of unbeatable strength.

He and Luke seemed to be getting quite a send-off. Sam couldn't help a grin. "You didn't have to do this, Pa. We'll be back. I just want to show him that old dugout down in the gulch."

"Not me, Sam," Luke said quietly. "I'm riding on when you head for home."

Sam stared at his father. "You knew about this?"

"He left a note under my door." Stoker pinned Luke with a stare. "On this ranch, we do not leave without a proper good-bye."

Luke opened a bulging saddlebag to drop something inside. "I don't do good-byes."

Stoker held the black gelding's headstall. "Luke, you're my son, and I'm damn proud to say it. Stay here. We'll fight this thing together. As a family. As it should be. I'll put all my resources to work in clearing your name. You don't have to go."

Luke glanced away and cleared his throat. Sam

suspected his brother wanted to take their father up on it, but that damn Legend pride wouldn't let him.

"Thanks, but I have to do this myself." Luke went to his father, clasping his hand. "I created this mess, and it's up to me to fix it. I'll never bring shame to this family. I want to earn the right to be called Luke Legend. And until I do, I'll stay away. If I don't go, I'll draw nothing but trouble, men seeking to make a name for themselves by killing me. Leaving is the only way."

Houston clasped Luke's hand and pulled him close. "Don't be a stranger, brother. If you need a hot meal or a place to rest, you know you're always welcome. We're your family, by God, and don't you forget it."

"Thanks, Houston." Luke's gaze found Sierra. "*Dulce*, don't let Sam boss you around. You've got a good head on your shoulders. I expect to see you in the family way next time I'm by." He winked.

She pulled away from Sam and looked up at Luke with tears in her eyes. "Be safe. You and I are kindred souls—I felt that from the first. Everything you need is here."

"All except for the man I have to track down." Luke's words were hard.

"Where will you go?" A little sob caught in her throat, the sound tearing at Sam. He put an arm around her waist to let her know she could always lean on him.

"To find my freedom." Luke kissed her forehead, then stuck a foot in the stirrup. "We're burning daylight, Sam," he said gruffly.

The fact that his brother hadn't had anyone to say

good-bye to in a long while made Sam's heart ache. Luke didn't know the impact he'd made on their lives. And he didn't know how much they needed him.

Sam kissed Sierra one more time and assured her he'd be back soon.

"Quit daydreaming, Sam, and let's ride," Luke barked, interrupting his thoughts.

"Waiting for you," Sam answered. Sparing one last glance at the barn, he galloped after Luke, taking a southwestern track toward some distant hills.

Three hours later, Luke stopped. "It's a little hard from here. You'll see a drop-off another twenty yards or so, and I'll have to give them a signal once we start down."

Them who? Sam glanced around and saw nothing but mesquite and cacti. Certainly no canyon. "What is this place?" He'd thought there wasn't a bit of Texas ground left he hadn't ridden over.

"I named it Deliverance Canyon." Luke opened his canteen and took a drink of water.

"Who's down there?"

"You'll see." Luke put the canteen away. "Let's go."

Sam didn't know whether to have his Colt ready. He decided to follow Luke's lead and keep it holstered. His brother parted some thick mesquite and rode through. Sure enough, they began a sharp descent. The steep winding trail made for difficult going. The horses loosened rock in an effort to keep their footing, sending the stones cascading down the hill.

Luke stopped and gave a loud birdcall. A second later, the same call came from somewhere below.

Sam grinned. "A strange way to knock on the door."

"Trust me. It's safer."

They continued another two hundred yards to the canyon floor. Sam couldn't believe his eyes. Probably a dozen women stood in front of crude shelters made of rough lumber and stone anchored amid the rocks. A clear stream ran along the opposite side. The women scurried for cover upon seeing him.

A flame-haired beauty somewhere in her mid-twenties, carrying a rifle and wearing a gun belt, marched toward them. If looks could kill, Sam would be dead. She aimed the rifle at Sam's chest. "Luke, I warned you about bringing people here. You broke your word."

Sweat rose on Sam's forehead. He prayed his brother would hurry with the explanations.

Unfazed by the hostility, Luke swung his long leg over the bedroll tied behind his saddle and dismounted. "Tally Shannon, don't get your dander up. This is my brother, Sam Legend. Only the two of us know about you ladies."

Keeping a wary eye on the woman, Sam slid to the ground. "Nice to meet you, Miss Shannon. Your secret is safe. I'm a Texas Ranger, at least for a few more days." He moved closer and stuck out his hand.

"Why are you here?" Tally glared, ignoring his outstretched hand.

"Luke wanted me to see why he's been so secretive," Sam explained, finally dropping his hand to his side. "You can trust me."

"We don't trust anybody," Tally spat.

"Except Luke," whispered a timid voice from the shadows.

"You saw what you came for, now leave." Tally jerked the rifle toward the trail.

Two more women stepped from a shelter, pointing rifles at Sam.

"Luke, you'd best do some fast talking," Sam urged.

"Darcy, Savannah, there's no call to threaten anyone." Luke walked toward them. "Put down those rifles. I mean it. Sam isn't here to cause trouble. One minute of your time, and we'll ride out. I just wanted him to meet the women I owe my life to. And to tell you I have to go away for a while. Sam is going to take care of you in my stead. Now, don't go to pouting, Savannah."

Though reluctant, the three women lowered their weapons.

"I don't want you to go away, Luke," Darcy sobbed. "Before you, we never knew a moment's safety. You keep the bad people away."

"I'm sorry, girl. Really, I am."

"They'll find us," Darcy argued.

Luke gently touched her cheek. "Sam will make sure they don't. When it comes to protecting women, he's the best."

"These women saved your life, Luke?" Sam asked, trying to understand the situation.

"They did." Luke draped an arm around Darcy and Savannah.

Tally still seemed a mite skittish and eyed Sam through cold, hard eyes the color of a winter sky. The breeze lifted tendrils of her flame-colored hair and settled the red strands across her cheek.

After a second, Luke continued, "After my mother

died, I got involved in a shoot-out and wound up with a gunshot to my chest and another to my head. These women found me, carted my body down the steep cliff—though I still don't know how—and pulled me from death's door."

"I don't understand why they're hiding down here." Sam's gaze moved from one to the other, and then to even more who'd stolen quietly up behind those. There must have been at least a dozen. The women were clean and well-kept, but each had what appeared to be the same small brand on their left cheek. He wasn't near enough to make it out, but he knew someone had put it there deliberately. Claiming ownership. A muscle worked in his jaw. Whoever'd done that better hope to God he didn't find them.

Though fear and distrust glittered in their eyes, all clearly fought to survive.

"They escaped from the insane asylum down by Church Falls," Luke said quietly.

"We're not crazy, mister," Tally Shannon snapped. "None of us. Our folks stuck us in there to rot. No one wants any of us. But the bastard who runs it put this brand on our faces, and we can't even go into town for supplies. They've got people scouring the country for us. They're offering a five-hundred-dollar reward—dead or alive. I'm not going back there. Never."

"If not for Luke bringing food and medicine, we wouldn't survive," Darcy explained.

"You're saying too much, Darcy, honey," Tally warned.

All this time Sam had been chasing Luke, he'd never

suspected the reason his brother needed the money. Not one cent had been for himself. That's why Luke had never taken more than fifty dollars, and even then he waited, every time, until that ran out. Now everything made sense.

Except one thing. Sam glanced at Luke. "You could've worked and earned the money they needed. You didn't have to steal."

"Yeah, right." Luke gave a sarcastic snort. "I tried that. But men looking to make a name for themselves for killing the notorious Luke Weston would always show up, and my employers wanted no part of me. The only way to stay alive was to keep moving. And the only way these women can stay alive is to never leave Deliverance Canyon."

"I guess you're right." Sam's heart ached for his brother and these women who yearned to be free and safe.

In the hour they spent with the runaways, Sam saw how desperately they wanted to live free as they chose. Each probably nurtured a secret dream deep in her heart. And Tally Shannon watched over them like a fierce mother hen, guarding her chicks from evil men who'd offered a reward for their capture.

This had to be some kind of horrible nightmare for them.

"I want to take you out of here and bring you to the safety of the ranch, where you'll be protected and cared for."

"*No!*" Tally shouted. "Too many people there, and it only takes one who needs the five-hundred-dollar bounty. We're staying put. If you won't bring us supplies once in a while, Sam Legend, we'll manage somehow."

"This is no fit place to live," he argued.

"Better than what we had. No one's complaining," Tally shot back.

Luke touched Sam's back. "Save your breath. You're not going to change their minds. This really might be the safest place for them."

With an aching heart, Sam told them he'd check on them in a few weeks.

As he and Luke said their good-byes and started up the canyon wall, Sam looked back. It took everything he had to keep riding. He wanted to bring them up from the depths, bring them to the Lone Star to rejoin the human race, bring them hope. Right now, they had none. But using force wasn't the way. Sierra could be his secret weapon. She could speak to them as women.

Yes, that's what he'd do. Maybe Sierra could convince them.

They rode in silence, each lost in his thoughts. Sam shot sideways glances at Luke, who shared so much in common with the runaways. All were hunted. "Sullen" best described his brother's mood, and his pale-green eyes held deep, haunting sorrow.

At the canyon rim, Sam turned. "I wish you'd stay. We're family."

"None I can claim yet. Not until I earn it." Luke laid his arm across the pommel. "I know the killer's out there, Sam. Sometimes I feel him watching me."

"It's too dangerous going it alone, Luke."

"Has to be this way. Thank you, Sam, for taking me in as a brother. It meant a lot."

"Still does to me." Sam pinned him with a stare. "Let us help you. If it's an extra gun, I'll be by your side before you can spit. No one can beat us Legends when we stand shoulder to shoulder."

"Ain't that the truth." It was Luke's turn to pin Sam with a stern look. "You know how I feel about *dulce*. Make her cry, and I'll whip you all the way to the Rio Grande and back."

Sam met his stare. "You don't have to worry. The only tears will be happy ones."

If he failed at that, Sam would pay the biggest, meanest, ugliest man he could find to lay into him with both fists and keep pounding until he was a bloody mess.

"Do you know my biggest fear, Luke? That I'll disappoint her in some way."

"You won't. She thinks the sun rises and sets in you." Luke set his big, black gelding in motion toward an uncertain destiny. Alone with men gunning for him and the law on his trail. Sam didn't know if he'd ever see him again. Or if Luke would be alive if he did.

Hell!

At last, Sam released a worried sigh and turned toward home and his beautiful bride. He wouldn't start off his marriage in hot water by missing the wedding.

Forty-five

Sam found Houston with a long face, waiting at the corral when he rode back. He itched to tell his brother about the women in Deliverance Canyon, but he knew he couldn't. He had to keep the secret if it killed him—for now, even from Sierra. Heaviness sat on his chest. Though he was certainly no authority on marriage, starting out with a secret between him and his bride could not be good.

"Did you show Luke that old dugout?" Houston asked.

"Yep." Sam led Trooper to the barn.

Houston followed. "Well?"

"Well what?"

"I know you didn't go there. When you thought we couldn't see, you turned south. What's going on?"

"I can't tell you. I promised Luke, and it's a secret I'm keeping, so hush about it." Sam removed his saddle and threw it over the rail. "Why the coon dog face? I noticed when I rode up."

"I figured I'd get accounts settled in case Luke ever changed his mind and wanted to come back to inherit. I didn't tell Pa—he's usually the one who handles this part—because I figured it'd get him down thinking about Luke being gone and all. The thing is… The books are all off. Pa's been taking large sums of money and gambling heavily in poker games with the other ranchers." Houston glanced away. "The ranch is in trouble—real trouble. I don't know if I can cover his losses."

Sam let out a low whistle. "Are you sure? Maybe it's not as bad as you think."

"He admitted it when I confronted him earlier. Soon we'll have no choice but to sell off sections. I'm not even sure how long we can pay the hands."

What good did it do to get all this land if Stoker was just going to let it slip through his fingers? Sam thought of the many sacrifices his father had made, the sweat, the fighting to keep every inch of the Lone Star. And for what? To let it go flat to hell? If he lived to be a hundred, he'd never understand the man whose blood ran through his veins.

"How can I help, Houston? Want me to talk to him?" This ranch was Houston's livelihood. It was all his brother had, all he knew, all he'd ever wanted. Sam laid a hand on his shoulder.

Houston straightened and pasted on a smile that never reached his eyes. "I shouldn't have brought this up on your wedding day. You know, just forget I mentioned it. And, Sam, he doesn't want you to know—thanks to his damnable pride—so don't say anything."

"Don't worry. Butting heads is the last thing I want today. I'll help you figure something out. You don't have to do it alone." But what could they really do?

Sam knew reining Stoker in would be next to impossible. But Sam sensed the problem was bigger than their father's vices. "What else is wrong on the Lone Star?"

Houston walked to the door and stood with his legs braced, looking out. "The main problem is overgrazing. Our herd is too large and gets bigger each year. Not enough rain, not enough grass, not enough hope. We simply can't feed them."

"How about joining a cattle drive passing through? Cut several thousand from our herd and take them to the railhead in Dodge City or Abilene. I hear they're paying top dollar."

"Pa's been fighting tooth and nail against the notion." Houston turned. "Sam, I don't think he knows the serious shape we're in, and I can't get through to him."

"By God, take that mule-headed man out there and prove it to him."

"The ranch is too large. It'd take a month to cover it. Besides, his solution is only to buy more land, which won't solve the problem. We're between a rock and a hard place." Houston scrubbed the back of his neck. "Hey, we were supposed to get you ready for your wedding. Get a move on. I'll rub Trooper down. Go."

With his thoughts whirling, Sam headed toward headquarters. He didn't know how to help either of his brothers, but he knew he'd do his best. He'd be there for both. No more riding off for the far reaches of Texas. He had no reason to.

Everything he wanted was here—and she was waiting for him with open arms.

❧

Sunset that evening was one of most spectacular Sam had ever seen. The oranges, purples, and golds blazed across the sky in such bursts of blinding color that it almost hurt his eyes.

Flanked by Houston and Stoker on either side, Sam stood beneath the bronze Texas star, the flag fluttering gently in the breeze. He didn't miss how Houston's eyes never strayed from Becky Golden. She was beautiful, in her dress the color of sunflowers to match her hair. His older brother was smitten for sure.

It appeared all the ranch families had come. Mrs. Ross and the housekeeping ladies wore their Sunday best. Hector stood proudly beside Sam, glancing up with a grin. Sam winked broadly, fighting the lump in his throat.

His son.

Though Sam was glad Stoker was going to keep the boy occupied until tomorrow, he worried what the boy might end up learning. Still, maybe one small orphan could fix what they couldn't.

As he waited for his bride, dark clouds blocked the dying sun. Damn! He'd wanted everything perfect for Sierra.

Ranger Tom Burdine unbuckled his gun belt, walked to the porch of the headquarters, and laid the belt on a chair. Opening his saddlebags, he took out a worn Bible that sported a bullet hole right in the center, then wearing his worn black Stetson and Texas Ranger badge, he stepped into place beneath the bronze star. That Tom had removed his gun was a miracle. In all the years he'd known the tough ranger, Sam had never once seen him without it.

How fortunate for Burdine to be a man of the cloth and to have arrived just when they needed a preacher. How quickly everything had fallen into place told Sam it must've been some divine plan. He felt his mother's presence.

The door opened, and Sierra emerged, clutching a bouquet of wild daisies, sprinkled through with some purple flowers. Sam's breath caught. No greater vision of loveliness ever walked the earth. The white satin-and-lace dress looked strangely like the one he'd seen hanging in his mother's wardrobe so long ago.

He leaned over. "Is that Mother's dress, Pa?"

"Yep. She wore it on her wedding day. I offered it to Sierra."

"It's really something." It seemed to have been made just for her. Sam swallowed the lump in his throat and blinked hard as Sierra took Rocky's arm and came to meet him.

Her blue eyes sparkled when she met his gaze and smiled.

One of the old rangers he'd ridden with had once said, "Life is a sum of all a person's choices. The good and the bad. It takes both to complete a life."

That must surely be so. And every choice Sam made had led to this moment with this gentle, strong woman. His heart swelled with love. Hector ran to meet her, and when she took his hand, leading him forward, Sam fought to swallow. A mist blocked his vision.

His wife. His son. His family.

When she stood beside him and took his hand, the

low sun's rays burst through the dark clouds, through the cutouts in the bronze star, and bathed Sierra in a halo of soft light. It seemed as though the good Lord had blessed their union.

Sam's throat closed, and when he spoke low, the words came out hoarse and bruised. "You, darlin', are without question an angel if I ever saw one."

A rosy blush colored her cheeks. "You told me that at the shack after we escaped from the train."

He lifted her hand to his lips and kissed it. "And I meant every word. I just didn't know how true it was at the time."

Sierra met his stare. "I knew even then that you were a handsome knight in shining armor, riding a buckskin instead of a white steed. You saved the damsel in distress, and I fell deeply and utterly in love with you."

Tom Burdine cleared his throat. "Is it all right if *I* conduct this ceremony? If you want to take over, Sam, I'll sit down."

"Don't be funny, Burdine. If you expect to get paid, I'd watch it," Sam growled.

"Paid?" The ranger chuckled. "You mean that's what those frijoles were? I thought you fed everyone who called on you."

"I'll take care of that little piece of business, Ranger," Stoker said with a grin. "And you can bet it'll be more than a plateful of frijoles."

"Thank you, Mr. Legend." Tom bowed slightly at Sam's pa. "Dearly beloved, we're gathered here today to unite this man and woman in holy matrimony."

Sam barely heard the rest of the ceremony. He

already knew he loved and cherished Sierra more than he'd ever thought possible. In fact, he worshipped the ground she walked on. His eyes never left hers as they spoke their vows.

At the end, Tom Burdine turned to him. "Do you and Sierra have a few words to say to each other, Sam?"

"Yep." Sam fought to control his emotions and found it quite a chore. He gazed deep into his bride's beautiful eyes, the color of the sky. "By all rights, I shouldn't be here, Sierra. I've cheated death countless times. But somehow I escaped, and I'm very happy to stand here with the woman I love. I fear I fall short in being good husband material, and can't imagine what you want with someone who's all horns and rattles and cussed god-awful stubbornness, but I will never give you cause to regret marrying me." He paused for a second to settle his quavering voice.

"Don't know what you see in me, but I'm mighty glad you do, darlin'. I'll spend every waking minute thinking of ways to make your life better. You're my lady, and I'm damn proud to be with you." He shot Burdine a glance. "I reckon that's all."

"I'd like to say something, Ranger Burdine," Sierra said. "Sam, you know the life *I've* had, and you know it didn't prepare me for this moment. I don't know how to be a wife, one who's strong and confident. I'm liable to be a work in progress, I'm afraid. But I'll stand beside you through thick and thin. I'll never falter, never run and leave you to face any problems alone.

"You're my husband, my friend, my lover. If anyone's unworthy, it's me. Through your patient caring, you showed me that everyone I touch does not die. I was broken, and you glued me back together and made me strong and healthy." Her voice cracked with emotion. "We have a son, and I'll be the best mother to him I possibly can. I'll give you more children to teach and love. We're a team, yoked together and pulling a load. I will always love you, my dearest Sam."

Sam found thickness blocking his airway. Why in the hell had he tried so hard to push her away? He deserved a good flogging. He didn't know what lay ahead, but he knew life with her would never be boring.

❧

They had barely said their "I dos" before Carlos and the other men whipped out their guitars and the party started. The women, dressed in their swirling skirts and white Mexican blouses, waved colorful streamers.

The scent of the night drifted around Sam as he took Sierra in his arms. He put his face against her fragrant hair, thinking of the night he'd told her to forget him for good. Thank his lucky stars she hadn't.

Her body swayed against him, creating a heat like no friction match ever did. This petite woman, with such strength and grace, was all he'd ever need.

Sierra looked up with a searching gaze. "Do you wish you were riding with Luke?"

"Yes, but not for the reason you think. I want to help him straighten out his life. Protect him from those who aim to kill him. Deep down, he's the most caring man I know." Sam thought of those women hiding out in Deliverance Canyon. At least he could look after them for Luke. In the near future, he hoped to persuade Tally Shannon to trust Sierra too.

But if she refused, he'd guard the women's secret.

Sam tightened his hold around Sierra. "Other than that, I'm perfectly content right here with you and our little man."

"I'm glad I have you, Sam. Glad we have each other."

"Me too. I can't even remember a time when you weren't beside me. The hanging and my life as a single man are only vague memories. Nothing out there equals what I've found here."

A smile spread across Sierra's face. "I'm very happy."

That made two of them. He didn't want to ever be alone again.

"Our future, my darling, twinkles as bright as my wife's pretty blue eyes."

"Do we have to stay for everything?" she asked, pouting.

"Nope." Sam twirled her around, grinning. "I'm whisking you away as soon as this song stops and making mad, passionate love to you. Anything you want to say, Mrs. Legend?"

Her glance up at him was quite innocent as she reached between them to fondle him. "How soon will that be, sweetheart?"

"Good Lord, woman, right now." Sam swept her up into his arms and sprinted toward her little school-teacher house and the bed's scripture quilt.

About the Author

At a young age, Linda Broday discovered a love for storytelling, history, and anything pertaining to the Old West. Cowboys fascinate her. There's something about Stetsons, boots, and tall, rugged cowboys that get her fired up! A *New York Times* and *USA Today* bestselling author, Linda has won many awards, including the prestigious National Readers' Choice Award and the Texas Gold Award. She now resides in the panhandle of Texas on the Llano Estacado.

Texas Redemption

by Linda Broday

New York Times bestselling author

— ❧ —

**Two brothers—One woman
A final chance to find...**

REDEMPTION

Desperate to escape her dark past, Laurel James agrees to wed the mayor of a small east Texas town. With him, life will be quiet. Respectable. Safe. It should be everything she ever wanted.

And it is. Until Shenandoah rides back into town.

Shenandoah never thought he would find the woman he's loved and lost...and he certainly never dreamed she'd be pledged to his brother. He knows he should step aside—he has nothing to offer a woman like Laurel James—but the moment their eyes meet, Shenandoah is lost. He can only find peace in her arms...but can redemption be more than a dream for a man who has known nothing but war?

— ❧ —

Praise for Linda Broday:

"Linda Broday's heroes step right out
of her books and into your heart."
—Jodi Thomas, *New York Times* bestselling author

"Broday understands the West and its lure. She brings
strong characters and deep emotions into a very
realistic western romance that pulls no punches."
—*RT Book Reviews* for *Redemption*, 4 stars

For more Linda Broday, visit:
www.sourcebooks.com

Left at the Altar

A Match Made in Texas

by Margaret Brownley

New York Times bestselling author

❧

Welcome to Two Time, Texas. Where tempers burn hot, love runs deep, and a single marriage can unite a feuding town…or tear it apart for good.

In the wild and untamed West, time is set by the local jeweler, but Two-Time, Texas, has two—two feuding jewelers and two wildly conflicting time zones. Meg Lockwood's marriage was supposed to unite the families and finally bring peace. But when she's left at the altar by her no-good fiancé, Meg's dreams of dragging her quarrelsome neighbors into a cease-fire are dashed.

No wedding bells? No one-time town.

Hired to defend the groom against a breach-of-promise lawsuit, Grant Garrison quickly realizes that the only thing worse than small-town trouble is falling for the jilted bride. But there's something about Meg's sweet smile and determined grit that draws him in, even as the whole crazy town seems set on keeping them apart.

Who knew being *Left at the Altar* could be such sweet, clean, madcap fun?

❧

Praise for *Left at the Altar*:

"A great story by a wonderful author." —Debbie Macomber, #1 *New York Times* bestselling author

For more Margaret Brownley, visit:

www.sourcebooks.com